THE ROGUE ENCHANTRESS

Amber Vonda

THE AGATE ENCHANTRESS

~ BOOK TWO ~

AMBER VONDA

© 2022 Amber Vonda

No part of this book may be reproduced without permission from the author except in brief quotations and in reviews.

CHAPTER I

"Hello, sisters, we have lots to talk about," Arianna said to the shocked faces as she pulled the cloak off and laughed, looking at Iris. "Clumsy as ever, I see."

Iris was speechless; she couldn't believe what she was seeing. Rubbing her eyes and opening them again, she allowed the tears to stream down her face when she realized it was really her.. Arianna was standing before them. Wasting no time at all, Iris walked straight to Arianna with her arms out, wrapping them around her as soon as she could.

"You're finally here," Iris sobbed in her sister's ear. Iris had been without her little sister for so long she had begun to believe that their reunion would never happen. She wanted to know everything Arianna had gone through and what she had been up to for all the years they had been apart. "Why did you wait so long?"

"I couldn't come out, Alister—," Arianna began to explain.

"Alister freed you over a year ago, sister," Angela cut her off.

"What do you mean...*freed* me?" Arianna expressed with the look of shock.

"He didn't chain you. He thought you'd understand when you woke up. After what you did for Atticus and his brothers, he came to tell us you were in his dungeon and that you were free. Alister just wanted you to wait for us," Angela explained.

"This entire time I could have been out here? With you?" she asked, moving her gaze quickly from Angela to Iris.

"Yes. Alister went back to your castle to tell you himself. He knows you had no control over the curse that consumed you. He completely understands," Angela said, smiling.

"No...these are lies. You lie," Arianna cried out.

"It's true. He said you were free," Iris added, backing Angela up.

Worried her little sister still didn't believe them, Iris studied her. She looked like she had slept little. What was it like for Arianna to live in fear all this time? Arianna was stronger than she had ever seen before. So grown up. Iris could also tell from her sisters' essence that she was extremely powerful, and that, above all, she needed to be careful not to alarm her.

***

Arianna shook her head furiously, still unable to believe her sisters. She had wasted yet again another year of her life in fear only to find out that she could have been reunited with the family a year ago. Looking at the absolute truthful expressions on her sister's faces, she pulled them both into a hug. All three let their emotions take over as they held each other.

"Where have you been all our lives?" Angela laughed. "We have so much to catch up on."

"That's an understatement. I know I have two nieces, a nephew, and you. I never knew I had a twin, though," she replied.

"We never told you. We didn't want you to blame yourself," Iris said regretfully, bowing her head.

"For what? Blame myself for what? What aren't you telling me, Iris?" Arianna asked.

Iris took a deep breath and began to tell Arianna about when she and Angela were born. She told how their father had to give up Angela to save her life, and that it was the hardest decision he ever had to make. They weren't exactly sure what was going on with the twins; all they knew was that every time they touched, it weakened Angela's life.

Arianna couldn't believe she had been sucking the life out of her twin. Or maybe sucking the magic out of her. She was, after all, a professional magic stealer. It was one of her best powers. That could explain why Angela had no magic because Arianna still harnessed all of it. Twice as powerful meant she had the magic that was still owed to Angela, yet she was not ready to give it back.

Iris went from how the twins were separated at birth to how Arianna, after she had lost her own child, had cursed all the women in the realm who were pregnant, causing them all to die. Iris explained she was literally possessed by the magic and that's why she couldn't remember; it was also why Arianna wasn't responsible.

Even though Arianna couldn't remember the facts Iris spoke, still sure that it was the dark side of her magic that'd caused the horrors that befell her and the realm, her own mind was twitching as if she was trying to bring the memory into focus. She forced it back, along with the voices that taunted her. When Iris finished explaining everything, Arianna could sense a magical presence coming closer to the colorful shop they were in called Bella's Boutique.

"Someone is coming into your store soon. I should go,"

Arianna announced.

"No, stay! Everyone is going to have to accept that you're back and here to stay," Angela said, offering a reassuring smile.

Arianna returned the grin, sensing the love and goodness in her twin's heart. Thinking about being like her, however, made her actually feel weak and naïve, being so open-hearted and kind. She had obviously never had to live a life like her own, so how could she ever understand? From what she had learned, Angela had a family of her own and an intriguing husband. In other words, her sister had everything Arianna had ever dreamed of, and she was envious.

"Mommy!" a sweet little girl's voice said, opening the door.

"Leah! How is my little angel?" Angela said, scooping her up.

Arianna watched the little blonde girl run up to her twin. Jealousy pinged inside her heart and soul, knowing she couldn't experience the same outcome with her own little girl. She did wonder how the children ended up with blonde hair when their family was so dark, with skin so tan. This made her think of Arik again. He dominated the features of the children, obviously. Pushing his appearance out of her mind as quickly as possible, Arianna questioned if now would be a good time to tell Angela that her husband was locked inside her very own castle.

"Who's that? She looks just like you," Leah asked, pointing at Arianna.

"That's your Aunty Arianna. Do you want to go say hi?" Angela asked.

Arianna watched as the trusting Angela sent the little girl over to her. Addressing her as "Aunty Arianna" made her heart warm and go out to her sister. Bending down to the girl, Leah walked right up to her.

"Hi, Leah. How are you?" Arianna asked, taken aback as the little girl wrapped her arms around her neck, hugging her tightly. Arianna could feel an intense rush of energy blow through her entire body. "Wow! What was that?"

"Just a little something I thought you could use," Leah said, as she winked at her.

Arianna sat on the floor once Leah walked back to her mother. In a daze, Arianna could feel her own heart crack and open, like a baby chick pecking at her shell and protruding from her dark surroundings. After all these years... Arianna began to glow brightly after her heart did a back flip in her chest. Looking at her arms and her legs, alarm spread through her as she watched this new, odd transition.

Her sisters just stood, watching and smiling.

"It's our mother's light magic, Arianna. Let her heal you," Iris spoke cheerfully.

Arianna's survival instincts kicked in as she fought the feelings. Terrified to allow her heart to heal, believing it would make her far too trusting and unable to protect herself, Arianna's fight made the glow dim, like a candle losing its war against the rising winds. Turning, she raced out the door. She used the light magic to her advantage, tapping into it to increase her speed so she could get home. She had her own light magic, but this was too much all at once for her to handle as the good tried with all its might to snuff out the dark.

Flying over the border of her castle after just a short time, Arianna tried to catch her breath. It felt like only seconds had gone by. How could she allow that to happen? Clearly not ready to let go, she stopped the bright light and held onto the pain and fear that'd made her powerful to begin with.

Arianna certainly did miss her sisters, and would like to get to know Angela and the children, but at what cost? Would they accept the strong, powerful woman she was now, or did they want her pure and good like them? Knowing the latter would never be possible, Arianna thought it best to stay away from her sisters...at least, for now.

***

After Arianna had left the store, Angela and Iris stood there, worried they had scared her off forever. They had stood still, excited but quiet as the light magic had tried to take over Arianna's body. They had no intentions of making a scene, but didn't think for one second that Arianna would run from it either.

"We have to get the king to make a formal announcement to the entire kingdom that Arianna is free. I think she just has lingering doubts and trust issues from all those years of fight or flee," Iris stated.

"I think so, too," Angela agreed.

Closing the store down for the day, taking Leah with them, they headed to His Majesty's castle after asking for a ride from the wagon driver outside Bella's Boutique. It was supposed to be a long ride, but halfway there they watched as Alister's large dragon shadow flew above the wagon and landed right in front of them on the road.

"Missed me already?" he asked as he transitioned back into a human before their eyes. "Found you first." He grinned.

"Arianna just paid us a visit, actually. We were on our way to your castle to tell you." Iris jumped out of the carriage.

"And I always miss you," Angela stated, observing the look of worry he now wore. Watching it go to his radiant smile after her statement, they told Leah to stay inside the carriage so the adults could talk.

"What did she want?" he asked.

"To see us. She said she was tired of being in fear for her life all the time. Angela and I told her she was free over a year ago," Iris said, smiling. "Then we all just talked and caught up."

Angela didn't like how her sister had left out the rest. How Arianna had taken off. Wondering if it was all that important, she was still determined to tell the truth to Alister.

"How did it feel to meet her after all this time?" he asked Angela.

"Like looking in a mirror. An immensely powerful mirror," she added, looking at Iris, giving her a stare that told her she was going to reveal the rest. "There's more."

Angela explained all that had happened with Leah and Arianna; she also described the beautiful scene that occurred before Arianna took off out the store doors with fear written all over her face.

"Can you announce Arianna's freedom to the entire realm? I believe she doubted it coming from us. Please, Your Majesty," Iris begged.

"Do you think I should, Angela?" he looked at her.

"Yes, I think you should. I also think when she hears about your announcement, she will come out of hiding, and then the two of you can sit down and have a serious talk," Angela suggested, even though the circumstances were awful being that his wife was one of the unfortunate women effected by a curse such as Arianna's.

He stood there, flaring his nostrils like he was going over the situation in his head. Looking from Angela to Iris—before he did what he usually does when he's ready to give in—Alister shook his head left and right with his eyes closed as a smile came to his face.

"Okay. I'll make an announcement. It usually takes thirty days to get the entire kingdom into town, though," he said.

"A month!" both Iris and Angela whined.

"Okay...fourteen days for you two, but I hope you're ready when the town turns against us," he said in a serious tone.

"I hope it doesn't come to that." Iris expressed her concern.

"Thank you, Alister." Angela showed her appreciation, walking to his side, jumping up, and kissing his cheek.

"You are both welcome," he said. Bowing, he transformed back into his dragon form and flew back to his castle.

CHAPTER 2

Neveah was walking with Carson to Blue Moon Mountain from her new stepfather's land. It was strange for Neveah to think of her mother married and that she had a new father figure in her life. Well.. kind of in her life. Being they were still on their honeymoon; she hadn't had the chance yet to know him as her stepdad.

The mountain wasn't a far trek, but when they reached the bottom, Neveah sighed. If the door wasn't so interesting to Neveah, she would have seen how steep the climb was and turned back around in order to enjoy a picnic in a bed of grass somewhere.

Hopefully, the hike would be a great way to get her mind off Nick. Finding it difficult as she took her first steps up the mountain, her mind wandered back to the moment when he had presented himself. She remembered how he had stumbled on his words, trying to explain to her how she made him feel.

Amused by the thought, Neveah still smiled at the memory of when she finally got to reach out and brush his soft feathers with her hand.

Later on, as their friendship grew, they had done everything together. Swimming and splashing like a couple of elementary schoolers, she'd been surprised at how much he had loved the water. Meeting his friends, he'd introduced her to ravens and crows, attempting to show her his leadership over all the flight shifters. He had spent hours just watching her write in her journal, staying completely silent. She was sure every time they'd been together—whether swimming, sharing picnics, hanging out on rooftops and just talking for hours—it would eventually turn into something. Yet every time she would sense Nick was going to do something or say more, he'd just turned away from her.

Shaking her head, trying to clear the thoughts about Nick from her mind, Neveah refocused on her walk. She hoped it would end soon; the heat of the sun was rising. Barely seeing her fellow journeyman now, Neveah realized that Carson had traveled far ahead without her. *Man, the guy is in great shape for getting his ass kicked. He never seems to care either.* Carson did surprise her. After all, what man can be dominated by another yet not be upset about it, but instead wants to learn from them and speaks of them with such admiration? Carson was sweet and was always up for physical activity. Sex was not among those activities, though. Neveah laughed to herself, wondering what kind of lover he would be. For some reason, she thought he would be awful at it.

"I think it's around here," Carson yelled back as Neveah increased her speed to catch up.

"Thank the gods...my calves are burning," Neveah expressed. Sitting down on a large boulder, she rubbed her legs and grabbed her water bottle out of her bag, guzzling most of it.

She sat there, wishing she had paid more attention to the

scenery on the way up instead of looking at her feet, lost in her own thoughts. The view was certainly breathtaking, with the sun shining through the veil of trees. Setting her drink down, Neveah noticed a shimmer coming from a dark rock perched right beside her bottle. Picking it up and turning it over, she began to feel excited. Neveah had never found this crystal in all of her rock-hounding days. Feeling the exhilaration consume her, she practically jumped up and down inside. She had truly found a geode amethyst.

"Carson! Is this an amethyst?" she asked, standing up and running over to him to show off her new treasure.

"Yeah, that stuffs all over up here," he replied, brushing the dirt from the crystal. "Now I know the door was around here somewhere..." His mind shifted gears away from the stone. "Want to help look?"

She almost gave him a piece of her mind at his slightly annoyed state. It wasn't her fault he was too submissive to win his jousting lesson and that he couldn't track worth crap—something most wolves should be a natural at. Rolling her eyes, feeling boredom settling in, she chose to stay quiet and started looking around for the door. As Carson seemed to do circles now, after changing into his wolf state and following his own scent, Neveah headed further up the mountain. Picking up her bag and bottle, she walked for what seemed like five minutes. Suddenly, Neveah heard the whisper of a woman's voice come from her left.

"Hello! Is someone there?" she asked, walking in the direction of the voice. She hit what seemed to be a dead end, until she moved the vines and brush out of the way and unveiled the door Carson was still trying to track. He'd been right; it looked like a door, but not from reading the writing carved into it, but because of the handprint. Putting her own hand up to the carving, it looked like the perfect match. Wondering how they'd etched such lovely writing into the rock, Neveah ran her fingertips over the strange language that appeared there. Stopping at the shape of the hand again, she placed her own against the print and pushed to see if it would open.

To her amazement, the door slowly opened before her very eyes. Stunned by the immaculate sight she was now viewing, Neveah stared into a room that looked like it was a dream come true from floor to ceiling.

***

Nicholas was up in the sky, orbiting like he was a vulture circling dead prey. He felt lost and confused. He missed Neveah and all the warmth she'd brought into his life. Now all he had were regrets for not telling her how he felt. It'd always felt like the wrong time. She was always being called off to do something, or he was. Or every time he would try to tell her he was ready she would bring up her ex-husband. That had instantly made him angry; not at her, but at the man who made her feel so insecure and had taken her self-worth. Nick had thought she wasn't ready for someone new in her life or her heart. Each time he thought she was, something she would say or a look crossed her face that would tell him otherwise. She became annoyed with his company as well, even though he'd just wanted to be near her, doing whatever she was doing. Ready to tell her about his feelings at her mother's wedding, he asked for her to come help him pick out a tux. Wanting it to be the best one, for her to be proud, he tried on many to see which one of them she would like most. Finding out she was going to the wedding with Carson, however, had toyed with his feelings. Then...watching her happy and giggling as she'd walked with Carson down the aisle had been enough for Nick. He did not volunteer to play games; he had enough of games with his ex-fiancée. All he'd wanted was a family and a wife that could fly by his side and have hatchlings of their own, so he'd used up the prime of his life on a woman that cringed at even the smallest idea of having children. Now he was doing the same thing, comparing his ex to Neveah. There was no comparison between the two women; when it came to Neveah, he desperately needed to talk to her, and soon. It had been too long. He missed being in the trees overlooking the best views of the ocean and sunsets with her, catching her as she'd snapped the last tree branch, and making her laugh with his silly bird dance.

"Nick, we still need your help. The young birds flew into the dark forest and all of them went to sleep. Who knows how many there are? We *have* to keep searching," Kenneth expressed his concern.

Kenneth, Nick's longtime friend and fellow raven was following up on a murder of young crows – a group that'd known perfectly well to stay away from the evil witch's dark lands. They had finally figured out there was a border around her living quarters. If you touched it, you would just drop and instantly fall asleep. It was Nick's primary job to help with all the issues concerning flight creatures. It was so sad to see all the boys and girls out cold along the invisible border, and he didn't want the number to continue rising.

Nick sighed. They had a lot to keep themselves busy for a while.

***

Neveah was standing before a room completely covered in amethyst crystal; it was the most beautiful thing she'd ever seen. Slowly stepping forward, she observed the floor once she got to the center of the room. Bending down, it felt much like an ice-skating rink. Blissfully happy, she went to twirl in a circle around the room, but suddenly the door slammed shut, turning the beautiful dream into a twisted nightmare. Running to the stone door, she banged on it with her fists.

"Hello! Can anyone hear me? Carson? I'm stuck in here!"

she screamed, slapping and banging on the rock until her hands hurt.

Putting her back to the wall, she slid down to the floor and began to sob, hyperventilating as the room's walls felt like they were closing in on her.

"Neveah...do not be afraid; you are not trapped. You can leave any time you please," the voice emanated from within the walls.

"Who's there?" Neveah spoke as her own voice seemed to match the one that echoed before.

"It is I, the maker of the amethyst family crystal. I am one of four original witches, Neveah. I am your ancestor," the woman's voice replied.

"Ancestor? But how can you be talking to me now if you're my ancestor from hundreds of years ago?" she panicked, not wanting to be the next victim of the crystal.

"My sisters and I separated the four realms long ago. In return, we were each punished by being consumed in our own crystal, never able to be free. We thought we were doing the right thing by separating the realms, but instead we ended up making each weaker and causing more damage than we could have ever imagined; damage that has occurred through time. We must fix what we have done wrong in order to finally be free."

"I want out of here! I don't want to die and be consumed in the crystal like you," she cried out to the voice.

"You can leave, as I said. You just have to admit your guilt and forgive yourself. Let go of your fear or the room will never let you leave. It will take over your entire body until it has reached your heart, if you do not admit your faults," the voice said, fading away.

"What do you mean? I don't understand," Neveah said, completely confused.

Somehow knowing she'd been abandoned, Neveah walked around the room; staring at her own reflection in the amethyst walls, she suddenly noticed that it wasn't just a room. There was a hallway. Walking down the path, she came to the end of the tunnel and witnessed a figure, looking much like herself, trapped behind the glass at the end of the hall. Taken aback by the image that looked like her own reflection, fear filled her body. Jumping backwards, she fell and landed on the floor, still looking at the woman's face. The face was hers...yet, upon study, Neveah could tell that the woman was older in years and dressed in different clothing. Getting up, she walked towards the unmoving woman. While Neveah was observing her features, the woman's eyes shot open. Screaming, Neveah ran back to the stone door as fast as possible.

"Neveah, you must hurry. Admit your guilt and forgive yourself. You're running out of time," the voice warned.

"Okay, okay!" Neveah shouted. "I know what you're talking about," she replied, crying. "It's *my* fault, but I can never forgive myself. I'm afraid I have ruined my daughter for allowing the abuse to continue for so long. I was selfish; I let her pain go on in order to live the glamorous and wealthy lifestyle. I didn't want to give it up, and in return I let him abuse me and Sylvia. I'm so sorry! I will never forgive myself." Neveah yelled and sobbed, letting out the well of guilt over the abuse that'd taken over her home before they'd arrived at the new realm.

Back on the floor Neveah went, laying her head on the cool rock as it sent shivers through her body. The room's temperature grew colder; she could soon see her own breath and felt her tears turn solid, hitting the crystal beneath her head.

"Neveah, you need to forgive yourself. What are you afraid of? Hurry Neveah!"

"I *can't*. I don't deserve forgiveness! I'm afraid I'm going to allow it to happen again. If I find someone real, I'm afraid it will just be another abusive relationship," Neveah whispered, as the room felt like ice.

Neveah's eyelids were heavy, and her body stiffened as the temperature dropped, making her bones ache with every movement. Ready to give up, ready to accept her fate and stay in the room forever, she suddenly spotted an amethyst-colored wave getting closer to her. Her eyes popped open wide as it creeped toward her unmoving form. Reaching deep inside, finding the will to live, Neveah promised to be a better mother and protect her children the best she could from repeating her own mistakes.

"I forgive myself," she whispered, listening to her announcement echo off the walls.

Watching the wave instantly stop, Neveah remained silent as the anomaly retreated and the temperature of the room returned to normal. Hearing the unmistakable creak of the door, alerting Neveah that it was now unlocked, she got up to run. Feeling the warmth now in her heart, Neveah pulled the door open.

"Neveah, please wait. Would you do something for me? Please..please bring us back together again? Unite us four sisters and free us so we can go to the afterlife together." The voice requested her aid in a heartfelt, desperate tone.

"But..how do I do that? What is your name?"

"You must find a way, or all of the realms will die. We must all be together to fix what we have done wrong. My name is Neveah, you are descended from me, which is why we look alike."

"I will try. I promise," Neveah replied. Turning back to the door, she took a step outside before once again shutting her ancestor inside.

"One more thing, Neveah. When you leave, your memory of this room will disappear. You will only have a..feeling; you will know that something has been asked of you."

"How am I supposed to find your sisters if I don't remember?" Neveah was now even more confused.

"You will know. When you are close to each of them, you

will feel the energy and each will call to you like I have done. Now go. Farewell," was the final word Neveah heard before the door slammed shut..all on its own.

Neveah stood within arm's reach of the stone door and couldn't remember what she was doing or what had just happened. Bewildered, she looked around and jumped as she heard Carson's voice break through her train of muddled thoughts.

"Neveah, where are you?" Carson yelled.

"I'm over here," she replied, listening to his footsteps getting closer.

"Where have you *been*? I have been calling your name for hours. It's almost sunset. We need to get back," he issued a stream of complaints.

"I don't..know. I didn't know it was that long," she replied, feeling like it had only been five minutes or so since they'd last spoke.

As the two of them walked back down the mountain, Neveah still couldn't shake the feeling that she needed to look for something. Not knowing what it was, she also couldn't shake the fact that her normal feelings of guilt and fear that weighed on her like boulders had suddenly disappeared. All she wanted now was Nick. Looking in Carson's direction as they reached the bottom of the mountain and stepped back on Jenisis lands, she realized she still cared for Nick and that Carson was just a wonderful distraction. Stopping down at the den diner where her mother had her wedding reception, she turned to Carson.

"I need to tell you something."

"What is it?" he asked, turning to her with questioning eyes.

"I don't want to be with you anymore. I'm sorry...I still have feelings for Nicholas, and I don't think it's fair to lead you on," she replied, choosing to take the honest route. Waiting for the tantrum, Neveah instead was surprised by his reaction.

"It's okay; I understand. I didn't really think we were heading to romance anyway," he said, lifting Neveah's hand and kissing the back of it. "Goodbye Neveah."

Carson turned around and took his leave. She stood in the middle of the grass beside the den, not at all sure of what the next step in her life was going to be.

***

Nicholas and Kenneth rounded up all the sleeping boys and girls far away from the witch's border; right before sunset, all of them woke up, stunned by the quick drop from flight. Luckily, none of them were hurt by their fall. Next on Nick's list was to notify Alister of the border and the safety measures they needed to make so this sort of thing didn't happen again. He tried to hide his excitement at the thought, knowing that a trip to Alister meant he'd be closer to Neveah—close enough to pay her a visit.

He was on his way to see the king of the realm when he noticed Neveah walking from Jenisis below him. He was in a hurry, but he figured he could at least say hello and then ask if they could meet up another time to discuss more. Descending, he landed near her where she could see him, or so he thought. Assuming she was lost in her own thoughts, he watched her keep walking, never breaking her stride.

"Neveah!" he called, watching her jump at the sound of his voice.

"Hi," she said, turning around to look at him.

"Are you okay? You looked...lost or something," he said, tilting his head in curiosity.

"I'm fine. I just broke things off with Carson and I'm looking for something. I wish I could remember what it was, though," she replied.

"Oh, I'm sorry," he lied, trying to keep the grin from his face at the announcement she was single. "Can I walk with you for a moment? I do have to see Alister soon, but I would like to catch up."

"Sure. I haven't seen you since my mother's wedding. You didn't even say goodbye."

"I know. I have been battling my own mind about that. To be honest, it hurt to see you with Carson, but I wanted you to be happy. You looked happy," he said, feeling awful at how he'd handled everything. He had just taken off after the ceremony; he didn't even stay for the whole event. Thinking she was going to be satisfied with another man, Nick believed that she definitely couldn't have the same strong feelings for him that he had for her.

"Then why didn't you say anything? You have just been a coward. I don't even want to talk about it anymore. I waited for you for a long time, and you showed no sign of wanting to be with me. I wasn't about to put my entire life on hold for you to decide. I'm sorry I told you my life story when I thought you were just an elegant eagle and not a clueless man. I can see now that you're just bored with me since I'm not mysterious like you anymore," she unloaded on him.

Standing there with his own mouth open for once, he was shocked by her explanation. How could he be so stupid not to realize how she must have felt? All this time, with everything he had mixed up in his mind, he'd overlooked that she had felt the same feelings but that he hadn't communicated with her. Maybe he was a coward and it *was* his fault that he had lost her. He would make it right; he would start communicating with Neveah. There was no way he would risk once again losing the beautiful gem that stared back at him now.

***

Neveah looked at his gapping mouth and shook her head. Walking around him to continue on with her stroll to town, she couldn't believe what she'd told him. It felt amazing, like she wasn't afraid to release her feelings on him anymore. She wasn't afraid of what he would say or how he would feel. Fearless...that's what she felt. The freedom of it was powerful enough to make her smile.

"Neveah, please wait," he called.

"I'm done waiting, Nicholas. I'm done. You either get off your high horse or you move along, cause this woman isn't waiting for anyone ever again," Neveah said, feeling the newfound energy build up inside her as she grew stronger with every word.

"I want to be with you. I won't make you wait. I'll leave you with that so we can communicate further after I speak with Alister."

"Of course, running away again," she sneered.

"No. I swear. There is a border around the witch's castle and a murder of young crows ran into it and fell to the ground. We need to warn the town to stay away from it."

"Oh my God! Are they okay?" Neveah said, feeling bad now for keeping him from what was a truly important mission.

"They're fine. They had a long nap and woke up recently, but I want to inform Alister so he can announce it and keep everyone away before someone gets hurt."

"Oh good. Well, get going. We can talk again soon. I don't want to be the cause of anything bad happening because I kept you from relaying the message."

"It was worth it. You mean so much to me and I'm sorry I gave you that impression. I will see you again, *soon*," Nick said, taking her hand and kissing the back like Carson had done before, only for the opposite reason. He was saying hello for the first time, not goodbye, and the feeling that produced made Neveah hopeful and grateful for her outburst of truth.

CHAPTER 3

Zackery was hanging out with Liam. He wanted to get away from the girls; they were just too dramatic for his liking. It made Zack grimace that Zinnia still hadn't tamed her personality. She still picked on smaller shifters. Zack didn't appreciate her attitude towards him, not to mention her lies. How could she have such a cool mom and be so awful to everyone? Was it maybe because she didn't have a father and never brought him up?

    Zack was standing in the middle of the field waiting for Liam to throw the ball, not realizing he was more focused on Zinnia and interested to find out why she was the way she was when the ball Liam had thrown connected with his stomach, knocking the air out of him as he rolled on the ground holding tightly to his tummy, trying not to allow the tears to fall.

    "Oh, no! Are you okay, man? You're supposed to pay

attention," Liam said, helping Zackery to his feet.

"I'm good. Guess I was just lost in thought," Zack replied, now standing. "Good throw though."

"Yeah, I've been practicing with the wolves. They are hard to play with if you're not tough."

"Guess I just don't have it in me. What's it like hanging out with wolves all the time?" Zack asked.

"They train a lot in both human form and wolf. Constantly wrestling or jousting. It's awesome to watch, but not much fun when they are so much stronger than me. It's a lot to be around them all the time. They make me tougher, though. You should come and train sometime," Liam suggested.

"You know me; I'm a lover, not a fighter," Zack laughed. Probably the answer behind why he hung out with the girls more than the guys.

"Well, I have a wrestling match with one of my boys at Grandpa Jenesis' rink. I'll see you later," Liam said, waving goodbye to Zack.

"Bye," Zack replied before heading out to the docks to see his sister.

***

Sylvia and Simon had been boasting all over the waters and land about their engagement. Sylvia wanted to get married upon horses and have them be the theme of her wedding. Simon wanted it to be in the water and have a witch bless the waters for the wedding so everyone would turn into a mermaid and merman. The couple couldn't mutually decide, and it was putting stress on them both.

Sylvia sat on the edge of the deck after Simon had gone back down into the ocean. They separated a lot to cool off; then they'd come back together and communicate further about their issues. She loved him and wanted him to enjoy the wedding as much as she did, but how were they going to have the best of both worlds? The water and land?

"Hey, sis. How's it goin?" Zack asked, coming up behind and sitting to the left of her.

"It's fine," she replied, kicking the water.

"You don't look fine. Where is Simon?"

All she could do was point down in the water and stare. Observing the reflection of her own face, she couldn't hide the truth from her brother, even if she tried. She looked up into his eyes, feeling torn up inside. The wedding was driving her crazy; it wasn't even something she would have ever thought she'd do at seventeen. She gave in and told her brother what was going on about the matrimony stuff and how she and Simon were handling the stress.

"Why don't you just have both?" Zack suggested.

"What do you mean?" Silvia replied with a question of her own.

"Have it here at the dock with horses, then jump into the water and have the rest of it. Sounds pretty cool," Zack added.

Sylvia lit up like the Fourth of July at her brother's recommendation. It was a genius idea; how she didn't think of it herself was crazy. She had to give props to Zack—he may not be the smartest when it came to girls, but he sure knew how to plan a wedding. The day was going to be perfect, and it was something her and Simon would both love and never forget for the rest of their lives.

Now that Zack had come up with the best idea, she needed to tell Simon right away. She jumped into the water and held the shell to her mouth that her incredible fiancé had given her in case she ever needed him. He had a shell wrapped around his neck as well so he could communicate back through it.

"Simon, come to the dock, please. I have the best news," Sylvia said excitedly into the shell before going back up to the surface to sit and wait next to Zackery.

She waited for Simon while going over the image of the wedding in her mind. Watching Simon pop his head out of the water made her remember their second encounter, with him on the dock and causing her to get goosebumps all over her body. She still felt shy at the memory of him laying her on her back and stopping things before they got too hot and heavy.

"Is everything okay?" Simon asked when he got out of the water. "Hey, Zack. How have you been?"

"I'm good. Was just talking to Sylvia about your wedding. I'm going to take off and leave you guys to it. See ya, sis. Simon," Zack said before he turned around to take his leave.

Sylvia, now bubbly, told Simon what Zack had suggested they do so they would both get the wedding of their dreams. She brought up having the wedding at the dock, riding down to it on horses before they jumped into the water for the blessing and the pronouncement of marriage. Sylvia could tell by the widespread smile on Simon's dimpled face that he thought it was just as fantastic as she did. Beaming at the image she now held in her mind—forgetting about any fuss they had before the moment—Sylvia knew she'd be forever grateful to her brother for coming up with the perfect plan.

***

Bella and Basil had spent almost all their time together in trees. He was now an amazing tree climber, and she wondered what other activity they could possibly do together. Today she had noticed he looked rather distracted and was more quiet than normal. He was a brave guy, but today he looked sad and distraught. Too afraid that she caused his distant attitude, she kept her own thoughts to herself. Knowing that the Halloween spirit was in full bloom right now in her shop, she came to the idea they should dress up and enjoy the festivities throughout the town.

"What are you dressing up as for Halloween?" Bella asked.

"Oh, I don't know. Anything that matches you," he replied, climbing to the branch she was sitting on to take a seat next to her.

His closeness still made her shy and turn away. This time, she was determined to stay calm. They had been buddies for a long time, yet she still hadn't admitted that she liked him, too; she was unsure what that meant when or if she finally told him. She had watched her own mother be in relationships and she didn't want that kind of complication in her life. Bella did not want to argue with her significant other, or end up wasting her time. She wanted communication, respect, trust, and someone who wasn't jealous of her having other boys as friends. Unlike her parents, she wanted only one love in her life, not have many throughout time only to settle on the least miserable relationship.

"Come on, let's take a walk," Bella suggested while she climbed down and out of the tree.

She watched the marvelous creature that Basil turned into before he flew into the air, gliding above her with all the colors of a blazing fire. She couldn't help but be completely in awe of how incredible he was. That's when she came up with the best idea.

"Come down. I have the perfect thing we can be for Halloween," she said excitedly.

"Yeah! What did you have in mind?" he asked, his eyes still blazing.

"I can create a costume as a phoenix, and you can be your shifter during the festival. What do you think?" she asked.

"I think I love it when you smile like that when you're completely happy. You're exceptionally beautiful," he replied.

Bella could feel the heat appearing again in her cheeks while he looked at her longingly. How could he make her feel so bashful? He still hadn't answered her, and his change of subject made her nervous when his face was so close to hers. She turned away to walk in the other direction before he could get any ideas. Hearing his footsteps behind her and feeling the touch of his hand as he wrapped his own fingers around hers, she didn't pull away, but she could feel the nervous sweat form on her body.

"Let's go spy on someone," Bella said, running towards the ocean, still gripping onto Basil's hand.

Spying on people was something the two were also good at; well.. at least Bella was good at it. She and Basil climbed the tree overlooking the docks and saw Sylvia and Simon talking at the other end. Bella couldn't hear what they were saying, but she could see what they were doing, and by the look on her cousin's face something overjoyed her.

"Can you hear what they're saying?" Bella asked.

"I can. Why? Would you like to know all the corny details?" he teased as he whispered in her ear.

"No corny stuff," she screeched and shook her head at his breath on her ear.

"It's just stuff about the wedding, and now it's about to get *really* cheesy," he said, once again whispering in her ear.

"Will you stop doing that! It feels weird," she said, flicking his forehead.

"Ow! How do you always know exactly where to do that?" he said, rubbing his forehead.

"Years of practice," she teased.

Turning away, she eyed her cousin a little longer. When she thought the situation couldn't get any more awkward after feeling the sensations from Basil's breath on her ear, she had to witness Sylvia wrap her arms around Simon and bring him into an intense make-out session. Observing Basil's face, his eyes looked like they were going to literally pop right out of their sockets. His back was straight and his head thrust forward, watching the couple move from kissing to laying on the wood deck. Bella covered Basil's eyes, and her own with her other hand, praying to the gods that they wouldn't be going any further into their entanglement with each other right out here in public.

Basil removed Bella's hand from his eyes as well her own

in order to face him. She still squinted her eyes shut as her head lolled forward. She could feel his hand on the right side of her cheek leading her to look in his direction. Finally, she opened her eyes to even more trouble. Never feeling the adrenalin and her heart race before now, she held her hand over her chest, thinking there was something wrong with it. Basil took her hand in his while he looked romantically in her eyes. She realized that this was it. This was the day she was going to have her first kiss—and in a tree of all places.

Bella leaned forward while Basil did the same. In that second, before a kiss could be shared, the tree branch cracked and snapped, making the two of them fall and land on the ground below. As if that wasn't humiliating enough, they heard the sound of running footsteps headed in their direction.

"Oh my gosh, Bella! Are you guys, okay?" Sylvia asked in a concerned voice.

"Yep. I'm pretty sure Basil broke my fall," she replied.

"Is he okay?" Simon asked, in alert.

Bella looked at the unconscious boy she had fallen out of the tree with. His eyes were shut and his chest wasn't moving. She shook him, yet he still wouldn't move. Turning him over to look at his back, that's where she saw it. Part of the tree had splintered and stabbed him in the flesh. Hearing the screams of her own cousin ringing in her ears, she couldn't move or release any sound of her own. Uncontrollably, she kept shaking him like he would wake at any moment.

"Basil! No!" the words came out in a horrific cry. "Wake up! Please! *Please*...wake up. I love you. Don't leave me!"

Bella cried, holding onto his body, covering him with her own. She was about to have her first kiss with him, and now he was lying flat on the ground, dead beneath her. He had turned her at the last minute so she could land on him and not be in his position right now. He could have flown.

Wait...he could have flown; he's a phoenix. Oh, please God, let the foinix and the phoenix have the same powers, she thought desperately.

Bella stopped the tears from flowing and turned him back over to remove the stick piercing his body, holding on to one last mythical fact that maybe, just maybe, he would come back to life. Once she had taken the splinter out, still holding it in her hands, she stepped away, still listening to Sylvia weeping. Basil's body went into the air and, *poof,* like a balloon filled with powder that popped, his body was suddenly turned to ash now laying in an enormous pile at her feet. Amazed as the ashes formed into a solid ice shell, they could barely speak as the shell melted away, leaving Basil completely naked now at her feet. She giggled and closed her eyes until she felt the warm hand remove her hand once again from her eyes.

"I love you more," Basil spoke.

The words rang in her ears. He was alive. Bella opened her eyes to see his fire ones and a tear drop down his face, before he pulled her close and lovingly kissed her softly on the lips and tugged her into a hug.

"You're still naked," she squealed, laughing and pushing him away. But now when she looked at him, she could see all of him. Turning away shyly, she aimed her gaze in a different direction.

Sylvia was turned away as well, while Simon came running back with clothes. She had forgotten they were still standing and watching everything. Certain that Sylvia had seen everything made her even more embarrassed. Simon ran by Bella and handed Basil clothes so she could turn back around. She was over the moon at all the events that had happened and the results that had come.

"I'm decent now. You can turn around," Basil laughed.

Bella turned around to face him again. This time he was only half-naked—the half that didn't embarrass her to her very core. She observed his strong build as he stood there, like a supermodel, wearing a pair of her designer jeans with his hands in his pockets. Up top she simply stared at his impressive six-pack of rippling muscles.

"Eyes are up here, darling," he said with his middle and pointer finger in front of his eyes.

All of them roared in laughter while Bella mentally slapped herself out of her own trance.

***

Leah and Izak were in the library. He wanted to learn the Greek language, and Leah wanted to look at books on magic. Surfing the translation section on English and Greek, he pulled out multiple books and walked to a table to sit down. Studying, he made notes addressing regular everyday use of Greek words. Izak was incredibly intelligent and book smart being a 4.0 student in high school and college; the new language would be easy for him to grasp. Watching as Leah took her seat on the couch across from him, he set his pen down to study her.

The smile on her face as she read and practiced simple magic with her hands. She was a fast learner, too. Seems when it always came to what the family really wants, nothing stands in their way when it comes to studying and learning something exciting. Watching Leah made Izak think of having children of his own with Iris. Of course, she had mentioned nothing more about having kids.

Izak could remember the day he broke things off with Iris. Quick but painful was the process: knocking on her door and asking to enter and talk, walking to the bed feeling torn between the right thing to do so she could find someone worthy of her. She was so upset when he told her he couldn't be with her, she had literally kicked him out of her room with magic and locked the door in his face. He had never felt more wrong about anything in his entire life and never wanted to see the pain he had caused her plastered on her beautiful face ever again. Like a coward, he ran to his mother's house once it was finally finished. Bringing random women into his life, not for sex like everyone had assumed, but to bawl his eyes out to complete strangers, made Izak a sensitive man. Not only in his temper but also in heart break emotions, he was never afraid to let the tears come from getting hurt.

"Hi!" Iris came up behind Izak, making him jump out of his skin.

"Why, you brat!" he said, pulling her from behind him into his lap so he could kiss her and hold her.

"Are you okay?" she asked in a concerned tone.

"Yeah. I'm just grateful that you gave me another chance," he said, looking up into her eyes.

"Awe. Of course. How could I not?" she stated, kissing the tip of his nose.

Izak looked at Leah when she started laughing. Bringing his thoughts to children again. Wondering if Iris wanted children. On Earth, it wasn't an option. His ex-wife couldn't have children and he was okay with it, deciding it would be best not to bring a child into the awful world of drugs and disease. But now was different.

"Do you want to have children?" he asked flat out.

Iris had stopped tapping her foot and stiffened in his arms. Did he say something wrong? She had asked him before they even realized they had feelings for one another, and he had stated his feelings on the matter. Iris hadn't expressed her opinion, though.

"I do want children," she replied after a few seconds.

"So do I. With you." He didn't realize he was going to tell her at that moment until he had opened his mouth and the words just released.

"Really?" she yelled, looking at him and making him let out a deep laugh.

"Yes. We can start now," he replied, whispering in her ear and softly kissing the soft skin of her neck.

"You're crazy. We are in the *library*," she giggled.

"Guess you will have to be quiet then," he teased, before she playfully smacked him.

"Aunty Iris, could you show me how this works?" Leah asked, handing her a book.

Iris took the book. Quickly, by the look on her face, it wasn't a good spell that Leah wanted help with. She was still and gazing at the page like she was going over a vicious memory in her mind.

"I can't teach you this kind of magic. It's defense magic...used against feelings for another. When someone doesn't return your affections, the spell helps your heart to heal and protect it. I had to do it for Aunty Arianna when she lost her husband. It's not good or easy," Iris replied, handing Leah back the book.

"I'm sorry, aunty. I have been practicing, though, and can do everything in this book." Leah showed her excitement.

Iris got up and walked to another section of the library to a locked glass cabinet, and used key magic to unlock the doors. Inside, she found a book for older witches. The magic would be perfect for Leah since she was already advanced way beyond her years. Some of the spells and chants in the book were even too hard for Iris. Aware that Leah was twice her power, and had guidance power, made it so the grimoire wouldn't be as difficult for her.

"Here. Take this one and practice. You should do it in the rink so no magic can exit and affect anyone else. You should be safe. Your grandmothers' power will only let you do as much as you can handle," Iris said smiling, hoping her own child would be as creative, intelligent, and magical as Leah.

"Thank you! Thank you!" Leah said, flapping her hands in excitement.

"You are very welcome," Iris spoke, walking to a hidden shelf door within the library and opening it. "The magic rink looks like a boxing rink inside, just use your magic to open the door to leave."

Leah ran inside without looking back at her. Iris smiled as she shut the door to return to Izak. He really had asked to start now on trying for a child. She couldn't believe it; with no doubt in her mind she was ready to be a mother. Iris always wanted to be a mother but spent most of her years taking care of Arianna, and couldn't imagine being with anyone in Drakous realm. Izak was the one she wanted to spend her life with, and now she had the opportunity to extend their duo.

CHAPTER 4

It was time for Alister's town announcement. As he made it through the crowd of people that showed up; nodding his head to them, they parted and bowed their heads in return. Angela and Iris were trailing close behind him. He had received news of Arianna's borders, making anyone fall into a deep sleep if they entered her lands. After Nicholas had informed him, he wondered if the witch was safe enough to be freed. Alister and Angela's family had spent the last two weeks delivering town meeting letters to every shop in Mood Town and every creature and shifter they came across. Donned with his own Drakon stamp as being official realm business, it was mandatory that everyone attend the meeting in the town's center to hear Alister's announcement.

  He stood in the square, with Angela and Iris on each side of him, as well as guards nearby in case anyone had an extra problem with the announcement. As time ticked by, it was now time for Alister to take a stand and make his speech to his entire kingdom.

Alister knew he could make the topic of his announcement a lot easier if he used the power within his voice to make the crowd more reasonable and understanding—slowly hypnotizing them to be agreeable. He would wait and see if it had to come to that and use it as a last resort.

"All of my fellow followers, I have brought on this town meeting for an important matter," he spoke loudly for all to hear. Glancing at Angela, he continued, "Arianna has returned to this realm to reunite with her sisters."

The sudden rumbling of whispers ran through the crowd. Talking back and forth, he could hear and feel all their concerns. Rumors had already spread about her being back in his realm, so it wasn't too much of a shock to many of his people. Of course, they still had their own opinions and feelings when Alister formally announced the news. And they didn't keep quiet about them.

"She's a murderer! She deserves her head on a stake," a man's voice rang through the crowd.

Alister could feel the pain in the man's voice. The curse had obviously hurt him long ago and he wasn't accepting of the news. Knowing that many would have the same reply, Alister continued, "All of you have heard by now that Angela is her twin sister. What you don't know is Arianna had no control over the curse she had cast. She has no memory of what happened and just recently found out herself," Alister explained.

"Does she still have her magic?" a woman asked loudly.

"Yes, she does. But she is no threat, I assure you. After all these years, she has control over it now. I give you my word as your King that she will not harm another. As you all know she restored life to Leo, Atticus's little brother, and she had punished the traitor of our realm and its people."

All were still acting out and hollering in the crowd about their wives and children that lost their lives. He couldn't blame them for each hateful word he heard. He, too, had been affected by the curse.

"I have suffered because of Arianna's curse along with all of you. My wife and unborn child lost their lives because of it. Most of you don't know this for I have never spoken of it, but Queen Alison died because of the curse Arianna unintentionally cast after losing her own beloved child. I will never forget the loss I have endured myself, along with you. But..if we do not let go of the hatred and grudges we hold against this woman, due to the awful accident that occurred, and move on with our lives," he paused to look at Angela peering up at him with sadness and apology in her eyes, "then it will consume all of us and make us no better than the dark force that took over Arianna. So, with all of you as my witnesses, I forgive Arianna and bid her free of all charges. That she, herself, is not guilty of this awful outcome that happened many years ago."

Exhaling, Alister waited to hear any more retaliation; instead, he heard the crowd slowly agreeing with him and watched as his people bowed their heads to his leadership of the kingdom. He was sure they knew if anything ever happened, he would protect them from harm. Even if it meant he had to sentence Arianna to death, even though he loved Angela, he would protect everyone from the witch. Determined to never have it come to that.

"Another matter. Unless you want to take the longest nap of your life, I would stay away from Arianna's borders. To protect herself, she has put up a shield surrounding her lands that will put anyone into a deep sleep if you go near her residence," Alister announced while he listened to the crowd speak to their neighbors.

"Bring up the Halloween party. Leave the meeting on a friendly note," suggested Angela.

"I look forward to seeing you all at the costume dance and what you all dress up as," smiled Alister, before motioning the meeting closed.

* * *

The crowd may have all been agreeable with Alister, but one person in the group was not at all thrilled. Marie, the underwater Queen to King Tarence, was not the least bit happy. She was out for revenge for what King Alister had done to her beloved husband. Seeing how he treated Angela motivated Marie to destroy their love and bond, just like he had succeeded in doing by killing her beloved Tarence.

Leaving the crowd with a plan in mind, she set out to look for the creature far from the near waters below. Making her way to the docks, she turned her head, speaking out loud: "You will pay, King Alister, and you're pretty human. I *will* avenge my Tarence," she vowed before diving into the water in search of the devil squid and its poisonous ink properties.

* * *

Arianna was in the crowd of people listening to Alister's freedom announcement. Surprised by everyone's agreement and acceptance of her so quickly, she had still heard the whispers and the screaming for her death, making her believe that no matter what they said to their king, they would never honestly pardon her for her mistake. With every right to be cautious, with some of Alister's followers still unhappy about the announcement, threatening if they had just a moment alone with her, she would pay.

Arianna couldn't blame anyone for their feelings towards her. His Majesty must certainly love Angela and is blinded by the possibilities she could unleash on the realm. If he knew what she was capable of and knew she had the family crystals in her possession, Arianna was certain that he would sing a different tune as to her being *free*.

She would wait and see the outcome of the announcement before she would allow her presence to be known to all. As she walked away from the crowd with happiness in her heart, knowing her sisters loved her and made this all possible for her, fear still controlled her decisions to stay put in her occupied castle.

Arik was her greatest supporter. They had built a friendship in all the time he had been her prisoner. It no longer felt like he didn't want to be in her company. They did everything together. Both lonely and always together made her believe they might have more than friendship. After all, Angela appeared to have a different man on her mind. Should Arianna feel guilty for the feelings that grew towards the hunky man that turned out to be more intelligent than she had thought? Perhaps muscle and brains were a dangerous combination that Arianna was not prepared for.

* * *

Watching the crowd separate, Neveah ran up to Alister and her sister, Angela. She was in distress; Nick had promised to meet up with her after everything that had happened between them so they could finally be together, and she hadn't heard from him since they last saw each other on her walk. Confused once again about the mysterious man.

"Impressive speech, Alister. I'm sorry you lost your wife that way. That's horrifying," Neveah expressed.

"Thank you, Neveah. It has been difficult for all of us...until your family arrived," he replied, looking in Angela's direction.

Neveah could see the dreamy look in Alister's eyes. She wanted to have that same feeling towards Nick..if they *ever* had time to be together. Wondering where he had been the last couple of weeks.

"Have you heard from Nicholas?" Neveah asked.

"No, the last time I heard from him he had told me about Arianna's borders and then he appeared to be in a hurry. He looked happy and excited about something," Alister informed Neveah.

"He was supposed to meet up with me, but he never showed. I'm worried about him." Neveah could feel deep down something was wrong.

"Hey, sis. Are you okay? You look pale," Angela reported, walking to Neveah.

"Yes. I think Nick is missing, though," Neveah replied with her head down.

"I promise, Neveah; I will investigate his disappearance. It's not like him to promise something and not come through. I know he has gone through a lot with his fiancée and brother. It was heartbreaking for him. I never understood why he wanted to be with the woman. She was certainly different," Alister said with a confused smirk.

"Thank you, Your Majesty." Neveah bowed and walked away.

If Nick ran away again, Neveah wouldn't forgive him this time. There was no room in her life for a coward. She had her own family to worry about. Alister was right, though. It wasn't like Nick to tell her he would meet with her and not show up.

* * *

When Neveah walked away from Alister and her sister, his Majesty continued to wonder about Nick, too. Distracted by Angela's excited voice going on about the party they were going to attend in just a short couple of weeks. Hearing Iris's hopeful voice that maybe Arianna would go with them. Alister couldn't help but hope she wouldn't show her face for a while in order to give the town a chance to register the news. Talking about her being free and watching her walk around free was going to be an entirely different story. Plus, anyone that distracted Angela from his attention made him jealous when he was having a hard time, as it was being "just friends" when he wanted so much to embrace her and enjoy her lips on his once again.

"What are you smiling about? Are you excited to dress up, too?" Angela asked, clearly oblivious to where Alister's thoughts had gone.

"Yes, of course. Anything that makes you happy and shows your big and full smile," he replied with flattery.

Angela blushed, making Alister hopeful that the adult party would bring their friendship up to another level. He was a confident man, but around Angela he felt like a teenage boy with multiple insecurities and uncertainties.

"Bye. Um..Izak's here and, well, we have things to do," Iris spoke, her cheeks turning bright red before waving goodbye to her sister and the King of the Realm.

"What do you think that was about?" Alister asked, noticing Iris's flushed state.

Looking at Angela, she just shook her head back and forth, smiling. Did he miss something? Was there a code between Iris and Angela he didn't know about? Now, Angela was red and embarrassed.

"I think they had quick, intimate plans," she laughed.

Alister laughed along when he realized what Angela was saying. That they planned to run off and have sex. All he could think was how lucky the couple was to have each other and be able to run off and do whatever they liked.

"Do you think they will have children?" Alister asked.

"I don't think so. I asked my brother years ago and he said no. Things may have changed since then. Usually, you don't plan for intimate relations, unless of course you have children and can't simply spontaneously get to enjoy that act."

Angela was feeling more and more embarrassed about their conversation. Her brother's sex life was the last thing on her mind. The idea of having more nieces and nephews to smother and love, however, was exciting for her to think about.

"Do you want more children?" he asked, like it wasn't a hard question to ask.

Angela looked into Alister's eyes. Nothing in his eyes said he regretted asking the question. He was just making conversation. It's not like he was asking to have a child *with* her. The question still made her mind go to continuing her family by bearing more children and having him father those little ones. Mentally taken aback by the sudden desire.

"Yes. Of course. Someday I would love to have more children," she smiled, answering his question. "How about you? Any desire to have little drakouns flying around your realm?"

The question seemed to sadden Alister. How could he ask her a question about having more children but look in distress for the question returned?

"I can't have baby drakouns. I can have children, and those I definitely want many of," he replied, smiling his biggest ever.

"Why can't you have drakouns?" she asked. Suddenly, she felt like an idiot; he was the only one of his kind. Wouldn't his gene spread to the offspring?

"It's too dangerous for the woman to have my species of children," he answered, looking somber.

Angela felt like she shouldn't press the subject. She was incredibly curious about it, though. What could possibly make it so dangerous to carry a dragon baby? She answered that question in her own mind. Thinking of the creature ripping you from the inside out made her cringe.

"I'm sorry. I imagine carrying a fetus drakoun in any woman's belly would be dangerous," she was apologizing, thinking it was comforting. She never expected Alister to laugh at the statement.

"Baby drakouns aren't carried like regular fetuses. They

hatch from an egg. You silly woman. It's dangerous because—" Alister couldn't finish.

A gentleman interrupted the conversation by whispering something in Alister's ear. All she could see was him nodding, and hearing him thank the man.

"Queen Marie is searching for a dangerous creature. I have eyes on her to make sure she isn't up to any wrongdoings," Alister told Angela. "I'm sorry I have to go down and ask around. See you again soon?"

"Of course. Do your royal thing." she smiled, saying her goodbyes. Still curious as to why it was so dangerous to have an adorable little dragon.

***

"Nick, please listen to me. I'm telling you the truth," his brother begged.

"How can I believe anything that comes out of your mouth, Bruce?" Nick snapped on his way to meet with Neveah.

Nicholas had just left His Majesty to see the beautiful Neveah when his brother flew out of nowhere to tell him that the realm was dying. Bruce and Natasha had run away to the ends of Drakous Realm, ready to leave everyone behind. After months, the two noticed everything dying and turning black.

"Look, brother." Bruce handed Nick an egg that was as black as onyx.

"What is this?" Nick asked, taking the dead egg from his brother.

"It's mine and Natasha's egg. We left it in a tree at the highest point. The darkness spread to our home and killed it," Bruce said with tears in his eyes.

"Show me," Nick demanded, ready to follow his brother to the end of the realm.

"It is a long trip. Are you sure you want to come with me?"

"Yes! Just show me, Bruce!" Nick barked irritably at him.

Taking one last look in Neveah's direction, he sighed. He was so close to her he could smell her in the air. Were they *ever* going to get the chance to be together? He had left Alister with his heart full of happiness and now he was following his little brother to the ends. A location where his brother truly believed the realm was starting to die.

CHAPTER 5

It was Halloween and everyone in the kingdom was buzzing around town, chatting on about what they planned to wear at the adult party. Children of the realm were also giggly and excited about dressing up in fun costumes for all to see.

Angela was inside the store with Leah and Liam, getting them ready. Liam was insistent on wearing a wolf costume, and Leah wanted to be an angel. She had ideas on how to make her halo glow with her magic.

"I could always turn you into a pesky wolf, for real," Leah teased.

"Really! Could you?" asked Liam excitedly.

"You're not turning your brother into a wolf. Take this and get in the dressing room," laughed Angela, handing Leah her costume.

"It would be so much fun, though. He would probably be

stuck permanently," said Leah, taking the white and gold fabric and walking into the dressing room.

"Do you need help with your costume, honey?" asked Angela, turning to Liam.

"No, I got it. I really do want to be an actual wolf, Mom," Liam whined and grabbed his costume, stomping into the other dressing room.

"When you're an adult.. if there is a way. You already have an amazing power as it is. Why do you want to be anything more than what you already are?"

"Because he already acts like a filthy canine. Why not be one for real?" Leah continued to give Liam a hard time while she walked out in her angel costume.

"Leah, are you an angel or not? That was mean," Angela said, warning her daughter if she continued there would be consequences.

"Sorry. Mom. I was just getting him back for all the years he picked on me and I could never tell him how it made me feel," said Leah, putting her head down.

Turning away from her reprimanding parent, Leah looked at herself in the mirror, twirling around in a circle. She loved her brother, but he was always mean to her when she was trapped in her mind. He would boss her around and yell at her for touching anything and everything. She was older than Liam by two short years, but ever since he was a toddler of two years, he'd taken on the daily roll to make sure she got to do close to nothing. No one could understand what she had gone through stuck in a dark room in her own mind with no real escape. The only one that could relate would be Aunt Arianna, and no one seemed to know how to contact her.

Leah snapped her fingers and brought her halo to a bright, luminescent glow; she strapped the back of it to her dress. Magic was all too easy for her. Her own grandmothers' essence wouldn't allow her to continue onto more advanced magic. It was annoying having to stop when she was progressing so quickly. She wondered on a daily basis if she would ever have complete control of her magic, and have no one limit her to what they thought was standard.

"You look glorious."

"Thanks, Mom."

It was Liam's turn to present himself. When he walked out of the room, he stopped in front of the mirror, like Leah. With a sigh, he looked at Leah and smiled. She was smiling, too. She waved her hand towards the back of Liam. When he turned around to look at his behind, he now had a tail. It was fluffy, full, and black, bouncing along with him as he jumped up and down in excitement.

"Oh, my God! Is he going to have that forever?" Angela screamed.

"No, just for tonight. I promise."

"Well, hopefully it gives you better balance than before." Angela took a breath and patted his head.

Leah and Liam just laughed at their mother's joke when the bell rang out from above the door. It was Bella. You could easily tell, because as soon as the door opened, so did her sister's mouth.

"Mom, is my costume ready?" Bella asked, rushing through the store. "Leah, you look amazing. Liam..is that *real*?"

"Yep. It's only going to be here tonight though. Unless Leah could make it permanent," replied Liam, while Bella grabbed hold of his tail and playfully pulled on it.

"Yeah, Mom would never allow that."

"Here it is, babe," said Angela, handing Bella her feathery costume.

"Thanks."

Bella took it and jumped into action. She was in a hurry to get out of her regular clothes and put on her red and orange outfit covered in feathers and plumage. Bella had been wanting and wondering if she could fly with them if she had the attributed, so she'd also made an exact mold of Basil's wings; the same length, height and weight, with feathers cast to match his own. Bella suddenly knew it could end up being a problem, seeing as that his build was so much different than hers; with her size and weight, it would definitely throw off her balance.

Exiting the dressing room, Bella went to show off her costume. Leah could see her displeased expression immediately. Circling Bella, Leah went to work; pulling out her magic, she made the feathers more realistic, gave her an orange tone to match Basil, and changed the size of her wings to match with her body type so she'd be safe.

"Thank you *so* much, Leah." Bella beamed with joy.

"Oh! I wish I had a camera. I could cry right now. You all look amazing," Angela said, giving each of her children a hug.

"*Mom*...you're going to mess up our costumes." The complaint was issued in unison as Angela rolled her eyes at the disgruntled faces.

* * *

Neveah and the kids were all dressed and ready at the castle, waiting for the evening to begin. Zack had dressed up as a great big, green Hulk character and Sylvia had donned the dress of an evil dark fairy. Leaving Neveah as a vampire queen.

"Do you think there's a realm where real fairies exist?" asked Sylvia.

"What about Hulk? Do you think *he* exists?"

"I think anything is possible at this point. Look where we are. None of us thought any of these mystical creatures existed. Now we walk around with them every day," Neveah answered.

"I hope your creature isn't lurking anywhere near us. We would all be doomed," Sylvia laughed, looking at her mother.

"How do you know I'm not real?" Neveah teased, acting

like she was going to drain her children of their blood.

They all laughed as Neveah pulled her almost grown children into her arms.

In the back of her mind the worry about Nick's disappearance was still beating against her brain. No one had seen him, and she couldn't help but fear the worst. What if he was passed out on the witch's land? Alister said he had sent a search party to look for him, but it had been over two weeks and still no news.

Neveah had been searching in magical books to see if she could use her powers to locate Nick and make sure he was okay. Unfortunately, without a relative's blood or one of his feathers, locating him was impossible.

"Are you ready to meet your sister at the shop?" Atticus asked, dressed up in his own warrior costume.

"Yes, we're ready," Neveah said with a smile.

Atticus had been a genuine friend of the family. Neveah thought of him like a brother, and the rest of the family would agree. There was something pure and honorable about him.

Atticus would escort them to town and meet up with his own two daughters, son, and wife in town after he dropped them off at Bella's Boutique.

Sylvia was excited to see her beloved Simon dressed up, and Zack was to meet the girls and a group of friends in town by the food. They had their own party to attend later that evening, and all the adults came to an agreement they could, *if* it was close to His Majesty's castle.

* * *

"You look breathtaking," Izak told the beautiful woman standing before him.

"No one is going to know who we are," Iris giggled.

"That's the best part."

Izak thought her idea of being a witch and warlock was too

basic, so he had taken control of what they would be, choosing the classic lovers, Romeo and Juliet. He figured the characters suited them well. Watching Iris doing her hair and makeup, he was a bit surprised that she didn't just use her magic to do all of it. A shot of worry hit his heart when he noticed that she looked sad sitting in front of the mirror.. and he knew why.

"Are you thinking about your sister?" he asked, taking a seat next to her.

"Yes," she sighed.

"Do you think she will show up?"

"No. If she were going to, I think she would have come out of hiding by now. I don't know what's keeping her from visiting us again."

"We should try to go see her soon. It's not right to be all alone during the holiday season coming up. We should all be together."

"I know." Iris stood up to wrap her arms around Izak. "Have I told you how amazing you are, lately?"

"Hmm, let me think. Maybe last night," he teased.

"You're awful!" she laughed, smacking him on the shoulder.

"Do you think you're pregnant?" he asked, reaching down to rub her stomach.

"No. It's only been a couple weeks." She smiled.

"Yeah, but can't you use your witchy senses to tell?"

"It doesn't work so soon," she laughed. "We should get going if we want to make it to the store with everyone else."

Izak couldn't help but imagine taking their little girl or boy trick-or-treating someday. He smiled and shook his head at how much he had changed. Never would he have thought the idea of fatherhood would make him feel so warm inside. Iris had reassured him that there was nothing wrong with him, and he was perfectly healthy to conceive a child. With that being said, he didn't understand why she looked so doubtful of his capability; certainly she was able, too. Right?

* * *

Arianna was tipsy. She wanted to join the festivities in town, but instead sat at home wallowing in her sadness. She definitely had the desire to see her family again, but was too afraid to face them and be honest about not being ready to go completely to the light side. After all, the dark could be fun sometimes, *if* you controlled it as well as she did.

"Do you have anything stronger than wine in your house?" she asked Arik who was sipping on his glass.

"Actually, I do. Come on. Let's go get it," he said, grabbing her hand to help her up from the recliner she had been sitting in.

Walking down the steps and through the hallway of her castle, she stopped at her nursery room. Standing there, in front of the door, the look of sadness washed over her face.

"Oh, no, none of that. We are going to have some fun tonight," he said, pulling her out of her trance and down the steps out of her castle doors.

The coolness outside hit her face, making the inflamed skin feel much better. She could already use a cold bath. Looking up at the man who was rushing her to his little green home, made Arianna smile.

Once they had made it to the steps and inside the abode, she could see the appeal. It was simple, with a small kitchen and gated room. He had let go of her hand to head to his long glass cabinet full of many kinds of liquor.

"Take your pick. I have it all," he told her, grabbing a bottle of Jameson whisky. "Hello old friend."

"I'm not much of a hard drinker. Is that any good?" Arianna asked.

"You have never had this? Oh, it's all we will need," he said, pulling her back outside and towards her castle.

Once inside, he rushed her into the kitchen. Still pulling

her arm, his grip began making her sore.

"Will you stop pulling me around so hard? Geez, my arm feels like its gonna fall off," she said, rubbing her wrist.

"Sorry. I guess I don't know my strength," he said, pouring them two double shots of the whisky.

She picked up her glass and smelled inside, coughing at the potent odor it emitted. Following his lead, she clinked her glass with his after he said cheers. He then downed his entire glass in one shot. Arianna followed.

"That's *so* gross and strong. I need juice or something." She looked around the kitchen for a juicy fruit. Biting into the peach, she laughed as the liquid ran down the sides of her face.

"That looks good; let me have a bite," he said, holding out his hand.

"No way, it is mine. Oh, and it's so.. good," she laughed, taunting him, daring him to just *try* to take it from her.

"I'm going to get it," he said reaching out to grab it.

He was too slow for her. She dodged his hand and took off upstairs to her power room—plopping in her recliner with her mother's grimoire.

* * *

Angela was getting ready for the adult Halloween party with Alister. She was beaming in excitement to see him come out of the dressing room in his black and red pirate outfit.

"I'm not coming out," Alister grunted from behind the door.

"What do you mean? You have to come out. *Please?* I know you look great," she said, laughing into her hand.

Angela knew it would be hard for the proud king to show not just her, but his kingdom, this side of him. He had been amazing these last few months, and she'd become happier and more relaxed with her heart around him, so she knew that softer, humorous side of him could come through.

"I look like a fool," he grunted.

"Come on. For me," she begged.

"Like, literally for you?" he said, a tone of interest resounded in his voice.

"I don't know. You never know what the costume will do to me," she manipulated in a fun way.

"Fine," he replied.

Opening the door, he stood in the opening looking at her with a patch over one eye. She had to admit, he was incredibly sexy in his costume. Angela had always had a soft spot for role-playing and the look of His Majesty dressed in pirate boots and the complete outfit, added with a hat, made her mind wander. She had planned to tease him a bit when he walked out; now all she could do was look at him like he was a large piece of chocolate she wanted to savor.

Shaking the steamy mental images from her head, she smiled. "You look amazing."

"Okay...but I'm not wearing the eye patch," he said seriously.

"Okay, fine. My turn," she said, running into the same dressing room with her costume in her hand.

Excited as she tried on the costume, her hope was that she looked as equally good-looking as His Majesty. He had really proven himself to her.

As she looked in the mirror at the pirate dress she was now wearing, she was pleased with her appearance. Unlatching the door to the dressing room, she walked out to show Alister but...he wasn't there.

*　*　*

Alister was waiting for Angela to get out of the dressing room when he heard a tap on the window of the store. When he walked to the front to see who or what it was, he saw a crow rapping on the glass. Stepping out of the store, the crow spoke to him:

"Your Majesty. We have found King Nicholas. He sends word from the end of the realm that the vegetation is dying and the sickness is spreading slowly. He informs us it has also killed the eggs of an eagle in a nest surrounded by darkness. Nicholas will not be returning soon," the crow finished.

"Does anyone else know of this?"

"Just the flight shifters, Your Majesty."

"Keep it that way. I don't want to worry anyone with this news yet," Alister demanded.

"As you wish," the crow nodded and flew away.

Alister was going over the frightening information in his mind. It wouldn't be long before everyone knew about the realm dying. He wondered why it was happening now. He had heard that the realm was sick when he was just a boy, but never thought he would be alive to watch it die.

"There you are. Is everything okay?" asked Angela, walking outside.

"Not really," he replied. Turning toward her, he stopped in his tracks and his mouth fell open. He was literally stunned by the short black and red pirate dress covering Angela's magnificent body.

He stared in awe, instantly wanting to cover her up so other, more unworthy eyes, couldn't take a gander at the beautiful form. The black printed stockings she wore he could see through, and as his pulse began to race, he forced himself to be calm and relaxed.

"What happened?" she instantly asked, apparently unaware of his reaction.

Alister's mind was racing over what he was going to tell her. He had promised not to lie to her ever again. But if he told her his realm was slowly dying, and everything in it, she would be upset and not enjoy the Halloween sprit.

"Could I get away with telling you after tonight?" he pleaded.

"Is it a serious matter? What's it regarding?" she asked.

"My realm. We are not in any instant danger, but we will have to figure something out in time," he replied, hoping it was enough to get Angela's mind off it.

"Yes. You can tell me tomorrow. I hope it's nothing dangerous, though."

He reached out for her hand and smiled. "Well, I must say, you look," he thought about what Basil would say, "hot!"

It seemed to work just how he hoped. Angela burst into a laughing fit. She couldn't breathe by the time he joined in the fun of laughing with her. Wasn't until the kids walked up to them smiling when they finally caught their breath.

"What's so funny?" Basil asked, smiling and laughing himself.

"Your uncle just called me hot," she laughed again.

"Way to go, uncle. He's *not* wrong," Basil smirked before it quickly was wiped off his face when Bella's smack connected with the back of his head.

"Ow! Why is your daughter so abusive?" he asked, rubbing the back of his skull.

Now together were Bella and Basil, Leah and Liam, and Alister and Angela. Soon followed by Neveah and her older children, with Iris and Izak.

"Wow, you all look epic," Sylvia announced. "Have any of you seen Simon?"

"No, I think that's him." Bella pointed at the boy with purple hair, wearing clown face paint.

"Oh my gosh, he's the Joker," Sylvia laughed loudly. "I'm guessing you helped him with that."

"Yep, sure did," Zack replied proudly.

"You look sexy," Simon said, approaching Sylvia and embracing her in a kiss.

"Thank you. You look perfect," she repaid the compliment.

"Well, let's mingle and find our friends," Angela suggested, wrapping her hand around Alister's bicep, taking his arm.

The family walked around town, taking gifts and treats offered to them by everyone. They left the witches to do tricks and offer blessings to the people. Zackery had met up with Ziara and Zinnia. Bella found Jacky and soon joined Zack and the rest.

"Where should we go?" Zack asked with his arm hanging across Zinnia's shoulders.

Zinnia covered her face in black- and orange-colored stripes. She was still representing a tiger, just not her normal white, snow tiger self. She had her claws extended and whiskers from her natural feline shift.

The group of children started walking towards the forest area to playfully scare the younger children. Zinnia brought along the idea of tormenting more than teasing playfully.

"Watch where you're going," hissed Zinnia, when another girl bumped into her while just playing with her group of friends.

"Sorry, I didn't see you," she replied, still laughing.

"You think it's funny stumbling into others?" Zinnia taunted, wanting to pick a fight.

Zack looked at the now startled girl Zinnia was being rude to. When he saw her push the girl down, laughing as the girl landed on her back, he knew he couldn't just stand back and watch. Grabbing Zinnia by the wrist, he jerked her hard backwards. Making her fall to the ground.

"What is *wrong* with you? You're an embarrassment. You said you would work on your bitchy attitude, but now you're just being flat out cruel," Zack said furiously. He had never been so mad before.

"Are you okay? I'm sorry she was so mean to you," Zack said, reaching his hand out. "What's your name?"

"It's okay. It was my fault. I should have been looking where I was walking," she replied, reaching up to grab his hand. Standing, she brushed herself off. "I'm Yalonda."

Now that she was out of the shadows, Zack could see her

face. She was gorgeous and looked to be the same age as him. Eyes a smoky grey, and filled with kindness, she wore the longest eyelashes he had ever seen, and offered a smile that made him speechless. He couldn't stop looking into her eyes, and because of how close she was to him, Zack was certain that she could see the affects she had on him. Her skin was dark like Atticus, making him think she might be related to him.

"Are you a horse?" he asked before he could stop himself.

"No. I'm an owl," she giggled.

"Really? That's amazing. Owls were my favorite animal back in my world. I collected stuffed animals and had stickers all over my wall." He smiled, talking too much until she looked confused.

"We can explain more later. Zack is just babbling," Bella teased. "I'm Bella and this is my...my boyfriend Basil."

Basil's eyes lit up; the fire in them seemed to inflame at Bella's words. The announcement seemed to mean the world to him because he grabbed her hand and kissed it before stepping forward to say hello to the girl.

"It's nice to meet you. Your costumes look amazing."

"This is my best friend Jacky, and Ziara, my cousin Sylvia and her fiancé Simon," Bella continued the introductions.

"Hi," all waved in unison at Yalonda.

She blushed at all the attention she was getting. Everyone had forgotten about Zinnia, still sitting on the ground. Finally she jumped up, acting like she was about to attack. Zackery jumped in front of Yalonda, pulling her protectively behind him.

"That's enough!" he yelled. "Go away! I never want to see you again, Zinnia."

Zinnia was in mid-shift when Zack stomped his foot on the ground and yelled at her. She instantly fell forward—not as her almighty tiger, but in her human form. She uncontrollably changed back into a human and stumbled, rolling into a ball on the ground.

"How did you do that?" She screamed in pain when she landed.

"What are you talking about? All I did was yell at you. You're the one who shifted back in midair…right?" Zack asked, disoriented by her words.

"No, I didn't. You're a freak. You did it. Or *one* of you did," she yelled at the entire group before taking off back to town.

Zack was stunned. What the hell was she talking about? The girl had loose wiring, that was for sure. How could he have turned her human by simply yelling at her? He had never felt so protective in all his life. A rush of power shot through him, but it wasn't an actual power. At least…he didn't think so.

CHAPTER 6

The family walked around town for hours; their journey ended when Leah and Liam became exhausted carrying their bags full of treats and gifts. The last friends they ran into were Atticus and his wife, Jessika.

"Hi, Atticus, what's up?" Liam asked, running up to him.

Liam always admired Atticus. He would never tell his friends that he would rather be a noble steed instead of a wolf, even though he loved the creature more than the canines.

"Well hello, little man," Atticus said with a smile. "I'm great, been busy. When are you going to come train with us?"

"As soon as I can. I have been training with the wolves a lot, so I haven't had much time for anything else."

"Have you heard from our mother?" Angela inquired.

"No. I haven't. I'm sorry."

"How long does a honeymoon last? What could possibly be

taking them so long to get back?" Angela asked out loud without thinking. Everyone's laughter at her made her realize how silly the question was.

"Hello, Jessika, we haven't seen you in a while," Iris said.

"Oh, I know. I'm sorry. I have been doing a lot of hiking and exercising. I'm on an energy kick lately."

Iris knew that Neveah would have a lot in common with Jessika if they ever got to know each other. They both loved to go on hikes, and they shared the same artistic talents when it came to making jewelry. Iris realized that Neveah hadn't made anything new since the family arrived at the new realm.

"We need to get together soon. You, me, and Neveah."

"I would love to." Smiled Jessika.

"Where are your little ones?" Alister asked.

"They are with the other teens. Going to that party at the cabin close to your castle," Atticus replied.

"That's great that all the children are getting along. Shall we head to our own party?" Izak asked, offering his arm to Iris.

"We shall." She replied, taking his arm.

* * *

When Alister volunteered to have the adult party at his castle, Queen Tiana had asked to decorate it. It was very different for Alister to have any event at his own residence, being that the last one he'd hosted was with his wife Alison. The entire realm was thrilled, however, to see what their king's home was like. Tiana had promised to make it 'welcoming and entertaining' for everyone to enjoy.

Upon entering the castle it was crystal clear that it had been touched by witches. Pumpkins floated along the ceiling, streams of candlelight decorated every inch, and live spiders even crawled along the walls.

"If I find any of those in my bed after this, I will be

vengeful," Alister warned Iris.

"Are you afraid of spiders, Almighty Drakon?" Angela snickered.

"Not at all. I just don't want to be sharing a bed with the creepy things," he lied.

"That's the point. Halloween is supposed to be scary and spooky," Iris teased, making crawly creatures with her hands.

The children were sent off to bed with a hug and kiss from Angela; the caretaker assisted them up the stairs. They sulked slowly up the steps, complaining of being tired with every step they took. Watching her two children fade from sight, she continued with her family and friends from the hall to the ballroom.

When they entered the room, Tiana ordered the music to begin, and Iris lit up the room by activating the crystals; she gave them an orange glow and put in a spooky ceiling, with the full moon and face skeletons hanging from the ceiling.

The audience clapped and whistled at the amazing display Queen Tiana and Iris put on; they had made the room perfect for the Halloween spirit. Shortly, the crowd moved out onto the dancefloor.

Angela's first instinct was to find her dear friend. She loved all the decorations and colors but, like Alister, she had no desire to have any of the crawly spiders anywhere near her either. They were huge and black, like tarantulas, but something you see in the desert. Shuddering at the creature's presence on the walls all around them, she walked towards Tiana who had chosen aptly to dress up as a black and gold spider.

"So, you're the mother of all these spiders," Angela said upon reaching Tiana.

"Oh, definitely; my creepy offspring. I would check every part of your clothing before you leave tonight. If you leave at all," Tiana teased, dropping her voice into a frightening tone.

"I can't say I *will* be leaving tonight, but not because of what you think."

"Oh *really*...?" Tiana raised her eyebrows.

"You brat," Angela laughed, turning red. "I meant; I'm not going to wake up my children to leave."

"Yeah. Sure. Totally," Tiana winked at her.

Angela was about to respond but was stopped by a soft touch on her shoulder. Turning around she smiled into the man's glorious eyes.

"Well, Hello Captain. Are you here to ask me to dance?" asked Angela.

"Why, yes I am, my lady. Care to join me?" he asked, offering his hand.

"I would be honored."

Alister and Angela joined the dancefloor, twirling around in their pirate costumes and laughing while they spoke of the outcome for the first Halloween held in his realm. The music had changed to a different tone of slow dancing, and the two embraced each other; Angela was wholeheartedly happy to be in his arms. She couldn't stop smiling and knew that she wanted to be with Alister in all ways, not only as friends.

Angela lifted her head from his chest to look up into his beautiful eyes. His eyes were closed and he wore a large smile upon his face. As if he could feel her gaze, he opened his eyes to look down into hers. Cheeks turned red as the mood in the room changed immediately; everything was suddenly moving in slow motion.

Alister cupped his hand under Angela's chin to lead her face towards his. Tilting his head down to meet hers, he brushed her lips.

"I have an announcement to make." Izak's voice suddenly came out over the intercom.

But before Izak could continue his announcement, it became clear that someone else had a bigger one to share with the room full of people.

"She's done it again! The witch has killed another

pregnant woman!" A woman's voice burst through the doors of His Majesty's castle.

Alister grew angry at the sudden interruption, already doubting the outburst. The voice belonged to Queen Marie, and he knew never to believe *anything* that came out of her mouth. Apparently the crowd thought differently by the sounds of their gasps and screams of fear.

"It can't be true, Alister," Angela fearfully spoke, shaking her head.

"Don't worry. I know. Let me take care of this and then we will continue," he spoke reassuringly to Angela and kissed the back of her hand.

"Let's not jump to conclusions. I will investigate the situation. Remember, this is Queen of the traitor who tried to kill me; she may do anything to avenge her husband!" Alister raised his voice, saying the words loud enough for everyone to hear.

With his words, everyone calmed. They now realized whose crazy voice had yelled out the news.

"It's true, Your Majesty. I would never hurt anyone. Not like this," she pleaded for him to believe her.

"Iris, come with me. I need you to check the body," Alister demanded, rushing outside to follow Marie.

"She's in town. In front of Angela's store," Marie informed.

* * *

The teenagers were gathered in the middle of the cabin, sitting in a circle on the wood floor with a bottle in the center. Bella had come up with a fun game so everyone could get to know each other. They would spin the bottle and whoever the tip ended up pointing at, they would ask the person across from them something about themselves, and vice versa. Getting up and moving round the circle after each spin would allow many secrets to be revealed by the end of the game.

"Ready?" Bella asked the group while she spun the bottle.

Zack spun and the tip of bottle landed on the new girl, Yalonda.

There had only been one question running through his mind from the first time he laid his eyes upon her. "Do you have a boyfriend?"

The other teens laughed but kept it short, turning to the now-flushed girl for an answer. She was shaking her head. "No."

"Do you want one?" Zack spat out, leaving the rest of the kids rolling on the floor laughing.

She still hadn't answered, but the piece of wood that landed in his lap coming from his sister's direction made him think he asked a dumb question, or at least an embarrassing one.

The girl was shy, shrugging her shoulders. The eyes that were all on her again waiting for an answer was too much. She just pulled her arms around her knees and hid her face.

"Now you did it, Zack. I'm sorry, Yalonda, sometimes my brother can be really stupid." Sylvia got up and walked to her, wrapping her arm around her back.

"I'm okay. I'm just not used to being around so many people. I stay in my owl form more than my human, so this is all a little much. I'm the sorry one."

"That's okay. No pressure. Just hang out and get to know everyone else. When you're ready, you let us know," Sylvia spoke sweetly to the girl.

"I don't want a boyfriend. At least, not right now," she tilted her head up to face everyone.

"You shouldn't have even asked that," Bella scolded.

"I was just being playful and teasing. I didn't know it was going to be such an upsetting question."

"Okay. Okay. Can we move on?" Jacky cut in before spinning the bottle.

The bottle landed on her this time. In front of her was

Sylvia. The room was silent for a moment when Jacky finally asked an even more embarrassing question.

"Have you and Simon had sex yet?"

Everyone seemed to be just as curious. Even Yalonda looked towards Sylvia with the same questioning eyes.

She looked from Simon to Jacky and just started laughing. Showing her bashful side, she replied, "I'm not going to answer that question. But, uh...what about you, Jacky? Any interest in boys. Or should I say girls?" sassy Sylvia asked an equally invasive question.

Jacky shot daggers at Bella who looked stunned and shook her head to reassure her that she had said nothing. But with that look, Jacky had given away her biggest secret. Now all her friends knew, and she wasn't at all ready to come out of the closet. Her thought process was telling her to get up and run or stand her ground.

"Yeah, so? Bella says it's perfectly normal in your realm for girls to like girls and boys to like boys," Jacky spoke confidently, standing up.

While all the teens were looking at her. The princess of all the land creatures announced she was a lesbian. Their mouths shot open, gasping in surprise.

"She's not the only one. I like girls, too," Ziara shouted, standing up beside her.

Silence had filled the room. Bella and Sylvia, being the only two that weren't surprised by the news, made their opinions known. Bella ended the silence by clapping loudly and whistling. Sylvia joined in, shouting, "Good for you guys!" The rest were confused but soon added in clapping and smiles of their own.

The game completely ended and all of them spent the rest of the night laughing and giggling; it was as if they had become the best of friends because of all the awkward questions. It had quite literally broken the ice between everyone.

***

The next time Arianna saw Arik he was carrying the two glasses in his hand and the bottle in the other. As he entered the room, she pretended like she hadn't noticed him at all.

"You didn't save me even a bite?" he asked complaining.

She shook her head while it was still in the book. Watching him out of the corner of her eye, he came up to the recliner in front of her. Setting his huge man hands on each side of the armrests, she could feel his eyes burning a hole in her mother's book, so she set it down to look at his face.

"Can I help you?" she asked because of how close he was and still staring at her.

"What are you reading?" he asked, picking it up to observe it. Appearing uninterested in it at all, he set it on the table next to her chair.

Facing her again with his beautiful blue eyes staring into her very soul., he remained completely silent. Confused at what he was doing, she shot him a critical stare.

"Oh, come on, don't pretend like you haven't thought about me kissing you," he said suddenly, leaning in.

Arianna dodged him, going out from under his arm; leaving her chair, she began backing up slowly. He was making her heart speed up as he walked in a determined gait towards her.

"You're drunk, Arik. Don't do something you might regret," she said. She tried to reason with him, until she met the wall behind her.

Her back now up against the wall, Arik still walked towards her. Her heart was racing in excitement. She had thought Arik was so charming and handsome, getting close to him these last few months as he listened to everything she had to say. Now everything was happening too fast.

"Don't make me throw you backwards," she said, lifting her right hand, ready to send him flying if he came one more step towards her.

He grabbed her right hand and pinned it against the wall. Lifting her left, he immediately grabbed that one, too. She really didn't want to fight. He was right...she had been dreaming about him and wanted him with every part of her body.

Pretending to struggle in his tight grip, he transferred both of her hands into one of his and pinned her arms above her head once again. She looked down at her feet, too afraid to face him. He reached up with his free left hand and stuck his thumb and four fingers up to her throat. She could feel his hand there as she swallowed, and he forced her to look up into his eyes.

Once she tilted her head back and opened her eyes, it was already over. He brought his lips closer to hers by halfway and waited a few seconds. She could have kicked him in the leg for being so slow.

Closing the gap, he firmly landed his lips on hers. Hungry, like he was trying to get a taste of that peach she had teased him with, he ran his tongue along the inside of her mouth. The heat erupted in her body as she replied to the unbelievable sensations he was sending through it.

Finally releasing her arms from above her head, she wrapped them around the back of his neck. Jumping up into the air, she proceeded to wrap her legs tightly around his waist. Feeling him grab hold of her thighs, he then walked her to the bed before dropping her down on top of it.

* * *

They reached the body of a woman lying on the ground in front of Bella's shop. Iris bent down to check her pulse. To her dismay, the woman had no pulse...neither did the fetus growing inside her belly.

Instantly feeling sick, she held her mouth and ran across the street to the nearest trashcan, releasing her absolute disgust. Crying, she shook her head and accepted Izak's offering of a hanky, wiping her mouth. This was not the time to be happy about her new possible realization *or* to announce it. Holding her stomach, she walked back to the body.

"You don't have to, Iris," Alister spoke.

"Yes, I do. I have to clear my sister's name."

Bending down once more, Iris used her magic to sense if the death of the woman was caused by magic. As soon as she touched the body, she felt almost deadly sick. She couldn't read or sense if there was *any* magic used or not.

In fact, she felt like she had lost her magic completely. Standing up and stumbling, she lifted her hand in the air and tried to make a firework. Nothing happened. Instead, she fainted, landing in Izak's arms who had never left her side.

CHAPTER 7

Waking up the next morning, Arik felt regretful with his head throbbing from the amount of alcohol he consumed the night before. Arianna lay next to him appearing to be deep in a peaceful sleep.

She may look like his wife, but her personality and strength were far from Angela's. Arianna was more confident and had a fire in her soul. Finding it to be a very attractive quality in the woman, it was hard to not wake her up and receive a repeat of the night before.

Angela's personality was very agreeable, and she accepted all his faults. Rarely did she ever speak against what he said, and always allowed him to take the lead and never put up a fight.

While he watched the woman sleep, he could tell she had been through many hardships in her life, yet she never told him much about what Earth had been like for her. Just that it was awful, and she would never want to go back.

Her face was stern and in control, like she knew what she wanted in life and was determined to get whatever it is she sets out for.

Getting up, Arik slowly slithered away from the bed to walk downstairs and guzzle as much water as he could find. Hoping when Arianna woke up, she could remove his hangover.

* * *

Arianna could feel Arik slightly pull on the blanket and remove himself from her bed. Pretending to be asleep so he wouldn't speak to her; not wanting to hear his regrets as he snuck out of the room. She didn't want him to know that the smallest pin drop or slightest movement on the bed could wake her up.

Luckily, she had been drunk when she fell asleep; if not, Arik's freight train of a snore would have made her literally throw the man out of her bed. Only hearing it early this morning already made her want to suffocate the man with the pillow. She would be ready to fix that medical problem if he ever wanted to continue to share her bed in the future.

He left the room and shut the door behind him. As soon as Arianna heard the click of the latch, she pushed the blanket off her naked body and walked to her vanity to look in the mirror. Holding her own head from the pain the whisky had produced, she decided then and there that she would never touch that kind of wretched alcohol again.

Her hair was a mess and the marks on her neck made her gasp at the silliness of them. What was the man, "a teenager" staking his youthful territory? None of that would do.

Now walking to her power station, she picked up a stone and pressed it to her neck, removing the hickey from existence. She then moved on to mix an instant hangover elixir that would stop the effects it had on her head and body; being nice, she mixed some for Arik as well.

Downing the mixture in one gulp took all of Arianna's might to not spit it out as it bitterly streamed down her throat. Like swallowing a rubber band, the bitterness lingered while the side effects of the night before disappeared.

Arianna fixed the rest of her appearance on her powerful and meaning business attire. Walking downstairs to join Arik in the kitchen, she carried his concoction in her right hand.

"I know it was a mistake. That will not happen again. No need to speak further about it. I brought you an instant hangover cure," she spoke, showing Arik the cup. Before she could explain more, he grabbed it, shooting it back like he had done multiple shots of whisky.

Waiting for his reaction, Arianna stood there with an amused look on her face. A wide grin came forth when he tasted it and the mixture flew back out of his mouth and nose, followed by a burst of uncontrollable coughing and gagging.

"Ha, ha! That will teach you to wait until I have finished instructing you on how to do things; in this case, how to drink a potion of mine." Still laughing, she abandoned him to go make another.

* * *

Alister was on his way to Julia's home, where Izak and Iris were staying, to see how Iris was doing. Queen Marie was untrustworthy. Knowing this was not enough to convince his followers, however, or to lock her away for good. Setting up a large group for an investigation was all he could do. If he didn't find out what actually happened, he feared all could be in grave danger. They would turn against Arianna, for sure, and could make her really cause problems for everyone.

Pondering everything in his mind, he lifted his fist and knocked on the door, listening to footsteps rushing towards it.

"Hi, Izak. How is Iris?"

"Hey, Alister. Please come in. She's awake."

As Alister walked through the house, he admired the solid interior walls. He was always impressed by the meticulous workmanship of his people.

"Is my sister okay? I know she didn't do it. That was poison, so I couldn't tell if magic was used. Incredibly dangerous. If I would have stayed by that woman much longer, it would have killed me. She would never do that to me," Iris spoke in a pleading tone while she lie on the couch covered in her blanket.

"I know. I know, Iris. It's okay. I believe it wasn't her either. I just don't have any proof to say otherwise. The people are getting worried and may try to go after her if I don't find out what really happened, and soon."

"I'm so glad you know that to be true," she replied.

"I have to take my leave. I promise I will get to the bottom of this. Just get better soon." He bowed to the both of them and took his leave. He was heading into town, where he knew his people were awaiting his reassuring words.

* * *

"There is *no* proof of Arianna being responsible for the tragic scene that we all saw on Halloween night. I have opened a kingdom-wide investigation to find out who could be responsible for the death of the woman. I do not trust Queen Marie and I urge all of you to follow my lead. I speak from experience, as you all know what happened when I had to take the life of the underwater king. She informed me I would regret what I had done. It's my belief she has done or had someone else do this unnatural act. All of you please listen for anything strange filtering throughout town, and if you come across something let me know so I can investigate myself. Thank you all for your time in listening to me today." Alister ended his speech and got down from the center of the town square.

* * *

Queen Marie listened to Alister's speech and became worried herself. She needed to build a group of followers that the curse had affected and make them see Arianna was indeed the murderer. Observing the surrounding, questioning chatter made her realize that it shouldn't be a hard task to accomplish. A group had already formed and now all she needed was to throw fuel on the fire that was already building.

"You all know that I am crazy, but I would never take a life of an innocent woman. Let alone a child. You know as well as I do His Majesty is clouded by his love for Arianna's twin and will do anything to protect her and her family," Marie interrupted the complaining group who seemed to believe Arianna was guilty of the crime.

The bunch looked at Marie like she had donned the hat of their leader; they wore a "what do we do next" kind of expression, waiting for her orders.

Smiling, feeling like she was taking candy from a baby, she proceeded to turn these people against their ruler and make them believe only her words.

"What are we going to do now?" A gentleman asked.

"We wait and go after the witch ourselves. But we must have patience. Choose a time when everyone will be occupied, and enough time has gone by that no one will expect a secret attack to be unleashed upon her." She thought quickly, "We will wait until Christmas morning and scare her enough to do something that will make the king take her head. You will all *finally* get your revenge;

the justice you deserve." With an awful, evil laugh, she concluded her plans.

This set of new followers smiled and clapped, as if grateful for her help. Taking advantage of the worst memory of their lives and using it to her advantage, she had a sick sense of satisfaction that her goal would be accomplished and the drakon would suffer as she did.

* * *

Angela, Neveah, the teens, and children got together to head to Julia's home to check on Iris. Angela was primarily worried that the poison used on the woman could kill a witch too. After all, Iris had only touched the body, and it made her so sick, she almost died. What if it had been Leah or Liam near the body? Would her children have lost their lives just because they had witches' blood? Or did the poison effect anyone in its presence? The sudden stop of the carriage brought her back to the current events at hand; the fears for her children faded into the background.

Stepping out of the transport, the crew walked to the already open door where Izak was standing with a smile on his face. Clearly grateful that his enchanting woman did not fall to her death.

"Hey guys. Iris is going to be so happy to see all of you."

"Oh good. We wanted to let her rest and make sure she was up for visitors before we decided to come over," Neveah informed before they entered the home.

Leah and Liam instantly ran to their aunty laying on the couch. All Angela could hear was the sound of coughing and ran into the room to witness her two children showing signs of immediate illness. Running to their aid, she grabbed them both like she was saving them from a fire to bring them outside and away from her sister.

"Are you okay?" she practically shouted. She'd fallen into

an instant panic that somehow, whatever happened to Iris was still lingering, and had somehow poisoned her babes.

* * *

Neveah was fine sitting in the same room as Iris. Confused as to why, Angela freaked out and rushed the kids out of the house as fast as possible. Bella, Zack, and Sylvia were together, just taking a seat on the other sofas littering the room.

Zackery wanted to talk to Iris and ask her if there were any strange powers that allowed a person to change a shifter, against the shifter's control, back into a human. On the other hand, the thought he should keep the question to himself and ask Liam more about his identifying powers; try to find out more for himself without alerting anyone. He didn't want to bring any attention to himself and have everyone make a fuss if he wasn't actually powerful.

Trying to remember the electricity of strength radiating over his entire body as he stomped his foot and yelled at Zinnia to go away, he was thinking it was just adrenaline running through him at that point that'd made something occur...not magic.

"Have you heard from Zinnia?" Sylvia asked, interrupting Zack's daydream.

"Nope. Not a word," Zack replied.

"I don't think I have ever seen you so protective and mad in all my life," Silvia giggled.

"I don't think I have ever felt that either. Guess I have a manly side." He grinned.

"Ha, you wish," she teased.

"Do you think Jacky and Ziara will be a couple after coming out?" Sylva asked Bella.

"I don't know. Maybe. They were friendlier with each other afterward," Bella said, staring straight ahead instead of at her cousin.

"Oh, is someone worried she would have to share her friend's attention?" Sylvia taunted Bella, sticking her bottom lip out.

"No. I am perfectly fine with us *all* being best friends. I'm just not as connected with Ziara as Zack," Bella replied, looking to Zack for support.

"She's awesome. She was the first girl I ever had a crush on. Until I kissed her and she was disgusted...wiping my germs off her face."

Bella and Sylvia reacted with a mouth covering snicker before they laughed loudly for everyone to hear. Poor Zackery should have realized then and there, Ziara was trying to tell him it was girls she liked before Zinnia interrupted.

"I'm okay, Mom! I just choked on my candy. We're fine," Leah replied to her mother's concerned state.

"Are you okay?" Liam asked his mother.

Angela jumped to conclusions, hearing the cough made her think the worst. So much about the realm scared her. With a face like her "evil twin," everyone treated her differently. If it weren't for the king, she would have been locked away in the tallest tower, never to escape. Some of that fear transferred on the safety of her children. Unlike her, everyone loved and accepted all of her family, especially Leah and Liam.

"I'm just being your worried mother. I thought that the poison still lingered around your aunty and made you sick," Angela answered, relaxing now.

"I'm fine, sister. I promise. See?" Iris was in the doorway listening before she shot a firework into the air, showing her magic was back to normal.

Angela turned around and ran to her with her arms extended, embracing her in a big sisterly hug.

"I'm so glad you're okay." Angela smiled.

The rest of the crew exited the house and planted themselves on the outside garden furniture to enjoy the beautiful scenery of their mother's home. As silence fell over them, it was as if they were all wondering how their mother was and why she had been gone for so long. Only to have their question answered when a pigeon flew down next to the picnic table; a string hung from its leg with a note attached.

Getting everyone's attention, the bird transformed into a woman, now holding the note in her hand.

"I send word from your mother and a letter for you, Miss Neveah." She handed Neveah both of the letters, bowed her head, transformed and took flight once more.

"Open Mom's letter first," Izak and Angela urged her to read.

"My Dearest Children and Grandchildren,

I know I have been gone a long time. By now you're probably wondering why. I will explain everything soon, I promise. I look forward to seeing you all at my house on Christmas morning and to finally open the presents from Earth. I just wanted you all to know I was okay, and happy, as can be with my new husband. So much has happened I couldn't possibly tell you all of it in this letter. You all just behave yourselves and do nothing that you know I wouldn't approve of; or at least make sure I'm there when you do it.

With lots of hugs and kisses.
All my Love,
Mom/Grandma"

Neveah finished reading the letter, making everyone excited about Christmas. The children were more interested in the gifts. That they would receive double, because of the marriage, and finally get to see what was inside the wrapping paper.

The letter wasn't very descriptive, but at least the

family knew now that their mother was still alive and nothing bad had happened.

Angela missed her mother dearly. Christmas wasn't that far away. Long enough to have no Christmas presents hiding in the closet yet. The family had waited to open their gifts on this Christmas after all. She desperately tried to remember if she'd wrapped any pointless gifts, like electronics, the year the earthquake shipped them all to Drakous. No matter. They were still beautifully wrapped and tucked away for safekeeping. The awkwardness did hit Angela, however, that one of those gifts was for her husband Arik, and vice versa.

"Well, I'm sorry, Mom, but I'm not waiting to do this. While you all are here, I have an announcement to make." Izak took a knee, holding Iris's left hand in his.

With that, he said the words that not one of the witnesses currently watching ever thought he would say, especially with an audience.

"Iris, my savior and goddess, you have always loved me from the moment we set eyes on each other. Nursing me back to health when I was a junky and restoring my self-worth. I still don't feel worthy of you, but if you give me a chance to show you for the rest of our lives, I promise I will surprise you and become the man you deserve. Iris Vickens...will you marry me?"

Like crickets were serenading the proposal, everyone enthusiastically awaited her answer.

With a screech and a "Yes!" Iris jumped into his arms.

Izak wasn't the most romantic man, but he loved Iris and she certainly brought out his best qualities so that, hopefully, the old Izak would never surface again. Everyone that knew the couple knew they were perfect for each other.

"I know this isn't much of an engagement ring, but it's the same stone you used to make me better when I was sick with withdrawal," Izak stated.

In a beautiful display of a white gold setting, the center

stone was an opal, offset by a diamond on each side. The opal was the same one Iris had used to make his fever subside when he was sick, along with the massage she applied with lotion to his body; breaking the ice between them as they playfully flirted with each other.

"It's perfect, and so much more meaningful than anything I could have picked. I would have never expected you were this sentimental." Iris beamed with happiness as tears of joy escaped her eyes.

Angela and Neveah stepped forward to give Iris a hug of congratulations and to see the beautiful stone with healing properties, as well as give Izak props for his choice of words to win her acceptance.

As the chatter continued with ideas about the wedding, it somehow got turned around to focus on the display of the dead woman on the ground outside the shop Bella and Angela had opened for everyone to enjoy. Even the teens wanted to know more about the unfortunate situation.

"Do you know why she was found outside our store?" Bella asked.

"Could have been Arianna," Sylvia joined in.

"There isn't any proof that it was Arianna. As far as I know. No one knows anything about the woman. It's very strange," Angela answered.

"Wasn't it like a curse that spread across the entire realm the first time? Wouldn't there be more dead pregnant women?" Zack asked.

Angela had an epiphany. They should search for another woman with child. If she was in good health, that should at least show people that Arianna hadn't caused another curse or outbreak.

"That's something we should talk to Alister about. Good point though, Zack," Iris said, nodding at Angela.

While Angela and Iris continued the conversation with the teens and Izak, Neveah ventured away so she could finally find out what had happened to Nick and why he disappeared.

In seconds after opening the other note, Neveah let out a bloodcurdling scream, and only Angela knew why. Alister had informed her of the news about the realm and what was to happen in the years to come.

"What the hell? What's wrong?" Izak grumbled.

"Nick says Drakous Realm is dying and everything in it!" Neveah sobbed, holding her mouth with one hand, she raised the letter up in the air with the other.

CHAPTER 8

It didn't last long. The statement Arianna made in the kitchen about the encounter she and Arik had being a mistake and never happening again, made him turn on her. In fact, he seemed more determined to make sure it happened again because of her statement.

Once sober, the actions made her feel even more guilty, but not enough to stop it from happening. Putting up a playful fight, the man ignited something inside her that she never knew she had.

This Christmas morning, she felt the extra enjoyment of his nearness. It would be so different to get up and out of bed with the excitement that she was going to spend the holiday with someone special. Especially after all the years spent without her family, being that they returned her to the institution she lived in most of her years on Earth.

Turns out when you explain your entire life story of magic, mythical creatures, and an entirely different realm to someone who doesn't actually love you, they think you're crazy and make others think so too.

Pushing the memories completely out of her mind, she focused only on Christmas dinner and her magical vegetable garden, before rushing outside to pick the healthy food groups.

* * *

Neveah rushed around her mother's home, keeping herself as busy as possible. Trying hard not to think about the mistakes she had made since reading the note Nick had written. She had memorized every word from reading it a billion times.

Nick informed her he would be gone for many moons and wasn't sure where that left the two of them, where they stood with each other. He just knew his place was with his followers at the far end of the realm. Drakous was dying as the darkness inched forward, killing everything in its path.

She would sit at her little table in her room in the castle with the letter in one hand and a bottle of wine in the other, allowing the depression to strengthen every time she reread the letter. Feeling guilty and ashamed of herself for giving in to the poison that had caused so many problems on Earth for her family and friends.

Getting herself back in control, she would project her addiction needs into making her jewelry. In the end, having enough to finally open her own store and share her beautiful gift of jewelry-making with others.

Regretfully, Neveah felt awful for holding such a large grudge against her little sister, Angela. Understanding that the realm was going to cease to exist was hard news to swallow, even for her perfect sister. Angela could have at least told her that Nick was okay and tell Neveah she couldn't tell her anything more. The promise she made to Alister would have been kept. She just wanted to stop stressing about Nick; stop worrying about his wellbeing.

When their mother arrived, Neveah would tell Angela that she forgave her and let go of the grudge she held in order to start over and be a close family again.

* * *

No magic was to be used to decorate the house for Julia's return home. Doing the work all by themselves was to make it more personal. Of course, being that there wasn't any electricity, they would use magic to activate the lights, but that would be all.

The teens and children carried in bins from the newly refurbished barn filled to the brim with all the Christmas décor Julia had collected over the years. Angela, adding the same reindeer that occupied the dinner table the same day the crystals transferred them all to Drakous, gave her a little humor as she placed it in the center of the table that was set with the best China plates, spoons, and forks.

Izak and Iris were busy at work, hanging mistletoe around every corner. Laughing, they stood under it from time to time to show their affection for one another with a kiss that brightened Iris's face.

The silliness of it all was fine until Angela remembered she had invited Alister to the festivities they would all share as a family. Certain that she would be caught under those scandalous traps with him, made her worry. She shot her brother and sister a critical stare of fake disapproval, only to be repaid with a sneaky smile and a fake expression of "we don't know what you mean; we are innocent, we swear."

Walking through the house, Angela stopped to watch

the children decorating the tree. They had been put in charge of that particular task. They added the lights that Leah happily made shine brightly, trailing after with purple and silver garland. The remaining glass Christmas balls Julia hadn't taken out of their boxes in years because Leah was autistic, she would grab them off the branches and throw them hard on the ground, enjoying the loud sound of a million pieces of shattering glass, had finally also found their place.

Angela's past memory of Leah dancing, with her arms in a fanning position above her head, once the ornament released from her hands, made Angela grin; the garland was also always a fun rope for her to tug on as she ripped it from the tree. But she never once did any of it to be mean; in fact, she hadn't even understood it was wrong, she was just entertaining herself.

They added the last of the decorations to the tree: Mr. Winnie the Pooh attached to his big red bell; the three snowmen that always made their grandma smile; and many pictures of the kids when they were a lot younger. With no way of taking more pictures, the ones set on the tree would have to last.

Heading back to the kitchen, Angela returned to her tasks involving the meal that would be shared as the family gathered. Coming around the corner, she ran into Neveah in her distracted...unfocused state. Ever since she read the letter Nick had sent, she had been beside herself; hating Angela for not telling her sooner, even though she'd promised Alister she wouldn't tell a soul. He had only told her a couple of nights before, so it wasn't like she had the privileged information for long. She, herself, was still trying to register the news. Adding more panic to all the family didn't sound like a good idea, but Neveah obviously thought otherwise when she gave Angela the silent treatment. Ever since that day, the only way Angela found out what Neveah had been up to was through Sylvia.

Sylvia said her mother had been throwing herself into her

creative jewelry making talent, planning on opening her own business near Bella's Boutique in the future.

Thrilled and proud of her, Angela hoped that their mother would help to mend their differences so they would be close once again.

Coming around the corner, Angela smiled at the happy couple. Iris and Izak had certainly been enjoying all their engagement congratulations. They were always so playful and teasing with each other; it made Angela giggle now just to see Izak chasing Iris around the table...until suddenly, she screamed, and dug at her hand in pain.

"Ow, make it stop!" She dug her nails into her left hand.

"What's wrong? I don't see anything," Izak said with so much fear in his eyes he looked like he was going to cry himself.

You couldn't see anything wrong with her hand, except for the scratches she was making herself.

"I need a mirror. A *big* mirror. Please...hurry," Iris cried.

Izak ran into another room as quickly as possible. Sounding like he was breaking things or ripping something off the walls, he rushed back into the room with a large mirror to put in front of Iris.

Iris looked in the mirror, putting her injured hand up to it, and chanted: "Deíte ta apróvlepta," until an image of Arianna appeared in the mirror.

"Iris, I'm so sorry I had to contact you this way. There is no time. I have done something terribly wrong and now I'm paying for it." A panicked Arianna rushed her words until Iris cut her off.

"Seriously! How could you be so evil? You were the one who killed that poor pregnant woman after all, weren't you? I thought the curse was an accident," Iris yelled at her sister.

Arianna showed everyone a completely baffled expression, while shaking her head left to right. "I did *no* such thing. I haven't hurt anyone, let alone murder any innocent woman. That's not what I was talking about," Arianna continued to explain until the realm trembled beneath their feet. "You all must hurry. Please, all the witches and Angela come through the mirror so we can stop this."

With the concern in Arianna's urgent tone, Angela was the first to step through the mirror. Iris, Neveah, and Leah followed closely behind.

"I will explain later, I promise. For now, I need to give Angela back her powers."

"*What?*" Angela gasped before Arianna embraced her in a big hug.

Stunned, Angela immediately felt the power running through her veins, taking over her entire body. The same view that everyone had witnessed in Bella's Boutique. The magic consumed Angela's body, mind, and soul... as they stood, watching.

While the transition took place, Angela could feel and see Arianna set a blue crystal in her right hand, a red crystal in Iris's hand, a purple one in Neveah's, and a yellow one in Leah's. Leaving Arianna holding up a black crystal.

"We need to link hands in a circle. Put your crystals in the hand that doesn't have one and hold tightly. Then, repeat after me: 'Apokroúste to kakó kai kleíste tis pórtes stin katastrofí'," Arianna chanted.

Angela was trying hard to chant, but her mind was getting cloudy; she felt like something was messing with her brain.

"You are a worthless, weak, unworthy woman. You are nothing compared to Arianna. I should have killed you when you were an infant. If it weren't for her, I would have succeeded in taking your life, giving me a body in return." Angela heard the words clear as day.

Looking around to see who the giver of the horrible words

were, Angela was shocked. She couldn't believe someone would say those awful things.

"You wanted magic. Now you got it. Look at yourself. You're useless. You can't even chant to save the poor realm from destruction and mayhem."

"I can, too. I'm doing it right now," Angela screamed back at the voice...without even opening her mouth.

"Ha, you're a disgrace. All this, 'Boo-hoo, Neveah's never going to forgive me.' Who the hell cares? She knows she's better than you ever will be. You will never measure up to her talents, beauty, or even the love she gets from your own mother. Oh, I mean fake mother."

Everything the voice was telling Angela inside her head was actually taking its toll on her ability to stay in the present. She felt weak. The voice was making her worst nightmares come true by saying all the things she'd thought of before.

"You can fix it. You can get rid of her. All you have to do is let me take control and I'll send her to a place where you will never see her again. All you have to do is give in."

"No! I love my sister."

"You're a sad excuse for a human being. If you don't listen, if you don't let me take control, I will go after your entire family. Your children, you're loving Alister, and your best friend."

"I don't even know what you're talking about. I don't even know how to let you take control. Please don't hurt my family. Don't hurt my sister."

Angela looked around at her family and grew sadder and weaker, she felt her eyes being pushed down and a coldness take over her body; she shivered as if she was being taken control of by the evil voice that still screeched in her ears.

* * *

The evil magic that Arianna had battled her entire life now resided inside of Angela, taking complete control of her mind and body. This particular magic had an unknown reputation for possessing Arianna and causing the worst curse ever, casting it throughout Drakous Realm – taking advantage of her during her weakest, most devastating moment in her life.

After years of experience dealing with that evil inside Arianna, she'd learned to control it herself with the good magic she had. Siphoning it out of Angela's body when they were born, just hours before, and saving her beloved twin's life.

Arianna was stronger in all aspects, even as a newborn. Having the lightest magic a witch could ever need in their lifetime. Giving her the extra strength, the ability for good to conquer the evil and trap it in its own little cage buried deep inside of Arianna. Waiting for the day it would be sent to a world with magic and be freed to bring down everything in its path.

The dark magic now had control of Angela. Tucking her away far in the back of the dark corners of her own brain where all her insecurities, fears, and doubts lingered.

To the left stood Neveah, who glanced towards Angela with a smile of forgiveness. Being that the evil now controlled Angela, all she shot back at Neveah was a sadistic grin, mouthing the chant that sent her to a faraway realm. Leaving only the magic, knowing where she was about to go, she waved goodbye to Neveah as she disappeared from Drakous Realm.

With a powerful wind and a flash of magical energy that closed the doors to Katistrofia and stopped the destruction and mayhem from continuing, every witch standing in the circle flew back, hitting the walls. Leah landed on Arianna's bed.

Among the witches was Angela's body. Hitting the wall, Angela was knocked back up to the surface where she would regain control of herself once more.

* * *

When Angela opened her eyes, she felt her head pulsing from the transition of control. Having no memory of the short time that another force controlled her, she was simply left with an awful feeling of sadness and despair.

Slowly getting up, feeling the pain in her muscles from hitting the wall behind her, she could hear the others laughing and hugging. They were congratulating each other for saving the realm and everyone in it.

Bewilderment at what had just happened, Angela was unable to wrap her brain around the scene as Arianna walked towards her, offering her congratulations with a tight embrace.

Still frozen, Angela's arms were limp by her sides; unable to fathom words or release the questions she now had for her sister.

"I'm so happy for all your help," she beamed. "I have a surprise for you."

Like looking at her own reflection, Angela stared into Arianna's eyes. Giving her a slight grin, which was all she could muster, she waited for her sister to continue.

"I brought Arik, your kids' father, to Drakous Realm." Arianna said, smiling.

Angela could tell Arianna was still talking because her mouth was moving. But after she had said Arik was in Drakous, she'd immediately become deaf.

Happiness had been followed by "oh no! no! no!" racing through her mind. Joyful for her kids to see their father after all this time, yes, but not so much for herself.

Knowing her heart belonged to another, and certain Arik would battle to get her back at all costs, she could feel the sickness rise in the pit of her stomach at the choices she would have to make in the near future.

Angela didn't want to go back to the life she shared with Arik. Forced to accept the issues they secretly shared. Going back to once again be the woman that brushed off her own feelings of situations because she would be chastised for her passions would not be her future. Any excitement would make her loud and any retaliation would make her regret it.

There was no way to keep up with her own feelings, thoughts, and confusion. The emotions overwhelmed her; all she wanted to do was hide and not deal with it. Seeing as that her mind agreed with her, she quickly passed out.

Right before everything went black for Angela, she could hear a cruel snicker followed by the sound of her daughter's voice asking, "Where is Aunty Neveah?"

CHAPTER 9

Neveah woke up on solid ground with pebbles and dirt sticking to her hands and cheek. She wondered why her sister had given her such a cruel look before floating through the air like she was on an invisible cloud and falling asleep. When the pungent smell of burning trees filled her nostrils, Neveah got up, brushed herself off and immediately observed her surroundings. Seeing and feeling the cold rock walls, Neveah glimpsed at what looked like the only way out, towards a flicker of orange light; she was sure she was in a cave. How she got there, she still had no idea.

Needing fresh air, she could feel the speed pick up in her legs as she ran towards the opening. Upon exiting, she gasped. Now her view was one of absolute fire, everything was burning or scorched beyond all recognition around her: the trees, flowers, grass, and so much more.

Her eyes widened as she viewed the outrageous scatter of the fire. Looking to the smoke-filled sky, she caught sight of an enormous bird covered in flames. Much like a dragon, it was now expelling fire across all the lands beneath it, continuing its destruction of the vegetation.

The bird could only be one mythical creature known; a phoenix, also known in Drakous as a foinix. Neveah now knew where she was. Her location was Basil's realm, the Foinix Realm; and the one soaring up in the sky was the king, Basil's father.

Basil had told stories of his father's recent behavior, that he was crazy and couldn't differentiate who was his enemy and who was his friend. Thinking up conspiracy theories that his followers had turned against him, and all wanted to kill him and take his kingdom for themselves. He was teaching them all a lesson by burning their lands, locking them up, or killing them if they tried to fight. Lunacy had already set in, seeing as that he'd recently lost his mind enough to go after his own son just for dropping a sword in training and making too much noise.

The creature was not something Neveah wanted to come face-to-face with even when the king had all his faculties. The bird, itself, could take her down in one swift shot. She felt the fear rising in her when it turned around and stopped projecting its stream of fire. Scared to death that he had spotted her and was looking at her right now, she turned on her heel and made a run for it.

Neveah didn't get very far. Someone came from nowhere...he jumped out of the bushes to her left, covering her mouth so she couldn't scream, and dragged her back into the brush.

"Now, I'm going to let you go but you need to be quiet. The foinix has incredible hearing. If you scream, he will kill us both." The man's voice whispered in her right ear.

He removed his hand from her mouth and let go of her waist, allowing her to turn around and face her kidnapper or rescuer – a title that remained to be bestowed.

She faced a man as tall as her brother, but with a medium build and bright red hair; his eyes shone with the same burning flames as Basil's. Having pale white skin adorned with freckles, the man also wore a friendly grin on his face. Realizing how close they stood to one another, Neveah took a quick step back.

"I'm Adonis Rubius, leader of my crew. You shouldn't be out here. There's a wicked magissa controlling our once dear king," he spoke.

Neveah still didn't say anything, unsure if she could trust the man. She just nodded her head in response.

"Are you mute? You can't speak?"

Neveah nodded her head once more.

"Come with me. I'll take you to our haven. You won't survive long if you're left out here all by yourself." Grabbing her hand, he led her deeper into the woods, away from the blazing fires.

Adonis basically dragged her through brush, trees, even things with mighty thorns. Neveah almost spoke just to get him to slow down and see how hard the travel was for her. He seemed unaffected by any scratch or thorn they ran through, whilst she seemed to bleed from everything she connected with.

Neveah needed to think fast about when she was going to speak and, if she did, whether or not she'd reveal her identity at that time. The only way she could determine if the people in this realm were good or bad is if she waited, watched, and learned all she could.

The unknown was frightening, and she knew nothing of the realm or its people. For all she knew the king *wasn't* crazy, and his people *did* really turn against him and try to go after his kingdom. She would wait and find out for herself.

Being hit with a plant that was literally thickened with incredibly sharp thorns, Neveah decided she'd had enough. Dropping to the ground, the man let go of her wrist, surprised by the sudden change in movement and weight, and stared down at her.

The pain she felt was intense; it was as if she could even feel the start of the mega-bruise that would appear on her wrist from the man pulling her around like a rag doll. Carefully, she ran her fingers along the scratches under her ripped leggings, feeling the warm blood that now ran from being carted through the dangerous foliage.

"*Gomoto!* I'm sorry. Why didn't you alert me that you were hurt? Why are you so fragile?" he asked, clearly confused, bending down to observe her injuries.

Pulling her legs away from his touch, she eyed the bare skin on his own legs; not a drop of blood or even a scratch marred the pale white man. How could he remain unscathed after all they'd run through? The thought hit her immediately: He was definitely not human.

"What are you?" the man's voice fell in a serious tone as he locked gazes with Neveah. "Even your eyes are unnatural." Shaking his head, he sighed deeply. His face was highly concerned. "Look, we need to continue; we cannot stay here. Get on my back."

Neveah's eyes widened at the request. Shaking her head, she knew there was no way he could carry her and run at the same time.

"Get on my back or I will carry you in my arms," he said in a warning tone.

Rolling her eyes, Neveah did as instructed and climbed onto the man's back. Wrapping her arms around his neck, he locked her legs in place by his sides.

Taking off like the speed of light, Adonis ran faster than any human being could possibly run. Neveah closed her eyes, hugging tight to the odorous man.

She didn't enjoy the stickers and the pain they gave her, but she didn't much like having the stranger's hands on her legs either. The ride was much smoother than running herself, until he jumped into the air, making her feel like they were flying, yet instantly coming to a safe halt.

"We're here! You can let go now," he chuckled.

Neveah opened her eyes and dropped slowly off his back, trying not to make her wounds worse. Another forest, more bushes, and straight ahead sat the biggest cave she had ever seen.

"Who is that?" A woman asked, walking out of the cave.

"I don't know. I found her running from the king. She's mute and..strangely fragile. I don't even know who or what she is," he replied.

"Then why did you bring her here?" she demanded.

While the two set to arguing about Neveah, she eyed the woman with curiosity. Appearing to be tough, Neveah learned she was definitely Adonis's sister who he referred to as "V." Finally giving in to her sibling, the woman stopped barking and looked at Neveah.

"She's exquisite. I'm Vera. Are you hungry?" she asked, walking closer.

Nodding, Neveah held her stomach as it grumbled. She did wonder why the woman would say something so odd as her being 'exquisite', however.

The woman peered at her like her brother had done, inspecting the scratches and bruising.

"Come with us; we have plenty to eat."

Neveah followed them into the cave that was filled with the amazing smell of cooked meats. As they entered, Neveah registered the spot where a table had been set; currently, ten adults and three children sat eating the plates of food set in front of them, taking a break from chewing only once to stop and stare at their new guest.

The darkness of the cave accentuated their eyes; each

person had a vibrant pupil color that ranged from yellow to orange to red. Neveah's gaze landed on the children, smiling at their innocent little faces. In return, they smiled and waved. Children were always a good sign; their presence meant the parents most likely had hearts of love.

An old woman stood from her seat at the table. Walking towards Neveah, when she stood in front of her, the woman instantly grabbed her head, flipping it from left to right. She was literally inspecting every part of her war-torn looking body. Lifting Neveah's arms and setting them back down to her sides, she continued to her legs. All Neveah could do was stare in surprise. When the woman bent down, running her finger along Neveah's scratches, it made her wince from the slight pressure, but in truth she'd always been a baby when it came to the smallest hint of pain. Back up to Neveah's face, the woman observed her eyes and then tried to pry her mouth open with her fingers. When Neveah couldn't take it anymore, she simply smacked her hand away, informing the woman silently that she did not approve of the invasiveness.

"This is a rare sight to see," the woman said with a smile. "She is a human."

The room filled with chatter and gasps. Talk of humans being a myth or extinct mixed with strange doubts and worries that she could be something called the 'wicked magissa' dressed in disguise. Whatever the hell that was. After their fears were clearly expressed, words of hope followed of being rescued and that Neveah was there to save them all.

Neveah felt for all the people in the room. Letting out a sigh, she decided they were just scared and wanted to stop being afraid for their own lives. The look of hope and care shined in their eyes when they stopped to peer at Neveah. With every expression she scanned, all she wanted to do was help them more.

"What is your name, dear?" the elderly woman asked.

"My name is Neveah Michelson." Choosing to make this

moment the time to speak.

"*What?* You *can* talk?" V asked, then turned to her brother. "Oh, you got me, brother."

"She nodded when I asked if she was," he replied, catching the dinner roll that came flying at his head, followed by the rest of the family laughing.

"I didn't know I could trust you. I'm sorry," Neveah admitted.

"We get it, dear. No one has trust issues as big as ours. Now tell us: Who are you? Where do you come from?"

"I *am* human. I originally came from a realm called Earth, brought to Drakous Realm by magic. I was recently sent here, although I don't know why, and woke up in a cave."

Just like it had been in Drakous, the looks of surprise and the gossiping of Earth and what they all knew of the realm broke out before they moved on to speak of Drakous and how a mighty drakon lived there.

"Are you a witch?"

"Do you know the drakon?"

"Will you send Alister to save us?"

The people knew Drakous well, apparently, even the leader by name. But Neveah had questions of her own. How did they know Alister, and why did they believe he would save them?

"That's enough. Let the poor woman eat. I'm sure she will answer all our questions in time." The woman still standing in front of her spoke to her family to calm them down.

"I will. I promise. I have questions, too." Neveah smiled, taking the seat offered to her. "Thank you."

They piled the food onto her plate. Smelling incredible, she began picking up the succulent morsels and stuffing her face. Thinking of her family and Christmas dinner that would be shared by all, Neveah still wondered what on earth she'd done to make Angela mad enough at her to send her away? But knowing her sister the way she did, she knew there was no way she would ever be that cruel. There *had* to be another reason. Yet the image of Angela's smile still made her shiver to her very core.

* * *

Adonis and Vera exited the cave. Jumping into the air, they transformed into two large lions, replacing their manes and tails with flickering red and orange flames of fire. With incredible speed they made it to the forbidden lands of their king's castle doors in minutes.

"You need to be in your o ánthropos form. Now!" two guards ordered, holding their stakes with copper spears at the tops that had the power to kill a lionix.

With a combined roar, Vera and Adonis transitioned back to human.

"We have news for Her Highness to report," Adonis spoke firmly.

The two men stepped aside. Adonis didn't want to spread news of Neveah's arrival, but he didn't really have a choice. The wicked witch had their little brother, who was only ten years of age, and the woman holding him captive had no heart, even for children.

"Next time the two of you come to the queen's residence in your shift form, we will strike," the man on the left warned, stopping Adonis by lifting his stake in front of him, allowing the copper to rub on his chest.

Adonis could feel the warmth forming under his clothes where the spear lay against his chest, but showed no pain when the man purposely held it in place, taunting Adonis to show his weakness. Even when a hole was burned through his shirt and the copper touched his bare flesh, he still wouldn't give the sick bástardos the satisfaction of seeing he was in any way uncomfortable.

"Please stop. That's enough. You're going to kill him," Vera begged the man to release the spear.

With a sadistic chuckle, the coward lowered the stake, allowing them to continue through the castle walls.

They didn't care about the pleasant interior design; in fact, the emotions they had for this location had long ago disappeared. The first time they'd set foot on these floors, they were honored, but now it was just a reminder of pain and agony. Remaining silent, keeping their eyes wide open, they marched toward the throne room.

The king no longer sat in his grand chair; instead, it had been replaced with the terrible woman that had taken their brother. Her amazing beauty was a trap for those that didn't know of the dark and evil heart and soul that lay within.

With eyes a smokey baby blue, skin softened with a peach tone, and glorious sandy blonde hair that lay perfectly curled on her shoulders, those who laid eyes on her were completely unaware of her age. And when she spoke in her soft, beguiling voice, the false advertising she emitted grew even more. Her appearance had long ago misled the king into thinking she was sweet as cherry pie, and everyone else that trusted His Majesty agreed with his thinking.

Standing before the woman who now called herself the Queen of Foinix Realm, Adonis and V presented her with forceful bows. Her evil grin showed them she knew how displeased they were and would never grant her that amount of respect, which meant she clearly saw their sarcasm.

"What do you have for me today?" the soothing voice spoke.

"We have news of a woman. She goes by the name of Neveah. I found her running through the woods," Adonis answered, trying to speak as least as he possibly could.

The mention of Neveah's name seemed to make the queen stir in her chair as a look of concern crossed her face. The fear in her eyes gave Adonis a slight bit of hope. She clearly knew who Neveah was or had heard of her somewhere. Adonis and

Vera didn't have the slightest idea of how, and they were doubtful that the true magissa would be sharing what she knew.

"What else?"

"She pretended to be mute when she was first brought to the haven. I believe it will take time for her to truly trust us before we could extract more information out of her," Vera spoke.

The queen was dissatisfied by the news. Neveah was smart, and that would mean the witch wouldn't be getting any information anytime soon.

"Adonis. You will make the woman trust you and fall in love with you. She will spill her entire life story at your feet, and I will get all the answers I need before I destroy her. You will report back to me alone, *after* the task is completed. Do you understand?" Her voice had turned demanding.

"How am I supposed to do that? She could already have a love. I don't think I can. She doesn't even show me any interest. That's an impossible request," he bravely complained.

"I will make you a potion that will help you on the mission. If you do not do as I demand, you will never see your beloved brother again."

"Please, Your Highness, is Everest okay? Can we at least see him?" Vera pleaded.

"You can when you do as I instruct. I will return your brother if you succeed in my request. If you fail, I will siphon his lionix abilities and take his human life along with it."

"I will, Your Highness." Adonis bowed in defeat.

Adonis was smart, too. He wanted to know all that the witch knew so he could hopefully use it against her. But how would he get her to talk? If he made a point that it would be helpful on the quest she had forced upon him, she would certainly have to give him the information...right?

"It would be much help in my success if I knew what you

know about the woman," he fished for knowledge.

Taking only a minute to think, she spoke: "Very well. The name Neveah comes from an ancient witch who lived at the very beginning. An original that was trapped, never to be found again. Before that, she had children of her own, and one day another by the name was going to be born from her line. There is no other research that is known. That's where you come in. I need you to find out if she has magic like her ancestor."

"Thank you, Your Highness. I will do my best."

She tilted her chin and stared at him. "I like you, Adonis. Something about you is just so...appealing and brave. Stop with all the formalities now. Call me Elinor; Elinor Butler. I so miss hearing my family name." She spoke as if they were now friends, and suddenly led them to the dungeon.

When they reached the floor, she pointed to the cell with the boy inside that was a member of Adonis's family...and the cell right next to it that held His Majesty, the supposed lunatic.

CHAPTER 10

Arianna moved quickly, catching Angela slowly and letting her faint gently to the floor.

Iris watched Arianna look from Angela to her with concern, still holding her head in her lap. Looking around the room, Iris tried to focus on the now missing Neveah. Instantly alarmed when she saw the windows were all broken out, she ran towards them and peered out each one, sighing with relief that Neveah hadn't been projected from any of them.

She spotted Leah sitting on the bed with her hands in her lap, her face a mask of shock. Maybe she saw what had happened, or had some idea as to where Neveah had gone.

"Leah, honey, are you okay?" Iris asked, taking a seat on the bed in front of her.

"I'm drained. Grandma allowed me to tap into so much

magic that...that I could see the demons and feel the darkness. It was cold...it made me sad," Leah replied, pulling a blanket up to her neck. "Neveah's gone...she disappeared even before the blast. Smoke. Somewhere with lots of smoke."

"What do you mean you could see them? I didn't see anything. How could Neveah go anywhere?" Iris asked.

Leah didn't answer, she just pulled the blanket over her head and laid down.

"It's okay, honey, we will figure it out," Iris said, gently rubbing her back.

Standing up, assuming Leah had fallen asleep from exhaustion, Iris walked towards Arianna. She wanted to ask for her thoughts on what had just happened.

"Do you think the magic was too much for her?" Iris asked, staring at Angela who was still asleep in her lap.

"Maybe. Or maybe I surprised her so much with my news of Arik that she fainted."

Iris took a step back. "Arik? What do you mean news of Arik? Arianna, you didn't bring her husband and the father of her children here? *Did* you?"

"I did. I was going to use him for my freedom. You know...collateral."

"The way you think. I *swear* you should be in a mental institution," Iris said without thinking first.

"Don't say that! Don't you *dare* say that! Hate to break it to you, sis. Been there, done that." Arianna shot at Iris, making her stop in her tracks. "Now help me get our sister to the bed."

Iris felt awful that her baby sister had to endure a mental institution. That meant she felt like she was going crazy, or her mind shut down again, leaving her in that dark room she'd always spoke of.

Arianna lifted under Angela's shoulders and Iris grabbed her legs; each walked awkwardly to the bed.

"Is my mom, okay?" Leah asked anxiously, watching as they got her mother on the bed, making both Iris and Arianna jump out of their skin.

"Oh my gosh, you little brat, you scared me," Arianna playfully scolded Leah.

"Sorry."

"The magic exhausted her. She'll be fine," Iris reassured her, turning to Arianna with her hands on her hips, waiting for an explanation.

"What?" Arianna asked.

"I might be guessing here, but I think she wants to know what happened when we first got here," Leah pointed out the obvious.

"Shouldn't we figure out what happened to Neveah instead of fussing over my big mistake? Long story short: I opened the Realm to Katistrofia. There was a riot of people after me just outside my borders and I overreacted; I tried to take over Drakous with an army of demons so I would survive and be the new ruler," Arianna explained.

"Are you serious? Why would you do that? You know what they did to our father and your husband. How could you?" Iris yelled, expressing her disappointment at her sister's ridiculous decisions.

"I don't *know* why, okay. Something in me needed to do it and become powerful. I thought I would just control the demons and..it seems so stupid now. I tried to close it. I messed up and closed it wrong. I was scared," Arianna explained, moving her right hand down to her belly.

"Arianna, I don't know how Alister is going to react to this one. If Angela doesn't wake up and protect you from his wrath and anger, he might lock you away for good." Iris felt scared again as she brought up Alister, memories of the last time flooding her mind.

"I will go and speak to him myself. I will even give him Neveah's family crystals that you sent me after. That way I won't cause any harm again. I'm sorry I made a huge mess. I *really* don't know why power and leadership were all I wanted. I don't want that at all anymore. I will tell Alister everything."

"Okay. Well, what do we do now?" Iris asked.

"Where's my father? I heard you say he was here. Can I see him?" Leah asked.

* * *

Arianna had completely forgotten about Arik. He was going to be so mad at her when she let him out of her father's locked bedroom. Well, technically it was his bedroom now, but she had walked past him, shoving him in his room and locking him in, like she was an angry mother putting him in a time out.

"Oh, sweety. Yes, I will go get him now." Arianna turned to run out the door.

Running down the staircase, she was more concerned about his wrath than Alister's. She stood in front of the door, putting her ear up against it to see if she could hear murmurings of pure anger. Thinking to herself that she was being ridiculous, knowing all she had to do was turn the knob and push and the door would automatically open for her, she tried to stop her hand from shaking as she prepared herself for what he would say. Opening the door and peeking in, she saw Arik sitting on the end of the bed with his head down, looking up slowly when he heard her step forward.

Disappointment radiated from his face. He didn't even have to say anything to make shivers run up her spine.

"I'm sorry," she spoke quickly.

"You had no right! You had no right locking me in this room. I thought we were past that. You're a self-absorbed childish woman who throws fits until you get your own way. I've had enough of you. I want to see my family. Now!"

"Stop it, you overgrown meathead. I stuck you in here for your own protection. How *dare* you speak to me that way? I'm not Angela. I won't take you bullying me." Stopping, she realized something was missing from her mind. A voice that taunted her, making her feel like Arik had just done. She was used to insults on a daily basis, but this time it was from someone she cared about.

Silence filled the room for just a few seconds until they heard what sounded like a riot being fought outside her boundaries. They sounded closer this time.. like they were just outside her front door.

"Who is yelling?" Arik asked.

"It doesn't matter. Your daughter is upstairs, with Angela and Iris. Leah wants to see you."

Arik left Arianna alone in the room, where she felt like she was abandoned again. She let the tears fall, holding her mouth so she wouldn't make a noise and her stomach because she felt like she was going to throw up.

***

Arik rushed up the staircase, not caring a bit about what he had said to Arianna before blazing past her to see his daughter. Jumping every other step, he made it to the door of the highest room in the castle. Just behind the door would be his little girl, yet he was unsure if she would show any signs of remembering him, with her autism.

Bursting through the door as quickly as possible, he was instantly bombarded by the unexpected squeal of "Daddy" coming from his very grown-up baby girl.

Falling to his knees, he took his daughter in a tight embrace, feeling her return the same amount of pressure as his silent tears leaked onto her left shoulder.

"Too tight," she gasped.

Surprised by her voice and how precise it was, he let go. Looking into her beautiful, happy, brown eyes, he could tell her autism was.. gone; yet he had no idea how that could possibly happen. Smiling, he allowed her to see he was not ashamed of showing weakness, that men cried too. Especially tears of joy.

"Oh, don't cry, Daddy. It's okay. We're all together now."

"I know. I'm just so happy to see you," he told her before looking up at a blonde woman walking behind his little girl.

He got to his feet, wishing to address the woman who Arik assumed he knew. Arianna had spoken about her often and loved her dearly. Nodding his head at the woman, he scanned the room in search of Angela, until his eyes landed on the bed.

Holding Leah's hand, he walked over to the side of the bed to peer down at his wife, sleeping peacefully. Now he could see the physical differences between the twins. He would have to tell her what had happened between him and Arianna eventually and hope that she forgave him. Not because he wanted to be with Angela and win her heart again, but because he wanted to be a part of his children's lives.

"What happened to her?" he asked Iris as she came to stand next to him.

"She has magic now and had to use all of it to help us close the doors to Hell. She fell into exhaustion. Happens sometimes," Iris replied.

"This is Angela's older sister, Daddy. She's going to marry Uncle Izak."

"Really? How is he? That is exciting. I'm happy for the both of you." He gave her a smile of congratulations.

***

Angela was stirring, starting to wake up. The voice that she could hear before she opened her eyes was familiar. Slowly opening them, she could see the man she had two incredible children with standing above her. Happiness spread through her body as she sat up to give Arik a hug. She had missed him more than she thought. He was, after all, her best friend. They may not have had the greatest relationship together, but they were friends, even when they separated a few times.

"Where is Neveah?" she asked, looking about the room for her sister.

Before anyone could speak, Arianna walked through the door and straight to Angela.

"Hey, sis." She smiled. "Feeling better?"

"Yeah. Kinda feel like I have a hangover," she replied, holding her head.

"Well, that's magic for you."

"Where's Neveah?" Angela asked for the second time.

"Leah said she was sent to a realm with smoke. Was probably an accident she did herself. She's very powerful. Don't fret though, we can find her with blood magic."

"I hope she's safe," Angela replied.

Arik walked away as soon as Arianna walked up to talk to her sister, completely ignoring his presence. Leah was chatting with her father about all that had happened since the day she first spoke; all from her point of view.

"We are going to need Sylvia and Zack to locate Neveah. When we are all stronger and our powers are energized, we can bring her back. With all of us, we should manage to only bring her back and not the area surrounding her," Arianna informed Angela and Iris.

"Well, what do we do now? Should we head to my mom's? I'm sure she's there by now."

"We should figure out what we are going to tell Alister so he pardons Arianna. Again," Iris suggested.

"Well, shouldn't be too hard. You and he are like a thing, right?" Arianna asked, wanting the answer to be "yes."

Angela looked towards Arik who was talking with Leah, hoping he didn't hear their conversation. She would explain to him that situation after they had all figured out what they planned to do about retrieving Neveah, Arianna's situation, and what the hell happened to start all of it. Why had she even brought Arik there?

"No. I don't know. Especially now," she whispered, still looking in Arik's direction.

"Well, either way, he cares about you, so you can use that to our advantage."

"I'm not *using* anyone! To *any* advantage. I don't know what you did, but I will not be saving your ass this time. I don't even know you," Angela bellowed at Arianna, shocking everyone in the room.

Angela was actually quite shocked by her own outburst. Annoyance was building up inside of her. She usually would have been all about saving her sister's life, whether it be sending her back to Earth or a dark dungeon she would be saving her from.

You tell them, girl, the evil voice spoke in her mind.

Angela thought she had imagined the voice speaking to her before the blast, but now she knew it wasn't her imagination at all. It was in there, in her mind, rooting for her to continue and tell them where they all could shove it.

Go away. Who are you? You're not me, Angela spoke back to the voice inside her own mind.

Oh, I'm not you at all. I don't belong in your pitiful mind. So weak, it sickens me. I want to go home. Where I was stolen from many decades ago. Your ruthless mother took me away from my true host, and all of you will pay.

Angela blocked the voice out of her mind the best she could, choosing not to entertain it any further.

"I will help, Arianna, but not at the expense of someone else's feelings. That's all I'm saying. Sorry for the rest..the snapping. I'm just overwhelmed," Angela spoke out loud.

"That was harsh. I definitely don't want to get on your bad side, girl." Arianna smiled mischievously at her.

"If you just talk to Alister and be honest, apologize and reassure him you're done with all your nonsense, then he will allow you to be free. You don't have to manipulate people to get what you want. If you do, it's not worth it."

"You're right," Arianna agreed.

"Hey, what's going on over here? You guys need to chill around my baby girl," Arik scolded.

"Funny. Not only is she not a baby anymore, she's the most powerful witch in this realm. I'm sure she can handle a little sisterly spat, you blockhead," Arianna grumbled.

"Geez, who is the married couple here?" Iris asked.

The silence was deafening suddenly; the room turned oddly awkward at the comment.

Your sister asked a good question. Who is the married couple? Whatever will you do, weakling? I'm looking forward to watching this play out, I must say. I know something you don't know. I know something you don't know, the voice tormented Angela.

What do you know? Angela waited. *Oh, now you shut up. Figures.*

"What's going on outside?" Leah asked from the window.

Everyone in the room rushed to the broken glass to look out. Somehow the boundary spell Arianna had cast for protection had broken down, allowing a mob of angry people to head through her doors.

"The magic to stop all destruction in the realm needed boundary magic. I had to bring down my own boundaries in order to close it. They left earlier, but it looks like they're back with more. Why are they even after me?" Arianna asked.

"They think you killed a pregnant woman in town. Someone framed you because of the past curse. We don't know who or why," Iris explained.

"That's sick. Who would ever *purposely* kill a poor, innocent woman just to have me killed? Especially one with child?" Arianna looked like she was going to cry.

"Tell Alister that. You are innocent. At least of *that* crime," Angela spoke.

"I said I would release the crystals to him. I would have no way of causing problems if he had them. I'm sorry. I wish I could explain why I did it."

"Because you're selfish and only think of yourself. You act without even considering the outcome that everyone has to suffer," Arik replied.

Arik wasn't wrong, but he didn't have to be so brutally honest with the way he said it. The tears shed from Arianna's eyes showed Angela that it hurt her, and the lack of response from her only proved he was right. The pain coming from Arianna's face could only mean one thing: They were more than just kidnapper and prisoner. They must have become friends, or even more.

Ding, ding, we have a winner. You guessed right. The voice popped in to annoy Angela once again.

I don't believe you. You are clearly the sick and twisted thing that was in Arianna's head, but I'm pure and loving, so you won't win, Angela fought the voice.

We will see about that, weakling.

"That's my sister, you..." Iris looked at Leah and stopped herself. "You're lucky Leah's here or else I would have so much more to say."

"Oh, I know exactly what you were going to say, Aunty. Daddy, that was mean what you said about Arianna. Did you know she was like me when she was little? Trapped in her own mind and called autistic? She has come a long way and now she is glowing with good in her heart. You don't have to worry about her anymore. None of you do."

"What do you mean?" Arianna asked Leah.

Just when she was going to answer, a rock came through the window, informing them it was time to go.

"Let's get out of here," Angela said, heading to the Mirror.

Angela walked through. Sitting next to it on the other side was Alister; he was waiting at the kitchen table for them to come back. His distressed state was apparent on his face when he got up and wrapped his arms around her, embracing her tightly.

Walking through the mirror next was Arianna, bringing anger to Alister's face before he started bellowing at her about the earthquake and demanding to know what she had done. Stopping in his tracks when he saw Arik, Alister went silent as the last unknown body came through the mirror..a stranger that emitted a displeasing odor.

Like two peacocks in a masculinity competition that was about to begin, the men simultaneously puffed out their chests.

Not knowing, sneering at someone who could truly kill him in a single second, Arik opened his mouth and addressed Alister: "Who the hell are you?"

CHAPTER II

Neveah was sitting outside the cave on a wooden bench with Edna Sofós, the same elderly woman who had physically inspected her before announcing to everyone that she was a human being. While they enjoyed the heat of the sun, they also had their fill of entertainment watching the children get chased by Adonis.

Adonis was running after each child, roaring and growling; as they came within arm's length, he would pull them in and tickle them until they laughed so hard they had to sit on the ground panting. The playful act made Neveah smile. Edna told her that Adonis wasn't the father of the children. They had lost their parents before everyone was forced to run to their own haven, but Adonis adored children and was a wonderful father figure in the little one's lives.

"What's his story?" Neveah asked Edna.

"Besides being a notorious gáidaros, what would you like to know?" Edna laughed.

"What does that mean? Gáidaros?" Neveah asked with curiosity; that was just one of the words bantered about that she didn't understand.

"That's right..Alister and his formal realm. It means donkey, or as you may know it, ass," she replied making Neveah laugh.

"So other realms do have their own swear words?"

"Yes...well, you will hear us use many different swear words and probably start using some yourself," Edna informed her. "Now, dear, are there any other words I can translate for you?"

"What about magissa and gamóto?".

"The first is our word for 'witch'; the second means, basically, your phrase: 'damn it'. It is used when we are frustrated. Who spoke these words to you, by the way?" Edna asked

"Adonis said them when he noticed I was hurt on our journey here. He seems to be a genuinely kind man, though." Neveah waited for Edna to tell her otherwise.

"Adonis has much to learn as a leader. Being a leader means you must put others before yourself. He will make many hard choices to keep us all safe. I believe his heart is in the right place." She paused as a slight worried look came across her face. "The boy has another sibling; a little brother, just ten years old. He was captured by the king, but for what reason we still do not know. Adonis will do whatever it takes to get him back and I fear it will lead to our eventual downfall," she further explained.

"Oh no! That's awful. Why would the king need a child?" Neveah expressed her concern for the child.

"We do not know. My guess would be to use as collateral. Family is everything and most of us would do anything to have the rest of our families united."

"When my family comes for me, I'm certain they will help in any way they can. We can bring all of you back with us and you can start over in Drakous," Neveah reassured.

"My dear, we want our home back. No offense to your new home, but our home was created for our kind. We wouldn't want to have bad blood between the realms if we are all *too* different."

Neveah couldn't understand why different species couldn't get along, but then she didn't ask what they were. Knowing that their shifting creature was their identity but was only shared when they wanted to show themselves, she dared not ask any invasive questions. After all, her having magic was still a secret so it wasn't fair to pry into others' lives if she was not willing to open up too. She didn't want to lie about her identity and that human wasn't all she was.

"Let me tell you a little about our realm," Edna began. "It was created by a powerful witch. One of four original witches. Her name was Talesman."

* * *

Adonis could tell he was getting Neveah's attention. It wasn't a difficult task to show that he had a playful, childlike side. He normally ran around chasing the children, but this day he wanted to make sure Neveah witnessed it.

He could tell she was fond of kids. He assumed, if she was like other women, she would be looking for a potential mate to bear children with. The instincts of his kind were all about procreating for the larger, stronger clan of their kind, so if he showed her he was father material, it would have to make him seem appealing to her. At least…that's what he thought in his own mind. She was smiling though, which made him confident his plan was already working.

The only frustrating thing about the day was the fact that

the old lady was taking all of Neveah's attention. Observing the two women's expressions he could tell they were deep in conversation. Thankfully, by turning his maximum hearing on, he could listen like he was right in the center of their intense exchange.

Laughing at first by the questions on Greek swear words, he was soon after annoyed and disapproving of the batty woman's description of his leadership. She wasn't wrong about Everest being the most important and that he would do anything to get him back, but unfortunately she'd said that it was at everyone else's expense. The fact she knew that about him annoyed him the most.

"Hey guys, come here." Adonis rushed the kids to his side. "I need a favor. I need you to ask the pretty lady if she has a special someone in her life. If you don't tell her I asked, I will owe all of you a favor. Lionix promise."

Adonis held up his right hand making a solid promise to the children. Listening to the giggles and laughter they emitted, he knew they were intrigued by his proposal. The kids stepped away from him to huddle in their own little circle. Turning back to him they replied, "You like the lady. You want to kiss her." The children chanted.

"Hush. Hush..they will hear you."

"Okay, we'll do it. You owe us, though," the oldest of the children spoke.

"Of course. Now let's go pester the old lady." Adonis said, rushing them towards Edna and Neveah.

The children took their seats on the left and right of Neveah on the grass. She had moved to face Edna and listen to the story she was telling about the realm. Adonis stood behind Edna as she was talking, he made puppets with his hands and then made them attack themselves, as he created funny faces behind the elderly woman until Neveah and the children all burst out laughing.

Edna turned around to give Adonis a critical stare. He was

prepared for her to turn, pretending he wasn't doing anything but swatting a fly. She was no fool, however, and immediately got up and started whacking him with her stick.

"Ow! I wasn't doing anything. Edna, ow! That actually hurts," he complained, blocking the stray hits that connected with the top of his head.

Rolling over laughing as Adonis jokingly cried for help, the kids cheered Edna on to 'get him'. As Neveah was on the grass, laying on her back looking up at the sky, she thought of the new adventure that had been forced upon her. The people were kind and generous. Funny and entertaining. Not to mention, the story that Edna told her about the original witches still stirred in her mind. Something about her story felt familiar, like she had heard a part of the tale before. She didn't have a clue where she might have heard any of it, so she chalked it up to a dream that had faded away in her memory.

As she almost forgot she wasn't alone, the kids suddenly piled on top of her. Giggling and tickling Neveah, they continued the cavalcade of laughter. Neveah was reminded of her own two children when she looked into the eyes of the innocent little babes.

"I don't think we have all been formally introduced. My name is Neveah Michelson. What are your names? I want to know everything about you." Neveah smiled.

"I'm Kyler. I'm ten; the oldest. The leader of my family," he said, standing tall and puffing out his chest to show he was proud and a tough little guy.

"I'm Petunia. I'm seven," the middle replied in a shy tone; her demeanor was far softer.

"I'm Rusty. I'm five," he said, putting his whole hand up to show her all five of his fingers.

"It's a pleasure to meet all of you," Neveah said shaking each of the hands offered.

The children followed suit and shook her hand as well. Confusion written on each face. Formalities weren't something they were accustomed to, but her motherly instinct was to start showing them how manners and a more proper custom way worked in the real world.

"Do you have children?" all of the little faces asked excitedly.

"Yes, I do. They're pretty grown up though. Sylvia is my oldest, she is almost eighteen. Zack is almost fourteen."

Neveah suddenly realized she might be missing her children's birthdays. The sadness hit her as she wondered if she would completely miss out on celebrating Sylvia's transition into adulthood. Each thought made her fear she would never see them again, never walk her daughter down the aisle, never watch her son turn into a strong, industrious man. She could feel the sadness overwhelm her as her eyes filled with tears.

"They are so lucky to have a mother and father," Petunia spoke, her face looking very much like Neveah's mournful one.

"What happened the night your parents disappeared?" Neveah asked.

Kyler spoke, "Our mother and father told us they loved us when they heard the king's men outside our home. Mother told us to run as fast as we could into the woods and not look back. They told us not to worry, that they would come for us as soon as they could. We crawled out the back and stayed together. Avoiding our shift so we wouldn't draw attention. But Adonis was the one who found us, hungry and scared."

The pain on the children's faces made her heart fall. She wanted to hold out hope that their parents were still out there searching for them, but from what she'd heard of the brutal king's behavior, she felt the chances were slim that their parents escaped that night. Most loving parents would have put up a fight and fallen to keep their children safe. She would have done the same in order to give her own children a head start.

"My children don't have their father in their lives either.

They only have me. But now I'm gone, too. I'm sorry you lost your parents that way."

"Adonis saved us and brought us here. We are all a family and now you are part of it, too," little Petunia spoke as all three hugged Neveah.

"Well, if Adonis saved all of you, he's a good guy in my book." Neveah smiled.

"You should be his girlfriend," Rusty practically shouted before all of them broke out into a fit of giggles.

"I don't think so."

"Why not?" Petunia asked.

Neveah thought about how she was going to answer without insulting their father figure. "I think…I think he's too fast for me. I mean, how am I ever supposed to chase him? I'm human."

"Do you have a boyfriend?" Kyler asked with a smile.

Neveah laughed. Answering that question was complicated. *Was* Nick her boyfriend? She couldn't answer that question for herself at this point in their relationship. They hadn't made any vow nor had they spoken certain words. Not pondering for long, she certainly knew she wasn't about to tell three children her man problems.

"Nope. Just us three, the rest of my siblings, and my mother," Neveah replied. She stared at them; apparently she'd answered correctly being that the kids now sat there with smiles of satisfaction on their little faces.

"Come play with us," they begged, pulling Neveah up by her arms. "Let's play hide-and-seek. You hide and we will find you."

"Okay, okay." Neveah smiled as she took off running, listening to the kids counting behind her.

Woods would be hard for the children to locate her in and she didn't want them lost. So Neveah found the first tree that was close and easy to climb. She grabbed the limbs and pulled herself up, going higher and higher until she could look over the entire forest. The cliffs, the rivers, and the sun setting was a breathtaking view from up high. She could even see the smoke of the burning lands. It seemed so small now; like a wood fireplace burning in a tiny cottage instead of the fiery inferno that scared one and all when you were standing right beside it.

She had climbed many trees before with Nick, something about Foinix made it seem like the first time, though. The river was glorious from where she stood. With the light's reflection, it glistened like diamonds lay on and about the river bed.

"Found you!" Three voices yelled from below her perch. "Now you have to find us."

"I don't think so. What cruel children you are to do that to the poor human, when you know you are master hiders and she will never find you," Adonis teased.

"You find us then," they replied, positioning themselves to make a run for it.

"No way, little ones. It's time for you to get ready to turn in for the night. Edna's waiting for you."

The unmistakable whining, complaining voices of children commenced while they slowly dragged their feet. Adonis picked up their pace by roaring after them, herding their bodies back to the cave.

Neveah laughed as they disappeared from her sight. Soon after, she walked out of the woods towards the cave to take a seat on the comfortable bench seat. This time, looking up, she witnessed the twinkling lights of the first stars appearing against the dark blue background.

Adonis returned with a smile plastered on his face, clearly amused by his own playful demeanor with the children. The man was a fool if he thought she couldn't see right through his use of the children to gain her attention. The manner was amusing to say the least.

"I swear that roar sounds real," Neveah said, turning in her seat to face him.

"That's because it is," he replied, flopping down on the grass in front of her with a gasp and a surprised expression. "No one knows, so don't tell."

Neveah couldn't tell if he was messing with her until a grin crossed his face. He was teasing her and it actually made her skin warm as she blushed uncontrollably and laughed. Bewildered by her own reaction, she forced herself to stop.

"What *are* you?" She finally asked.

"I'll show you mine if you show me yours," he said, like he had some knowledge he shouldn't have.

Alarm spread through her that somehow Adonis had figured out she was a witch. She had been so careful not to use her magic, or to use it far away from the unknown creatures she now shared a home with.

"I'm just kidding, you silly woman." He laughed.

* * *

Adonis waited for Neveah to begin asking questions about him and their kind. Deciding he would play a guessing game with her in order to get her really wanting to know more about him and what he was, he awaited the questions impatiently.

He used the quite time to study her. The woman was gorgeous. Adonis had stated that to V when him and Neveah had arrived outside the cave. V had made fun of his weakness for a pretty damsel in destress, explaining to him if he didn't check himself he could end up bringing the wrong woman into their haven.

He was ordered to find out if she was a witch and that is exactly what he planned to do with his brother's life and freedom on the line. Planning a trade with the words, I'll tell you what I am, if you tell me what you are, he hadn't assumed that his flirty attempts would go further than he'd originally planned.

"I'm a Lionix," he answered before he ended up with his

foot in his mouth.

"What's that?" Neveah could make out the lion part, but what made him different from an actual lion was the interesting part that confused her.

"I'd rather show you than tell you," Adonis said, jumping into the air from his sitting position and shifting into the mighty creature.

He could tell Neveah was completely astonished by his transition. He wasn't able to communicate to the woman in his current form, so he couldn't reassure her not to be afraid. She didn't seem to be showing fear in her eyes, however, just admiration as she walked around him, observing him with complete interest.

He wanted to show her his wild side and everything it was capable of, so he began by running around like the proverbial cat chasing a mouse. Showing her his speed, he took off into the forest and climbed to the tippy top of the tree she'd sat in when playing hide-and-seek. Jumping off of it, he landed right in front of her. Walking towards her like the lion he was, he stalked her as if she was his prey. Growling under his breath, he focused on her intently as she walked backwards.

Stumbling, Neveah fell, landing softly on her butt. His chuckle sounded more like a cough outside of his own ears; but when the look of pure fear entered her eyes as his fuzzy face came two inches away from hers, he backed away. Turning from her, he made sparks of fire in the shape of little fireflies hovering in the air. Making them grow larger and combine into the size of a tennis ball, he then changed the shape into a beautiful flower, bringing it to Neveah's face for her to blow out. After all, the natural reaction to fire is to extinguish it so it won't burn you.

Transitioning back to his human form, she started clapping. Taking a bow and then another, and another even though she was the only one present, Adonis listened to her clapping and felt like a god as she gave him props for his wonderful demonstration, making him proud.

"Thank you, you're too kind," he bowed again, teasing. "Stop it, you're making me blush."

Once the initial excitement left Neveah's eyes, he suggested they take a walk and talk. He told her all about the different fire shifters that existed: from the lionix to the fire lizard to various snakes and reptiles that had similar powers of toxic saliva and body armor. He completely opened up, telling Neveah about all the different species.

"What about the children? They have got to be something that's actually cute," she asked, beaming, really wanting to know.

"Really? The lionix isn't cute enough?" He pretended to be highly offended.

"Hah. Good try."

He wasn't sure how to tell Neveah about Kyler, Petunia, and Rusty. He had been protecting them from the queen since he'd first found out what they were. The mighty woman wanted their kind more than anything, and Adonis knew why. When their parents had sacrificed their lives to protect the little ones, they'd taken down many of the armed guards with one screech. Instead of echo locations, these bat-like creatures could kill their prey with an echo, making all their enemies senses melt from the inside out.

"I'm afraid the children's identity is not going to be discussed tonight. I can tell you one thing, though; those three innocent little ones are the very last of their species," he said in a serious tone.

He needed to change the mood. It was getting stuffy, and he needed it to be fun and cheerful. Needing to change the subject quickly, he focused on Neveah.

"What about you? Tell me the life story of the damsel in distress, lost in the woods, awaiting her knight in shining armor to rescue her." Proud of himself for that one, he laughed.

"Oh, yeah, and I have the scratches and bruises to show for it," she laughed with him.

Adonis put his head down showing his defeat; all he had left to say was that he was sorry. Watching the moon hover above them, he observed Neveah's sleepy state as she let go of a yawn and rubbed her tired eyes.

"Well..it's late. We should turn in for the night. My bed is this way; let me show you," he teased.

She was walking with him until he said the last part. Laughing, she pushed him where he pretended to fall over. He was still chuckling as he headed to his quarters to have himself some sweet dreams. On his way to his bed, he stopped and held the witch's potion in his hand, melting its container into nothing.

***

Neveah walked in the opposite direction as she still softly laughed at Adonis' sense of humor. The man did make her smile non-stop; laughter came naturally around him. She couldn't remember the last time someone made her laugh so much, but that was probably because there had never been a man in her life so amusing.

She had been looking down at her feet until she reached the cave. Now looking up, she could see Edna was in distress about something. Pacing back and forth in front of the cave, she rushed to her to find out what was wrong.

"Is everything okay?" Neveah asked concerned.

"Be careful, dear. Don't trust everything Adonis or Vera say. Might be nothing, but both were seen in their shift quickly going towards the king's castle when you first got here. If you have any secrets you're wanting to share, I suggest you keep them to yourself for now."

Neveah could tell that Edna knew more and was keeping her safe, just in case being what she actually was would somehow backfire and bring danger to her doorstep. Even though she was unsure of why the information would be dangerous, Neveah heeded her warning.

"You know, don't you?" Neveah asked.

Edna nodded.

"You know I'm a witch?"

"Oh, I know much more than that, my dear." With her pointer finger over her lips, Edna hushed Neveah's words.

CHAPTER 12

Arik saw everything from the other side of the mirror, waiting for the man to stop yelling at Arianna. He should have no right to be jealous, but when you see something with your own eyes, it does tear at the heartstrings.

The man wasn't big compared to Arik, so he was sure if it came to a fight, he would be on the winning side.

"Who are you?" the man demanded, overthrowing Arik's question and attitude.

"I asked first," Arik shot back.

Arik had actually realized who he was talking to the moment His Majesty's eyes turned gold and actual steam came from his nose. Now he was mentally kicking himself in the ass for asking the King of the Realm who the hell he was. *Damn it!* This is *not* the way Arik had wanted to meet this guy.

"Okay, boys... Alister, this is my son-in-law and father of my two youngest grandchildren. Arik, this is Alister, the King of Drakous. All egos aside; get it together." Julia jumped in and cut through the tension.

Arik was shocked to see Julia after all these years. Instead of getting older as nature would have it, he peered at her youthful image and was surprised that the elderly woman now looked to be in her mid-thirty's. He stared at Alister, who seemed to be just as confused as he was.

As Alister and Arik looked into each other's eyes, they both shrugged at the same time, as if placing Julia's shocking appearance on the backburner. Shaking hands respectively, Arik was impressed by the firm grip Alister possessed, especially when it hurt enough for him to make a face.

Yeah. Yeah. You're a strong and mighty dragon who could crush a human like me. I get it. You overgrown reptile. The words raced through Arik's mind, knowing better than to say them out loud.

* * *

Who does this human think he is addressing me with that tone? Alister growled to himself. Alister felt like he was about to lose control and shift to show the man a lesson. If it weren't for Julia stepping in to resolve the situation, Alister would have transformed into his drakon in seconds and made the human fall to his knees – which is exactly where he belonged when in Alister's presence.

Lucky for the man he was part of Angela's family. Not so much for Alister and Angela's progress towards being together and making a family of their own. Alister needed to find out how Angela felt about her husband being in the realm now. *How did the man even get here?*

Alister let go of Arik's hand. He had proved his point; he had made it crystal clear who the alpha of this realm was.

Without uttering a word, the men had an understanding.

The woman and Leah had already abandoned the standoff between the two men in order to sit Julia down and explain what'd happened in Arianna's castle. He would have to find out the rest in a formal meeting. For now, he would let Arianna enjoy the holiday with her family.

Moving closer to the living room, Alister observed the family huddled on the furniture; watching the kids' faces light up when they saw their father after all these years made Alister's heart drop. He couldn't compete with a family reunion. Even Angela smiled at his presence, getting the children even more excited as they yelled: "It's Daddy!"

The others were absent from the family in the living room. Izak and Iris were walking Julia and Arianna around the house, mostly Iris, as she talked about her decorating skills. Julia hadn't seen her home since the day they'd arrived in the realm living in the castle with the land queen, Tiana, or with Jenisis.

Alister wasn't the kind of man to stand in the way of matrimony. If it were any other woman, he would have given up as soon as the man's name was mentioned and walked out of the house. When it came to Angela, however, something in him wouldn't allow Alister to take any steps towards the exit. He certainly held honor and respect for her, but right now all his brain could do was work hard to come up with a plan as to what he would do now.

Moving closer to the couple and the children to watch from a distance, he felt as if he was already licking his wounds from the pain he was experiencing...until Angela looked in his direction, standing to the left of the doorway like a wallflower waiting to be asked to dance.

"I'm sorry." Angela silently mouthed the words. She wore a look of sadness, wanting him to know that she understood the mirror sight of her husband was hurting him.

With a nod, Alister lowered his head, turning away from

Angela's gaze. He was certain if he engaged in a conversation with her right now, without putting proper thought into it, words said would certainly end up leaving them both heartbroken.

***

Julia, witnessing the silent conversation Angela attempted to have with His Majesty, felt sympathetic. On a mission, she walked directly up to Alister.

"Hello, Alister," she whispered.

"Your Highness," he bowed. "I see your wolf has given you the youth of a thirty-year-old woman. How do you feel?"

"Dear, King Jenisis and I have much to report, but for now I want to talk about my daughter. And you need to listen."

The statement shocked Alister. Her dominant tone was highly noticeable in her voice; he actually wanted to obey her every command. Not much had been said after the wedding of the Alpha shift king.

"I love my son-in-law. He is a good man, but *you* need to win my daughter's heart. I'm not a fool. I know they had many issues and that they even hid some from me. They are not good for each other. Angela deserves better, and you can give her that," Julia whispered, telling him what he needed to do.

"With all due respect, Julia, I have no intention of being anything more for Angela than a friend from this day forward. He is the father of her beautiful children and she is...she is his wife. Angela must stay with the family she has built." Even just listening to his own words said out loud, Alister knew he was full of it, but there was nothing else that felt *right* for him to do.

"That's bullshit and you know it! Have you even asked her what it is she wants or does it even matter?"

"Do not speak to me in that hostile tone. You may be the Queen of the Shifters, but I am still your king. Do you understand?"

"Yes, Your Majesty. I'm sorry. I just want you to be honest with yourself so my daughter doesn't suffer," Julia replied, attempting to calm her tone.

"You can't talk to me about honesty when you still have secrets that need to be shared with your family from the moment you got married. How is that marriage going, by the way?"

"You know everything?" Julia asked in utter bewilderment.

"Yes. I haven't spoken a word of your business to anyone. While we are offering advice, however, let me give you some. Don't shut your family out because you don't want to burden them with your problems. Together, your family can work to resolve them."

Bowing her head, Julia submitted, but still had words of wisdom to speak. "Angela's happiness is in your hands. I know Arik better than you do. And I know it's up to you if you want Angela's life to be easier or harder in the future."

The last bit of advice that Julia left Alister with hit him hard. He didn't want Angela to have a hard life at all. He wanted to give her everything she could want, and more. Looking back up at her, she was still in conversation with her children and their father.

Alister was about to leave when Angela looked back at him. Pointing at the door to exit the house, she clearly wanted to speak with him alone. He was trying to avoid this conversation that was potentially going to ruin their friendship. But it was too late to run.

* * *

Angela knew by the look on Alister's face that the conversation they were about to engage in was going to be one of distress. She needed to tell him quickly how she felt about him or she was going to lose him. Watching him take off towards the exit as soon as she pointed to the door, she stood and rushed after him.

When Angela made it on the porch, she didn't even get a chance to express herself. His expression was one she had seen many times before. The one when you break up with someone but really don't want to. Feeling like there is no other choice.

"I have honor and respect, Angela. I will not come between you and your family's success," Alister spoke, already knowing Angela was going to bring up the situation with Arik.

"You're not. There's nothing to come between. I want to be with you." Angela finally admitted out loud what she'd wanted to say for years. "I know I've been difficult, Alister, and it has taken me a long time to tell you but.. I don't want *anyone* but you."

Alister showed a hint of excitement before a frown quickly replaced it. He was stubborn. If they had already been established in their relationship, they wouldn't be having this conversation to begin with. He wouldn't be giving up on them so easily.

"I have to be honest with you. If it were me, and Alison came back to life with our child, I would at least try to make it work. How many times have you gone back to make it work with your children's father?"

"The circumstances are different this time." Angela thought about how many times she and Arik had reconciled. She couldn't count how many times anymore because the amount was great. The last year had been their best and even that had issues.

"Because you believe you have more options. If I took myself out of it, you would choose him. For your children and your family. He would be your choice."

"No! I have changed, living in your world. Your realm. I'm telling you the truth, Alister. I choose you. Why isn't that enough?"

"It would have been. I have waited so long to hear those words release from your mouth. But now he is here, in this realm. What kind of example am I showing my people if I just take what I want, when I want it? You taught me to think before I act. To see things from all perspectives. Now you must take your own advice and think about how many lives will be affected by the choices you make for those little ones' futures."

He was passionate in his words. Angela knew him well enough to know that he would not change his mind at this point and time.

Angela didn't have time to reply; she was not even sure what she would or could say against the powerful speech he'd made. Zack, Simon, and Sylvia walked up the steps, cutting their conversation short. They were ready to go into the house.

"Hey man, what's up?" Zack asked casually, walking by.

Simon bowed, walking with Sylvia who screamed "Grandma!" when she entered the house. Following behind were Basil and Bella.

"Uncle, I'm starting to see wrinkles from all your frowning. You should loosen up a little," Basil teased, *almost* lightening the mood outside.

"You're mean." Bella glared at Basil, reaching out to hug His Majesty. "Your uncle doesn't have wrinkles at all. Merry Christmas, Alister."

"Merry Christmas, little one," Alister hugged back.

Angela couldn't take the sight of the embrace. It felt like the tip of the iceberg she was standing on the edge of before she turned around so no one could see the tears she no longer could hold. Angela's lips quivered at the sadness that was now consuming her body. The stillness in the air was worse than any argument Angela had ever been in. He said nothing, but she could still feel his presence behind her. While she got control of her breathing and calmed her shaking body, the silence ended.

"I will always be here for you, but we will never be more

than friends from this day on. I'm sorry."

With those words Angela felt the wind of his wings as he took flight. She couldn't bring herself to turn around when he stood as a man. When she knew he was in his drakon form and flying away, she turned around and ran after him.

"Please Alister. Don't leave me!" she screamed...with no reply.

Angela fell to her knees when he was out of her sight, past the ocean and the mountains beyond. Covering her tear-coated face with her hands, she'd never felt more broken and alone than at this moment. She had truly never thought he would reject her. To make matters worse, the evil laugh filled Angela's ears, breaking the silence all around.

"He's right, you know. You would go back to Arik because of your custom to take on only the complicated and difficult. Anything else is just going to be boring and too easy for you. You're a weakling. Soon Alister will be one of the past and you will give in," the voice mocked.

"No, I won't. Not this time."

"Well, not without my help. You need me and you know it. I can be your strength and stop all of those who take advantage of your innocent heart. No one will mess with you, with me on your side."

Angela thought about what the voice was saying. Breaking her train of thought, the sound of the outside door slamming shut made her turn around to face her mother, who was rushing with her hands extended towards Angela.

"He's gone," Angela sobbed.

"I know, honey. I tried to talk some sense into the man, but he didn't listen."

"Oh, damn! What did she do? Your fake mother scared him off and ruined your chances at a happy life."

"What did you say to him?" Angela gasped, feeling the anger that the voice's words had brought upon her.

"Nothing. I promise. I told him to stay and fight for you, is all," Julia replied, taken aback by Angela's outburst.

"Right, because dearest Mommy always approved of everyone you have ever loved. How many has she ruined a future with? Making you settle for a man like Arik because no one else was good enough?" The magic stated, full of sarcasm.

"Come inside, baby. Spend time with the family. We need to figure out how to get Neveah home."

"No! I'm going to lie down. Why don't you just go ahead and find a way to get your one and only daughter back yourself," Angela snapped at her.

Instantly regretting the words she let come out of her mouth, Angela blamed the magic who was now laughing and thanking Angela for letting her play. The sick and twisted thing in her mind needed to go, just.. not yet. Even the feeling of her own mother trying to comfort her by rubbing her hand on Angela's back was making her sick.

"Just stop touching me. Go away and abandon us like you did before." Angela ran inside the house, leaving Julia standing alone with her mouth agape, shocked and hurt by her words.

Angela reached the spare bedroom that was much larger than it had been when it was her own bedroom. The bed was like heaven as she buried her head into the pillows and covered herself in blankets, hiding from anyone and everyone.

The voice continued to taunt Angela until she was weaker and ready to let the magic take control. She was tired of fighting and telling it to shut up. All she wanted was sleep. A time of happiness with her family on this merry day had taken a turn for the worst, and now all she wanted was silence.

Angela sighed, knowing she had to make a deal. "If you don't do anything bad, I will let you handle certain situations. You will never be in full control, but I will allow you to take part in my life mentally. If you don't listen to me, however, I will have all the witches lock you away and never let you out. Do we have an agreement?"

The magic sighed. "We have an agreement. Your pitiful

mind is better than nothing, I guess."

"Good, now let me sleep and leave me the fuck alone."

* * *

The power quieted, letting Angela sleep, settling her mind only to bring nightmares to the surface just before she was woken by a knock on the door.

"Who is it and what do you want?" Angela barked

"It's Iris. We have a plan to get Neveah back and it's all set up. We need you."

"Why? My blood won't help."

"Yes, but your magic will."

"Get your ass outta bed; let's go!" Arianna yelled, now banging on the door.

"You don't have to be so pushy," Iris spoke.

"Well, you don't have to be so coddling," Arianna shot back.

Arianna rolled her eyes at Iris. She wanted to get it all over with. If she could get Neveah back, it would help her situation more. She was sorry for Angela's heartbreak, even though she could relate at this time. But she decided that now wouldn't be the best time to bring up her own situation while they already had another to face that was overflowing with boiling water.

Angela opened the door. Dark circles ringed her eyes, and her angry attitude was apparent on her face.

"Good," Arianna spoke. "The negative energy and mean attitude you got going on will power the magic you have inside, making it stronger so we can get Neveah back. Use it," Arianna ordered, pointing at her sister's face, trying not to laugh at the irony of their switching positions. She no longer felt and looked like Angela.

"Yeah, whatever. Let's get going and get it over with." Angela slumped her shoulders, shutting the bedroom door behind her.

Arianna led the witches, Zack, and Sylvia through the mirror. All she would need was the blood of the children to visibly find out where their mother had been sent to.

"Are you okay, Mom?" Leah asked.

"I'm fine, honey. Just a little sad," Angela said, trying to smile slightly.

"It's all going to be okay," Leah reassured.

"Wow! Witches have cauldrons?" Sylvia asked, walking over to the huge vat sitting in the middle of the room.

"Yes, and much more that you have probably seen on TV. Other witches use different things. Our line usually only uses crystals and stones," Iris spoke.

"And blood. Speaking of, I need yours now. Step up to the cauldron," Arianna said, rushing the process a bit.

"Is it going to hurt?" Zack asked with a fearful look in his eyes.

"No. Just a prick of the finger. Don't let her scare you." Iris answered quickly in case Arianna had decided to tease him.

Arianna grabbed Sylvia's left hand. First using a stone needle and pricking her ring finger, she allowed a few drops to drip into the cauldron. She repeated the process with Zack.

"Why do you get the blood from that finger?" Leah asked.

"It's the only one that goes straight to your heart. When trying to find family that you love and who are lost, you keep your feelings for them directly in your heart, which is why we need those emotions the most. You still have much to learn, little one." Arianna smiled, showing her soft side as she spoke this time.

Arianna led the four witches, Zack, and Sylvia to circle the cauldron, hand-in-hand. With the power of all four witches, they shouldn't have any problem seeing Neveah and her location. Beginning the simple spell and the chant, Arianna assumed they'd only have to be uttered once.

"Vres poios agapiétai kai chánetai. I dýnami tou oikogeneiakoú aímatos mas deíchnei." Arianna spoke the words to find Neveah. Instantly, the sight of her face would show inside the bowl.

But when peeking inside, there was no sign of anything. No picture or location, just dark, black silence, not even a heartbeat could be heard. The news was scarce. Only Arianna knew that something was wrong.

"Is our mother dead?" Sylvia started to panic.

"No, she's not. If she was, this would show us her body. This is...different. It feels like my magic is being blocked. Which could only mean that wherever Neveah is, someone doesn't want her to be found. But it would take the power of a hundred witches at the very least to make an entire realm invisible to all outsiders," Arianna answered, more than a bit confused herself.

"Neveah is in a realm with witches that don't want to be found. That's not good at all," Angela added the obvious.

"There is no way to find Neveah or even go to a realm that is guarded with such hardcore power. We can't do anything until the spell is broken in whatever realm she's in. I'm so sorry, children," Arianna spoke.

"Are you saying our mother could be trapped, dead, or with a hundred witches that don't want to be found and there is no way to get her back or even find out?" Sylvia spoke with a blank look on her face, repeating what they had all told her.

"Yes," Iris spoke, grabbing Sylvia and Zack, embracing them while they cried in her arms. Angela and Arianna joined them.

"We will never stop looking for her. I will never stop training; I'll work harder and harder every day until we can find a way. I promise." Angela spoke, holding them tighter.

"We all promise."

"Don't worry. I have a feeling at this moment she's happy and surrounded by others that both accept and care for her. It will take time to find her...but I know she's okay," Leah stated her odd report before adding herself to the long-lasting hug.

Arianna listened to her words and couldn't tell if she was being positive or if she actually knew Neveah was okay.

Sadness still filled the room, even after Leah's words were released. Not one person in the space could honestly say if Neveah was going to be found or coming home anytime soon. All they shared was hope.

CHAPTER 13

Neveah didn't understand why it was taking her family so long to come to her rescue. She felt like it wasn't her that needed the rescuing, but more the people she had come to know, like family. She was definitely ready to do something—*anything*—to help them at this point.

The people were all fire shifting creatures, a mass of immaculate colors in a variety of shapes and sizes. Gigantic reptiles that could burn you with one touch. Spit and slime that was like acid that melted any part of your body. The sight of them wasn't pleasant in the least bit either. She had never been much of a reptile pet owner, personally. Although she did have an iguana growing up that went by the name of Maryjane. If you even tried to hold her, she would whip you with her tail or try to sink her razor-sharp teeth into your skin.

After that incident she tried to stick with the basic, cats and dogs, and one attempt with a rat that didn't work out well either. Why Neveah focused on her pets as a young girl was just to keep her mind busy from her family, especially her son and daughter.

The people all around Neveah trusted and accepted her; being more comfortable that she knew all their abilities and forms, they could now train in front of her. They could never kill each other with any powers related to fire, but it certainly looked painful after each contact followed up by a fast-healing ability. From all the chatter, no one thought they would be fighting their own kind, especially their dear king they spoke highly of until he went mad. Most still thought it was never the king that was in control of all the damage, death, and mayhem caused; they believed it was all the magissa's fault.

For Neveah, Adonis had been incredible to watch. Strong and powerful in his leadership, he was also the biggest flirt she had ever seen. By now, it was apparent that Adonis wanted to be with her. Getting to know him each day for months, she'd found it becoming an increasingly difficult challenge not to give in to the mostly carefree man. He did bring out her silly and playful side, making her feel like a young teen once again.

"Hey beautiful. Thinking about me?" Adonis asked, fluttering his long eyelashes over his fire red eyes.

"Ha! Not at all. I was just thinking about my family," she lied.

"Can't blame a guy for hoping." He winked.

Shaking her head with a blush upon her cheeks she looked down to the left of her. Adonis sat in the soft bed of grass, watching the equally matched opponents while they jousted. She could never tell when Adonis was joking or being serious. Unable to shake the feeling that he was trying too hard to gain her affections, each time she rejected his attempts he would show signs of annoyance but make them disappear quickly. All she could wonder was...why?

"Adonis, I do care about you. I'm just broken, and there are still many things you don't know about me. My heart had been broken and my mind had been completely brainwashed for years by my ex-husband. He made me feel like I was nothing without him and that I could never amount to anything. Holding my children above my head.. threatening to take them from me.. and there was nothing I could do about it because I had no money from being a stay-at-home mother for years. I completely depended on him." Neveah stopped, awaiting Adonis' response.

"He's lucky I wasn't there. I would have made him wish he was never born," Adonis replied, displaying his anger in both expression and voice.

"My divorce was only finalized a month before we were sent to Drakous, and there I fell for a man that was just as broken as myself. I never understood him and thought he was rejecting me and just wanted a friendship. Then I found out he was scared and hurt from his own past. He wanted to talk before I ended up in this realm but then, he disappeared, and sent letters telling me the realm was dying and he had to stay away and report to the king," Neveah stopped right there. She had said too much too quickly.

The look on Adonis' face while his eyes bulged in shock was a clear sign that he caught up to the last part of her story. It was like a stack of heavy books had been weighing her down; Neveah actually felt relieved to finally let it all out.

"The Drakous realm is dying?" Adonis asked quickly to confirm.

"Yes. No one can explain why, but apparently it will take decades for it to consume all of Drakous."

"That's unreal. Looks like our realm isn't the only one in trouble."

"That's why I need to get back. My two teenagers are growing up and I'm missing it. I need to start putting them before my own desires until they're happy and content with their own lives."

"I'm sorry you're missing them. I know how that feels. As far as the man that didn't make it clear he wanted to be with you, he's a coward intimidated by your strength and your beauty. What kind of shifter was the man anyway?"

"He's an eagle."

"He needs to have his wings clipped for making you confused. I'm more right to the point with my endless charm and flirtatious nature," Adonis added a teasing note.

"I figured that out," Neveah laughed.

"It doesn't work on you though, does it?" he asked; his eyes were pleading.

Before Neveah could stop herself, she admitted, "It actually is." She smiled longingly into his excited eyes until the world seemed to come to a complete halt, and the noises faded into the background.

Leaning in to seal the deal with a kiss was shockingly interrupted by a man who had left earlier to go on a look out with Vera.

"Vera was captured! I told her not to go!" A distressed shifter ran towards the couple. "She said she saw your brother and..took off. I'm sorry, Adonis. I tried to stop her!"

The man was building an audience of concerned faces all around. Practice had stopped to listen and huddle towards the three of them. Waiting on Adonis to reply to the scarce news, he seemed to be waiting on others to speak before he reacted.

"What do we do now?"

"We need to move."

"No. We need to fight. We're ready," the last of the crowd shouted his opinion.

Neveah looked to Adonis, like everyone else did, with questioning eyes. For someone who'd now lost his sister on top of his brother, he was certainly handling the news unusually well.

"There's nowhere to go. All we can do now is fight," Adonis

spoke for the first time.

"We will all fight to the end." Noises spread throughout the crowd.

"We need a witch to fight or we don't stand a chance." A woman with sense was heard.

"Everyone calm down. I will hold a meeting and all will have a chance to speak. Right now, emotions are high and none of us are thinking clearly. Use that energy you feel and train like your life depends on it," Adonis instructed. "Now go. We will touch base soon."

* * *

Adonis watched his people slump back to training in an agitated, angry state. He regretted what he agreed to with the witch regarding his sister. How could he trust her to release Vera and Everest?

The queen's plans were not working. As he left the safety of the cave to have a meeting with the queen he knew there was no valuable information to report about Neveah. After all, Neveah was a tough egg to crack. With his overly confident nature, he'd destroyed the potion the queen gave him and decided he could get Neveah to fall for him all on his own. Irritated that she had turned him down many times, he realized destroying help in his case was a bad idea. His visit with the information was displeasing to the magissa but he had no other choice than to make a new bargain.

Elinor informed him she would be handling everything herself, all she needed was to get Neveah to come up the right side of the castle where she would be waiting to capture her. He had agreed he would make it happen and lead Neveah to the location the queen stated. Although it was supposed to be an easy task, the witch was smart; she requested assurance of a trade. She wanted Vera or she would get rid of his little brother, with a promise she would return both of his siblings after she had custody of Neveah.

Adonis had no choice but to bow his head and agree to her demands. Vera couldn't know the plan, and the witch would handle everything to do with her. The rest was up to him to get creative. She had suggested that he get the people riled up for a fight, giving him a chance to take down some of her followers – enticing him with revenge at her guard that could have killed him the last time.

Lost in thought, he hadn't spoke about anything more. Neveah had got up and walked to Edna to express her concern, too. All he could overhear was that her family wasn't coming, and something was stopping them. She didn't know exactly why it was taking them so long. Adonis hoped that they would arrive soon, he really didn't want to hurt Neveah. He'd rather be with her and make her a part of his family, but his blood was at stake and even that topped his romantic affections.

The queen sat in her chair using Edmond to torture and motivate Adonis. He could almost feel his little brother's pain from one touch by the witch's magic. He watched as Elinor siphoned the life magic out of Edmond slowly and painfully, until nothing but screams filled the air. He had tried to refuse her requests before she used his brother as a literal bargaining chip.

Adonis felt responsible for his brother's capture. If he hadn't pushed Everest to be faster, stronger, and constantly been hard on him, he would have never run away and ended up in the witch's grasp in the first place. They were all powerless against her, even Adonis was realizing that the people's lives were only safe if he agreed to all her terms, adding the safety of everyone in his haven.

"Edna, Neveah, please join me for the start of the meeting. I fear that a fight is all we can do to protect ourselves." Adonis spoke after getting up and walking towards them.

* * *

Elinor was in her quarters making quite the mess. Picking up and throwing everything around the room with her magic, broken furniture pieces and clothing lined the floor of her room. She was having her own childlike temper tantrum as she screamed with anger at Adonis' disappointing news.

What was wrong with the stupid woman who seemed immune to the man's charms? If *she* was younger, Elinor would take the man as her own and force him to be her king – force him to take over and rule this useless realm. The potion hadn't worked from what he informed her, which meant Neveah had a love stronger than her magic or she was unaffected by the potion – which only proved she had some sort of magic. The love in Neveah's heart is all she would need to rip from her and produce a powerful magic to be used on a powerful drakon. She'd own even more power if she retrieved the hearts of the couple in love before she ended both their lives. She would take both Neveah's and Adonis' hearts, just to be sure they shared more than just a friendship connection, and make an irresistible potion that even the drakon couldn't refuse. It was indeed a shame that the handsome Adonis had to die; she'd so enjoyed using him as her personal beck and call boy.

None the less, Elinor had to make plans regarding Vera's capture. With the fight that was certain to come, soon after she would need extra power and strength in case they came after her. There was a powerful foinix that had all the might and vigor she would need with her name on it.

Sighing, she snapped her fingers and cleaned up the room, restoring it to its former glory, before turning to walk down to the dungeon to have a little chat with the king. The frustration building up inside her could be far better used on him. With a laugh at her own sickened thoughts, she entered through the doors leading to the king's cage and stood directly in front of him.

"You will never win. I have built a grand kingdom with loyal followers. My neighbor realms will come, and they will destroy you." King Thaddeus spoke with far more strength than days before.

"Glad to hear your strength is increasing," she replied with a wicked smile. "You're going to need that."

* * *

Adonis brought in the rest of his warriors to hold a meeting inside the cave. Explaining the plan to them and addressing their attack locations – who'd be stationed on the left and right, front and back – he then volunteered to be part of the front group. Showing them all the instructions on a handmade map.

"We don't have enough shifters. We're going to be slaughtered," one man spoke.

"That's not true. When Vera and I scoped out the area of the castle we noticed the magissa had a small number of followers; maybe ten in total, including the two in the front guarding the doors. We can handle them," Adonis reassured them.

"We could send the three children. They have the power to quickly end it all."

"No way in Hell are we sending those young children! They are too young and have minimal control over their abilities. It's dangerous for them and we could *all* be killed if it backfires." Adonis hoped his words were fearful enough to prevent his little ones from being sent into the witch's grasp.

"We can't fight the witch without another of her kind, or the drakon who witches' powers have no effect on."

"What chance do we have if we sit and wait to be picked off one by one? We have no choice either way; right now we are sitting ducks."

"Here! Here!" Everyone hollered, throwing their support

behind their leader.

Adonis was thrilled by their excitement for battle; a chance to really use all they had and show what they were all capable of. He believed they could kill whoever they wanted, and the queen would not stand in their way. She just wanted Neveah, and the rest was all a gift to them.

"Could we at least find another haven and ask for help? Others might feel the same as we do and want to fight for *their* freedom."

Having outsiders who didn't know Adonis and who might question his authority was an idea that made him stir inside. Concerned that they would find out his secret and expose what his real plan was. He couldn't risk it, but he needed to give the people something. Without a witch he had no other motivation or valid reason to deny the correct option of accumulating a greater number of warriors. He would just have to tell them that he was the leader and they either followed him or they could get out.

Neveah hadn't taken her eyes off Adonis, watching him intently. He didn't yet know that Neveah was already suspicious of him; she just didn't know why. Adonis barely looked her way and, if he did, he quickly left her gaze. It was like he was a different man, or acting like someone who had completed his task regarding her. It would be natural to think that his sister's abduction had changed his mood. But then, he hadn't shown any emotional distress to her being captured. She sighed. *Who am I to say how someone grieves, though?*

She wondered how her own family reacted when she disappeared suddenly. If they missed her, and what exactly was stopping them from coming for her and being there, standing beside her. They should be there to attend the meeting and be part of the fight. With the witches in her family, and all the manpower Alister had in his grasp, the magissa in Foinix wouldn't stand a chance against them all. Neveah really hoped that Edna would give the go so she could tell everyone she was a witch and hopefully relieve their stress. She needed to train with them. Her magic was weak from not using it in order to hide her identity. She needed to strengthen her power soon; if not, she would be worthless in protecting her newly built family.

* * *

Elinor couldn't stop laughing at Thaddeus's words. She, of course, knew something he did not. Information that would make him lose all hope in his eyes. No one could, or *was*, going to save his realm, or *him*, from her demise. Not even his son, Basil. Not that he would even want to help the man after he'd almost killed him – after Edna had made Thaddeus believe Basil was an evil demon, even making him unable to tell the difference between an actual monster from Hell and his own beloved son. Dark fairy dust had done the trick after blowing it in his eyes. Bless her evil soul.

Basil had escaped into Drakous with the help of a witch. From what Elinor could see through the window it was a powerful witch, and she was trying to enter Foinix. That just wouldn't do, Elinor hunted down two of the battonix shifters and used their echo and pain, connecting their life force to the crystals that helped power all of Foinix. The fire agates, along with the shifters, helped her build a strong shield around the realm. All she had to do was keep them connected.. and alive.

"Oh dear, dear, Thaddeus. You are so clueless. No one is coming to your rescue. I made it so no one can enter or exit from your realm." She laughed, watching his eyes change. "Not without my blood magic, and the only line of mine died a long time ago. And, of course, a handful of special family crystals from the original witches. As for your followers, they are all going to be dead soon, so you don't have to worry about them."

"Burn, you evil magissa. I should have never trusted you;

you're a cruel, twisted excuse of your kind."

"Well, thank you. I do love the compliments. I'm feeling quite parched now. I think I'm ready for some of your power now," she replied, unaffected by his words.

"Go to Hell! If you think I'm going to—." He stopped dead in his speech.

Elinor grabbed his arm, harnessing every drop of his abilities, giving herself the powers of a foinix. She let him fall to the ground so she could take in the sensations now running up her arms and down her body and legs, like shots of pure ecstasy.

When Elinor opened her eyes and looked at her own reflection in the eyes of Thaddeus, she replaced her smokey blue eyes for his fire red ones, changing his to a shade of green. He was now just a feeble human being in her eyes.

"Why don't you just kill me?" he asked, on his hands and knees before making it to a standing position.

"No. That would be all too easy. Plus, who would hang out and watch your kingdom crumble with me, while I soak up every bit of power from each shifter that suffers and dies?" she asked, adding a sickening laugh that could make anyone shudder in pure disgust.

"Why my realm?"

"Honey, yours is just the beginning of many more to fall. Yours wasn't even my first choice, actually. If it wasn't for my foolish sister taking all of my dark magic that took years to harness, and then running away to a world without magic so I couldn't claim what was mine, I would be talking to an entirely different king, you brainless man," she replied, getting angrier as she spoke.

Words could never explain how much hatred she had for her sister and having to grow up in her perfect shadow. Elizabeth Butler, one and only angel to one and all, was the owner of beauty, mind, and soul and exceled in everything she did. Her being the golden child that could do no wrong, left her being the helpless mistake of a younger sister that received all the disappointing looks from their parents. The complete opposite of Elizabeth was the definition of Elinor Butler.

Although beauty was the one thing Elinor finally triumphed over her sister for, catching all the eligible men's eyes and enjoying every bit of it, her father forced her into a marriage to settle her down. Of course, the joke was on her dear, old dad when the husband who'd been forced upon her met his maker through Elinor by trading his life for everlasting youth and beauty and placed in the glorious lands of the pixies located in the most radiant realm of all. There, Elinor earned the dark fairies respect..and received a bag of dark dust to honor her.

* * *

Neveah was silently asking Edna if the time was now to reveal her secret. Edna raised her hand and lifted her index finger, instructing her to wait a little longer. It was apparent she wanted to see how Adonis was going to reply to all the questions from the people.

"We will search for another haven and recruit as many shifters as we can to help in our battle to come," Adonis agreed. "If no one opposes to the plan, or has more to say, I will end the meeting and send a search party to locate the closest haven to ours."

It was obvious that Edna had received the reply she wanted, because as soon as Adonis

finished his speech, she nodded to Neveah and gave her the go.

"I have something to say." Neveah stepped forward observing all the eyes that shot in her direction.

"Well, out with it. We don't have time to play guessing games anymore." The statement sounded more like it was directed from Adonis and not from the people at all.

"I'm a witch, and I am ready to fight for everyone's lives," she hastily replied, aiming her words directly at Adonis. "What do you have to say about that?"

CHAPTER 14

Arianna woke up every morning happier and more cheerful than she had been in many years. The voices in her head had stopped; finally, after so many years, she was free of the evil that'd occupied her own mind. She wasn't sure if it was her unborn child or it was the magic she gave Angela that was obsessed with power had brought on mental illness, but her constant need to rule the world and make everyone bow to her was gone.

Arik hadn't come back home with Arianna. He visited with the troubled Izak in his own home on Arianna's property, but she didn't want to think about Izak at that point and time. Arik was far too busy enjoying much deserved time with his son and daughter, Angela was not present around him. Arianna could tell he wasn't in love with Angela anymore, but he had a duty at least to try.

Sleeping in this morning, Arianna laid in bed wondering what exactly it was that she wanted out of life, feeling like she had an opportunity to go after those things now. She wanted her family and to be connected with her nieces and nephew. Above all, she wanted a love in her life that wasn't selfish and would cherish her always. Someone that would love her in return.

Rubbing her own belly, she pondered over her meeting with Alister the day before. Arianna was completely shocked by his sudden pardon of her mistakes, holding his hand out for her to drop the family crystals in. As promised, she gave up that incredible power the crystals possessed and hadn't cared one bit about discarding them from her life. She had been honest with Alister..for the most part. The only exception was not telling him about her pregnancy and that Arik was her unborn child's father.

Regarding Neveah's return, only then would she need the stones back to perform the spell. Alister promised to return the stones when the time came, and he would be present for the entire scene. Returning the stones to their rightful owner once she returned safely.

Marie, the underwater mermaid queen, was still loose in Drakous, assuming she was somewhere waiting for Arianna to make one wrong move that she could use against her. Marie might be the guilty one, but Arianna wasn't about to underestimate the followers she had who wanted nothing more than to see Arianna burned at the stake.

Arianna's home was a mess and in dire need of a makeover. Sitting up slowly, careful not to get a head rush from the excitement of a remodel she would be doing to fill the hours as well as her mind, she slid her legs off the bed and set them on the floor, ready to conquer the day.

* * *

Alister couldn't calm himself down, so he wasn't able to shift back into his human form. If he couldn't resolve his issues, he would be stuck in his drakon form for a long time.

Lighting things on fire or freezing everything in his path were only a couple things he wanted to do at the moment. The other was to turn around and kidnap Angela, never letting her go again. It took all his strength not to do the latter.

Trying to justify his decisions and how he had treated Angela was difficult in his drakon form. The human side of Alister had a different outlook on love than the almighty drakon. Morals and integrity as a human being not to break up a house already built with two happy little children. The other more primal side of him, without a doubt, would do *anything* for Angela and knew he wanted only her.

Alister couldn't do anything right lately. He was unable to prove Arianna's innocence, his loyal people were disobeying his royal commands, and above all he couldn't give Angela what she needed from him, even though he wanted to. Well, at least he could do something right and pardon Arianna at the meeting she was to attend with him.

Still depressed, but somehow done battling himself, he flew down for a landing in front of his castle. After a little work, shifting back into a man, he walked towards his castle doors to sit and wait for Arianna's arrival.

* * *

Arik walked around Julia's house. He was staying in a guest room that the laborers and construction workers had added to the lovely home. Well, now the home was Izak and Iris's, it was to be their wedding gift, Julia stated before leaving to be with her husband. All she had said to Arik was, "Welcome back to the family." Nothing more. Arik didn't feel welcome though. Angela seemed to be avoiding him, his children were the only ones both overjoyed to be around him. Arik couldn't help but admit life was easier being with Arianna and he hated it, but he missed being around her, playing house. He missed being wanted.

"Where is everyone?" Arik asked Izak when he came out of his room. The poor man looked like a walking zombie.

"They're gone. Training. Some shit like that," Izak mumbled his response.

Arik knew better than to press Izak when he was in an agitated state, but to be fair, that was in the past and he had been on drugs.

"Fuck," Izak burst.

"What's up, man?"

Izak didn't answer, he was bent over with his hands on the kitchen counter and his head between his arms. It wasn't until Arik heard sniffles that he realized Izak was crying.

"Why? Why my sister? Hasn't she been through enough?" Izak turned to look at Arik with tear-filled, red eyes.

"I don't know, man. Why don't you come sit down next to me and we can talk?"

"I don't want to sit! I wanna break shit! My sister could be dead! Don't you get it? I already lost my brother," Izak stated, calming just a little at the end.

"You don't know Neveah's dead," Arik raised his own voice. Going back to when he thought his family was dead.

"She might as well be."

"Just hang in there, Izak, you've come a long way. Your fiancée and family will get her back. Give it time,"

Izak was still upset. The anger and fear were written all over his face. Arik had seen it too, looking at his own reflection, before he made everything numb and couldn't feel any more pain.

"How did you do it? Cope, I mean, when you thought we were all dead?"

"I didn't. I got fucked up and did a lot of drugs until

nothing else mattered. Had a lot of meaningless sex; even ended up in prison for beating a man to death. That was my life until I got out of my cage and straightened myself out."

Arik could tell he got to Izak. His eyes focused and widened in surprise. Now he was walking to the table and taking a seat.

"Shit, man, I had no idea. I'm sorry you went through that."

"Don't repeat my mistakes. I lost everything and had no one to help me pick up the broken pieces. You got a great woman. Don't fuck it up. They're hard to find."

"Yeah, thanks. I'll try not to. It's just hard, you know. Every down moment I go straight to thinking about getting high. I'm sick of it."

"It's addiction and you have to battle it for the rest of your life. Day by day, step by step. Just keep saying no." Arik laughed after reciting his N/A mantra.

Izak seemed to be more relaxed and calmer now. He knew the same chant; it was something they all said at the beginning and end of the meetings. Arik thought his words of wisdom worked and that he had proved his point.

"Did your house come with you like ours?" Izak asked.

"Yeah. Why?"

"I just want to get away. Could we go chill at your house?"

"Sure, man. Anything you need."

The men packed a couple of bags and walked out the door to head to Arianna's land.

* * *

Alister could hear the carriage pull up outside the front of his castle. Arianna would be getting out of it soon and joining him in a discussion. They both had their differences and needed to talk. Remembering Angela's advice, that when Arianna came out of hiding they both needed to sit down and have a serious talk, made him smile.

"Your Majesty." Arianna's voice cut through the memory. "Are you okay?"

"Yes. Why do you ask?"

"Because you were wearing an odd..smile. I'm sorry, I thought you would have a different look on your face," Arianna ended on an awkward note.

"To be honest, I was thinking of a memory I shared with Angela. She loves you and was on my tail about having a talk with you so we could move on."

"I love her, too." Arianna smiled.

Alister grinned, he had hoped Angela was enjoying having both of her sisters in her life.

"How is she?" Alister asked.

"Miserable. Crying all the time. Wouldn't come out of her room. Now she won't come out of the magic training cages. She's obsessed," Arianna answered.

Arianna's words sent pain through Alister's chest. 'Don't kill the messenger' was all he could think. She was being honest after all. He was the one to blame, not Arianna. He remembered that too.

"I think it has a lot to do with Neveah's lack of return. Missing her, she keeps feeling responsible for her disappearance. I don't really understand why. I'm sure she's a little upset about you, too, though." Arianna wanted to remind Alister about Neveah, and he knew it.

Alister was mad at himself now for selfishly thinking what Angela was going through was all about him and not the love of her sister. Looking at Arianna, he could feel her emotions. She was doing this on purpose. He chuckled inside at the sisterly traits of feistiness they all shared, not blaming her in the slightest.

"Right. Okay. Well..shall we take a walk? I want to show you something and have a talk," Alister asked, standing up.

"Of course, Your Majesty. Lead the way."

Walking past Arianna, he smiled at the resemblance

between her and Angela, when just a couple of years ago he was locking Angela away, refusing to release her because of his own arrogance. Now the woman that all his anger was meant for was walking beside him, though he had no desire to punish her. That feeling had disappeared the moment he had romantic feelings for Angela. That was within days of meeting her, which he didn't realize.

"Your Majesty, I thought you wanted to talk. Not lock me up," Arianna's panic was rising as she realized he was leading her down to his dungeon.

"I do want to converse. I just wish to show you where it all started with Angela," he laughed. "I confused her for you the first day she arrived in my realm. Even kidnapped her."

"She must have been so frightened; I certainly was. Thinking you were coming for me. So, I can only imagine how Angela felt under your wrath."

"We have come a very long way from that. I was stubborn and unreasonable. I never thought about anyone else's pain except my own, especially after the curse and what happened. I have grown a lot over the years."

"You knew me before everything, before that awful curse. I know I was trouble, but I never would have intentionally hurt Alison. She was a sweet and generous queen. I admit I was jealous of the love she gave to everyone she spoke to, but I have changed that part of me. It's gone."

"I know. I can feel your emotions, all of them. I never was able to before. What's left of you feels good and pure. Your intentions are clear and selfless." Alister told Arianna what he could see about her, and she believed it.

Alister opened the cell that was once occupied by Angela, her bedroom in his castle. He had cleaned it himself since she was last there, but no matter what, her natural scent filled the air. Seconds after, thinking about a scent, he started laughing uncontrollably, completing confusing Arianna.

Still laughing, Alister tried to explain, "I once gave Angela warm milk and it came flying out her nose and mouth. I swear that's the day everything changed for me."

"Yuck, I never liked warm milk." Arianna laughed, too, joining in the fun.

"Well, you know, you don't have to worry. I'm going to make an announcement that you are free and not responsible for the death of that woman. I will also announce my concerns about Queen Marie. Someone is responsible and my people need answers; hopefully, soon, I will have at least some answers to relieve their stress. In the meantime, you need to sit tight and put your boundary back up. I don't want to have any more trouble."

"Yes, Your Majesty. Will you be visiting Angela soon?" Arianna asked with curiosity.

"Arianna, call me Alister. As far as Angela goes, I will keep my distance and give her space..for her and her husband to rebuild what was taken from them."

"Alister, she doesn't want to be with Arik, and he doesn't want to be with her either. He just wants to be with his children. You will see," Arianna said calming herself.

"How do you know what they want?" he asked, hopeful but still guarded. Could Arianna have the words to make him drop everything and go scoop up Angela so they could finally be together?

"Well, she hasn't spoken to him since you left her on Christmas. I'm sorry, I really can't tell you any more than that, but please keep an open mind. The rest is my business in the situation and I'm not ready to share it."

"There is a lot of that going around lately. I won't press. I suggest you get your business resolved before it turns into a big thing, though. With that, let me walk you to the carriage."

Arianna nodded in agreement and proceeded to walk side by side with Alister. Waving farewell to His Majesty, she finally released a sigh of relief. The wagon ride home was relaxing now that she had resolved issues with Alister. She could also finally see how appealing he was, but nothing compared to Arik's looks and demeanor, something she hoped Angela wouldn't realize.

Arianna's mind raced, still thinking about Arik when she arrived home, stopping the wagon when she watched the door to Arik's little green house close. Someone was inside Arik's house and she didn't know who.

* * *

As soon as Arik opened the door, Izak had a one-track mind. That was to search his house for alcohol.

"What do you have to drink in here?"

"Oh, let me show you. I could use a drink, too," Arik replied, walking to his cabinet.

Izak followed closely behind looking around before he saw the large cabinet completely full of liquor.

"Damn, man. That's like hitting the jackpot. Got any Red Bull? Jager bombs?" Izak seemed excited now.

"Yeah, but its sugar free and probably expired."

"Fuck it. Let's do it anyway. My fiancées a witch, so we will be fine," Izak replied.

Arik grabbed the jager from the cabinet, along with two shot glasses and two larger glasses. Walking to the pantry, he grabbed the Red Bull and poured it into each glass, adding the jager in the shots and then handing Izak a set.

"To Neveah's safe return," Arik said, clinking glasses with Izak's before dropping the shot glass into the energy drink and downing it all.

One after the other, both men indulged in the consumption of alcohol. Playing board games, they finally moved the party of two into the garage to play some sloppy darts.

"Hey, man, I got to go inside. I gotta take a shit," Izak announced.

"Cool. I'll stay here."

Izak ran into the house, he didn't need to use the restroom at all, he just wanted to search. He looked under Arik's bed and in every crack and crevice of his bedroom, finding what he wanted in a pair of old shoes stashed in Arik's closet. Which is exactly where he would hide his own if he had any. He lifted the small bag of white powder from the shoe and sighed.

Walking over to the bed and sitting on the edge, he fought with himself to dump it and never look back. The addiction talking to him in the back of his mind had other plans. It wouldn't hurt *just this time*. Plus, the bag had very little in it; chances were, he wouldn't find anymore. He just needed the pain and hurt of worrying about his big sister and what could have happened to her to just go away. The last thought running through his head before he snorted the drug up his nose and laid flat on his back, was that Neveah was dead, and when they found her body it was already going to be too late. Closing his eyes, he took in the high of what he had done.

Little did Izak know he wasn't alone. Someone had witnessed his actions while standing just outside the window.

* * *

Arianna no longer wanted dark colors to fill the interior of her home. This time it would be bathed in a palate of warm colors, like ocean blue and sunset orange. Colors of the places she loved to be on a hot summer day. Anything cheerful to offset the unfortunate images running through her head. The change wasn't difficult at all. With a whip of her magic, she had the window puzzle pieces of glass back together and reset. The walls and pictures were altered that hung along the hallway, kitchen, bedrooms...all decorated to her liking.

Satisfied with the makeover inside her home, she then moved to the outside. Covering the front lawn with lilies, sunflowers, and fire-colored roses in a rainbow of orange, yellow, and red, added even more to the warmth she now had running through her.

Arianna headed out to the spot where she would put up the invisible shield again, as Alister instructed. The anger running through every part of her mind, body, and soul was no longer there; her power, alone, wasn't strong enough to put the walls back up because her desire to have walls had disappeared. She didn't want to keep people out anymore, welcoming them was what she would rather do. The next time the riots came for her she would be ready, apologize kindly, and prove to them that she deserved their forgiveness.

The number of people wanting Arianna's head was the least of her problems at this time. Her biggest concerns were for her beloved sister Iris and how distraught she was going to be to hear about Izak. Most of all, she wondered if Iris was even going to believe Arianna for what she saw Izak do inside Arik's house. It was certainly going to be a relationship changer or a new struggle that the couple had to work through. Arianna hoped, for everyone's sake, that it wasn't going to be a bad situation confronting Izak about his addiction. After all, Arianna had heard stories about Izak's temper. Either way Arianna had much to talk about and only hoped Iris wouldn't kill the messenger.

CHAPTER 15

Vera was out cold and being dragged to the castle because she fell for a trap while her little brother was used as bait. She was coming to when she heard the sound of steel bars opening and closing, while she was set behind them. The newest addition to Elinor's prisoners.

"I brought you a friend to keep you company," the witch spoke to the young Everest who was trapped behind the bars of the cell next to his sisters.

"Vera!" Everest yelled. "What did you do to her?"

"She's fine. Just a little disoriented from a light supply of knock out powder. Thanks to the help of Adonis, we knew she would be out on watch today." Elinor sneered wickedly.

"He actually did it. I really didn't think he would," Everest said solemnly, putting his head down to look at the ground.

"My brother would never betray me!" Now fully awake, Vera had heard everything.

Vera tried to use her shifting power but she was shocked by the effort. It was like an invisible collar was wrapped around her neck preventing her from barking, but in her case, stopping her from being able to shift by sending a painful feeling through her body.

"I wouldn't try that again. The air behind these bars are enchanted. None of you can shift and, if you try, the pain will increase every time you do so.."

"She's right, sister. Adonis made a deal that if he gave you up, she would give him another chance to get Neveah. He had no choice, or she would have killed me right in front of him. He's going to trade our freedom for Neveah."

A sadistic laugh filled the room. Echoing off the walls, making both Vera and Everest shake inside. Both siblings looked at each other, knowing that the evil woman had no intention of letting *anyone* go.

"You silly child. You have no idea what I have in store for your kind. Adonis is just prolonging the inevitable. You will all meet the same fate, all the shifters in this realm will fall. So, enjoy what time you have left. Goodbye for now, my little mice," Elinor waved with a satisfied look on her face before she turned around, walked up the steps, and out of the dungeon.

When Elinor was out of sight, she left the two lionix's shivering in fear, knowing that at any point in time, they were both going to die.

"At least we have each other until the end. I have been really lonely down here, all by myself," Everest stated, reaching his arm through the bars to his sister.

They had one another. That was the only plus to their situation. Vera slightly smiled and reached out to connect with her brother's hand. When they touched, their eyes suddenly glowed and their teeth extended, briefly giving them hope that together they could somehow shift and escape the prison they were in.

***

Adonis froze in place when Neveah confessed to everyone that she was a witch. He didn't know how to feel about the news. Hopeful? Angry that she hadn't told them sooner so the evil magissa didn't have both his siblings? Sad for what would happen to her now that her secret was known by all?

"You can save us all."

"We're not going to die."

"We're saved."

The words of hope were expressed by all of Adonis' people. They surrounded Neveah, offering her embraces of affection and bowing at her feet.

"Please, none of you have to do any of this. I will do all I can to help us and get your freedom back. I promise," Neveah announced while looking at Adonis, who smiled and nodded his head.

Neveah nodded back before receiving more praise for her witch identity. Adonis knew she hadn't trusted him enough until now. It was clear she had known better to do this in front of an audience and not alone with him.

"How many witches are in your coven?" Adonis asked.

"Five, but one is just a child. She is my niece. I don't know how I can contact any of them," Neveah replied.

"Well, you must try. You are not enough to defeat the witch dwelling here. We can take out her followers, but you will need all the strength and power you can harness in order to take her down."

"We will help you, dear. You can harness what you need from us. Our abilities can become yours," Edna reassured her.

Adonis left the cave after Edna's words. He knew he was beat and knocked down a peg in leadership. By everyone's reaction, Neveah was the new savior and leader. He still had a job to do, which was to get his family back if it was the last thing he did. Nothing had changed, but he wouldn't be reporting this new news to the magissa, in hopes that Neveah would somehow have the upper hand and be able to defeat her.

* * *

As time went by, a group of the shifters went to recruit more of their kind in order to help in the battle to come. They were successful in finding one haven and getting ten more shifters to join them. With knowledge of a witch to help with the fight, the new arrivals were more willing to put their lives on the line.

A plan was made with Neveah's attack from the west side of the castle. She had never used defense magic before, nor had she used anything that would kill another of her kind. Thus, it was going to be more than a challenge. Neveah had to put her kind heart aside and learn to get her hands dirty or she would have no chance to win and save the people.

Adonis changed his tune and was back to the charming and flirtatious man he had been before. He expressed his frustrations with Neveah and chalked his behavior up to coping with his sister's capture. Neveah forgave him, making sure if there was a next time that he would talk to her instead of making her suspicious of him.

The shifters all lined up like they were eager and ready to get their blood drawn, even though drawing power made one far more exhausted then being hooked up to a bag slowly leaking blood into it as an offering. The extraction of the fire shifters abilities, even just a small portion, was far more demanding on each one's body and mind.

With a touch from Neveah, wrapping her hand around each shifter's wrist, she was able to siphon the power. Slime, spit, fire...she could harness it all and feel it running through her veins each and every time. The heightened senses and ability to heal quickly were not among the abilities Neveah could take without crippling the person. Each shifter showed signs of pain and weakness, while Neveah gained strength and sensation. But there was a point where she couldn't go any further. She had enough of watching her people suffer.

"All your abilities are making me sick. I feel like I have more than enough," Neveah stated, trying to sound truthful.

"We want you to be ready, but we can't have you immobilized either," Adonis spoke. "Everyone, give Neveah a break, she needs rest."

The line moved away from Adonis and Neveah. Neveah pretended to take an exhausted breath of fresh air while Adonis stood watching with his arms across his chest, grinning at her while she plopped down on the ground.

"What?" Neveah asked looking up at his knowing face.

"Oh, nothing. I just know you're full of it. You can see what your powers are doing to my kind and you don't like it," Adonis stated, sitting down next to her. "You're faking that it's having negative effects on you, when you know that you feel untouchable and more powerful than any of us right now."

"Is that right? How do you know?" Neveah asked in defeat.

"Because your selfless, *and* I can smell how strong it has made you," Adonis replied, looking at Neveah, he placed his right hand over her heart. "This is pure and good."

Neveah looked down to avoid his gaze. She had never felt like she was selfless, quite the opposite, in fact. The new adventure gave her a new purpose in life. Helping others was an incredible feeling and that made her the *most* powerful.

The strength that Neveah could feel made her believe if she extended her arms out and thought about flying, she instantly would be able to. Her legs felt strong, like she could kick through a brick wall. The skin on her body was steel armor that nothing could pierce through. She was ready for war and to fight alongside everyone else.

"Thank you, Adonis," Neveah said, a tear escaping her eyes.

"You're welcome."

"What do we do next?" Neveah asked, standing up.

"We practice. Give me your best shot." Adonis encouraged Neveah while taking a strong stance in front of her.

"You want me to use magic on you? No way! I'll hurt you," Neveah protested.

"Aw, that's cute. You think you can hurt me," he chuckled right before his eyes turned primal as he activated his senses.

Neveah still couldn't bring herself to strike him with any powers that could hurt him. What if she did more than hurt him? What if she accidently killed him? Knowing he would never leave her alone, Neveah lifted her hands up, palms facing Adonis, and shut her eyes to concentrate on her magic. She barely got to piece together a plan before she was knocked to the ground.

"Dead. You're dead!" Adonis said, pinning her to the ground. "In seconds, in a snap of a finger, the witch or one of her shifters would have killed you!"

"I wasn't even trying! I can't..not with you," Neveah yelled back at him.

"You need to treat me like your foe and not your friend. Right now, I am your enemy. Now get up and act. Now is *not* the time to think." Adonis got up and walked a few feet away, taking a battle stance once again.

When Adonis' eyes glowed again Neveah concentrated, this time with her eyes wide open. He charged at her, while she used the powers of a lionix on him. Hitting him with his own fire, she accomplished nothing; instead, he connected with her and knocked her down yet again.

"You can't use my *own* abilities against me. I was prepared for it. You need to channel my power and reverse it. Hit me with the opposite of my power."

"Okay," Neveah said, getting mad.

"Use that emotion, get angry. Scream if it helps," Adonis instructed before getting ready for his third attack.

Neveah whipped her hand like she was lassoing cattle, bringing the invisible rope down and wrapping it around Adonis' shoulders. Turning fire into ice, the switch appeared around him, binding him, until he melted it with his flames.

Neveah ran from him, dodging his attempts to stop her and bring her down. Throwing boulders of ice in his path, she slowed him down a bit. She continued to run, looking behind her.

The two were getting attention and an audience was forming to watch them train. Cheering and whistling at Neveah was not helping when she was trying hard to concentrate. Slowing him down wasn't helping either, his speed was not subsiding. Tapping further into her abilities, she suddenly stopped and turned. Using the power of the wind, she lifted him into the air where she then trapped him in ice. The wind stifling his flame under the ice had worked. Neveah watched Adonis's face turn white and, for the first time, the ice wasn't melting. The color in his eyes was fading, and all around her had become silent. Neveah had beat him, finding the weakness of the fire shifters. Wind and ice were their downfall.

Releasing Adonis from becoming a permanent ice sculpture, she lowered him safely to the ground. Allowing his surroundings to melt away, she left Adonis unharmed on his knees in front of her.

The audience applauded Neveah's performance, admiring her quick thinking and action. Adonis looked into Neveah's eyes and smiled, offering a nod of respect. She was ready and more powerful than she had originally thought. The magic that she had created was incredible. Anyone standing in Neveah's way was doomed; they would wish they'd never messed with her, or her newfound family.

***

The day to defeat the witch was upon everyone in Adonis' haven. He hoped Neveah was strong enough to defeat the evil that kept his people in fear. She was, after all, an amazing force of nature on his side of the battlefield. He would warn Neveah to be prepared for anything on the witch's turf – the fact that she could be anywhere, in any form. Adonis felt the need to at least tell her that so she would be ready. He couldn't tell her the truth in case Elinor was able to extract information from Neveah with her witchy powers. And if there was one thing Adonis had learned, it was to never underestimate the power of smart women, or smart witches in this case.

On the witch's land Adonis prepared his troops, dividing them into select groups for their defense. He knew that Elinor had stated she wouldn't fight against his people. It was to be a free-for-all as long as she had Neveah. The weaker group he put together for attack on the east side of the castle, the group forming to the north, at the back of the castle, would have to be more prepared in case they came across the witch on her way to Neveah. Adonis sent the slime and acid abilities to them. He left the strongest fighters to the south, in front of the castle. The land shifters, where he knew a certain someone would be guarding the front. Adonis had a bone to pick with the guard that burned a hole through his favorite shirt and had left a permanent scar on his chest.

"Are you all prepared to take your stations?" Adonis asked the people.

"Yes," they replied in unison.

"Then go and be careful. Neveah, you wait," Adonis added, while everyone parted.

"What? I'm ready," she turned.

"I know you are. Just...whatever happens, just know that I want you to give it all you got. If the opportunity arises, don't hold back," Adonis spoke as if he was telling her goodbye.

"We can do this. I'm ready," Neveah reassured him.

"I know. One other thing," Adonis paused. With no words to describe his emotions, Adonis used action. Scooping her up in his arms, he placed a soft kiss on her lips before setting her back down on her feet.

"That's for good luck." He winked. Turning to join the rest of his crew, he left her speechless, making her forget her mission entirely for a brief moment.

* * *

Neveah smiled as she walked through the woods behind her little group of shifters to the west of the castle. She was distracted by her mind racing on about Adonis and the kiss. Did he want that kiss to be what sealed them together or did he really only kiss her for good luck? In her mind she wanted it to be real and not complicated, but did she want to be with a man like Adonis?

Stumbling through the woods she tripped and scraped her ankle along a thorny vine. It made clear little drops of blood. Neveah sat to inspect the scratches and didn't see anything out of the ordinary, but bleeding from a normal thing like thorns wasn't supposed to happen when she had shifting armor as skin. How could the plant make her bleed if that were true? She could only think that she must be losing the shifting abilities and the witch needed to show up before they were completely gone.

Neveah got up from inspecting her wounds. As soon as she was standing, she could hear the sound of a light, evil laugh coming from all around. She couldn't pinpoint where it was originating from until it echoed loudly behind her. Turning, she shot magic through her hands, connecting with nothing but bushes.

"Oh, dear, you are not even close to being as powerful as

me," the voice spoke.

Neveah threw her hands to the left and then the right. Trying to obliterate the person behind the voice. She wasn't going to capture the woman; she was doing all she could to destroy the threat. This time the witch was projecting herself somehow. Messing with Neveah's sight, making her believe she was standing right in front, then behind, and then all around her.

"I know what you're doing. Come out and fight me, you coward!" Neveah yelled at the top of her lungs.

"I'm not going to waste any of my energy on you. That would be foolish when I have already won," the evil drone continued. "You will feel it soon."

Neveah began to feel dizzy. The trees above were moving and her vision slowly faded.

"You were so distracted by my spy's kiss that you didn't watch where you were going and got scratched by my poisonous thorns. I have to hand it to Adonis; he sure knows how to knock a girl right off her feet."

"Spy? What?" Neveah's speech was slurred as she bent down and sat on the ground so she wouldn't fall.

"Oh you poor dear. That's right. You don't know a thing. Well, before you fade away let me tell you one last thing. Adonis is my spy, and he was in charge of bringing you to me. You thought he really liked you, didn't you?" Elinor taunted Neveah one last time before she was completely paralyzed by the poison.

* * *

Elinor bent down to observe Neveah in her slumber. Her guards arrived, perfect timing. Neveah was unmistakably beautiful in Elinor's eyes. Looking down at her new prisoner's hand, she also noticed the lovely jewelry adorning her fingers. The amethyst ring, in particular, intrigued her enough to take it from Neveah.

"What a beautiful ring." Elinor bent down and grabbed Neveah's right hand in an attempt to remove the ring but gasped in shock when her skin touched Neveah's.

"You have been touched by my magic. Where is it?" Elinor grabbed Neveah's shoulders, screaming at her. "Who has my magic?"

Neveah couldn't answer Elinor's questions while unconscious, but that didn't stop Elinor from yelling at her and slapping Neveah as if she was only a petulant child pretending to sleep and not actually under the control of poison. Elinor glared at her, only stopping her brutal actions when she heard a light cough come from one of her guards.

Turning around to set her gaze on the gentleman standing nearby, watching her like she was going crazy. Elinor stood up and straightened her clothes, running her fingers through her hair, and fluttering her eyelashes at her followers.

"What news do you have for me?" Elinor asked.

"We have the lionix you asked for, Our Queen," her head guard stated.

"Oh! I'm so pleased. How is Adonis?"

"He is severely injured. He put up a massive fight and killed one of our own in front of the castle."

"Tisk. Tisk. That naughty man."

"What would you like us to do with him? He is going to die if you don't heal his wound, being that he was injured by a copper point blade."

"I do need him alive. I suppose I will heal him after he is safely in the dungeon with this one," Elinor stated, pointing at Neveah. "Put them in the same cell. I'm sure she will want a word with him."

Elinor laughed at the explanation Adonis was going to have to come up with as he faced the pure and goodhearted woman that now lay at her feet. Adonis was to be Elinor's king, or he was to fall like the rest. He would have no other choices.

"What would you like us to do with the rest? They are still lingering around the premises."

"Kill them. Kill them all. I have no need for any survivors," she said with a wave of her hand. "Pick up this mess and bring her to the dungeon."

Elinor walked away from the guards with no concern for Neveah waking up. On her way to the castle, she came across many shifters putting their lives on the line in order to defeat her. Of course, they were no match for her when she turned them to ice and shattered them like glass, or dissolved them like puddles into the ground without actually exerting any real effort. Most that had stepped up to her from out of the bushes had no training against someone like her. Neveah should have at least taught them how to sneak up on a witch.

Her mind turned back to her newfound knowledge. Neveah had been touched by Elinor's evil magic. That meant her other half was close by. The magic that she once had before her own sister stole it from her. There must be more of their line alive, and Elinor would have to bring down the magic keeping them hidden from all other realms. She would use blood magic to locate what belonged to her and bring it back home. With her magic complete and all in one vessel, no realm would then be able to stand against her. She would have it all. They would all bow down at her feet and call her queen, or they would suffer all the way to their last dying breath.

Once inside the castle walls she sat in her bedroom preparing the concoction. Once in the cauldron, she added her blood.

"*Vreíte aftó pou cháthike,*" Elinor chanted to find what was lost.

Looking down into the bowl an image appeared with three women standing around, talking. She couldn't hear what they were saying, but she could tell with one look that the woman with peach colored skin and sandy blonde hair was definitely her niece. The other two standing next to her, however, were strangers. All she knew was that they were identical twins and would be incredibly dangerous to her if they so happened to be witches. Closing the image to the other realm, she walked to a small cage in her room.

"Looks like I will be all powerful once again, Your Majesty," she spoke to the small mouse inside her cage while she fed it crumbles of bread. "We are going to have visitors very soon, King Thaddeus."

CHAPTER 16

Sylvia was waiting at the dock for Simon. She had devastating news to tell him. She missed her mother and feared the worst. There was no way she could get married now, or ever for that matter, not without her mother. She was coming up on eighteen quickly, and with that came the honor of being crowned Queen of the Waters with her king, Simon, by her side. But she wouldn't do it without Neveah.

With a splash in the water breaking Sylvia's train of anxious, fearful thoughts, a happy Simon exited the ocean; lifting himself, he hovered above it. He appeared to be overjoyed by something, but when he observed Sylvia's face, his gleeful look faded into a frown.

"What's wrong? Is it your mother?" Simon asked, rushing to her side and grasping her hand.

Sylvia began to cry. When she looked up into Simon's eyes, she couldn't speak. Quickly she turned away, knowing she would be unable to tell him what she was going to say while facing him. He tried to hold on to her hand, but she jerked away before she spoke.

"I..I can't marry you," her words came out in a rush as the weeping sound followed; she covered her mouth with her hand.

"What do you mean, Sylvia? You mean you *won't* marry me?" He asked with concern in his voice.

"I can't do it without my mother. She could be dead or alive; no one knows anything and I have no way of finding out," Sylvia spoke quickly. "I can't do it until she's home...safely. If she's gone forever, then I will never get married."

"So you will never be happy because your mother is missing? Sylvia, they will find her, and then all of this will be for nothing. Do you really think Neveah would want you to be miserable for the rest of your life? She loves you. She would want you to live a full and happy existence, you know that."

Sylvia thought about what Simon was saying and the complete sense he made, but she just couldn't bring herself to agree. In her mind, all that mattered was her mother's fate and her own pain that felt like it would never go away.

"Simon, you don't understand. You never had a parent that loved you unconditionally...the loss is different."

"I may not have, but I know what Neveah would want for you."

The anger was boiling up inside of Sylvia. Her sadness was turning into hatred. The feeling was like nothing she had ever felt before. Finally Sylvia felt that she had the strength to turn around and face Simon to express herself. He had no right to tell her about her own mother. What her mother would want was to be home with her children, celebrating every part of their lives together.

"You know nothing!" Sylvia screamed at Simon, sending him flying backwards, far into the sea.

"Oh my God! Simon," she yelled in panic.

Sitting down on the wood, Sylvia brought her knees to her chest, sobbing uncontrollably. Everything was a nightmare..a horrific dream that she wished she would wake from at any moment. "What did I do?" she cried.

"Hello," Simon spoke in a lyrical voice.

Sylvia looked up from her knees, offering Simon an apologetic smile. She thanked the gods he was okay.

He smiled back. "Who are you, my lady?"

Sylvia couldn't believe her ears. Simon didn't know who she was? Chills froze her heart. What in the world did she do to him? *Was* she a witch, or had she screamed so loud he'd somehow forgotten who she was? Everyone she knew always told her that her scream could break windows when she was a little girl, but she never thought she could break a human – certainly not a beloved boyfriend.

"I'm Sylvia. Simon...you don't know who I am?" She stared into his oddly blank eyes. They still sparkled yet..like those of a baby just waking up to a world they'd not yet explored.

"Who's Simon? I know nothing of this person you speak about," he replied.

Needing to get help, Sylvia knew only her aunts could somehow fix whatever she had done. Not entirely sure *how* they could, she felt awful for what she had done to Simon and hoped beyond all hope that it was reversible.

"Wait here..please. I have to go get someone. I promise I will fix..this." Sylvia jumped up and ran to find Iris, Arianna, and Angela to help.

* * *

Zack spent all his time with Liam, training with horses and wolves. His opponents beat and bruised him, but he kept at it.

Never backing down, he kept running at them for more. On multiple occasions, an adult shifter had to step in and tell Zack he had enough and must get medical attention.

But the pain and agony of losing his mother was too much to bear. He wanted to feel a different pain besides the emotional. Zack still hadn't figured out what he was...what kind of magic he possessed that could turn a shifter human in mid-transition.

"What are you doing? Are you trying to get yourself *killed*?" Liam scolded Zack.

"I have to tell you a secret, but you can't tell anyone. Promise me!" Zack said, changing the subject.

"What?" Liam asked, annoyed that Zack had brushed him off.

"I can stop shifters from transitioning into their beast form," Zack admitted. Saying it out loud gave him a sense of relief, like his secret had been weighing him down.

After hesitating a moment, Liam smiled. "That's amazing! Can you make them shift when they're human too?" Liam asked. "You're like me!"

"Wait. I don't know if I can. I never tried," Zack replied with a shrug.

"During the next match you should try. Concentrate extremely hard to make him shift."

"Okay. Yeah, I will," Zack said, although remained a little unsure as he stepped up to the fighting rink.

It shouldn't be a hard task. Zack looked at his new opponent and concentrated on his wolf form. He knew what the boy looked like as a wolf, with his grey markings running down the right side of his body. Repeatedly chanting in his mind to turn the boy into a wolf, he realized quickly that it wasn't working. Instead, the boy tackled Zack, bringing him down to the ground.

"Get mad! Trigger your emotions!" Yelled Liam from outside the rink.

The more Zack concentrated on his mother's missing status, his father's abandonment, and the years of abuse his mother and sister had put up with, the more he could feel his own power rising. Becoming fast enough to dodge the hits coming at his body and face from the other boy, all of his emotions built up to an even greater scale. Projecting it all on his jousting partner, he screamed in his own mind to turn into a wolf; to shift..NOW!

At that moment he could feel the power again, just like the night when he'd stopped Zinnia from making her transition. The same intense sensations ran over his body. Right when the boy ran straight at Zack, he stepped to the side, grabbed him with one arm, and threw him to the ground.

The feeling was amazing..mixed with confusion. Zack was shrinking to the floor. His hearing and sight were magnified and everyone was watching him. In a split second, Zack was on his hands and knees, or so he thought.

"What the heck? Zack, you're a wolf!" Liam cheered.

Zack looked down at his feet, shocked to see a new set of paws where his hands should be, planted on the floor of the rink. His power was more than he had bargained for, and all he wanted at that very moment..was his mother. Laying down, Zack covered his eyes with his big, black paws and cried; the noise came out like a series of soft howls in his ears.

The boy that Zack had been wrestling with had already taken off before Zack covered his face. Jenesis was soon by Zack's side, along with Zack's partner. Walking up to Zack, Jenesis bent down to sniff him.

"Zack, my boy, can you speak?" he asked.

Removing his paws from his face, Zack let out a small, shrill whine as he moved he looked up at his grandfather.

Liam could tell his cousin was scared, and he felt bad for him, but he also felt completely envious for the power and skill Zack had just discovered he owned.

"He's not an actual wolf," Jenesis announced. "I don't

know what this is, but it has something to do with magic – not a new transition."

Jenesis picked up Zack with no difficulty and jumped over the net around his rink, landing directly in front of Liam with questioning eyes.

"Did you know about this?"

"He just told me, Grandpa. He didn't know what it was, just that he had a power he didn't understand," Liam answered, showing complete respect as he held eye contact, even though he thought Jenesis was scary and intimidating.

"Don't worry. Zack will be okay. I think he fell asleep. We need to get him to the rest of the family and ask the witches."

"Okay. I'll walk with you," Liam agreed.

"I got him," one of the other adult wolves said, picking up Liam and setting him on his shoulders like he was a young child.

"Thank you. Let's run so that we can figure out what's going on quickly," Jenesis instructed.

The men took off and ran with the power of their wolves. Their destination was Julia's home, in hopes that Iris would be there and be able to help.

"Have you ever seen anything like him before, Grandpa?" Liam asked, watching Zack turn into a human right in Jenesis' arms.

"No. This is strange. He smells like a normal boy. His wolf had no scent at all.. almost like the beast was nothing more than an illusion. It was only visual, as if wanting to make everyone *believe* he was a wolf and not a boy. However, I could feel his fur and his nose was wet." He sighed. "I don't understand. All I can hope is that someone in the family can give us answers."

Liam was annoyed, being handled like a child. He was getting older and wanted to prove to everyone he could be just like the wolves and horses. That he could be fast, and an asset to the pack. Liam wished his grandfather would turn him into one of them. Or, at the very least, tell him it simply wasn't a possibility.. if it wasn't.

"Grandpa Jenesis. I have a question," Liam began.

"What's your question?" Jenesis smiled.

"How do I become like you? Will you turn me into a wolf one day?" Liam blurted out.

"Well, my boy, you have to marry a woman and have your wedding blessed, like Grandma Julia. Or blessed by the Blue Moon when we recruit new wolves. If your heart is pure and your intentions selfless, the moon will turn you. If you want to turn for selfish reasons, the moon will reject your request."

"Wait. Are you saying my grandmother is a wolf, too?" Liam asked excitedly. "What is she like? I bet her wolf is beautiful."

Liam waited for Jenesis to reply, but he soon realized something. The look on his face was clear; Jenesis had given him more information than he meant to.

Jenesis' face turned into a frown. Sighing, he looked back at Liam. "I wasn't supposed to say anything until Neveah returned safely, so this will remain our secret. A *binding* secret."

Liam nodded at the firm tone and strong jaw of his grandfather. "Of course."

"Your grandmother is the most beautiful beast I have ever seen; powerful, too. No one has seen anything like her before. The moon blessed her and accepted her into our pack. I can't say anything more," Jenesis concluded, still looking worried.

How could the alpha king of the animal shifters be worried about anything? Liam thought. Julia was scary as a human; Liam could only assume that she was even more scary as a wolf. His grandmother *always* had control and took charge of *all* situations in her family. For Liam to think she would be any different as a wolf would mean underestimating her – something he would never do.

***

Bella was in the shop all by herself. She spent a lot of time alone lately, what with her mom's obsession with magic and training with Arianna or Iris to get her aunt back. If Angela wasn't on the magic training court, tucked away in the library, she was locked away in her room, avoiding everyone. Bella knew her mother was hurting, but when she happened to run into Angela, she seemed like an entirely different person.

Basil was absent from Bella's life, too. He was ordered to go with his Uncle Alister to inform the King of the Sky that Neveah was missing and to check on the darkness that was creeping across the land of Drakous.

The boredom Bella felt had to be obvious when her two best friends walked through the door of the shop. She had been leaning behind the counter with an elbow placed on the top, holding her face in her hand as she looked down at the paperwork showing her shop's success.

Jacky and Ziara entered the store, bringing happiness to Bella's face. She was saved at last from her slow, boring day. The giggling couple were obviously happy to see Bella too.

"You look so entertained. Are you sure you want to hang out with us today?" Jacky teased.

"Well, aren't you funny? If you don't rescue me, I'm pretty sure I will die of boredom," Bella played along. "Don't you two look adorable?"

Ziara blushed at Bella's compliment while Jacky acted completely unaffected by the words.

"So, I told my mom and..get this. She asked what took me so long to tell her. Can you believe it? Mom already knew!" Jacky screeched. "She said whatever makes me happy, she's fine with.."

"That's amazing," Bella said, turning to Ziara. "How did Delphine take the news?"

The image of Delphine, Ziara's mother, came back into

Bella's mind. They were the first set of moodamorphs they'd met when first arriving in Drakous. Bella still smiled when she recalled that day, being brave enough to call Ziara over when her cousins were too shy to break the ice first. And then Zack ending up being better friends than Bella and her. Even though he spent all his time with guys now, Bella was sure they would all get together again someday.

"She doesn't understand it at all. She says she's going to speak to the queen and marry me off to a male moodamorph," Ziara replied, putting her head down.

"Mom will never do it. Not if she truly supports me," Jacky spoke with confidence.

"Does she know that you have feelings for each other?" Bella asked.

"No, but still, my mom's smart. She has a gift, but says she won't tell me unless I have it, too." Jacky pouted.

"Moms always say that." Bella laughed.

"Speaking of moms, how is yours? Mine has really missed yours and she's worried about her. They haven't seen each other in like, forever," Jacky stated.

"I know. We have to set them up somehow."

"Like put together a spa day," Ziara suggested.

"Perfect! We should also go try to visit Zinnia again today. Has anyone seen her since Halloween?" Bella asked.

"No, her mom sold the shop too," Jacky informed them.

"Well, we have to do something today or I'm going to go crazy," Bella said with a theatrical sigh.

"You already are," Jacky teased.

The girls decided to do one of Bella's very favorite things: spy on people. Their targets being Sylvia and Simon. As they exited the shop, Bella wondered if Sylvia was okay. She had been out of sorts since her mother got trapped in another realm. She couldn't blame her, though. Bella wondered how she would feel if it were her own mother missing. Of course, it already kind of felt like her mother was gone with the way she'd been acting...

* * *

Iris was at her house trying to reason with Izak. Something was wrong with him. Arik had told her he was never the same after they'd left his house. Apparently, they got drunk and Izak passed out in Arik's bed; Arik had found him curled up on the covers.

Leah was spending a lot of time with her father and, unfortunately, had witnessed the consistent arguing between Iris and Izak. And being that Izak drank a lot, he could quickly have violent outbursts when Iris only asked him simple, calm questions...like what was wrong; or why he was acting the way he was. And now here he was, doing it again.

"Why am I acting this way? Are you *blind*? My sister is missing and you can't figure out how to find her. You just sit around here, asking me stupid questions. You're useless," Izak yelled at Iris. "No, I'm not okay! My sister's probably dead and you're doing *nothing*!"

Iris was shocked; her mouth was hanging open. Leah knew that he should really watch out. The last person he would want to be mean to is a witch.

He watched her reaction and wore a disgusted look on his face. Leah could tell he regretted saying it and he was angry with himself now.

Izak went to turn away from Iris, only to face Leah standing in the doorway. He had already cried, but somehow seeing her made his emotions even worse.

"I'm fucking stupid! What's wrong with me?" he yelled, covering his head in shame.

Leah looked at Iris with confusion, but Iris simply shook her head. They continued to stand in silence until they heard a loud *thud* and looked towards Izak. His attempt to put his fist through the strong wall had been unsuccessful; instead, the gnarled bones clearly showed that he'd broken his own hand.

"Oh, my God! Let me help you," Iris gasped as she looked at the torn flesh and the bruised, disfigured limb.

"Stop! Don't help me. I don't deserve it. I'm sorry. I'm so sorry," Izak cried, grabbing onto Iris while they slowly sank to the floor. Iris held Izak like she was holding a doll, not a grown man. "Don't leave me. I love you. I'm sorry."

"Hush, honey. I'm not going anywhere," she replied.

Leah couldn't believe her eyes or ears. There were times where she knew things the others didn't, but at the moment she could only think her uncle was crazy and needed more help than Iris could possibly give him.

"What's all the commotion about in here?" Arik asked, walking into the living room from outside.

Iris looked up at Arik and her eyes darted to Leah. She wasn't dumb; she read the message in Iris' eyes loud and clear. She could tell that the moment Izak and Iris shared was something most adults tried to hide from children.

"Come on, angel. Tell me more about your grandma's voice in your dreams," Arik said, trying to guide Leah away from the obviously disturbed couple on the floor.

"I would wait. We're about to have some bewildered visitors," Leah answered in a hazy voice.

"What do you mean?" asked Arik.

Before Leah could answer, the front doors burst open and Liam ran inside. Jenesis was close behind, holding an unconscious Zack in his arms. He walked to the couch and laid him upon it.

"Zack turned into a wolf and now he won't wake up," Liam blurted.

Everyone hovered over Zack. He looked like he was sleeping. Iris got up and went to Zack's aid. Checking him all over, she forced an eyelid open and jumped back in surprise when the canine eye was unveiled underneath.

"I wasn't expecting that. He must have wolf blood. Zack might sleep a couple of days. Transitioning, especially for the first time, can be tough," Iris gave her diagnosis.

"There's more." Liam stated.

His tale was interrupted as Sylvia rushed inside the open door. "Something's wrong with Simon! We had a fight..I screamed at him..he flew backwards into the ocean. Now he knows nothing, not even who he is, or who I am." Sylvia spoke so fast she finally had to stop and take a breath.

Now everyone's gaze had turned from Zack to the terrified Sylvia. Leah smiled to herself, thinking there were far more witches in the family.

"Iris, something's wrong with me. I want my mom," Sylvia cried, running into Iris's arms.

Trouble kept coming. While Iris comforted Sylvia, Nick, the King of Sky, rushed into the room.

"Iris, we *need* you. The darkness is spreading." Nick stopped himself as he stared at the many faces looking at him from around the room. He witnessed tears, a passed-out body, a broken hand, and a myriad of stunned expressions.

Leah's mind drifted away from the present. Images were flashing in front of her eyes. The act had happened before, but the pictures were always fuzzy and she couldn't make them out. Now that all the faces were in front of her, however, the pictures cleared and allowed her for the first time to see what the future held. Without thinking, she smiled and laughed, breaking the awkwardness in the room. The outcome of all that was going to happen was crystal clear now.

But everyone else was clueless; the images were only for her to see. Leah wanted to tell everyone how everything was going to turn out, but when she opened her mouth to speak, no words came forth. She couldn't speak about the future because..she shouldn't. Her guidance magic informed her that telling them would only alter the future and do an obscene amount of damage to all involved.

Smartly, Leah shut her mouth and kept it all inside, while the others attempted to figure out this insane, phenomenal mystery for themselves.

CHAPTER 17

Elinor was furious. She'd felt the remaining energy of her magic when she had touched the woman, but her poison had put her to sleep before she had the chance to get any answers. Patience was not one of her strong suits; in fact, it felt like being locked in her own personal Hell while waiting for the pathetic woman to wake.

Getting answers out of Adonis was out of the question. After he had been stabbed with the copper coated dagger near his vital organs, he had been absolutely useless. All that growling and snarling he did was dangerous with an injured animal. She would need to heal him soon if she ever wanted to have him sitting by her side on the throne.

The only thing that would heal his injury was something rare she had inside her special cabinet of unique potions. She needed a few drops of sap extracted from the Tree of Life that she had collected on her journey to the Realm of Fairies.

Inside her bedroom, she had a hidden room behind a bookshelf. An unoriginal cliché of a hiding place for important items, crystals, and liquids. She didn't care because no one in their right mind would ever try to enter her room, let along steal anything from her. Even people in their craziest mind knew not to mess with her, seeing as that she held the medal of the craziest of them all and was proud of it.

As she collected the ingredients, quartz and opal ash, Elinor mixed in drops of sap, adding the filtered water in a bowl completely made of agate crystal. The use of crystals immediately made her think of her sister. Which was never a good idea in her mind because the memory of her would project bad magic onto everything she touched. Crystals were always used for good, and that kind of magic was hard for Elinor to handle. In addition, she was a hand witch, meaning the most useful of her powers was projected or syphoned through her own hands, not by using gems or crystals to achieve success.

Once finished with Adonis's cure, she began working on a truth potion for Neveah. There was no way the woman would tell her what she needed to know to finally be reunited with her precious magic. An honest potion was going to be simple to contrive; the ingredients only consisted of a container made of amazonite that forced honesty and tears of the tortured— her own personal twist in the concoction. The tears would allow a painful consequence to be brought down upon Neveah when she lied. Whatever the victims were tortured by, would happen to Neveah. The game would provide an intriguing show for Elinor. Setting both containers in the pocket of her black and red dress, she heard the voice of her prisoner. She was finally awake, and Elinor was ready to take her rath out on her traitor.

With an evil snicker, Elinor made her way out of her secret

room and down to the dungeon to begin her interrogation.

* * *

Neveah stirred awake on a hard, cold concrete floor and had no idea where she was. All around her was dark. She snapped her fingers in an attempt to light up the room, but instead she received a shocking pain for her efforts. Reaching up, she felt the metal contraption wrapped completely around her neck. As her panic kicked in, so did the tightening of the collar.

Neveah pulled at it, coughing and scared that it would choke her to death, but panicking was not helping her situation. Realizing she needed to calm herself, she forced her arms and hands down to her sides and took in small breaths, trying to relax in the hope that it would allow her to breathe regularly again.

Controlling her breathing and relaxing was the trick to get the contraption to loosen so she could finally take in air normally. Neveah reached up slowly to touch the collar once again, but it had completely disappeared. She assumed her attempts at using magic had triggered the effect it had on her; she wouldn't use her powers again until she figured out how to remove the invisible choker.

"You handled that well. That's good," a struggling voice spoke. Even though she recognized the voice, she still jumped at the sudden change in the silent room. The voice she knew perfectly well belonged to Adonis.

Anger built up inside of Neveah after realizing Adonis was sharing the same room as her. If what the witch had said was true about him being her spy, Neveah was certainly going to give him a piece of her mind. Anger was only the beginning. She reached her hands out to feel her surroundings, reaching toward the sound of Adonis's voice. Neveah could tell she was in a cell by the feel of the bars her hands struck. Rising, she walked slowly along the steel barrier; her legs stopped when they reached a hard object, knee-high. Lowering her hand to feel what she'd walked into, the touch of human flesh announced that it was, indeed, her cell mate. His skin was wet and hot to the touch, and she couldn't help but worry about him.

"Are you hurt?" Neveah asked in a concerned tone, but remained mad.

"I'll survive," Adonis replied.

"Good, because I'm going to kill you! You traitor!" Neveah yelled at him. She didn't even bother to ask if he was the witch's messenger boy. She had felt something 'off' about him and now the witch had confirmed her fears. "How could you do that to all your people?"

"Will you be quiet! She will hear you. I had no choice, Neveah. The witch would have killed both of my siblings. It was you for their freedom," he whispered, struggling with his words.

"You could have at least warned me or told me the plan."

"She would have known. Plus, it wouldn't have made a difference. She's just too powerful."

"You didn't even give me a chance; you should have trusted me. Now we're all going to die and it's your fault," Neveah spoke louder, regretting it quickly when she heard the sound of the door above creak from opening followed by the quick steps coming down the stairs to see what the commotion was all about.

"Fos," came the sound of her captor's voice, then light appeared all around soon after.

Neveah could see her surroundings in the room now. She was a lot closer to Adonis than she had thought. Saying he was okay was another one of his lies. The blood dripping from his stomach and darkness all around his eyes were clear indicators that he was going to die, and soon, if he didn't get medical attention.

"Hey beautiful," Adonis said, smiling in his charming way,

obviously trying to distract Neveah from seeing how serious his injuries actually were.

Shaking her head was all Neveah could do. She couldn't even look at him in the awful condition he was in. All she wanted to do was let out a cry of fear that he was going to die at any moment and needed help. Neveah turned her head away and met the face of her attacker outside the bars.

She gasped. Not only was she stunned by the woman's lovely appearance, but also her resemblance to Iris. They could have been considered twins.

"Please save him," Neveah begged for Adonis's well-being.

"Oh. I assumed you would enjoy this sight of him, considering he did betray you and lead you straight into my poisonous trap," The evil witch spoke while wearing her sickening smirk. "You must really love him."

"No. I just don't want him to die. He doesn't deserve to die when he was only trying to protect his family. I would have done the same thing." Neveah spoke even though she was lying. At that moment, she hated him, but she did love him and wanted him to live.

"I will, but not for you. For myself. I have plans for the courageous lion." She smiled at Adonis before turning back to Neveah. "Right now, I am a lot more interested in you. Let's get acquainted, shall we? My name is Elinor Butler, the most powerful witch in all the realms. You will do well to remember that. What is your name?" she spoke now with a forced smile.

Neveah could see right through the witch's mask. She was pretending to be a decent human being, but in reality, she was just toying with Neveah to see if she was dumb enough to fall for the 'good cop' method. Neveah would play her little game and see if she could turn it around and trap her instead.

"My name is Neveah Michelson," she spoke with the mirror smile Elinor had given her.

"Well, Neveah, it is a pleasure to finally meet you in person. Tell me, where do you come from? More importantly, how did you enter my realm?"

"Oh! I'm from around. I have been here this entire time. Born and raised in Foinix Realm," Neveah lied.

"You are a lying wench!" Elinor spoke coldly before splashing a jar of liquid on Neveah.

Neveah instinctively ducked down, even though it made no difference. The fluid got on her, soaking into her clothes and wetting her skin. Prepared for any type of pain or burning sensation sure to come, Neveah closed her eyes. But to her surprise, no agony burst forth; the witch had fooled her into thinking it was going to be something magical that would force her to her knees.

"Now, let's hear you lie to me again," Elinor taunted. "How do you feel about Adonis?"

"I feel nothing. I just want him to live." Neveah answered and an uncontrollable itching sensation began.

"Well, that was a lie. I didn't need the potion to tell me that. It will only get worse, by the way. The more you lie, the stronger the side effects. It's a fun game I like to call 'Truth or Surprise.' Yay! Ready to play?" Elinor looked like it was the Fourth of July and fireworks lit up her eyes from all the excitement.

"You are a disgusting excuse for a witch," Neveah spoke; still scratching. The truth had made her symptoms go away. The rash disappeared and the itchy feeling faded.

"Looks like that one was the truth. Now tell me, do you know where my magic is?"

"I was telling the truth. I don't know what you're talking about," before Neveah even completed the sentence, she watched as a spider crawled out from under the skin on the back of her hand. Screaming in surprise, she shouted: "Somewhere on Drakous. I don't know who has it."

Neveah was hopping around the room attempting to flick all the creepy-crawly things off her that'd appeared. She never liked to hurt any living thing, not even a slug on earth that was trying to eat her garden vegetables. Seeing the spiders, however, made her instantly want to squish every eight-legged critter emerging from her own skin. It was worse than the uncontrollable itching, but the fixing of it was the same. The symptoms disappeared as soon as she answered the question truthfully, but the spiders that had arrived were still crawling around.

"You have no idea who has my magic in Drakous? Only a relative with my blood could control my magic. Did my sister have children?" Elinor demanded answers.

"Yes, she had children. I don't know which one has your magic, though. I can only assume that the one who has it transferred me to this realm." Neveah hoped that was enough of the truth to make her not suffer any other magical visitors.

"Oh, my baby is trying to tell me where it is. My sweet, perfect, little magical essence." Elinor spoke of her love for the magic she had lost long ago.

Listening to the crazy woman speak of her power like it was an innocent child trying to find their way back to a loving mother, was a little on the disturbing side. The witch had done a complete three-sixty with her personality. One minute, she demanded answers; the next, she was excited and sounded completely harmless. The woman had some serious issues.

"I'm going to go get it back now. Chow," Elinor said, turning to leave.

"What about Adonis?" Neveah begged for the antidote to cure his injury.

Elinor looked at Adonis still full of fight laying on the cot in the cell. "Fine. Make him drink this," she instructed, pulling a small jar from her dress pocket. "When he is better, he is to be my husband and take over all the realms in the universe...or he will die. Bye now," Elinor said, leaving Neveah in complete shock, with her mouth hanging open.

"I would rather die than marry that disturbed magissa," Adonis spat.

* * *

Elinor left the room looking satisfied, but inside she wanted to kill something or throw a huge tantrum. She certainly loved to make a dramatic scene. Calming herself, Elinor knew she could definitely do both when she brought down the shield that blocked all the other realms from looking in on Foinix Realm. That being the only way to get her magic back.

The walk to the lighthouse was a short one from the dungeon doors leading outside. She was feeling excited that she was going to be reunited with her magic very soon. The day was looking up in her favor. After all, now she was about to visit her two favorite shifting creatures—the battonix parents of the three little brats that had escaped her guards. She would be finding them later when she needed the fully charged power they possessed.

Once Elinor made it to the bottom of the brick lighthouse, she used a knife to cut her hand and pressed the emerging blood against the wall; a door opened, revealing the staircase leading up to the top of the tower.

Walking up the steps, behind Elinor the door closed, and the stairs faded away until she reached the two battonix. They looked helpless with the magical chains wrapped around their powerful shifting heads, forcing them to make an echo nonstop surrounding the entire realm. The chains were connected to the stones of strength and sound to keep them from dying.

"You beautiful creatures have served your purpose," she spoke, reaching out to put a hand on both of their shoulders, sucking the life force out of them both until they dropped to the ground, taking their last breath. In her mind, she believed she was setting them free, doing the honorable thing. Even with that belief, however, Elinor couldn't help but enjoy watching the fear invade their eyes right before they fell.

"Now, with that done, it's time to see what little harlot has my magic," she continued to speak to herself while she got her cauldron prepped, before slicing her other hand and squeezing her blood into the giant vat.

Almost instantly, the faces of three young women came into focus. One highly resembled her own self; clearly it was her niece and therefore must have the magic. Her anger built watching the other two. They showed similar features that reminded her of her sister. Twins made her even more concerned; twin witches were known to be the most powerful of their kind. The smiles the three wore enraged Elinor and, before she could stop, her emotions took over and made her open her mouth to alert them she was watching.

"You thieving witches have my magic! I want it back. If you don't return it to me in thirty days, I will put Neveah's head upon a stake and make an example out of her. I will show you what happens to those who think they can steal from me! You have thirty days to return my magic to Foinix Realm. This is my final and *only* warning," Elinor announced, not waiting for a reply before she closed the window between the two realms.

She was furious her sister had so many powerful children that she picked up the cauldron and threw it out the window of the lighthouse. Hitting the bricks and breaking down on the blocks, it finally crumbled all over the ground. Elinor was already prepared for the destruction to come, and hovered. As the lighthouse completely fell apart, she landed on the pile of rubble it made.

Still enraged, she walked towards the west wing of the dungeon entrance and entered the area where she held Vera and the boy, Everest. When she opened the door, she found both in their lionix forms. Somehow the two had found a way around her powers to keep themselves able to transition into their beast side. Everest jumped at her, catching her off-guard before he flew past her and escaped. The boy had made it out, but she still had his sister. Vera had apparently stayed back to keep her little brother safe, and the attention focused on her.

Vera paced left and right, trying to find an opening, but the anger built up in Elinor made her even more powerful. Adding to that, she now had the battonix powers Vera wouldn't be prepared for. Elinor screeched, sending her penetrating echo off the walls all around Vera. Instantly submitting to the piercing noise, Vera fell to the ground and covered her ears with her paws until she shifted back into her human form.

The power that Elinor now had was like nothing she'd ever felt before. Her voice had a new strength that could come in handy in the war she was sure would come. If she was going to have any chance against the witches and shifters on Drakous, she was going to need all the power of every last shifter in Foinix to go up against them, as well as the twin witches.

With a mask of sick satisfaction plastered across Elinor's face, she picked up Vera with floating magic and led her to the cell that held Neveah and Adonis captive. This was the perfect time to make a point and show Adonis what would happen if he denied her again. She had heard him tell Neveah that he would rather die than be her king; after seeing this, she should hear it no more.

When Elinor made it down the steps to the couple, she slammed Vera up against the bars. Enraged that not one of them was paying attention, she stared at the pair that messed up her entrance before her announcement. Neveah was crying and holding her hands over her face; Adonis was laying on the cot..fast asleep. She had expected Adonis to be up and on the alert for her return so he would now gasp at the sight of Vera being hung up on the cell bars like a puppet without strings. Now she had to start from the beginning after waking him up.

More annoyed that Adonis still hadn't woken up, she looked with her magnified sight and realized that his chest wasn't moving up and down; he wasn't breathing.

"Did he not take the elixir I made?" Elinor bellowed, dropping the unconscious Vera on the floor.

"No, he didn't. So now he's dead. All of us would rather die than be forced to be with someone like you!" Neveah yelled back at her.

"Don't worry. Your time will come, especially since your family knows where you are now. They will come and they will meet the same fate." Elinor snapped.

Listening closely to Adonis, Elinor projected her enhanced hearing all over his body, searching for a pulse or even a faint heartbeat. There was nothing. She sent an electric bolt at him and zapped his entire body to make his heart start up again, but it didn't work. She needed his heart in her hands, but she couldn't allow the doors to open and risk Neveah's escape or Vera's sudden awakening where she could run. Right now, neither woman could escape. She needed to weigh her priorities and take risks only when necessary. Should she bring Adonis back just to kill him later? Or leave him be and end the life of his sister who lay inches from her feet.

She wrapped a magical chain completely around Vera and looked at Neveah. "I'm coming in to bring him back. If you try anything, I will kill him and her. Do you understand?"

"Yes." Neveah nodded in agreement, quickly stepping aside.

Elinor opened the door and rushed to Adonis's aid. Reaching in his chest, she could feel the life still in his heart. She zapped his heart with a shock of electricity and his eyes suddenly shot open. Instantly, he showed all signs of life. The elixir she made still lay on the floor next to the cot. She picked it up and forced it down his throat until ever drop was gone. Stepping back, she raced from the cell, locking the door behind her.

Neveah ran to his side and held him in a long, lasting embrace.

Jealousy pinged Elinor as she picked up Vera and walked her back upstairs to make her dramatic, theatrical entrance once more. She walked slowly down the steps to build the suspense, knowing she had their full attention this time. Adonis and Neveah watched her bring Vera to the bars and smash her against them. Waking up, Vera made a sound of pain when the metal connected with her body.

"Adonis, you will join me and take over the realms. Be my king or this will happen to your dear Everest, too," Elinor warned before extracting Vera's power and ending her life along with it.

Adonis reacted as she had expected. Rushing to the entrance of the bars to pull and pound on the steel poles, he screamed and cursed at her evil.

"Well, you shouldn't have refused me the first time. You forced me to do this when you knew perfectly well what I'm capable of."

"You will pay for this. Mark my words you evil magissa. You *will* get what's coming to you." Adonis warned.

He didn't intimidate Elinor one bit, but she did admire his attempt to frighten her. That was the part of his personality that really made him appealing to her. No man or beast had ever spoken to her like Adonis did. All her childhood boys chased her and did everything she wished; as an adult her beauty grew, and men simply couldn't resist her. It was rather boring until she had met the man standing before her and sensing the hatred radiating from his entire body.

"What I get coming to me better be you, or the next time I come down here it will be with the young Everest—who has so much life to live—and that life will be in your hands." she laughed "Bye, bye now. I have a wedding to plan."

Neveah couldn't bring herself to watch what Elinor had done to Vera, but she watched the witch leave...or almost leave. The door opened but then they heard her footsteps coming down the stairs once again. This time, when she stopped walking, she was staring through the bars at Neveah. Neveah couldn't help but look away, the witch intimidated her and scared her more than she would ever admit. The unpredictable actions that she had shown, without an ounce of care in her eyes for anyone's life, showed she couldn't be anything less than a demon straight out of Hell, itself. The horrible feeling she got when she looked directly into the witch's eyes was pure darkness.

"I almost forgot about you. You're certainly a quiet little thing, aren't you? You have spent more than enough time with my fiancée. I'm done allowing that. How do you like cheese?" she asked Neveah.

The question threw her. "I...like cheese," Neveah replied, trying to be agreeable.

"Good. Pontiki," she stated, pointing a finger at Neveah.

Neveah felt herself shrink to the ground. Inside, her stomach twisted and turned. making her feel queasy. Suddenly, without another warning, Neveah found herself completely transformed into a little brown mouse, sporting very tiny paws and tickly whiskers she could feel when she tried to speak. Nothing came out except a squeaky sound that even she didn't understand.

"That is the perfect little animal for you. A rodent," Elinor spoke, reaching out to lift Neveah from the floor. She was startled when Adonis grabbed Neveah in midair, stopping Elinor from getting to her first.

"You don't need her. She's just a mouse now. I will marry you, but Neveah stays with me," he demanded, holding the mouse carefully in his hand against his chest.

"Very well. It's not like she can use any magic while in that form. You can keep her as your little pet. Call it an early wedding present." Elinor smiled. "Take care, my husband to be."

When Elinor left, this time Adonis made sure she was gone. He set Neveah down on the cot and turned around to pace the bars again. He wasn't going to give the magissa the satisfaction of hearing him cry or show weakness, but looking at the pile of ash that was once his sister, brought him to his knees. Vengeance on the witch was the only joy he would ever feel until the day he died. Right then, he made a vow: The witch's blood line would also end, so she couldn't resurrect herself from any of her living relatives, when he finally had the chance to kill Elinor with his own two hands.

CHAPTER 18

Everything was happening too fast. Iris could only handle one thing at a time, and multiple things were going on. She needed to take Sylvia aside and fix the King of the Waters. That was one thing she could fix instantly if she knew exactly what Sylvia had done. Next, she would help save the realm; bring with her all who had power with Nick, and meet up with Alister and the rest. Being head witch when her own life was crumbling down around her made it more than difficult to focus on all other problems.

"Nick, I will get all the witches together and help. I know you have many questions about Neveah, but we need to settle a couple of other issues first," Iris spoke, letting go of Sylvia.

"Take your time. I know what happened already. I just..can't believe it," Nick said, putting his head down.

"Sylvia, bring me to Simon and we will see if you can reverse it yourself or if we need something stronger. It sounds to me like you're a Siren witch. You hypnotized him to forget everything, you can reverse it if you try." Iris told her with confidence, leaving out the part that she had never seen a Siren witch in person.

"Okay. He's at the dock. I told him to stay there while I went to get help," Sylvia said, still sobbing, ready to show Iris the way.

"Everyone, stay here and keep an eye on Zack. I'll be back soon."

Iris followed Sylvia out the door and down the dirt path. The docks weren't far from Julia's house so it wouldn't take them long to reach Simon. She wasn't prepared for the day to be so complicated, though. Thinking about Izak with his broken hand, and how it ought to teach him a lesson until she could mend it. Zack being a wolf, and how Jenisis didn't believe and was unheard of, were just some of the confusing situations she would have to figure out.

"What's wrong with me, Iris?" Sylvia asked.

"Nothing is wrong with you, my dear. You finally found out you have magic. That's a wonderful thing," Iris replied, smiling at her.

"I'm scared. What is a Siren witch, anyway?"

"Well..in the books, a Siren is supposed to be a water creature, and a powerful one at that. She had a voice that could be used for both bad and good. Their voices could bring in ships to crash and men to die, or they could be used to end wars between men and bring peace to realms."

"But I'm not a water creature. How could I do any of those things?" Sylvia looked at Iris. confused.

"I don't really know. It's the only thing I could think of when you told me your voice is what did that to Simon. Are you sure no one else was near or in the water? Other creatures are known to come to our realm from other realms every so often."

"Yes, I'm sure. I could feel the power release from me and attack him. I will never forgive myself if I can't fix him. I went there to tell him I couldn't marry him, and he was only telling me that my mother would want me to be happy. What if I *can't* fix him?"

"You can. If you caused it with pain in your heart, you could fix it with the love you have for him. You will see," Iris reassured her, hoping it was true.

"Why are Bella, Jacky, and Ziara here?" Sylvia asked, pointing at the dock.

Sylvia and Iris ran to the end of the dock to see what the girls were laughing at. Simon was swimming around, being silly with a piece of seaweed attached to his face to look like he had a green mustache and goatee. The sight made Sylvia laugh, too, which was very helpful in getting her magic under control so she could help Simon get his memories back.

"What's wrong with Simon? He's like...acting and talking like a two-year-old," Bella asked.

"I cursed him and made him forget everything in his life. I guess I'm some kind of witch, and my power is in my voice," Sylvia stated, looking down again, feeling the guilt.

"She's here to fix him, though. Sylvia, think of all the times that made you exceptionally happy when you were with Simon. Make sure you keep all negativity out of your mind," Iris instructed. "Your power is in your voice, so once you have all of the happy memories in your mind, call for your magic."

Sylvia closed her eyes and concentrated on the happiest memories she could, all that included Simon. The day they met and how he had playfully messed with her. Their first kiss and being busted by her mother. Her mother being gone now...

Sylvia's eyes shot open and all she could see was dripping darkness in her vision. "What's wrong with my eyes?" Sylvia panicked.

"Sylvia, calm yourself. Close your eyes if it helps," Iris

spoke.

"No! I'm afraid of the dark. Please don't let it go dark."

"You can do it. Listen to the pretty lady." Simon said, swimming toward her, jumping onto the dock, and taking Sylvia's hand in his own.

She could feel his touch. The feeling of his soft hands was helping her fear subside.

The wonderful memories came flooding back through her mind. She forced herself to believe her mother was okay. She viewed the day Simon had proposed to her, which proved to be the memory that called her magic forth. It was like she was dreaming but awake at the same time. She was speaking but nothing was coming out.. or she couldn't hear her own voice.

Sylvia stared into the blank eyes of her beloved Simon as she spoke: "Come back to me. Reverse the wrong I have done and make it right again."

The voice she finally heard escape her lips was unreal. It was a prolonged, beautiful echo to her own ears. The smiles on the faces of Iris and the others showed her that they thought her voice was lovely, too. Simon's eyes, however, told her a different story. One of hurt and pain, causing her to feel guilty all over again.

"I will always love you, but you have cursed me. Now, I want nothing more to do with you." Simon spoke his heart-wrenching words and then backed away from her, dropping into the ocean below.

Sylvia followed him until she reached the end of the dock and looked down into the water. He was nowhere in sight. She had done it; she'd started all of it when he was only trying to help. And now that she wanted his love all over again, Simon was gone and unwilling to forgive her.

Standing up, Sylvia made a vow to come back every day and beg for his forgiveness until he remembered all that they had shared together and would be willing to come back. He couldn't stay mad at her forever.

Could he?

* * *

Angela had heard everything that happened the day before, but really couldn't care less because all had been resolved. She was rather curious about Sylvia's new powers, though.

"We have to go and stop the darkness from spreading, but we need to make sure the men are good—able to keep an eye on the kids," Iris said in the meeting Angela was forced to attend in Arianna's power room.

"Arik can handle his three. Or does he still consider my beautiful niece, Bella, to be one of his own?" Arianna asked.

"Of course, he does. Even if we aren't together, that doesn't change how he feels about Bella. Why are we even talking about this?" Angela asked, glaring at Arianna.

"Maybe because you don't even talk to your children or do any real grown-up things, like speak to your husband.. or ex-husband. Whatever you plan to do with him, except leave him in limbo."

"Okay, you two are completely off topic. Angela will handle her business when she's good and ready. *Her* business," Iris repeated, looking at Arianna.

"Don't look at me like that. You are both avoiders when you know it's wrong. Izak is still an addict and obviously got his hands on something to make him act the way he does," Arianna spoke to Iris, then switched to Angela,. "Arik used a lot of drugs when he thought his entire family was dead. Did either of you think that maybe those two are connected somehow?"

"You think Arik's using drugs from his past with Izak and they won't be able to handle the children while we are off saving the realm? That's okay, I can stay here," Angela spoke with less concern in her voice than Iris was about to express.

"Oh my God! Izak found Arik's stash from a long time ago

and that's why he's been acting this way," Iris gasped.

"Arik seems fine, though. I don't think he knows what's going on," Arianna spoke quickly to defend him.

Angela sat in complete boredom while her two sisters made the plan to do an intervention with Izak. She could only think about more power, and perhaps how she could siphon the darkness that was consuming the realm and turn it into her own dark magic—making her even more powerful than before. She fantasized about all the realms she could take over while she watched everyone scurry in fear...

"That's enough! What a sick thought. You are seriously a dysfunctional evil that was never meant to be created. I told you I would share my mind with you, but that doesn't mean you can fill it with so much horror," Angela spoke to the magic in her mind.

"Well, I'm bored, and all this mushy guy nonsense is just as disgusting to me as my horror images are to you." The evil complained.

"Then go away. Don't you ever sleep or want time alone?"

"Fine, but if anything interesting happens, you better wake me." The magic spoke before fading into the back of Angela's mind.

Angela was back in the present with her two sisters, listening to their plan to anchor the darkness to a living being. Someone whose lifespan was long. It would stop the darkness from continuing until the life of the anchor ended, then it would have to be transferred to someone else until they could find another way.

"We need to link it to Basil. It won't hurt him, and he will live many lives. He's a foinix, after all," Arianna suggested.

"That's right. What do you think, Angela?" Iris asked, turning her attention on her.

"Why don't you take light and snuff out the dark. I don't want Basil turning dark because we connected him to a force that kills everything in its path. There has to be something light to keep the dark at bay." Angela didn't want Basil to be a victim because something they did turned for the worst.

"We can try to find an equally light force, but it might be difficult and take time we don't have. We need to be prepared for anything," Iris spoke.

"We have enough light magic to conquer the dark. Shouldn't we at least try?" Angela asked, hoping it would work.

"We can try. I don't want anything to happen to Basil just as much as you don't. He's been through a lot, with his father trying to kill him, forcing him to come to our realm." Arianna agreed with Angela.

"Well, let's talk to Nick and get prepared for our departure," Iris said, abruptly ending the meeting.

The three ladies walked over to the mirror to enter into Iris and Izak's home to speak to the men waiting there about a plan. The mirror had been moved into the living room, so it wasn't in the way sitting in the kitchen. When Angela, Arianna, and Iris walked through they were greeted by the trio of men.

Nick jumped up and off the couch, while Izak and Arik followed suit to hear the plan the women had come up with.

Iris was the first to speak. "We have devised a strategy. We will head back with you, Nick; that means you, Izak and Arik, will be in charge of the children while we are gone. Sylvia and Bella said they will help, too. We will try to project light magic onto the dark, but if that doesn't work, we will have to anchor the darkness to a living person in order to stop it from spreading," Iris explained.

Izak and Arik nodded their heads in agreement, while Izak stood with his broken hand near his heart. Iris still hadn't healed it, thinking it would teach him a lesson before he went hitting another wall. She squinted in sadness when she could tell he was hurting.

"Whatever you do, we need to get going soon. The longer

we stand here, the faster the darkness spreads," Nick informed the ladies.

"I'm coming with you, Mom," Leah spoke as she came from around the corner. She had learned a thing or two about eavesdropping from her big sister.

Silence filled the room; everyone looked at Leah, and then to Angela. She had the final decision on whether or not to allow Leah to join them on their perilous journey. Her light magic would certainly be incredibly helpful, and she would certainly be the one to complete the spell they needed to cast. Angela was ready to agree; besides, there wasn't any real threat to her if they stayed away from the line of death.

But her other half had other ideas..forcing Angela to refuse.

"No! It's too dangerous for you to come along. What if something happens to you? I can't allow it," Angela's 'other half' spoke up.

"I agree. You're too young to handle such a large amount of magic," Iris added. "I'm sure you can do it, but how you feel after will be a lot on a little vessel."

Leah didn't fight the answer her aunt and mother gave, but she did look at Angela with a long stare that indicated she knew something. That her mother was off, and that Leah knew why. Angela hated the look in her eyes, it made her bow her head in shame. The evil that lingered in her mind was so much stronger than her, she couldn't even gain control of her answers with her own child. Leah knew something would have to be done about the voice..and soon.

"That's that, then. Shall we take our leave?" Nick asked with impatience.

"Yes, but before we go, I need to help Izak," Iris spoke.

Iris walked to Izak and held his hand with another healing stone inside, centering them between their hands. Looking into his eyes with pure sadness and concern, she chanted "giatrépste ta spasména." As the words were uttered, instantly

Izak's fist healed, repairing the broken bones.

"I promise I will do better. I'm sorry," Izak told her.

"You have told me that before.... When you broke my heart the first time. We will talk when I get back," Iris whispered.

Izak nodded in silence.

Without another word, Iris turned to Nick and told him they were ready to go.

* * *

When they arrived at the camp where everyone was stationed before the darkness, many shifters were present. Mostly all flying shifters, among them was His Majesty, there to greet them all.

"Thank you for coming! It's spreading and we need to stop it as soon as possible," Alister spoke, looking very excited to see Angela.

Angela stood as still as she could behind Arianna and Iris. She wanted to run away and hide somewhere—anywhere that Alister couldn't see her. She called for an escape in her mind, only to get an evil laugh in response. *"You're the one who told me to go away. Now you need me?"*

"Yes! I don't want to be here. I can't even look at him."

"I know because you're a pathetic weakling. This will be fun for me. I will help under one condition. You don't stop me, no matter how ridiculous the man looks when I completely shatter his heart,"

"You have my word. I won't stop you," Angela replied, wanting her escape more than anything else.

"Run away and hide, you little mouse."

Angela went to the darkest part of her mind. She didn't want to be involved with the situation at all, nor witness what the evil was going to do. She wanted to feel strong, but anything to do with Alister feeling pain—she already knew—was too much for her.

Angela stepped forward, in between Iris and Arianna, cutting the conversation short. The unnecessary chatter of "catching up" wasn't what they came here for.

"Well, we need to get to work. We didn't come for a reunion; we came to save you dying realm since you are incapable and too bull-headed to realize you needed to call us sooner," Angela spoke with the new 'angry spice' that now took over her personality.

The insults worked, Alister's face turned sour when he looked into Angela's eyes. She repaid it by raising her left eyebrow and preparing to beat him when he was already down. He didn't fight her words or stand up for himself, he just sighed with a glum look on his face.

"Of course. I'll lead the way," Alister said, tuning around.

Angela shocked both Iris and Arianna with her words and tone, but they proceeded to follow Alister and their sister toward the line of darkness.

"I'm sorry I upset you, Angela."

"Well, I don't know what I was expecting from a coward that can't own up to their own feelings. What kind of king allows another man to take away the woman he *claimed* to love, if he is not a coward? I can care less about you now. I'm here to get a job done; not for you," Angela spoke, adding an angry tone. "As far as upsetting me. I'm over it already, I guess I didn't really love you either and just enjoyed the idea of having such a powerful man show interest in such a simple woman like me. I have magic now; I don't need anyone."

Everything Angela had said was really upsetting Alister—she had insulted him in all the ways she could think of. The only thing she hadn't topped her attack off with was adding his wife to the mix. He was already flaring his nostrils, allowing the steam to escape while he looked at Angela with glowing eyes.

"Could you imagine if your precious Alison was here? She would be so disappointed in what kind of weak king you have become. Bowing to another man and allowing him to take what was yours."

Angela couldn't finish her speech, even though there was so much more she wanted to say. Alister had suddenly transitioned into the beast he was born as and grabbed her around the waist, picking her up with his talons and raising her in front of his great big dragon nose.

"Enough! You don't speak of my wife. You're lucky I don't take your head for that."

"Go ahead! Make an example out of me. Taking my head would help, actually; it would take me out of the misery of being in your presence and in your ridiculous excuse for a royal realm."

"This isn't you, Angela," he spoke, lowering her down to the ground but keeping his talons around her. "Something wicked has consumed you. I can't feel anything coming from you that is kind and human."

"I am what *you* created. If anything is different about me, it's *your* fault. Now let me go, you overgrown lizard!"

"Angela, stop!" Iris screamed, showing her concern.

Angela didn't stop staring directly into Alister's great big, gold eyes. But nothing was working; he wasn't overreacting like she'd hoped. Magic wouldn't bring him down, but she couldn't defend herself and destroy him if he didn't attempt to attack her. Instead, he loosened his grip and let go of her. She knew why.... An audience was building around them, and now wasn't the time to lose himself when his kingdom needed him so desperately. Wounded was all Angela had succeeded at doing—nothing more than hurting his pride and feelings.

"Nick, please lead them to the darkness and be done with it," Alister spoke, still in his drakon form.

Leaving the crowed, he took flight and left the witches in the hands of his noble King of the Flight Shifters. He would take out his anger in a different location, where his people couldn't see him.

Angela laughed in her own mind at all the facial expressions looking at her now. Straightening her clothes and hair, she showed no remorse for what she had said or done in stirring up Alister's emotions. With a small grin, she finally broke the silence.

"Let's get going. The realm's not going to fix itself," Angela stated, turning and walking in the direction Alister had flown.

No one stopped her or tried to speak to her. Both Arianna and Iris knew that she was beyond upset and the emotions were dangerous, but they were also powerful and useful in the huge task that was before them.

When they reached the darkness, Iris gasped at the sight. All the vegetation showed signs of death. She could *feel* all of it. Putting her hands up to the line, with Arianna and Angela copying her every move, she tried to bring light to the scene.

Angela had other ideas, of course. While Arianna and Iris were trying to counter the darkness, she tried to suck it in. So much magical energy came from the area; she couldn't let it go to waste. Determined to get every last bit of it, she moved closer. If she could just set her hand on something solid the darkness had consumed, she would be able to harness it.

Arianna and Iris had their eyes closed in concentration as they chanted, so Angela took the opportunity to bend down, reach her hand across to the other side and set it on the ground. Feeling the sudden power race through her, she watched the darkness recede and thought it was working.

Unfortunately, the darkness only backed up about a foot before it roared toward the trio of witches, knocking them backwards and sending them tumbling through the air. Angela screamed in pain while her hand turned black. The evil in her mind swiftly retreated, leaving Angela to pay for the consequences of touching the darkness.

"My hand! Oh my God, what's happening?" Angela cried out, completely oblivious to what had just occurred.

Iris ran to her aid and grabbed her hand. Arianna ran

behind Iris to use the rest of their light magic to save Angela's hand and bring it back to its original state. It was too painful for Angela to comprehend. She had allowed the wicked to control her mind for so long that everything overwhelmed her and brought her to the ground. Angela fainted as soon as her hand was repaired, barely hearing Iris yell: "What did you do?"

When Angela woke up, she was completely herself. The evil magic didn't linger anywhere in her mind. She sat up to observe her surroundings. She was inside a tent, by the looks of the light shining through the top and sides. Instantly, she remembered her hand and how it had disintegrated like it was burning away before her very eyes. Now it was whole again, with no signs of turning to ash. She sighed in relief and swore to handle herself from then on.

Shortly after she made the silent vow to herself, Alister entered the tent with concern written all over his face. Angela was stunned by his appearance, looking at him like she hadn't seen him in years when actually it had only been a few minutes. She could feel the pain and tightness pulling at her heart while they stared at each other in silence.

"How are you feeling?" Alister spoke first.

"I didn't lose my hand." Angela smiled, rubbing the healthy skin.. "So, I guess I will survive."

"What were you doing?" he asked.

"I don't remember. It happened so fast. I guess I was trying a different method when the light wasn't removing the dark magic. I thought I could be the anchor and remove it. It was working at first, but then it..backfired. I was wrong."

"Well, that was stupid! You could have killed yourself," he scolded.

Angela looked away from him in response to his words. She didn't like him mad at her, especially the last time...when he broke her heart. She remained silent and avoided his eyes until he came closer and bent down, making her look at him.

The confusion in his eyes made her even more uncomfortable. Apparently, the evil hadn't made the sparkle leave his eyes when he looked at her. It had promised to be brutal and make him care nothing for her..but obviously the evil was a liar, too.

"Basil is now the anchor to the darkness. He will live a long time and the risk of the darkness spreading is gone. We can all live our lives without fear of it continuing," he whispered.

"I told them that was too dangerous. I felt the darkness enter me when I touched it. What's going to stop it from doing the same to the innocent boy?" Angela spoke with worry.

"He never touched it. The others took care of everything. It has no effect on him and it stopped spreading. Only the area will be a death trap for anyone who attempts to enter that part of my realm. But I'm glad you're feeling better. We can all go home now," Alister said, offering his hand to help Angela.

Angela looked at his hand with sadness and anger building in her own soul. Looking up into his eyes, she showed her disgust at ever touching him again, let alone taking his hand no matter how injured or weak she felt.

"Go to Hell, Alister, I don't need your help," Angela stated, before she turned her head away. There was no escape this time. The evil voice inside her remained silent.

"As you wish. Goodbye Angela," Alister said before he exited the tent.

Angela listened to him take flight before she let the tears rain down, releasing the wails of a broken heart..all over again.

CHAPTER 19

Sylvia, as promised, went to the docks to plead with Simon for his forgiveness. Every time he rejected her cries of apology, it was worse than the day before. She acted like a desperate damsel in distress. The harder she tried; the more Simon ignored her. ...Except for today.

Simon was happy when he exited the water, bringing another man out to join him in the rays of the sun. Sylvia was going to the dock to tell him she was ready to leave him alone and let him live his life without her, but the smile he wore made her rethink her decision.

"Who's that?" Sylvia got up and walked over to the two men.

"His name is Rodney, and he has answers for the king," Simon spoke proudly. "Marie is guilty of killing that poor woman and he will inform His Majesty of all that he knows."

"Could I..." Sylvia hesitated, clearing her voice. "Could I come with you?"

"Do what you wish. Not like anyone can stop you," Simon spoke in an irritated tone.

"Simon, *please*, I told you how sorry I am and that I'm okay now. I'm learning about this new magic, and I think my mom is still alive. I was just upset.. I was losing hope, but you helped me." Sylvia smiled, hoping he was in a listening mood today.

"Well, at least one of us is better. I spent a lot of time thinking about it, too. I think that you're not mature enough to be Queen of the Waters. I wish I would have seen it before, so we didn't waste all this time trying to figure it out," Simon spoke, regretting his words as soon as he saw the devastation upon Sylvia's face.

She said nothing. He had really meant nothing that he'd said, the words were simply an immature way to make her feel bad. But when he moved forward to apologize, she turned away immediately and ran off, sobbing. Simon felt terrible, but instead of beating himself up about it, he tugged hard on Rodney to move with him. He was Marie's accomplice in finding the devil squid. He would pay for his crimes along with the wicked queen.

When Simon made it to His Majesty's castle and entered the doors to his Throne Room, he was not met with the king in his human form. Alister was in his drakon form, pacing back and forth in front of the throne. He stopped for only a brief moment when Simon walked in to present the guilty man in his grasp.

"Your Majesty, I have a merman here for you. He has information about Marie. Would you like me to come back another time?"

"No! Bring him forward," Alister spoke in a deep voice. "Who is this man?"

"This is Rodney, a shining star and traitor. He was helping

Marie to contact the devil squid. Tell His Majesty what you told me," Simon demanded.

"I had no choice; the queen has no sympathy for anyone. She would have killed me if I refused her orders. I'm sorry, Your Majesty, but King Simon speaks the truth. I helped her and found the creature in the deepest depths of the sea, where only a star could reach and shine brightly enough to bring it out. It volunteered its supply of ink to me. When I brought it to Queen Marie at the dock, she informed me it was going to be used to lock up the evil witch in a place where she couldn't hurt anyone again. She never told me it was to kill an innocent woman. I accept my fate, Your Majesty," the man said in a regretful tone. Bowing his head, he readied himself to feel the blade of the drakon's tail slice through the back of his neck before his death.

"Where is Queen Marie now?" Alister screamed as he approached the man.

"She is hiding in the caves..behind the waterfall,"

"You are to set up a trial in the center of town, Simon. I will be back in fourteen days to sentence Marie. You are to get everyone in my kingdom together in order to view her trial and punishment. Do you understand?" Alister instructed Simon.

"Yes, Your Majesty. What would you like me to do with the star?"

"Lock him away. And *you* need to learn how to control your waters, or I will remove your title faster than I killed Tarence," Alister said, belittling the King of the Ocean right before flying away to go after the mermaid.

Simon heard Alister's threat clearly. He didn't want to lose his new title, but he knew His Majesty was not joking. King Tarence's torture sell was something Simon never wanted to set eyes on again. He hadn't had to deal with anyone's treachery since his new title had been granted to him.

Rushing Rodney back to the dock to reenter the water,

Simon couldn't stop thinking about Sylvia—how much he wished she was there with him, to be there when he locked up his first prisoner. But when he arrived at the dock, Sylvia was nowhere in sight. She obviously had chosen to stop trying to make him see how sorry she was.

The star held tight in his grasp, never once tried to escape. In fact, he walked willingly and showed no desire to be released. Even when Alister took off after Marie, the man seemed unafraid of what his consequences would be from the part he played in the woman's death. *Maybe the man wasn't guilty after all...?*

Simon took one last look behind him to see if Sylvia was there. When he saw no one, he jumped into the water, still holding on to the star man with plans to bring him to his father's old cell; the place where Tarence held anyone who fought against his demands to stay away from the land creatures.

* * *

Bella rushed Angela down the streets of Moodamorph town. Now that Angela was back to her normal self, the voice had been only a small fraction of her mental state. She was free to enjoy being around her children and not worry about the dark side coming out.

Bella had blindfolded her, telling her to get ready for a wonderful surprise. Laughing, she chatted with her mother. Telling her a good surprise was something she could use, especially after everything that had happened with Alister and at the end of the realm.

"Where are you taking me, you silly child?" Angela laughed, hoping she wouldn't run into a pole at any moment.

"You're fine, Mom, don't worry. You all just need a special day after what you went through."

"All?" Angela asked, bewildered by her choice of words.

Bella didn't answer the question. Instead, she opened a door, came to a stop, and took off Angela's blindfold. Angela was still smiling when she opened her eyes to see where her oldest child had brought her.

"Surprise! Iris, Arianna, and Queen Tiana are all here. It's a spa day, Mom," Bella spoke excitedly, looking at Jacky and Ziara who'd helped get everyone together.

Angela was surprised, but her other side wasn't happy. The magic knew Tiana had a power that might expose it, which was far more dangerous than the others who simply believed Angela was just heartbroken, not sharing her thoughts with another.

"This is great, honey," Angela responded with a fake smile.

Queen Tiana got up from the chair she was sitting in and walked towards Angela, making her incredibly nervous. With a sympathetic expression, Tiana wrapped her arms around Angela, embracing her tightly. Angela repaid the hug while the magic made a sick gagging sound inside her mind.

"You don't have to pretend with me. I know how you feel. I love you, sweetheart. Things will get better. Just wait and see," Tiana expressed her positive outlook on the situation.

"Thank you. I love you, too," Angela spoke wholeheartedly.

"We are so glad to get you two together. It's been forever. Now that our work is done, we're going to take off. Bye, Mom," Bella spoke for all of them.

"Bye, darling. Thank you," Angela said once again, smiling.

"What are you three up to today?" Tiana asked.

"To spy on someone. Or go find Zinnia and see if she's okay," Jacky replied.

"Stay safe. Something is going on with that family. I don't know what, exactly, but..be careful," Tiana expressed her concern.

"We will. Bye, Mom," Jacky waved, rushing the other two out the door.

"Where's the wine at?" Angela asked, rubbing her hands together with an excited smile.

The ladies laughed in unison when Angela showed signs of lightening up. All of them walked to the table set with a variety of fruits, cheese and crackers, with bottles of wine to drink. Angela poured four glasses, handing one to her sisters and Tiana. Lifting their glasses in unison, they cheered to saving the realm from destruction yet again. Only three of the women took a drink of the liquid.

"Ladies, take your seats and we will begin," Rose spoke with her rosy, cheery tone.

Four soft and relaxing seats sat in a row, ready for them to pick a chair. Arianna walked to the far end, with Iris following her lead. Then Angela and Tiana took their chairs. Once they were all comfortably seated, the quartet of mood ladies reclined the chairs, allowing them to lie flat.

"Close your eyes, please," Rose instructed, before smearing a thick paste on Angela's face and setting two round, cold objects upon her eyes.

"What is this stuff?" Angela asked.

"You don't want to know," the other three replied in unison before an outbreak of giggles began.

Angela smiled at the response. Whatever the ointment was, it relaxed and soothed her skin, so she wasn't complaining. Even on Earth she had never been able to enjoy a spa day with a facial cleansing before.

While her face felt like it was calmly soaking, Rose brought a straw to Angela's mouth to drink through. When she took a drink, she was happy to taste her wine.

"This is some royal treatment," Arianna sighed in complete bliss.

"*More like torture treatment. Why are we here?*" the magic spoke to Angela. "*You know that pesky friend of yours is going to figure me out and then they will make you give me up. Are you really this stupid? Of course, you are.*"

"I'm quite enjoying this outing, thank you very much. Why are you here if this is torture for you?"

"I'm making sure you don't out me just in case you have a grudge from the other day about disintegrating your hand. You can't get rid of me that easily."

"I didn't plan on it, but now I'm thinking about it. After all, if it weren't for my sisters, you would have killed us both because of your greedy need for dark magic."

"Did you hear me? Angela?" Tiana's voice broke through Angela's mental conversation.

"Sorry, I was lost in thought. What did you say?"

"I asked how you feel about Arik being back? Must be really confusing for you."

"It's awkward, and I do not know what to say to him. We have talked little. He hasn't pushed a conversation either, which is unusual for him. Maybe you should talk to Arianna. She seems to know more about him than I do these days."

"What do you mean by that?" Arianna asked defensively.

"I'm not stupid, that's what I mean. I know something went on between you two. The thing is, I just don't care to know what it was exactly. I don't care about any of it; I'd rather he just stayed on Earth," Angela spoke in a cold tone, with no help needed from her other half.

Crickets filled the room, and no one wanted to put a stop to the silence; this only confirmed that Angela was right about what she had stated. Her heart belonged to another, and she wasted none of her energy on something as dumb as jealousy. It wasn't in her nature to feel jealous when she didn't have romantic feelings about the father of her children anymore.

"Time to wash, ladies. Then we'll take a small break before nails, hair, and massage." Rose spoke in a hopeful voice as if wanting to remove the tension in the room.

Rose and the others removed the objects from their eyes before they sat up and moved along to the next station of the royal treatments, where they washed their faces in water with daisy petals floating upon the surface. The process was all fascinating to Angela. She couldn't help but find amusement in how silly..how girly it all was.

Once the wash was done, Angela walked over to the table to enjoy bites of cheese and fruit, being joined by her twin shortly after.

"I was going to tell you, Angela. I just didn't know how to address the topic without butting into your life," Arianna spoke in a whisper; a hint of guilt was in her voice.

"I honestly don't care. I'm not upset with you. Other things are literally clouding my mind and I'm overreacting."

"That's not possible. You have to care a little. Don't you?"

Angela laughed at Arianna's shocked and somewhat impressed expression. Smiling at her sister, she had only one thing in her mind—how sorry she was for Arianna to be fooled by Arik's charm, alluring personality, and physical appearance. She would find out soon just how selfish the man could actually be. If they became an official thing.

"That's not the best part either," the evil filled her head and began to chant. *"I know something you don't know..I know something you don't know."*

The diatribe brought on curiosity, but nothing more. Angela learned not to play or entertain the voice's taunting. She wished someone could figure out what was really going on with her and give her no choice but to part ways with the magic she possessed. It wasn't good for her to have it inside her head. But like a drug, she couldn't shake the need it had brought into her life.

Iris walked towards Arianna and Angela, smiling, wanting to get in on the sisterly gossip. Arianna smiled at her while Angela tried not to give in to her mental curiosity.

"What's going on over here? You two getting along?" Iris asked.

"Arik's charm has enticed poor sister. What are we going to do with her?" Angela teased, making a fun joke out of it.

While Iris and Arianna laughed, Angela looked around the room. Tiana wasn't anywhere in sight. She missed her dear friend and wished she hadn't stayed away for so long. Tiana had obviously noticed no difference in Angela; she'd simply boiled it up to man problems, like the rest of them.

"Where did Tiana go?" Angela asked.

"She stepped outside. Said she wasn't feeling well. Something about the energy in the room," Iris replied.

"Everything is fine between Arianna and me. I hope she comes back."

"Why Arik, of all men, by the way? Did you have to be interested in our sisters' husband?" Iris put Arianna on the spot with her inquiry.

"We were stuck with each other for so long…. He listened to me when I had no one else. I don't know. We tried to put an end to all of it."

"Sure it wasn't the peacock dance?" Angela laughed. "Did you two drink at all?"

"Oh my God," Arianna started laughing.

"Probably want to ask what happened after the dance. You should ask her more questions. See if she lies to you."

"No thanks, think I'm going to just enjoy this time with my sisters. Go away," Angela demanded the voice to get lost.

The sisters continued to laugh and chat about Arik. Angela told them she'd clean up the mess that was still lingering with her and Arik. Alister shot into her mind. If he knew that Arik and Arianna were together, how would he react? Angela smiled, thinking of the possibilities it would bring to her and Alister. Even though she was heartbroken still, maybe they had a chance after all.

Angela joined the girls in laughter. Their smiles and laughs ended only when a voice made an announcement, like it was over an invisible intercom that screamed into the room:

"You thieving witches have my magic! I want it back. If you don't return it to me in thirty days, I will put Neveah's head upon a stake and make an example out of her. I will show you what happens to those who think they can steal from me! You have thirty days to return my magic to Foinix Realm. This is my final and only warning," the voice spoke, loud and serious.

At first, Angela thought it was the magic speaking in her mind, for it matched the dark magic that only Angela knew she possessed.

"What was that?" Tiana asked, rushing through the doors to Angela and the others.

"We just found out where Neveah is. She's alive." Iris smiled.

"Doesn't sound like it's for very long. We need to get the information over to Alister. He has the crystals," Tiana spoke urgently.

"We need a plan. This woman wants a battle. She doesn't care about peace. We need to take these thirty days she promised to prepare," Arianna spoke, remembering the same voice clouding her own mind..her entire life.

"Poor Neveah. How could any of us have known it sucked her into a portal to Foinix? I had no idea," Iris said sadly, with Arianna and Angela agreeing with her.

"Why are you lying?" Tiana asked Angela, calling her out on her agreement.

"What are you talking about?" Angela said, suddenly even more uncomfortable.

"You knew this entire time where Neveah was," Tiana spoke.

Angela looked from Arianna to Iris, then back to Tiana. She didn't know what to say or how to defend herself. She hadn't known where Neveah was, but something obviously did. And when Angela thought she was speaking the truth, a part of her knew damn well that she was lying.

"Seriously, I do not know what you are talking about. Did you get drugged somehow?" Angela defended herself.

"This is not only Angela. Trust me. Something has control of Angela's mind," Tiana said, pointing at her.

"Oh, my God! I know exactly what is going on. Why didn't you tell us? I could have helped you with the evil magic inside you," Arianna yelled at her.

The magic was panicking, while Angela was thanking any God that was listening for the secret to be out; finally. Angela was happy until the evil attacked her mind and pushed her to the back, locking her up in the darkness.

"None of you know what you are talking about. I'm fine, just emotional because Alister and I broke things off. Nothing more. So just get out of my way," she yelled at Tiana, who blocked her path.

"You are not my best friend. You're an evil that needs to be destroyed."

Angela glared at Tiana's statement. Thinking quickly, she threw her hands up and out towards Tiana, but before she could chant and curse, Arianna and Iris attacked her from the left and right side, instantly knocking Angela out and protecting Queen Tiana.

Arianna felt terrible again. She knew something was up with Angela and didn't mention it to anyone. Something was missing from her own mind, too. The same tormenting voice she had from the day she was born was taking over at times.. the voice that matched the woman who had spoken to them over the invisible intercom.

Putting all of it together, Arianna knew that the moment she transferred the magic into Angela was the first time in her entire life she felt sane. Arianna had never claimed to be a saint or a very honest person. And feeling bad was one thing, but would she have given Angela her magic back knowing that an extra evil essence would go into her mind too?

Absolutely.

* * *

Bella, Jacky, and Ziara reached Zinnia's new home. Walking up to the house, Bella felt suddenly uncomfortable. Something was wrong; the hairs on the back of her neck were standing up, as a layer of goosebumps covered her arms.

"Are you going to knock, Bella?" Jacky asked.

"I think we should go," Bella replied. "Something doesn't feel right."

"Don't be silly," Jacky said. Walking in front of Bella, she rapped hard on the wood before stepping back to wait for Zinnia or her mom to open the door.

There were sounds of items being dropped on the floor inside, so they knew someone was home. When they didn't hear footsteps coming to the door, however, Bella knocked. Slowly steps appeared, taking their time...they were sure it was Zinnia's mother. Bella thought it was weird that she was so hesitant to answer the door.

"Who is it?" Zinnia's mother asked.

"It's Bella, Jacky, and Ziara. We wondered if Zinnia wanted to come hang out with us," Bella spoke.

"We want to apologize," Jacky added.

The door handle wiggled before she opened it just a crack. The smell inside was appalling; a potent mixture of vinegar swept through their nostrils. The girls had to plug their noses with their fingers so they wouldn't smell it anymore.

"That's so sweet of you, girls. Zinnia isn't feeling well, though. Please don't come back...she has to rest. Bye, girls," she said quickly, attempting to close the door.

"No, wait. If we can get Iris or someone, we would like to help," Bella thought quickly, knowing something was wrong.

"No!" Her reply was panicked. "I mean, no thank you, dear. She just needs her rest. Please don't come back."

Zinnia's mother shut the door in the girls' face, leaving them to look at each other in confusion. The smell was familiar to Bella, but she couldn't remember where it had come from.

All she knew is, whatever it was, it scared her from the inside out.

The girls didn't talk as they walked back down the steps. Only Bella lingered, moving slowly away from the porch. She couldn't help but wonder why Zinnia's mother wouldn't want help if her daughter was sick. Looking up, Ziara and Jacky had already made it around the corner and out of sight. Taking one last look at the house before moving along, Bella noticed a figure in the attic window. Locking her eyes upon the moving image, she watched as the person dressed in a black cloak waved out at her, as if to say goodbye.

The original creepy feeling returned. The hairs on her arms and legs were standing up and her skin was tingling. Soon, Bella's curiosity outweighed the fear, and she walked back towards the house with a fake smile on her face. She waved back. Her steps ceased as she watched the figure breathe on the window, making a cloud of fog appear on the glass. Raising a finger, the image she now knew was Zinnia wrote H-E-L-P in the fog.

Bella's heart began to race, as her eyes widened in concern. She felt like she needed to tell Zinnia's mother that something was wrong with her and she needed help, but as she got closer to the porch, Zinnia shook her head from left to right.

Bella mouthed, 'Why?'

Zinnia's face was plastered to the window now. It was pale and sickly looking. Bella looked back at the door and then back up at the window. This time, Zinnia's face did not meet her gaze; instead, a skeleton stared down at her.

Screaming, Bella stepped backwards, tripped over a rock and fell on her back. She scrambled backwards, away from the house, before she got back on her feet, turned around, and ran from the property as fast as humanly possible.

This time, she didn't look back.

CHAPTER 20

Angela woke up and groaned at the throbbing pressure in her head. Lifting her hand to rub it, she realized she couldn't. As she looked down at the chains confining her wrists to the chair, and her ankles in the same condition, she gasped. Catching her breath, she attempted to recall memories to the surface of what had happened before she'd blacked out. She knew..if she was ever in the presence of Queen Tiana, she could tell something was wrong with Angela and she'd be able to tell the others that a darkness was controlling her. But the spa day had turned for the worst when Angela made the mistake of telling lies in front of Tiana.

Wiggling and pulling, Angela tried to get out of the chains. The weight of them felt like the chair was bolted to the floor; nothing budged. She didn't enjoy feeling trapped, and it was making her feel like she was suffocating.

"What's going on?" Angela yelled when the room's walls began to close in on her. "Hello, is anyone there?"

Angela could hear quick footsteps up the staircase of Arianna's house. Angela called out to the magic in her mind, trying to figure out what they'd plan to do now, but it did not answer her. Even though Angela could still feel its presence, she knew that it, too, was trapped from communication. She assumed the chains had something to do with it. They had to be magic, she thought.

The door opened slowly, making Angela look up to see who would enter. Iris walked through it and Angela couldn't help but smile. Even though she wasn't completely sure why she was tied to a chair, she was grateful the burden of holding onto her secret was finally out in the open.

"You must feel like you have one hell of a hangover," Iris spoke, walking up to Angela with a cup in her right hand. "Swallow this; it will help."

Iris brought the cup to Angela's lips and tipped it, allowing the liquid to pour into Angela's mouth. Soon the throbbing headache disappeared and Angela could think with a clear mind. Watching the other two walk through the door, she felt sorry for what she had said to Tiana. It was a foggy memory, but she had a part in the first response when Tiana had exposed her.

"How does she look, Tiana?" Arianna asked. "Is it gone?"

"Like Angela," Tiana smiled. "The chains are keeping the evil from coming out."

"We can get rid of it now," Arianna spoke quickly, walking forward.

"No! Please. I don't want it to completely go away. I can handle it," Angela begged. "I don't want to be useless again."

Angela looked into her sisters' eyes and pleaded with them. She could handle the magic now, especially if they knew about it and helped her with it. There had to be a way for her to keep the magic and get rid of the evil. She would do anything to make that happen.

"Angela, you can't control it. I lived with it my entire life. She will find you at your weakest point and take full advantage. All the good you have inside you...she will turn it and make it dark and uncontrollable. Having it for a few months is nothing compared to having it for over thirty years. Trust me, sister, you *don't* want this in any way, shape or form," Arianna stated.

Iris, Arianna, and Tiana walked away to talk about it in private, where Angela couldn't hear them. But she couldn't risk losing the power. There *had* to be something it could be useful for. Perhaps she could use it to help get Neveah back to Drakous Realm.

"Wait, before you guys remove the magic, just think how it could help in saving Neveah. It is so strong, stronger than anyone else's power. Think about it. It could be used to our advantage instead of causing chaos. Is there *no* way we can control it?"

"We could make you a necklace. Lock all the power into the pendant," Iris suggested. "At least it would be out of her head and have no control over her mentally."

"I have already tried that. There isn't a powerful enough stone to stop it from burning back into you. The most we can do is box it up until we need it, but then it will be even more unpredictable and antsy than before. There is no telling what it will do. The safest way is to destroy it," Arianna spoke.

"What if we make a deal with it? She seems like she will do anything to survive. If we threaten her, or tell her we'll do something hideous in return, we could lock it away inside of me and only let it out when we need it." Angela said.

Arianna shook her head. She knew what it was like to have all that power and not want to let it go. No matter how much she hurt the ones she loved, it always made itself more important. Now that the power was out of her own mind, she never wanted it back. She could love and be loved now. And she wanted the same hope for her sister.

"It could work. I remember that magic always wanted to go home. To its original host. I can guess the voice we heard at the spa shop was its witch. The voices match."

"I noticed that too. You can't forget that voice after it becomes a part of you."

"We need to remove the chains and talk to it. What do you think, Iris?"

"I think you're both crazy and we need to destroy it before someone gets hurt," Iris changed her answer, no longer wanting to store it in a pendant. "But I do understand we could use it to get Neveah."

Stepping back, Arianna remembered the contract paper on her desk. She was going to use it on His Majesty, but didn't think it was necessary now. Walking towards her desk with magical use objects, Arianna grabbed a piece of paper and created a binding contract with a pen that connects you to its words. After writing the terms and conditions, she wanted the magic to follow. She poked her finger and signed it with her blood.

Walking back to Angela, with the paper and pen in her hand, Arianna removed the chains and stepped back with Iris—prepared for an attack if it came their way. The magic would have heard what they'd talked about even if it was suppressed in the depths of Angela's mind and unable to reply.

"Is it still her?" Iris asked Tiana.

"Not at all," Tiana said with a sad expression as she stared at Angela. "You are seeing pure darkness. Be cautious, it doesn't look happy."

"You sneaky thing. I knew there was something about you. What I would do to harness that power of yours," the magic spoke in its evil tone before turning to the others. *"I have behaved; I have only done what Angela has asked me to do."*

"You heard our proposition. What is your answer?"

Arianna got straight to the point, waving the piece of paper in her face.

"What exactly do you plan to do with me?" she replied with an amused look.

"We are going to lock you up inside of Angela. That is not negotiable. You will have no control over anything Angela does or says. Nor will you be able to hear her conversations." Arianna spoke in all seriousness before getting to what the magic would want to know. "I promise to make it a horror show for you in your prison world; give you all the hideous images you love so much. Then, if you help us when we need you, in exchange we will return you to your rightful owner. Do we have a deal?" Arianna asked, handing Angela the magical pen and paper to seal the deal.

Magic can't break a signed contract between a witch and its word. If it does, it will be destroyed for real. Here, Arianna had to sign it too. If she wasn't true to her promise as well, she would die. The deal was, simply stated, that the magic would return to its original host if it did what the contract stated. The only thing that would void Arianna's end of the deal is if the host died, which is exactly what Arianna planned on happening.

"My dearest, Arianna. Why so glum? We had some great times, didn't we?" the magic spoke, changing the subject. "You were my favorite, you know."

"Are you going to sign it or yap until we mute you completely?" Arianna said hastily.

"Yes, I'll sign it. Geez..no time to catch up, I see. Just give it to me." Angela held out her hand and grabbed the paper and pen. Looking at the contract, she read it before signing in the same manner as Arianna had, smiling from ear to ear. Like a genie in a lamp, it was only allowed to come out of its prison world when Angela called for it.

"You better make my prison gory. I don't want no child's play. Give it to me murderous and bloody," the magic demanded, dramatizing the description and handing the paper back to Arianna.

"You're disgusting. I would rather destroy you. If it weren't for you agreeing to help us, I would have taken pleasure in watching you disappear for all eternity," Arianna spoke, setting her hands on Angela's forehead and wrapping her fingers around her temples. Iris walked behind Angela and set her hands on the back of her head, spreading her fingers out as well.

Both closing their eyes, they chanted: "Pagidépste to skotádi kai to kakó sto myaló sas. Dimiourgíste énan kósmo trómou gia aftó. Na leípeis tóra méchri argótera."

Removing their hands from Angela, they knew the magic was gone and trapped in the prison of its own choice. Angela was free and able to make her own decisions, thinking only for herself. Arianna knew Angela wasn't going to like it when she found out the only magic she had was locked up. She was back to being a normal human until she called for it.

"Welcome back, Sis." Arianna spoke, smiling along with Iris and Tiana. They didn't need to confirm with Tiana to know Angela was back to normal.

"You're free," Tiana cried, holding Angela tightly; Iris and Arianna joined in.

"Thank you all so much. I'm sorry I have been such a pain in the ass," Angela spoke, issuing a laugh.

"A royal pain, actually," Tiana beamed. "Speaking of royal, we need to go see Alister about everything we learned. He's going to be *so* happy to know that the words you spoke weren't actually your own, and prepare to get Neveah back."

"Can we leave my side out of it for now? I'm not..ready for him to know," Angela spoke. She worried about his reaction, and she wasn't sure if she was ready to forgive him. "I don't want him to stress about me when he has so much more to deal with. We need to train and get prepared for whatever battle we will be up against."

"Angela, you have to tell him. He is losing his mind. I haven't seen him outside of his drakon form since he got back from the trip when you all stopped the darkness."

"Tiana, I will tell him when I am ready. Please understand. I made the evil talk to him. I told it to do whatever it took to make him leave me alone and hate me. It was my doing as much as the magic. I can't take it back yet until I know how to fix it completely. I don't know if I'm ready to fix us either. Whatever it said or did, I'm not ready to have him back on my side. You just don't understand," Angela pleaded. Tears built up in her eyes from the pain of losing Alister.

"Okay, okay. We won't say a word. That's your business. You can handle it however you decide. I'm here for you and love you both. I just hate seeing you or Alister hurt."

"I promise I will. Let me talk to Arik and clean up my mess; let me take care of my responsibility. I will see where we stand and where he and Arianna stand. Then, I can move on."

"You still want him?" Arianna panicked.

"I still want Alister. Not Arik," Angela laughed as soon as she watched her sister's frightened eyes turn to pure relief.

The rest of the girls joined in with the laughter while the three made fun of Arianna and teased her for being so gullible. Arianna needed to tell Arik how she felt about him; she just needed to wait for Angela to say her part first. She didn't want Arik to feel obligated to be with her for the child. She wanted him to stay with her because he loved her as much as she loved him.

* * *

When Alister reached the waterfall the star had mentioned, he could already smell the woman fish laying in wait behind it. He hovered at the entryway of the falls and slowly, without a sound, popped his head through the water, making it land on the back of his neck. Marie sat there in her mermaid form, brushing her hair like she hadn't a care in the world, with her back to him. Alister let a slow steam out of his nostrils, just enough to make her hear and stop in mid-brush.

Like a cat playing with its prey, Alister waited for her to turn and scream, or try to make a run for it. Thinking about how she would react amused him. What he didn't plan for was the brush being thrown over her head and straight at his face, so she could distract him and try to disappear.

Alister caught the brush in his mouth, like the dogs did, catching a stick. When Marie rushed to his left, he jumped right in front of her, making her scream for dear life. Annoying him, he headbutted her and sent her flying through the air, bouncing off the rock wall and landing on the ground. It was then that the screaming stopped—when Marie was knocked unconscious. He walked over to the woman and snorted, before he picked her up with his claws and flew off with her in his grasp, headed for home.

It took all his strength not to chop her into pieces with his talons. His anger grew the more he thought about what she had done. The only thing that could stop him was thoughts of Angela and the times they'd shared while he was in his drakon form. Reminding him of the first day they had met. The anger he'd felt towards her was the same murderous feeling he had now, until he found out for himself who she really was. However, this situation was different. There was nothing controlling the mermaid except her own carelessness for anyone else brought on by her own vengeance for losing her beloved husband. He would lock away the mermaid and she would never see the light of day again.

He flew over the crowd in the middle of Mood Town's square. Already he could hear the people yelling from below in anger: "Sentence her to death!"

Simon had done well listening to Alister's demands. Everyone was surrounding the stage, where he could finally remove the traitor from his list of things to worry about.

Simon was finishing up his ties, securing Rodney to the second pole placed on the right side of the stage, leaving the left for Marie.

Alister landed in the center of the stage, dropping Marie onto the floor instantly, looking at Simon to take care of it and tie her up as well. He couldn't guarantee that he wouldn't accidentally slice her if he had to create the knots himself. Alister then looked out at his people to listen to what they had to say.

Their loud voices continued to cry out:

"She's evil. She deserves to die!"

"Hang her!"

"Light her on fire!"

The same things they'd yelled when he had announced Arianna's freedom. You think they would have anything else to say by now. Of course, he wouldn't be doing any of those things they recommended. His people didn't need to see more death being displayed, even if the woman deserved it. He was happy to hear most of them agree with him, that she was guilty before even hearing the facts. Until he heard the few others who still blamed Arianna.

"It wasn't her! It was that witch that killed our wives and children!"

"She's innocent!"

Alister emitted a roar, silencing the crowd. "My people, I have brought the traitor of my realm. She is guilty of treason and murder of an innocent woman and child. I will let her speak."

Marie was still unconscious when Alister demanded Simon to tie her to the stake. He would pry the confession out of her and regain an understanding with his people when she woke. Simon tied her with the black ropes, beginning with her wrists behind her back, then securing her feet to the pole. While Simon was working on the final bond, Marie slowly stirred awake, shaking her head and body as if attempting to clear the fog from her brain.

"Get away from me, you stupid boy. Untie me this instant! I am *still* your queen," Marie ordered.

"You're no queen of mine. You're a murderer and will be sentenced as such. Say hello to Tarence when you go *straight to Hell*," Simon spat back at her.

Simon moved out of the way so everyone could look at the traitor and Alister could unleash his wrath upon her. Marie looked at the eyes of the crowd upon her. Some showed pure disgust, while others still looked like they thought she was innocent. Turning her head, she looked at Alister with his glowing, primal gaze. When she looked behind him, she spotted Rodney tied to a stake of his own.

"Queen Marie, I sentence you to imprisonment for the rest of your years to think about what you have done. You are a traitor; you are the killer of an innocent woman and her unborn child, and you should have to dwell on that for the rest of your life. Do not try to deny these allegations. We have a witness." Alister walked over to Rodney. Turning, he glared back at Marie once more. "A shining star who states you forced him to contact the devil squid and return with the ink it possessed in order to kill the woman—failing at your own attempts to kill the witch known as Iris who came to the woman's aid. How do you plead?"

* * *

Angela, Arianna, Tiana, and Iris made their way to the front of the stage while Alister was stating his facts. Angela was shorter than the rest of the ladies and couldn't see a thing. She walked more to the right, so she would be behind Alister and in front of the mermaid. When she heard his statement, Angela couldn't help but feel sorry for him having to deal with the hideous woman. She was glad to know he wouldn't be killing her, however. He was bigger than that, and Angela was proud of him for not just burning her at the stake.

"How do you plead?" Alister repeated in his most angry tone. Even Angela hadn't heard that tone before.

She wished he would turn around so he could see her. She wanted to be up there on the stage to hold his large hand and tell him everything was going to be okay. It took all her strength not to take the steps.

"I'm not sorry for the crimes I have committed. I would do it all again until every last thing you ever loved was dead. I'm only sorry I won't get to see them suffer and fall when that thing gets ahold of them. You will *all* suffer and die," Marie's voice was clear. She laughed wickedly after her threat and then spit in His Majesty's face; taunting him to do something he would regret.

Angela could tell Alister was losing his control. His eyes went completely primal, turning black as night, as streams of fire began exiting his nostrils. Angela tried to hurry to him, but she was too slow. She couldn't stop him from making a huge mistake. Alister had killed the woman with his bare claws. Separating her body into multiple parts, blood sprayed out of each section before they scattered across the stage floor.

The sight shocked Angela, whose mouth was hanging open and her face was covered with the dark blood of the mermaid. Most of it had sprayed in her face and was dripping down her skin. She couldn't see anything but the dark red glaze. Angela didn't think she had made a sound, but the sudden turn of Alister's body was a sure sign that she had released a scream.

Whipping the substance and chunks of God only knew what from her face, she could finally see clearly. Looking down at her hands and feet, only to see them covered in blood as well, Angela's shock slowly wore off and allowed her other senses to kick in. The smell was unbearably strong and burning her nose. The taste in her mouth was enough to make her vomit.

Her ears still didn't function; the world still sounded like she was under water. Alister was saying something to her and looking very sorry. But when he tried to reach out and touch her, she saw his talons and jumped back, scared to death, only to hit hard against the edge of the stage, instantly making her throw up. The landing must have knocked the blood out of her ears because she could suddenly hear Alister's voice, along with the crowd's frightful gasps echoing behind her.

Everyone scattered like a herd of horses, running left and right, fearing for their own lives. Leaving Angela on the ground in pain, Alister came down from the stage and offered his claw.

She immediately backed away, crawling across the ground. "No...please! Get away from me. Your eyes are still black. Transition back. Please...Alister. Don't touch me," Angela begged, covering her eyes with her hands because she could no longer crawl without feeling the excruciating pain in her bones.

"We got her, Your Majesty. You should go home and cool off." The sound of Tiana's voice brought calm to the situation.

"Iris will heal her?" Alister spoke with sadness.

"Yes, of course I will." Iris walked up beside Tiana

"I don't know what happened. I'm sorry, Angela. I'm sorry to everyone," Alister said before lifting off and flying away from the frightened eyes of the woman he loved.

Angela could feel the wind from his wings and breathed a sigh of relief that he was gone. She had never seen anyone die before her very eyes. It was awful, and not just because of the blood and horrible smells. The death of someone murdered by another was something your brain would never stop seeing. The image of Alister squeezing the human form of the mermaid would forever be embedded in Angela's memory. She could never again see Alister as anything more than a cold-blooded, killing drakon. That could have been her...if he didn't believe she wasn't Arianna when they'd first met. Or it could have been Arianna if Iris wasn't there to protect her.

Angela now knew what the almighty drakon was capable of, and she never wanted to see it again.

The pain in Angela's back was unbearable. Her adrenaline was wearing off and she could feel every ache. She could tell that the pain was apparent in her eyes when she looked at her sisters' anguished faces. She didn't even have to speak before they blew a powdery substance in her face, putting her to sleep, and placing their hands upon her.

CHAPTER 21

As if making Angela and all of his people completely afraid of him wasn't bad enough, now Alister had to deal with war against his brother, and he was stuck in his drakon form, unable to transition back into a man. He'd already tried to calm himself down on multiple occasions, but nothing worked. His biggest concern this time was perhaps he wouldn't ever be able to get out of his beast form ever again. But whether human or drakon, he still had a kingdom to run, no matter how afraid everyone was of him. Alister needed to plan a meeting with all his royals so they could defeat the Foinix Realm and get Neveah back.

Alister flew over Queen Tiana's castle. She would be the first he would contact for the meeting. Perhaps she and King Dustin could help him with his transitioning issues, too.

Usually, after landing upon the roof of the castle, he would transition; this time, however, he had to make it through the roof access doors in his enormous form. It was more difficult than he had expected. More embarrassing than anything else, he got stuck and had to break the door in order to go through. Helpers to the queen and king heard the commotion, but fled in fear as soon as they saw him.

Apparently, word of what he'd done had traveled fast.

He walked swiftly down the steps and into the throne room, ignoring the fear in everyone's eyes as he kept his composure as best he could. He couldn't blame them. No one had ever seen him be so murderous before. In fact, he had never felt that way except for when he took the life of Tarence under the water, but that was self-defense.

"Queen Tiana," Alister bowed, entering her throne room. Once again, she was alone.

"Alister, dear. How are you?" Tiana spoke, getting up to greet him with a peck on his scaled cheek.

"I'm sure you can guess."

"That's true. I know you're miserable. I'm sorry, Your Majesty."

"I need your wise advice, and we need to set up a meeting. Where is your king?"

"He's already begun ahead of you and is getting the others gathered. He thought it would be better if he approached the other royals, under the circumstances. You must keep your strength, Alister. We are going to need it in the battle to come."

"You're not afraid of me?" He lowered his head with his question, feeling nothing but sadness now. Before, he would have held his head high, having no problem with the fear he ignited in the eyes of others.

"Hah, as if you could scare me." Tiana winked at him. "Your strength is more intense with how long you have been in this form. I'm afraid you will not be getting out of it, Your Majesty."

"What do you mean by that, Tiana?"

"You are no longer human, Alister. You won't be returning to your human body again. I'm sorry," Tiana spoke sadly, answering his question before he could ask.

Alister was quiet, and Tiana had never seen him without words before. The silence was more concerning to her than the primal behavior. It was in a drakon's nature to be aggressive towards those it did not love. The past few years, she had noticed Alister suppressing his nature and becoming tamer, as a ruler and defender of an entire realm. In her opinion, it was important to keep his reputation of being the cold-hearted beast he was before he met Angela. Although, his color wasn't making her any less concerned. She knew he would never hurt her, but she would need to make sure that her kingdom wouldn't be a part of his tantrum, either.

"Take it easy, Alister. If you damage my home, I will kill you myself," she teased. "The witches could help you. Your humanity isn't lost, you just can't transition on your own—that's all I'm saying. Their powers, however, could be the key."

Alister bowed his head and dampened his emotional color to show Tiana he would not be destructive. He still couldn't speak. He didn't know what it would be like to be just his drakon side. How would he be king if he couldn't transition back and forth? The questions racing through his mind were endless.

"You could leave Jenisis and Julia out of the meeting. I know they have enough of their own problems going on," Alister finally spoke.

"Little late for that," Jenisis' voice echoed through the Throne Room. "How are you, dear friend?"

Alister turned to see Jenisis and Julia standing in the doorway. He smiled at his longtime friend and felt warmth fill his heart. He'd already seen Julia when they returned but hadn't had the chance to see the newly married groom.

"Jenisis, it's a pleasure to see you," Alister spoke happily.

"You, too. Seems I have missed some events during my absence. Have you doubled in size, Your Majesty?" Jenisis teased.

"Seems I have." Alister chuckled.

The rest of the nobles arrived during Alister's and Jenisis' heartfelt reunion and remained quiet as they looked on. The animal shifters bowed in the alpha's presence and the King of the Realm. Jenisis smiled at the show of respect.

"How are you taking it? Seems I'm not the only one with problems, King of the Shifters. You are still king, right?" Alister teased, slightly hitting a soft spot with Jenisis.

"I suppose I'm taking it the way any alpha would when they have to step down. I am still king, but now I have an incredibly powerful queen by my side."

"You couldn't have known Julia would become the new alpha when you married her. Any regrets?" Alister asked, thinking of Angela and how he would never be able to marry her now.

"I can hear you both. I hope you know that." Julia walked towards Jenisis and Alister.

"Well, then you can hear me tell Alister I have absolutely no regrets and I would marry you all over again if I could," Jenisis smiled.

"Your Royal Highness. Alpha of all the shapeshifters. I meant no disrespect. I was only joking." Alister bowed with a fun smirk, even if no one else could tell. "Plus, I knew you could hear me."

"You're full of jokes today." She smiled before her face fell. "I still wish you would have taken my advice about Angela. You wouldn't be such a mess if you would have listened to me at the very beginning."

"My dear, maybe you shouldn't poke the drakon when he is already paying for plenty."

"You're right. I'm sorry, Alister. I'm pissed off, too, but I'm sorry for everything that has happened. Right now, we have the major issue of my daughter being held captive by another witch. You can count me in," Julia spoke hastily, like she was ready to rip the witch's head off that had the nerve to cage Neveah.

"It won't concern you, for you are not going."

"The Hell I'm not. That's my daughter you are going to rescue."

"You have other children to think about, not just Neveah. You are not going. Neither of you are. So go," Alister bellowed. "Send back your right-hand man and your strongest warriors. I will lead them into battle."

"Yes, Your Majesty," Jenisis bowed.

"No! This is bullshit. You can't tell me not to help rescue my daughter."

"Yes, I can! And I said go. Now!" Alister roared, making Julia cower slightly but not submit.

Julia snarled back and transformed into her beast side. A glorious shining shimmer of silver fur; the largest wolf form anyone had ever seen. She succeeded in completely throwing Alister off his game. He had never seen Julia in her wolf shift before, and she was definitely a sight to see, but what she was doing was also incredibly dangerous. As history stated, challenging the King of the Realm was a fight to the death. And if Julia struck first, she would sign up for a joust she simply couldn't win.

***

Iris was furious with Izak. He refused to hand over his stash. He claimed he was out, with no way of getting more. So she was taking her aggression out on Arianna and Angela in a practice of defense magic. They set up a large magical circle where they could practice high energy and dangerous magic to defeat the witch in Foinix Realm. Arianna was doing a great job defending herself, but she feared for her child and was holding back. Receiving a painful hit, she guarded her stomach the best she could, but it was no use. She was going to need to stop and tell her sisters she wasn't feeling well.

"What's going on with you?" Iris asked irritably. "You can't fight like that against the evil witch. She will kill you."

"I'm not going with you," Arianna replied, walking out of the ring and towards her home without any further explanation.

She had expected Angela and Iris to follow her. Instead, they continued to attack each other. Arianna could see them out the window of her power room while she held the healing stone in her hand to make the aches and pains go away. What she really wanted was a nap. The little being growing inside her tummy was taking much of her energy, and she couldn't keep up with even basic magic.

Walking to her bed, Arianna laid down, completely prepared for a nap when she saw a bright light suddenly shine through the entry mirror. Looking up, she watched her little niece walk through the glass.

"Leah! Hi, honey. Come here." Arianna motioned her over to the bed.

"Hi, Aunty. How are you feeling?" Leah asked, walking towards the bed and sitting down beside Arianna.

"What do you mean? I'm fine," Arianna said, looking down into Leah's big, brown, all-knowing eyes.

"The baby, of course. How's my little cousin...or is it brother or sister?" Leah asked, rubbing Arianna's belly.

"How did you know, Leah?" Arianna gasped in surprise.

"Don't worry about that. For now, I need you to sneak me into Foinix. If you don't, I will tell my mom and dad that you are carrying my little brother or sister...or cousin. I need to go with you, and I know my mom will never allow it."

"Nice try at blackmail," Arianna said, completely ready to play her game. "I don't know how you knew, but I'm not going to the other realm and putting my child in harm's way. The same way I would never put you in harm's way."

Leah rose from the bed and sat on the floor. She stretched out on her stomach so she could headbutt the floor in anger.

She may be mature for her age and her magical intelligence beyond her years, but she was still a child. Her tantrum, on the other hand, could be dangerous if she got overly dramatic. Arianna thought a magical timeout would teach her beloved niece a lesson. She couldn't help but hope her own child didn't have any strange ticks like little Leah.

Once Leah was done, it was like it never happened, except for the light redness on her forehead.

Returning to the bed, Leah spoke, "Aunt Arianna, I'm sorry. I don't know how to convince everyone if they don't allow me to go. Many of our realm creatures will die. I'm more powerful than any of you know. I have a special power I can't speak to anyone about. Grandmother says if I tell anyone what I know, it will be dangerous for the future. I literally can't speak of it."

"Holy God...you're an eye! We have to get Angela and Iris in here. Now!" Arianna said, standing up and rushing Leah towards the window.

"Angela! Iris! Come quick," she yelled out the window.

They both stopped throwing magic at each other and ran towards the house.

Well, that got their attention. About time they showed any concern for me.

"Promise me you won't say a thing about the baby. Promise," Arianna pleaded.

"I promise," Leah replied, rolling her eyes.

"Thank you. I'll tell everyone soon."

"Sure you will." Leah stated knowingly.

"I will...right?" Arianna asked, now that she knew Leah was an eye for the future.

"I can't answer either way. Sorry," Leah answered.

The fast-paced steps raced to Arianna's power room.

Barging through the door, it surprised both Angela and Iris when they looked at Arianna and Leah and saw that they were both...just fine.

"What's wrong?" Iris asked.

"Is the magic still present? Call it back in your mind, Angela," Arianna said. She knew if the magic found out Leah was an eye witch, it would stop at nothing to get it.

"EPISTROFI!"

"What's going on now?" Iris asked.

"Leah is an eye witch," Arianna spoke excitedly.

"No way." Iris said in complete shock.

* * *

Julia paced in front of Alister. The room went completely still. No one moved when they saw Julia transition into a breathtakingly beautiful wolf. Alister couldn't help but be in awe of her appearance. He could only hope that she would stop. Breaking royalty rules was not something he wanted to deal with, and he would be breaking the rules if he allowed Julia to live after challenging him. Not only that, it would show his weakness. But then again, if he showed mercy to her after what he had uncontrollably done to the guilty mermaid, it might prove that he hadn't completely lost his mind.

The drakon side wanted to have the fight, urging him to take the challenge. But Alister stood his ground. The side of him that was at all human, refused to move. It reminded the drakon that this woman was Angela's mother, and if he killed her, not only would the love of his life want to kill him, he would also lose all of his people and his kingdom. Julia had more power in the entire kingdom than Alister did, and he knew that. All he could think to do was bow his head in respect.

"I bow to thee. Not as the King of the Realm, but as an equal. I refuse your challenge, Julia. I will not fight you,"

Alister spoke loud and clear for all to hear.

Julia stopped snarling and transitioned back into her human form. Her eyes were full of tears and fear consumed her of what could happen to her oldest daughter. She sat on the floor and cried. Alister curled up by her side and tried to comfort her.

Her strength surfaced again, just enough to threaten His Majesty. "You better bring her back to me alive. If you don't, I *will* challenge you, giving you no choice but to fight me until I kill you. Do you understand?"

"I understand. I will bring her back or die trying. You have my word." Alister lifted his head and looked Julia directly in the eyes to assure her he was serious.

Jenisis walked over to Julia to offer his hand in help. Julia got up and took her husband's hand before nodding to His Majesty and turning away, leaving him with the rest of their pack and strongest warriors.

Alister watched Julia walk away; he witnessed the amount of respect she'd earned from her challenge when everyone parted to create an aisle for Julia to walk down. A secret smile crossed his face. Grateful his beast loved Angela as much as he did and knew what was at stake. The drakon knew he was beat as soon as Julia transitioned. He wouldn't harm any member of that family. One day he would be a part of it, and he would not burn any bridges that prevented him from getting that chance. Even though he had already set a torch to quite a few, he still had a slight chance to rebuild the best he could.

Angela had been coming onto the stage for a reason. Whether it was to stop him or comfort him before he had taken the life of that traitor, he didn't know. All he knew was she still cared and wanted to talk to him. If he could get close to her and communicate, maybe she could free him from the beast he had become. Perhaps Angela was the key to it all.

* * *

Leah was confused and completely lost in thought by what Aunt Arianna said. *What was an eye?* Obviously, it was something to do with seeing. In her case, a visual of the future was exciting if she could ever speak of anything helpful. All she could do was seal an opportunity to be transferred to the Foinix realm with the rest of the army. She didn't even acknowledge the others' arrival before she spoke.

"I need to come with you to Foinix. I can't explain why, but if I'm not there, the outcome of the war will be different. Mom, please take me with you. I'm old enough. I can help," Leah begged.

"We can handle the one witch. The three of us will be unbeatable if Arianna would quit being so safe. Why are you so afraid of being hit?"

"We aren't talking about me right now. Leah needs to be in Foinix to help. If she is an eye for the future and we mess up the outcome, we might as well be killing our people on purpose," Arianna snapped back.

Leah looked up at her aunt and smiled. She knew what was at stake for the lives of everyone. Excitement ran through Leah when she noticed her mother's look of agreement. If she could convince her mother that she would stay out of harm's way, and only help if she was absolutely needed, she knew now that her mother would agree.

"What is an eye?" Angela asked.

"It's where the person can see glimpses of the future, but it's forbidden to speak of it. They could only help to make the outcome stay the way it was supposed to be. If Leah saw herself in the other realm, she must go," Iris informed her.

Leah could tell that Angela was caving. It was two aunts against one mother who didn't know the ways of magic as much as the others. Leah couldn't come up with another reason to convince her mother to allow her to go.

"I guess you *have* to be there. If it is crucial, you must be there. I don't see how I can stop it. However, you are to stay as far away from the action as possible. Do you hear me?" Angela spoke sternly.

"Yes. Of course, Mother," Leah bowed her head.

"If I find out that you are lying about being this eye thing just because you want adventure, I will have your magic removed from your body faster than you can apologize."

"I promise, Mom, I'm not lying."

"Good. Looks like you two have another defense trainee," Arianna spoke, patting Leah on the back.

"Don't you mean all of us?" Iris asked. "We *all* need to practice, even you."

"I don't need to be practicing because I'm not going. I can't risk my health."

"That's ridiculous! We're all risking our lives and you're the one who got us into this mess to begin with. You are going," Angela demanded, ready to lose it on Arianna.

"It's not that I'm afraid of risking my life. It's…it's another life I am concerned about," Arianna spoke, holding her stomach.

"Oh my God, Sister! Are you pregnant?" Iris beamed.

Leah was smiling at all the tension in the room. Emotions were still a fascination she couldn't understand completely. Even on Earth, a tense situation always intrigued Leah. She could never understand why. Watching her brother throw a fit and start crying always made her have an uncommon response. It was fascinating when he would cry and she tried to knock him over so he would continue, even though she knew it was wrong to poke him when he was already emotional.

While Leah's family was talking over who was going to Foinix and who was staying, Leah could already sense that Arianna was going to announce her pregnancy. What was even better was someone else would be present for the announcement. Leah's father was walking through the glass mirror like she had done prior to talking to Arianna. Her aunt was confessing at the perfect moment.

"Yes, I'm pregnant with a human child. I'm sorry, Angela. It is Arik's child. We didn't mean to. It just happened. I'm so sorry," Arianna spoke with her head down while twiddling her fingers nervously.

A sly smile appeared on Leah's face when she watched her father's expression go from shock to illness. He had heard every word and was handling it like any man who had impregnated their wife's sister, creating a mess of a family. Leah looked from Arik to Arianna just in time to watch her mimic his response.

"Why didn't you say anything?" Arik spoke, finding his words once he gained eye contact with Arianna.

"Surprise," she replied, like they were at some party he didn't know she was throwing for him.

Arik didn't have time to respond; Angela burst into an uncontrollable laughing fit. She couldn't stop. Every time she tried to speak, she would snort and laugh even harder. The laugh was not out of amusement, however. Leah knew that her mother would laugh at situations that seemed like they couldn't get any worse, and she was expecting that when the rain started, it would pour down. Not everyone knew that about Angela. The laughter always came before the freaking out moment.

"What luck I have. Nothing should surprise me. Just look how things have been turning out for all of us," Angela spoke when she caught her breath. "It's ridiculously ironic."

Arik pulled Arianna behind him in case Angela used her magic and did something she was going to regret. Everyone in the room was on edge when Angela's laughter stopped, ready for anything that she might do.

"I told you before, Sister. I don't care what the two of you have done with each other. What I do care about is how the Hell you could keep that a secret for so long. Alister and I could have avoided the entire split up, heartbreak, torture, and more! He broke my heart because he thought I would go back to Arik. Turns out, he had nothing to worry about to begin with."

She took a deep breath and balled her hands into fists. "You both enjoy each other. Happily fucking ever after to you both. God knows, you have ruined mine because of your secret. I will never forgive you for this."

Angela walked towards the couple. Arik stepped aside, keeping Arianna blocked behind him, protecting her from what may erupt.

But Angela didn't stop or even look back at the traitors. She just opened the door and slammed it shut behind her, leaving them all to wonder and feel terrible for the parts they played in ruining Angela's shot at having her own fairytale come true.

CHAPTER 22

Sylvia was next to the ocean, avoiding the dock in case she ended up running into Simon. She was trying to avoid him as much as possible so they could move on with their lives. Training her voice on the water creatures looked to be a success; stars, fish, and other mermaids volunteered to be the testing subjects for her voice magic. Even though Sylvia and Simon weren't together anymore, some of the creatures still felt like they had no choice to partake, seeing as that their own king used to be with her. Of course, fear of Simon was the least of their worries. Land and water shifters were more afraid of Alister; they knew if they didn't cooperate with Sylvia, they would have to deal with him.

She sang to all the creatures in the water with simple requests, such as doing tricks, like jumping out of the water doing flips in the air, or going to the bottom of the ocean to retrieve a shell, rock, or pretty stone and bring it back to her. The magic of her voice had become a very useful weapon in mind power, and by testing and honing the skill, she made it so they wouldn't remember what she had asked them to do. Sylvia already felt different from everyone else. She didn't want the water creatures to think she was odd, too.

Another power she practiced on the creatures was transition control, by using a pitch in her voice, only comparable to a dog whistle that only a canine could hear. In her case, it was a whistle that only the water shifters could hear, forcing them to shift into their human form. Once Sylvia realized it caused them physical pain, however, she stopped and swore to use her pitch voice *only* on her enemies. By halting the process, she let the water shifters relax and moved on to the land shifters.

Walking away from the beach leading into the photogenic ocean, she made her way to the field where everyone else was training to go to Foinix Realm. Sylvia looked at all the land creatures and found herself annoyed. She thought, *Why couldn't I have just been a cool shifting creature?* She walked around to find which land creature she would practice on. Once she made it to the center of the field, she just needed to take her pick. Choosing the bears to begin her hypnotizing magic on, she concentrated on the thoughts in their minds and then sent her voice soaring through the air.

"Beautiful bears, bring me a stick from the forest," Sylvia sang.

Some of them heard her and turned around to just smile. Others who heard her moved to do exactly what she'd ordered but stopped halfway to the task, shook their heads, and looked back at her in complete annoyance.

What had she done wrong? Sylvia was confused as to why her powers were failing on the land creatures but worked perfectly on the water shifters. Maybe her voice was hoarse from all the practice on the others. She was standing their mulling it over when she heard sudden footsteps coming up behind her. Her heart sped up in her chest; Sylvia knew who it was before she even turned around.

"You are a siren witch. Don't you need water to activate your power?" Simon asked stepping beside her with a smile on his face that still made her melt inside. "I can help."

Simon had his own power with water. He could produce water from his hands just by imagining the water from his ocean. If he consumed a land creature in water, Sylvia's magic could work. Simon observed their surroundings and stopped on the herd of horses. Lifting his hands, he pointed his fingers at them, drenching them all in water. "Try now."

Sylvia stepped forward while Simon stepped aside. Just knowing Simon was there by her...helping her...warmed her heart while she sang her lullaby.

"Rock-a-bye baby on the tree top...," Sylvia sang her childhood lullaby, putting Atticus and his herd to sleep, turning them human so that now their physical forms lay comfortably on the ground.

"I did it! I did it!" Sylvia screamed excitedly, jumping up and down. Turning to Simon, ready to leap into his arms, she awkwardly remembered that they weren't together anymore; or even friends, for that matter, and stepped away. "Sorry, I... I forgot."

"It's okay. I don't mind," Simon said, smiling from ear to ear. He'd gotten excited for her accomplishment, too, and had almost grabbed her and pulled her into a tight embrace.

He was still smiling, with his eyes locked on hers, before he noticed the very large drakon glaring right at him who was now standing just a short distance away. His Majesty was walking angrily towards him, and Simon didn't even know what he had done wrong.

* * *

Zack hadn't been able to transition into a wolf for weeks. He'd confused Jenisis, who was trying to train Zack and figure out if he was one of the pack members. Zack could tell his grandfather wasn't convinced that he was a shape-shifting wolf. He was being too gentle with Zack; if Jenisis really thought Zack was a wolf, he would be training him harder. Even the pups got trained more aggressively.

"This is useless. You're not a wolf. It should come naturally for you to shift into your form. Let's take a break, son. You look exhausted."

"Thank you, Grandfather," Zack spoke, pretending to be worn out before exiting the rink and joining his excited cousin.

"That was great. I don't think you were trying, though. Why didn't you tell him you can stop a shifter literally in their tracks?" Liam boasted.

"That was a fluke, Liam. Something to do with Zinnia. Not me. Remember? I tried it and turned into a wolf instead?"

"Yes, but...." Liam couldn't even finish his sentence.

"But nothing. You're just a kid. You don't know what you're talking about. You're a wannabe. Can you even see anything different when you look at me?"

"No, I can't. It just means your abilities are undetectable, making them so much cooler. You're wasting it. But how would I know anything about a special power when I actually have mine under control? You saying I'm wasting your time? You're wasting *my* time, man. If you are too afraid to face your abilities head on, you're just a coward and letting everyone down. Goodbye," Liam defended himself strongly, stomped off, and ran away from Zack before he could reply.

"Come on, man! I'm sorry, don't go. I'm just frustrated. I didn't mean it," Zack yelled, hoping Liam heard him and came back. He had always been there for him and supported him when he was afraid.

Zack did try to apologize because Liam was right. He had

been holding back because he was afraid. Turning into a wolf and being stuck in hibernation mode for days was scary. What if he was stuck in a deep sleep forever the next time he used his powers? Zack had to remind himself constantly that the risk was worth it; it was all to get his mother back from their rescue mission, and he needed to be strong for her.

"You ready to try again, son?" Jenisis asked, breaking through Zack's train of thought. "We could try using your other senses. Smell or hearing, instead of physical strength, if you would like?"

"Can we get right to the base? You can shift into your wolf, and I will try to copy you. Trying to force my strength with wrestling obviously isn't working. I don't see or even feel any of my other senses working until I can feel that the inner animal. Does that make sense?"

"Sure, at this point I'll try anything to help you. What we know is that you *are* something and I'm glad to help you find out what." Jenisis smiled. Patting Zack on the shoulder, he led him back to the rink.

Zack thought about stopping Jenisis from shifting, but he still doubted that he had that ability. He still couldn't even admit to himself that all the power had come from him when he'd helped the owl girl.

Jenisis and Zack entered the rink. Seconds later, Zack got distracted by the sound of two fighters snarling and hissing. He turned to watch the large cats in the other rink practicing and pouncing on each other. Zack could only imagine how exciting it would be to turn into a great, big, black jaguar like the two of them, and join in with their fun.

Turning back to Jenisis, Zack's heart leapt into his throat. His grandfather had already shifted into a wolf and was now running directly at Zack, forcing him to think quickly. The images of the black cats popped back into his mind and before Jenisis could connect, Zack pounced in the air and landed right on top of his grandfather before he felt his entire body transition into the grand feline creature.

"Incredible, Zack!. You're a jaguar!" Jenisis spoke loud and proud while looking up into his eyes. Then Jenisis observed their surroundings to see if there were any jaguars nearby. Zack must have copied his shift from them. The black cats were already looking in their direction when Jenisis waved one over, while still pinned under Zack.

Once Zack got off Jenisis, he sat down and held his paws up to observe his new body. Extending his claws and retracting them was the coolest thing ever. He got up and tried to look between his four legs at his tail. Swaying it left and right, he was excited to learn that he had control over every movement of his body, like it was completely natural. He wondered if he could communicate this time.

"Can you understand me when I talk?" Zack asked through his new whisker-covered mouth, taking a seat again.

"Loud and clear, son," Jenisis laughed.

"He doesn't smell like one of us. What is he?" One man, who had transformed from the jaguar, asked Jenisis.

"This is my grandson. Zack. He can turn into a wolf *and* a cat, apparently."

"How is that possible, King Jenisis?"

"I'm guessing he has a type of magical power running through his veins that makes that question one only a witch could answer."

The man's eyes darted back to Zack. "How are you feeling, dear boy?"

"I feel good. Just like the last time, but this time I'm staying calm and not freaking out. I'm cool, but could you find Liam for me? I want him to see this."

"You're the fastest creature on four paws, aside from our king, of course. You can find him yourself. Jump over the rink and be on your way." The man told Zack, stepping out of his path.

Zack got up from his sitting position and ran towards the

bars; jumping, he cleared both the barricade and the man standing next to it. Landing safely on his paws, he took off at full speed in the direction Liam was running. It all felt like natural instincts, the speed and the enhanced eyesight. He could see for miles, and tapped into his honed hearing, where he swore he could hear the ocean and his sister's beautiful singing voice. Zack was sure that when he reached Liam he would be excited for him, and accept his apology for being a jerk.

"Follow my grandson and I will meet you later. He's headed toward the battle training field," Jenisis ordered.

"Yes, Your Majesty."

* * *

Sweet Leah was gossiping to her big sister about the breakup between Sylvia and Simon. How their sibling had cried because Simon kept rejecting her, yet now the two of them were awkwardly working together. She had been unaware that Alister was listening to every word she spoke. Instantly becoming enraged with the boy for breaking his promise that he would never hurt Sylvia, even emotionally.

A king is always true to his word, and Alister had told Simon that if he ever caused Sylvia pain, he would come for him. Spotting Simon, he could already tell the boy was afraid even though it was all for fun, though he would scare him even further by showing him an angry face and build up the anticipation.

Something in Alister's mind switched, though. His amusing tactic to put the fear of life into Simon was turning to actually threatening the boy's life. Genuine anger built up in Alister as he rushed toward Simon. Reaching him, he lifted him up off the ground with his sharp talons.

"I told you what would happen if you ever hurt Sylvia, did I not?" Alister bellowed, looking into Simon's terrified eyes.

The boy went speechless. Alister suddenly heard a voice yell back at him that wasn't Simon's.

"No! We *had* a fight and it was *my* fault. I'm the one who broke it off with Simon. Please Alister, don't hurt him!" Sylvia begged, pulling on Alister's neck.

Alister removed his eyes from Simon, who was struggling in his grasp, and darted his gaze upon Sylvia's frightened eyes.

"Alister, my mother's loss brought me emotionally down and I mistakenly ended our relationship. I still love him. Please don't kill him."

"I love her, too, Your Majesty. Nothing has changed," Simon found his words.

Alister's drakon side relaxed, although people looking in from the outside couldn't tell any difference. He was still determined to make the couple get back together, even if he had to force the unity and have the two marry this instant.

"You will still marry. That is an order, not a request."

"Absolutely," both Simon and Sylvia spoke in unison.

Alister lowered the boy and let him go. He looked at Simon's scratches and cuts, realizing how close he'd come to chopping the boy into pieces. Meddling in others' love lives wasn't a situation Alister had ever got involved in, yet now he'd almost killed a boy over it. It seemed he couldn't even be playfully mad without going full-on primal and losing more of his human side every day.

Sylvia covered herself over Simon, comforting him so Alister couldn't hurt him again. Simon slowly stood up and, once on his feet, tried to regain his posture and dignity by showing Sylvia he was strong, but still allowing her closeness.

"I'm sorry, Simon. I'm not myself. I hope you can forgive me." Alister bowed before flying away. Alister never meant to create such a huge crowd of his people or have them all eyeball him like he was a monster. He watched as the people surrounded Simon to see if he had been seriously injured.

Liam joined his sisters and Basil at Simon's side to see if

he was okay like the rest of the crowd who had been training. After Liam left Zack, he went straight to the field to join his siblings. He was worried about Zack, but they needed their space. He hadn't expected the field to be even more dramatic than Zack's attitude, though.

"My uncle has a lot going on. He hasn't been in his human form since we came back from the encounter with the darkness. I'm sorry you ended up in his clutches," Basil apologized when they reached Simon.

"I'm not sorry. Remind me to thank him later," he spoke, looking down at Sylvia still clinging to him like she was holding on to dear life.

Everyone relaxed once they saw Simon's joyful reaction. If it weren't for Alister, Simon and Sylvia would have still been awkward by normal standards. They had no choice but to marry now, and Simon couldn't express how happy he was about that as he returned Sylvia's affection.

"I can heal your wounds. I saw everything," Iris spoke, walking in front of everyone to reach Simon with her healing crystals.

"I will heal fine, but I'm grateful for your service, Iris."

She worked on his deepest cuts, running the crystal over the top of each one—five on each side of his body were deeper than the retreating scratches Alister had made through his clothing—only stopping at the sudden sound of an enormous cat's roar.

Sylvia looked up for the first time since everything had begun. The big, black cat had its eyes trained directly on Liam. It was ready to pounce, so Sylvia had to think quickly.

"No, no, turn back to your rightful form," she sang loud, in her hypnotizing voice.

No one had a clue it was Zack within the black jaguar's body. So, when he turned into his human form and landed, rolling onto Liam, both boys began laughing hard while grumbling from the slight pain felt when they connected.

"Hey, no fair, Sis," Zack whined. "Surprise! It's me. I'm sorry, Liam, for being so mean to you earlier."

Liam laughed at Zack. He was also very proud of him for getting over his fears. He knew it was him coming and saw how happy he was when he attempted to playfully pounce on Liam.

"So cool! I knew it was you the whole time. I saw you running through the trees," Liam informed.

"You could see me then?" Zack asked.

"Yep. Even the funny grin on your face as you ran. You looked free and happy."

Zack was still grinning when he looked at Sylvia. "Thanks again, Sis. It was really hard to turn, you know?" He teased.

"How was *I* supposed to know? I was protecting Liam. I didn't know that beautiful creature would turn out to be my silly brother." Sylvia stood, messing up Zack's hair.

While the others were gossiping about Zack and his exciting experience of turning into a wolf and now a jaguar, Iris walked away from the group to observe from afar and let the kids enjoy their glory. She was smiling in a daydream kind of way while she listened to everyone ask Zack to try other creatures, wanting him to turn into every species they could think of.

Iris was still smiling when Jenisis joined her quietly, looking at the young boy before he spoke, "What *is* he, Iris?"

"He's a mirror shifter, and if he can control his abilities by the time we start the war against the Foinix Realm, he will be our savior and it will be over before it even begins," Iris answered, still smiling. Her concern for anyone's future, now that she knew exactly what Zack was, had lessened tremendously. What a rarity the Michelson family were turning out to be.

CHAPTER 23

Now that Arianna's secret was out in the open, the next thing to do was tell Alister. She knew the way Angela had reacted was only a small fraction compared to how Alister was going to respond. Arianna just knew he would lose it and possibly murder her for keeping the secret. He would take it as her ruining his and Angela's life together. She did tell him before that Angela and Arik were over, but he chose not to listen because she couldn't explain her connection with Arik yet.

"Are you okay? You look stressed," Arik asked, turning on his side and propping his head on his elbow to look at her before checking her forehead for any sign of a temperature with the palm of his other hand.

"Just lack of sleep," she lied. "We really need to do something about that snoring of yours, though, or I might just smother you with my pillow," Arianna threatened, but it was hard to look serious when he was so close and rubbing her belly.

"Do you think it's a boy or a girl?" Arik asked, without offering a reply to her comment.

"I don't know. I could use magic to find out, though." She smiled at him.

"No magic! I thought just by being a witch, you could automatically tell. We could wait until it's born," Arik suggested, with an expression of concern on his face.

"The baby is human, like you. I meant I could use urine or blood and test it with magic to find out if our baby is a boy or girl. I wouldn't be using magic on myself," Arianna said, rolling her eyes even though she loved how concerned he was for her and their unborn child's wellbeing.

Arik handled the news better than she had expected. While she was looking longingly into his eyes, she could read how protective he was towards her. The refusing to leave her alone and banning her from using any magic while carrying their child was beyond irritating. She didn't mind the need to take care of her, but the constant barrage about every little thing she did was making her truly want to suffocate him.

Arianna got out of bed to sit in front of her vanity. She needed to prepare herself both mentally and physically for her confession to Alister about what she had been hiding this entire time. She would be bringing along her sisters and as many witnesses she could in case he had a murderous reaction to the news.

Rising, she walked to her long, standing mirror and turned to the left and then to the right, running her hands down her growing belly. Arianna thought of the perfect maternity clothing she could create with just the snap of her fingers. Lifting her right hand above her head she was ready to do just that, but before she could even get a snap in, Arik's barking voice stopped her.

"Don't you dare!" he demanded. "No magic. You will have to dress like the rest of us for now."

"How do you expect me to do that when none of my clothes fit?" She glared at him.

"Unless you want me to go and see Alister in this, I suggest you let me do this small amount of magic to get dressed for the day."

Arianna was wearing a lavender silk nightgown that barely made it past her buttocks. Arik looked at her up and down, like eye candy, giving her his seductive grin before shaking his head to clear the images. She found his response most amusing and silently laughed.

"As intriguing as that would be, I don't think that's going to work. We will have to go see Iris and see if she can help. If her and Izak have made up yet and she's in a helpful mood," Arik suggested, pointing at the mirror that made it feel like they were in the room next door.

"Fine," Arianna grumbled, not wanting to start a fight that she wouldn't win. "Let's go then."

"Wait a minute," Arik said. Getting off the bed, he grabbed her long robe thrown over the side of the bedframe, reached her, and covered her with it. Treating her like a child, he wrapped it around her and tied a knot in the front.

Arianna pouted and stood still until he was standing above her where she could give him a critical stare. "Thanks. Can we go now?"

"Of course," Arik replied to her sarcastic tone with a smile, showing off his dimpled cheeks like he didn't care or even hear her annoyance.

The smile was more enticing to Arianna now that she was pregnant. Before, she felt like she had control over her emotions. *Stupid hormones*, she thought to herself before smiling at the thought that he probably wouldn't even touch her because he thought it was dangerous...or something silly along those lines. His gaze, however, told her a whole different story while they stood in front of the mirror not moving, just staring longingly into each other's eyes.

* * *

Izak was done going through withdrawal and more reasonable than he had been, substituting wine for the drugs. But Iris had refused to help him this time, no matter how much she wanted to, because she thought he needed to learn his lesson and take the consequences for his actions. Iris wasn't naïve, she knew he was lying when she told him to hand over his stash and he told her he was out. They needed to talk and either fix their relationship, or cut the ties and leave it behind. She really didn't want to leave him, but if he continued to be dishonest with her, she wouldn't have any other choice. The only thing holding her back from chastising him was her own secrets that she was keeping from him and the rest of her family.

Today was the day to communicate with Izak. She walked out of the guest room in Julia's home and down the hall to her and Izak's bedroom. Iris took a deep breath before knocking on the door.

"Izak, are you awake?" She spoke loudly in case he was sleeping.

"Yeah," Izak grumbled. "You can come in."

Apparently, Izak didn't think before he invited her into his room. Lifting his head from the pillow, he looked around the space covered in dirty clothes; wine bottles adorned every surface, along with cigarettes in the ashtray in front of the windowsill. If that wasn't enough of an embarrassment, the odor in the room could knock out anyone who had a normal sense of smell.

"On second thought...I'll be right out," he said, rolling over and doing a sit-up, before standing and walking towards the door. "What's up? Do you need something?"

When Izak cracked the door open and looked at Iris's face,

he noticed the dark circles around her eyes showing him she hadn't slept much in days. He knew she was working hard every day to empower herself even more than she already was. Izak wanted to embrace her in his arms and comfort her this time. But the image of her slapping him across the face when he'd last tried made him keep his feet glued to the floor. She wouldn't be ready for that, and he knew it.

"Do you want breakfast?" She asked awkwardly, moving her feet from side to side. "We could talk?"

"I would like that very much. Just let me freshen up first and I'll meet you in the kitchen," he spoke, smiling in hopes that she would forgive him. Offering to make him food was a promising sign, unless her intention was to poison him.. then, not so much.

"Yeah! Okay. I'll see you soon then." She smiled back, flashing her perfect white teeth.

Izak stood still grinning like a fool. He could get lost in her eyes for days and never want to escape. They stood staring at each other in the doorway, like they were a new crushing couple that didn't want to leave the other alone for a second. He rolled his eyes at Angela's sudden interruption, killing the mood.

"There you are, Iris. I have an idea," Angela spoke hesitantly.

Izak shut the door and leaned his back flat against it, He had no intention of eavesdropping, but couldn't help it when they chose to continue their conversation right outside his door. He was grateful for another chance and hoped his sister didn't have anything stressful to talk about with Iris. Iris had done well with making him clean up this time, and every cramp and strain of his muscles would all be worth it if he could hold her once more. The alcohol helped very little in his recovery; the potency and percentage were nothing compared to liquor on Earth. He had to consume three times as more than he would on Earth to feel even slightly numb to the effects of the physical withdrawal.

"What's your idea, Angela?" Iris asked.

"You know that devil squid ink that made you sick?"

"Yes. It'd almost killed me because I'm a witch, and being so close to the poison seeping in the air from that poor woman was made for the taking of magic and life. What about it?"

"Well.. technically, I'm not a witch, right? I just have magic that Arianna transferred into me, none of my own."

"Get to the point, Angela."

"Okay, I could harness the ink and transfer it into the evil witch on Foinix Realm. It would kill her, or at least weaken her so the rest of you could finish her off."

"No freaking way! That poison is too dangerous and unpredictable. We don't know how it would affect you, and I'm not willing to jeopardize your life to find out. You still are of witch's blood. Do you have a death wish?"

Izak was still listening—with his ear now pressed against the door, about to open it—when he heard what Angela said. Luckily for Iris's wise reply, he was able to refrain from throwing the door aside and yelling at his little sister. If another one of his sisters got hurt, kidnapped, or disappeared, he wouldn't be able to handle it.

"No, I don't have a death wish, but this magic is not going to participate in killing its own host. As soon as I let it out, it will realize what's going on and freeze up on me. How the Hell do you presume we win this war without another back up?"

"Fine, then. Run it by Alister and find out what he has to say about it. It's the King's decision on what further actions we're allowed to take," Iris spoke, taking the answer out of her hands.

"This is bullshit! He will never let me do that." Angela cursed, before stomping back down the hallway and slamming a door behind her.

Iris shook her head at the tirade. Angela may not be Izak's biological sister, but she sure had a temper like him.

Once Izak heard Iris in the kitchen preparing breakfast, he abandoned the door to get himself groomed before he was in her presence. Optimistic that his foolish sister hadn't messed things up for him and Iris.

Iris was mixing eggs and milk in a bowl while the sausage cooked, thinking about what Angela had said. It upset her, mostly, because she knew Angela was right. Being careful not to light the kitchen on fire or burn the food because of her emotions, she moved from the eggs to chopping up green peppers, onions, mushrooms, and spinach, throwing them in the egg mixture and tossing it into the pan with the sausage. Cooking always calmed her down when she was stressed.

Angela's plan was brilliant, and if it worked to their advantage, that other witch wouldn't stand a chance. If it backfired, however, and poisoned Angela, it would kill her quickly, and Iris would never be able to live with herself. Of course, she *could* create a pendant using Neveah's family crystals with all the ingredients to keep her safe, such as maximizing the strength of a labradorite crystal by combining rose quartz with it. The magic that Angela harnessed would never allow her to destroy its home; Angela was right about that. But even if that was the case, Angela would be as good as dead either way.

"Smells fantastic in here," Izak spoke, making Iris jump when she was stirring the pot of ingredients to make her egg scramble.

She turned around quickly, thankful for the sudden distraction from her own thoughts. Izak made all her concerns and worries go away and instantly they were put on the backburner when she laid her eyes on him. He was so handsome in his button-up green shirt, with his hair smoothly combed. Knowing how much he hated combing his hair, Iris knew this was an extra attempt made just for her.

"Perfect timing. Just finishing up," Iris told him before turning back around to the food, mentally reminding herself not to forgive him right away. She needed him to realize everything he'd put her through, and feel how much he'd hurt her and jeopardized their future as a couple.

"Let me take over. Sit and tell me what's bothering you. What is it you would like to talk about? I'm all ears."

Iris turned around again and bumped heads with Izak and they burst out laughing.

"Sorry," Iris spoke, still giggling at the goofy display.

"Nope, my fault. I snuck up on you. I was too close, but you smell great," he said.

"Thank you," Iris took the compliment and walked towards the kitchen table, allowing him to wait on her. She watched while he added the scramble to the plates and pressed oranges for juice. He then proceeded to walk to her, with the plate and glass in his hands, placing them in front of her.

"The fruit is perfect and has that smell of pure goodness," Iris told Izak, while he walked back over to the counter to retrieve his own plate of food.

Izak laughed. "I'm glad it meets your expertise," he said, before returning to the table and sitting down to eat.

Both ate in silence, as if neither was ready to be the first to start up the conversation that could perhaps save their relationship. When they finally spoke, it was in unison.

"I just want to say…"

They exchanged smiles for talking over one another. Usually they would jinx each other and be more playful, but this time they needed to have a serious conversation.

"You first," Izak urged. "You came to me, so I know you want to say something."

"Actually," Iris paused, "I want to hear what you were going to say, please."

"Okay." He took a deep breath. "I wanted to tell you how sorry I am. I had no right, treating you with so much disrespect. There is no excuse for my actions. I just want you to know that I have learned my lesson and promise I won't fuck up this time. Please give me another chance. I won't be one of those cowards who hurt their woman, apologizing and then doing it all over again the next night. I *refuse* to follow in my father's footsteps and be all talk. I will make a change for myself and *our* family."

"You haven't mentioned your father in years. I didn't know he was like that." Iris looked down in sadness.

"I know if I continue down the road I'm on, I will become abusive, and I refuse to be anything like him. Drugs and alcohol.. I'm done with them both if I want *any* kind of life for us."

"You're not that bad. I know you would never lay a hand on me. You're not your father, Izak. You just throw a fit like a child sometimes," Iris teased, trying to lighten up the conversation.

"Thanks for that," Izak laughed.

"Thank you for opening up more to me. I know it's not easy for you. But there's just one thing you have to remember," she leaned forward, whispering.

"What's that," Izak inched forward, as well.

"You never piss off a witch," she answered, flirting with him.

"Duly noted," he added, closing the gap quickly between their lips.

* * *

"It's in my blood, Arik. What do you want me to do.. drain my blood of all magic?" Arianna's sarcastic tone interrupted the couple reuniting in the kitchen.

"No, of course not. But magic is exhausting, and I won't have you risking our child's life," Arik barked in response to Arianna's anger.

Iris rolled her eyes at the loud voices of the new couple joining them who were already arguing about something that

Iris could agree with Arik on. Arianna had already lost one child to magic, she didn't want her to lose another.

"And just like that, the drama has returned to our lives," Iris smirked.

"Her and Angela are definitely sisters," Izak laughed, still looking at Iris.

"What's going on in here? Something smells good," Arik asked, walking into the kitchen and looking around for the obviously scrumptious meal.

"Sorry, Sis. I tried to stop him. He just has this ridiculous need to poke his nose in everyone else's business."

"He's not the only one," Iris stated, looking at Arianna.

"Ha, ha, very funny. He won't even let me get dressed. He believes *any* magic could hurt the baby," Arianna mocked.

"He's right about that. Any magic *could* be harmful to the baby. Don't want a repeat of last time," Iris spoke in a very serious tone.

"That won't happen. I don't have the dark magic anymore, but I need something to wear," Arianna said, mixing her whining and complaining together in her own special recipe.

"Of course, you do." Iris snapped her fingers and, in the blink of an eye, Arianna was dressed in a long skirt matched with a loose fitting, pink blouse.

Arianna looked in the mirror at herself with disgust.

Iris couldn't help but laugh because the choice of wardrobe wasn't anything Arianna would ever be caught dead wearing. When she turned to look at her with a "What the Hell is this?" look on her face, Iris spoke, "I know it's not anything you would normally wear, but you look innocent in it, and we need to meet Alister."

"Because looking like an innocent church girl is going to make him *not* want to murder me when I tell him I have completely ruined his and Angela's happy ever after? That *I* could have saved him from all the personal heartache that got him stuck in his drakon form? Maybe I'll start with the fact that by carrying Arik's child, he never has to worry about Angela going back to him. 'You're welcome, Alister. Have a nice life. Bye.'" Arianna dramatized how the encounter was sure to play out.

"I wouldn't be so direct, but if that works for you, go for it," Iris delivered in her equally sarcastic tone.

Arianna stuck her tongue out at Iris. "Good thing Alister gave us direct access to his castle through the mirror. That long ride would have sucked, even worse than this outfit," Arianna sighed.

"Are we ready then?" Izak chimed in.

"If we want any chance of saving Arianna and Arik, we need to get Angela," Iris spoke, marching down the hall to grab Angela for the journey.

***

Alister was patiently waiting for Angela and her sisters to arrive at the castle. Just imagining talking with Angela and somehow making things right between them was all he had to hold on to. Even if it was a fantasy created in his own mind, he was determined to make it come true. He wondered why they had wanted to talk, when they'd already discussed and trained all who was going to be fighting in Foinix.

Excitedly, Alister walked to the window for the twentieth time to see if his guests had arrived. This time, he waited. He watched Arianna walk through the mirror first, with Arik following, holding her hand. Confusion and rage instantly consumed Alister when he locked his eyes on the loving hands of the couple. It was only Angela's smile and cheerful energy that stopped him from running outside to rip off some heads. Iris and Izak were last to step out, appearing to have made up with each other. As great as it all was to see them wearing happy expressions, he did not expect Arik to be holding the wrong woman's hand.

Snorting, sending the signature steam out his nostrils, he left the window and raced outside to hear exactly what was going on.

"What is the meaning of this? I demand answers, now!" Alister bellowed, pointing at the clasped hands with his eyes locked on Arik.

"Personally, I don't think it is any of your business. It's not me; it's everyone else who insists you know everything." Arik stepped up to Alister, pulling Arianna protectively behind him like he had when Angela found out about them.

If this man's plan was to piss off Alister, he had succeeded. Alister didn't even have to step forward to get in Arik's face and give him a fearful glare that would send any normal being, creature or human, running away.

"It's not worth it, Your Majesty," Angela spoke in Alister's right ear.

Alister turned his head to look at her. "Explain to me why this man is holding Arianna's hand and not yours?" Alister asked, with a hint of desperation in his voice.

"I will if you promise to stay calm and see the bright side of the situation. Promise me that and Arianna will be happy to explain it all to you. What's done is done and can't be changed. I wouldn't want it to be either," Angela said, smiling back and forth, between Alister and Arianna.

Arianna moved Arik out of the way, reassuring him she would be fine, and reeking of fear and deceit that she knew Alister could smell. Her fidgeting meant she was hiding something, and he wouldn't react pleasantly to her confession. He knew her words had to be a big deal or Angela wouldn't have gotten involved and calmed him down.

"Your Majesty…please don't be mad. Remember when I told you Angela and Arik were done, but I couldn't tell you more because it was my mess to clean up?" Arianna asked, lowering herself to her knees and begging him from a praying position. "I'm pregnant with Arik's child and have been keeping it a secret for months."

Alister didn't even have a chance to think rationally; his mind was completely taken over by his primal side's instincts to destroy something...or someone.

Apparently, he wasn't the only one to notice this change inside of him. Angela wrapped her arms around his neck as tightly as she could and whispered sweetly in his ear. Yet the words that struck him were not kind, but threatening.

"If you hurt my sister who is carrying my niece or nephew, I will find everything in my power to bring you down. That goes the same way for Arik. He just found out too and we are all trying to register the news. I don't care what they have done, because my heart still aches for you...even though we will never be together."

Listening to Angela's voice and her words made Alister calm, but sad. She let go of his neck, offering a slight smile and a nod, awaiting his response.

He wanted to nod back; to tell her he wouldn't touch the new couple. He wanted to obey her every word. But when he looked back at them...holding each other, the fury was once again inflamed. In his mind, that should be him and Angela embracing each other. Once again, the witch had taken everything he had ever wanted away. All this time he could have been with the love of his life. Flames shot before his eyes. *Not this time.* He wouldn't allow the witch to get her happy ending. He would take Arik away and send him back to Earth, or lock him up for all eternity.

Pushing off with his back legs, Alister jumped into the air to circle his prey, before swooping down in order to grab the man so he could throw him in the dungeons. The man was no fool, though. Arik pulled out a dagger from a knife clasp in his boot and jabbed at Alister once he was in arm's reach.

The dagger surprised everyone, including the drakon. Alister tried to disarm Arik the next time he came down from the sky, but Arik sliced Alister's paw, making him roar...increasing his rage once again. Alister was not willing to be nice anymore. Arik had been given many chances to surrender, but now Alister would tumble into him—literally knock him over and hope he didn't die so he could keep his promise to Angela.

The closer Alister got to Arik, he let go of his flight control, readying himself for impact with the human body. Before he could make the connection, however, little Leah came out of nowhere, running to guard her father.

"Don't hurt my daddy," Leah screamed, surrounding her and Arik with a protective bubble.

Alister hit the brakes in midair, just enough to crash behind Leah and Arik and land hard against the rock, dirt, and trees surrounding his home.

CHAPTER 24

The kingdom was down to its last day before it was time to open the doors to enter Foinix Realm. There was a massive sense of tension in the air, and everyone was ready to release it on the evil witch and her followers awaiting them in the neighboring realm. Alister was at risk of losing his title for putting multiple people in danger because he couldn't control his temper. But at least he could take his frustration out on his enemies when he returned to Foinix.

Angela convinced Iris in secret that they had no other option; they needed to seek out the devil squid to save Neveah. The dark magic that Angela had would never join their fight, and there was no stopping it from turning on her once it figured out what they intended to do to its host. But there simply wasn't enough manpower to take down all of the witch's followers and the witch, herself, without the extra security.

Iris and Angela agreed to walk to the dock and call for Simon in order to ask for Rodney's help. Instead of locking the star up, Simon had given the star a choice to be locked up for the rest of his life or serve him in any task that he asked. Of course, Rodney had taken the second choice—to be loyal to his King of the Waters.

Bending down to touch the water at the end of the dock, Iris closed her eyes and sent vibrations into the depths below so King Simon would rise and meet her. While waiting for his appearance, Angela paced nervously on the wood. Iris watched her in hopes that she would change her mind the longer they waited for Simon.

"What's taking him so long?" Angela complained.

"Are you having second thoughts?" Iris asked.

"No. I just don't want to get caught. Alister could have spies on us or something."

"You don't want to get caught? What about me? What's stopping him from disintegrating me if he finds out that I put you in life threatening danger?"

"I know, Sis. I'm sorry. We don't have a choice. Zack doesn't have complete control over his ability to make shifters transition or turn human yet. We might as well be fighting this entire war ourselves, so no one else gets hurt," Angela panicked.

Just then, Simon popped his head above the water line; Sylvia was beside him, holding his hand. They both wore huge smiles on their faces and didn't hide them when they laid their eyes on Iris and Angela bickering on the dock.

"Iris. Angela. How are you?"

"We are well. Just having a little disagreement. It looks like my hands are tied, though," Iris spoke. "How are you two?"

"We are splendid. What can I do for you?" Simon asked.

"We need your assistance in getting Rodney to locate the

devil squid again. We wouldn't ask if there was any other way...," Iris spoke.

"Does His Majesty know what you're doing?" Simon asked, immediately shaking his head and raising his hand. "Wait. Don't answer that. I don't want to know. How much ink do you need?"

"The smallest amount possible," Iris spoke.

"Maybe a little more," Angela edited her request.

Iris sighed and nodded in agreement. If Angela didn't have enough to put down the other witch, the danger would have all been for nothing.

"I'll tell Rodney and have him work on it right away," Simon replied, a little worried.

"Thank you, Your Majesty," Iris spoke. She smiled at Sylvia and Simon. "I'm happy you two are back together."

"You're welcome, Iris. I expect a very large wedding present from you after this one," Simon teased before receiving a playful smack from Sylvia on his shoulder.

"We don't charge family," Sylvia said, acting disappointed.

"I was joking. Well.. sort of," Simon laughed.

"We don't expect a thing. We are just happy to help, Auntie," Sylvia said.

Iris and Angela left, waving goodbye to the happy ones, so Iris could work on a strong pendant to protect Angela and store the ink from the devil squid.

***

Zack continued to work with Liam, but this time trained with Atticus, hoping to get his powers stabilized. He was determined to get it completely under control. Zack couldn't just think of any animal and turn into them; he had to see them first before transitioning was possible.

The amount of emotion it took to use his ability to stop others from shifting or force them to shift was difficult when put on the spot. Zack tried to force all of his protective instincts onto the creature he was trying to make human, but only once had he been successful. It wasn't 'on the spot,' either.

Liam was rough housing with a young wolf that was learning to control its aggression. When things escalated and Liam cried out in pain from being bit by the pup, Zack jumped in and forced the shifter into their human form. He had exhausted the canine and made it sleep when the transition was complete. Everyone who witnessed Zack's powers praised and adored him. He didn't care much about anyone's "oohs" and "aahs," except for Yalonda. The beautiful owl girl he met and saved on Halloween noticed him more and more, even though she remained shy.

Her playing witness made Zack become even more confident in his abilities; he felt like he was going to be useful in the battle. Even if he couldn't get all of his powers under control, he could at least mirror their enemies and use their own powers against them.

"Want to really put your shifting ability to the test?" Liam asked a daydreaming Zack who was lying flat on his back in the grass, looking up into the blue sky

"What did you have in mind?" Zack asked. Intrigued, he propped up on his elbow to give Liam his full attention.

"I was just thinking you could try a mermaid or an eagle…or maybe even the dragon!" Liam jumped up and down in excitement.

Flight creatures were one of the shifting animals Zack hadn't thought of, but he definitely wouldn't dream of turning into the king of the entire realm. If he could turn into a merman and breathe underwater, that would be really cool. He could even join his sister and Simon on their adventures below.

"We could ask Nick and see if he would let me practice with him," Zack thought out loud.

"Nick's pretty cool. Let's go ask around and find out where

he is," Liam suggested.

The boys both ran to Atticus to ask him if he knew where to find Nick. Zack thought about how Nick had been feeling—how concerned he was for Neveah. He looked pretty torn up about her being held captive by another witch. They all were, but they were going to get her back, and soon. Zack didn't know much about Nick, but he knew that the two wanted to be together for life.

"Nick might be in the forest near the meadow. He spends most of his time in a tree nearby," Atticus answered.

"Thanks," both boys said, ready to run into the forest.

"Wait, what do you plan to do?" When the boys remained quiet, Atticus trained his stare on Zack. "You haven't taken on a flight shifter before. Make sure you ask Nick first, okay? Don't put your life at risk," Atticus instructed, looking worried.

"Of course. I wouldn't have tried without his permission. I promise," Zack reassured him, confused as to why he thought he wouldn't ask first.

Atticus only nodded his head in reply before returning to his herd and galloping away.

When Zack and Liam found Nick, he was indeed in the tallest tree near the meadow. His large eagle form stood out like a sore thumb in the big branches above. The boys ran until they were directly under the tree, looking up. Zack assumed that Nick was sleeping and maybe they shouldn't bother him. Perhaps they should go to the dock instead and ask Simon if he could mirror his species. But before Zack could tell Liam what he was thinking, Nick's eyes opened wide, and he spoke.

"Hello, boys. What brings you to my neck of the woods?" Nick asked, before lifting off the branch and soaring down to them.

"I was wondering if you knew about my new abilities to mirror other shifters?" Zack asked.

"Of course. Who *hasn't* heard of your new magical abilities?" Nick smiled. "You're here to ask if you could copy my eagle side, correct?"

"Yes. I haven't tried a flight shifter yet. It sounds so cool to be able to fly." Zack beamed in excitement.

"Zack, I would be honored to teach you. In fact, I wish your mother was here to see it, too. Did you know.. this is the spot where I first showed your mother who I was? In this very meadow," Nick spoke with a longing look in his eyes.

"Don't worry, Nick. We *will* get my mother back and then you two will be together again."

"I hope so."

"Enough of this mushy stuff. Let's get down to the fun stuff," Liam begged.

Liam was so quiet that Zack had almost forgot he was there. Looking up in the tree, Zack suddenly felt like he was afraid of heights. The tree was super high. What if he found out he couldn't fly and fell to his death?

"Don't worry. We are going to start here on the ground first. I'm not going to do what my mother did to me and kick you out of the nest. We can take it slow," Nick offered reassurance like he could sense how Zack was feeling.

"Oh, thank God. I was holding my breath looking at that tree," Zack laughed.

"Let's start with your transition; how do you do it?" Nick asked.

"First, you transition into your eagle and then I concentrate on your form. I will look at your feathers and think of them surrounding my entire body, too. It shouldn't take long," Zack explained.

Nick, in a snap of the fingers, transitioned into an eagle. Zack was surprised at how quickly he could change; it took at least a couple minutes for Zack to completely transition into any shifting creature. While Zack focused on Nick's appearance—his beak, feathers, color, and size—Zack could feel his own body change and turn into a bird.

"Dude! You're doing it. Why is he brown, though?" Liam

asked.

"He's young," Nick answered before talking to Zack. "Even though you can mirror my species, you're still a young one, so your feathers don't look like mine. It's incredible."

"Thanks," Zack replied.

"Okay. Now spread your wings out and try to take in the air around you, flap them up and down and concentrate on lifting off and taking flight," Nick instructed.

Zack looked at Liam, who was flapping his arms and jumping into the air to encourage Zack to soar. The action made Zack laugh while he tried to flap his wings and jump, too. The boys were being silly, until Zack felt his feet leave the ground. Instantly afraid, he dropped back onto the grass. Good thing he hadn't gotten very far from the hard earth.

"That was a great first try. Believe me when I tell you that it's even hard for us actual eagles to fly our first time. The landing can be even more tricky, too, so you must practice a lot. There's no hurry. I'm here for you all day," Nick assured him.

"That was so rad, Zack. You're going to be flying over the mountain and into the clouds, while I'll be stuck down here on the lame ground," Liam teased, even though Zack could tell he really wanted to have his powers, too. He would be more than happy to share his abilities if he could.

"What did you feel when you were floating?" Nick asked.

"Fear. I'm afraid of falling, not being strong enough, disappointing my family when they count on me to be this amazing savior…I just feel like I'm going to fail." Zack lowered his beak and head down to the ground.

"Yes. That would do it; even to me. That's a lot of weight you have on your shoulders. Fear is great, though. It's a strong emotion that has a huge effect on all of us. Once you realize it's okay to be afraid and accept that emotion as normal, you will realize how much power it actually gives you. Anyone who says they are fearless are lying or just dumb." Nick laughed, as

Zack and Liam joined in the fun. "Just trust and believe in yourself. You got this."

Zack continued trying to fly, getting frustrated with each failed attempt to get off the ground. So many people were counting on him to get all his powers under control so he could be helpful. If the sifters in Foinix had any flight abilities, his friends and family wouldn't be able to count on him.

"Let's try something else. You're getting too frustrated. You're going to start molting if you keep stressing," Nick teased, showing his patience and kindness. "Do you even like your new ability, Zack? Or is it all work; a complicated new thing in your life that you really don't want?"

"No one has ever asked that before. I do like it, but I think it has been so stressful trying to control it that I really haven't had time to enjoy it much." Zack continued to think about it.

"I tell him all the time to chill. He needs to loosen up, be silly and have fun. You floated when you were playing with me, cuz'. So, quit thinking about it so much," Liam advised, still flapping his arms in a circle. "I'm going to be a pro if I ever become a bird."

Nick and Zack laughed at the carefree, not a worry in the world, Liam. He was more useful than he knew. He made everyone laugh in any situation and encouraged others to enjoy life and be free. Emotions everyone under stress seemed to forget.

Deciding to try it his way, Zack ran around in a circle with Liam, putting all the stress and expectations on the back burner to just have fun. Before he knew it, he was jumping into the air and taking the wind under his wings. Fear hit him again, but this time he used it as a goal to achieve by accepting his fear and using it to his advantage.

Liam was clapping his hands and cheering for Zack when he turned his head to look down at his cherubic face. When he turned to look forward again, Nick was in front of him on his right-hand side. Looking back, Nick winked before he let out a loud whistling sound. Zack replied with a 'caw' that made Nick laugh.

***

Angela walked to the wooden bridge to meet with Simon alone. She wanted to observe the ink while she was by herself in silence. When she arrived, Iris was already standing at the end of the bridge with her hands on her hips and disappointment written on her face.

"Don't look at me like that. What are *you* doing here all by yourself?" Iris asked.

"I'm here with the pendant so I can get prepared to transfer the ink into the crystal. What's your excuse?" Iris stood still, waiting for her answer.

"I was just coming here to wait for you," Angela lied.

"I'm sure you were," she replied sarcastically. "Angela, you have no idea how dangerous it is. Tomorrow is doomsday and you were coming to play with fire," Iris spoke loud, shaking her head.

Bowing her head down, Angela looked at her feet in shame. She couldn't hide anything from her big sister. Except the magic that was controlling her. How did Iris even *know* she was coming to the bridge?

"How did you know I was coming early?" Angela asked. It was her turn to be suspicious.

"I have a magical tracker on you now. Ever since we found out you harbor a killer in your mind, I don't fully trust your actions," Iris admitted.

"Remove it! I am not a child. You can't just keep tabs on me and make decisions for me. I have had plenty of controlling people in my life. I don't need that anymore," Angela spoke with frustration.

"That's enough, ladies. Time to cool off," Simon said, coming swiftly out of the water and spraying both. Making them scream, he drenched them.

"Oh my gosh, Simon!" Both yelled at him for his actions.

"If you two can't stop bickering, I'm going to have this destroyed and *no one* will get the ink again. Do you understand?" Simon threatened, holding up the shell in his hand. "The ink is stored in this. Sylvia couldn't be around it. It was making her dizzy. Now, what are you two going to do with it?"

"I'm sorry, Simon. Thank you very much. If you could just set it down, I'll transfer the ink into this pendent," Iris requested, holding the jewel up in the air.

Watching Iris work her magic, Angela took note of her actions. She was envious of Iris's magic. Knowing she wasn't born with her own wasn't fair. As the ink was being transferred into the pendant, you could actually see it moving through the air, like a black string going directly into the crystal. Once Iris was finished, she stood up, pendant in hand, and held it out to Angela.

"There is only one way to find out if it's going to harm you. I brought a few rose quartz stones with me to heal you quickly if it starts draining you," Iris spoke with a look of worry in her eyes.

"I'm sorry," Angela said, apologizing to Iris because she was making her do something she didn't want to. Taking the pendant from her, Angela said, "I feel fine."

"I am not leaving your side until I know for sure that it's not going to negatively affect you," Iris spoke stubbornly.

The sickness the ink caused was already having internal symptoms that Iris couldn't see. Angela wasn't going to mention the feeling until she absolutely needed to. If Iris knew it was making her body ache, she would remove it in a split second and the plan would be ruined.

"What should we do in the meantime?" Angela asked.

"How about we talk? I know it's not right to treat you like a child. You're a grown woman and can make your own decisions. I'm sorry for keeping tabs on you; I will remove the tracker when we get home," Iris said.

"Um. It's okay. I understand. Don't sweat it," Angela replied slowly.

"Angela, you're slurring your words. Are you feeling okay?"

The dizziness Angela was dealing with pissed her off. It was supposed to work. Why couldn't she have just *one* win in her damn efforts to help? All she wanted was to save her family and the people with a guarantee they would all live and go back to their lives.

Iris grabbed a rose quartz from a little silk bag and grabbed Angela's hand, projecting all the healing properties the crystal possessed into her body. Instantly bringing Angela back to the surface, she removed all the side effects the ink was having on her body and mind.

"How do you feel now?" Iris asked.

"I feel incredible! Even better than before." Angela wasn't lying. She felt a hundred percent better, which brought her hope that she would be able to do it after all. Convincing Iris was going to be a different story, though.

"I don't know. Are you sure you're okay now?"

"Yes, but just in case, let's stay close to each other and use the crystals again if I need them. Even if it makes me sick again, we can fix it."

"Let's go to Arianna's. She has more crystals in case you get worse," Iris suggested.

"Great," Angela replied in a sarcastic tone and let her eyes roll.

CHAPTER 25

Iris, Angela, Sylvia, and Leah stood in the middle of the meadow. Each of them possessed a crystal from Neveah's bloodline, which would allow them entrance into the Foinix Realm. Iris used a special chalk crystal to make a large circle in front of the four witches, big enough for all sizes of Drakous Realm creatures to fit through. The witches then joined hands and the portal opened.

Alister was the first one in line to walk through the door. Iris informed him to be on high alert; she didn't know what would await them on the other side. All she knew was it would bring them to a location where Neveah's emotions were strongest. Her happiest memories.

Once Alister walked through the portal, the rest of his people followed. Hundreds of warriors ready to defeat the threat and save Neveah. When everyone else had entered, the quartet of witches proceeded forward together, joining the warriors on the other side.

The process was easy for the witches, and they celebrated with glee—all except for Angela. She was weak from the devil's ink slowly draining her life. Dark circles already formed around her eyes. Only Iris knew what was happening and she walked toward Angela to see how she could help.

"You look like death is eating you itself."

"I'm fine. Just give me a boost," Angela lied.

"There are only four crystals left. Are you sure you want to use one now?" Iris asked.

"Yes, I'm sure."

Iris set a healing crystal in Angela's hands. Cupping her own hands over the stone, she forced the mending properties into Angela's system quicker.

Angela could already feel the color returning to her face. It felt like a hot blush on her cheeks when she lifted her hands to touch them.

"Better?" Iris asked.

"Much." Angela smiled.

"Let's join the others and explore," Iris recommended, reaching her hand out for Angela to take.

Together, they walked around, wandering among Foinix Realm's finest fire shifters, watching their every step. Fire creatures surrounded Alister when they saw him, like they already knew him. The children were bouncing on him like a jungle gym, making him laugh along with them. Iris and Angela giggled at the sight before they continued on their walk.

While still observing their surroundings, an old woman holding carefully to a walking stick somehow strutted towards them. Angela smiled sweetly at the appearance of a completely harmless old lady.

"Which one of you is Neveah's sister?" she asked; an

ornery expression plastered on her face.

Iris pointed at Angela without a word. Angela smiled and stepped forward. "I am. I'm Angela," she replied, reaching her hand out in greeting.

Instead of repaying the formality, Angela got something completely unexpected. The old lady used her stick and thumped her right on the top of her head. Angela quickly backed up and rubbed the sore spot. "What was *that* for?"

"What *took* you so long? Neveah has been waiting months for you to rescue her," she scolded Angela.

"Nice to meet you, too," Angela replied. "For your information, we just found out where she was and built an army to save her. The witch had a lockdown on this realm; she surrounded this entire kingdom with an invisible shield to stop anyone trying to peek in or enter into Foinix."

The hag's face became even more annoyed, as she spat, "I'm Edna. Good luck. You're going to need it!" With that, she turned her back on them and walked away, leaving Angela completely dumbfounded.

She looked at Iris, confused as to what had just happened. Were all Foinix creatures going to be weird and hit Angela with objects? She didn't know anything about them, but like her sister had warned—they needed to be prepared for anything. Even harmless looking old ladies.

The army soon found that they had landed smack dab in the center of a haven. From the count of heads, there were only twenty to twenty-five fire creatures fighting for their freedom. Some were even sporting wounds from their last encounter against the witch and her servants. Talk of a traitor in their midst, who was supposed to be their leader and guide them to victory, instead had led them to their death and injury. The people desperately needed to be saved. Angela only hoped she could survive long enough to do that for these people.

Putting the odd meeting with the hag behind them, Angela and Iris continued on their way, doing a perimeter walk around the camp to see what was nearby. They could see a river and located the direction of the castle. Men and women sent unusual stares their way. While they walked, they even heard whispers about Iris's appearance. The people seemed to think Iris was the evil witch who had caused all the damage to their lives; this was most concerning. Thank goodness for Alister's sudden appearance beside them, silencing all the doubts that were spreading around like wildfire.

"What's their problem?" Angela asked Alister.

"Rumor has it, Iris is the mirror image of the evil magissa," Alister replied.

"How could that be possible?"

"I'm not sure. Maybe they are related. Wouldn't be the first time something like this happened. I'm going to fly to the witch's territory and find out what she wants. I'll approach friendly, but I'm certain she will want a war, so we attack at dawn tomorrow morning. Get your rest. You'll need it."

"Yes, Your Majesty. Just be careful," Angela added her instruction in a worried voice.

Alister smiled upon hearing her concerned tone. "I will. Plus, she can't hurt me. Remember? I'm immune to witches."

"Their magic used on you, maybe," Iris teased. "Be wary of temptations you won't be able to resist."

Alister missed the point that Iris was trying to make. Instead, he got defensive, like Iris was somehow insulting his intelligence. "I am no fool. I won't be tempted, no matter how beautiful she is." Alister shook his head in annoyance before taking his leave.

* * *

What was Iris talking about? Alister tried to make sense of what she had said. How could another woman even slightly tempt him when he still only wanted Angela? He was almost to the castle when he realized what she had meant. He desperately wanted to be in his human form again and she must have known the evil witch would be powerful enough to turn him back. Even the thought was absurd. There wasn't a witch in the world who could convince him to allow *any* spell to be cast upon him.

As Alister set his thoughts aside, he looked below him at the scorched scenery of the Foinix Realm. He wondered why someone that planned to take over such a glorious location would destroy it first. ...Unless she planned to leave the realm after she'd turned it to dust.

By the time Alister was in sight of the castle, he could already see the woman outside the walls in a grassy area, seemingly alone and unguarded. He thought her brave to be unaccompanied by solders of her own, or powerful enough not to worry about anyone swooping in from the skies and coming after her.

She surprised him once more when the witch smiled up at him with her hand blocking the sun so she could see. "You gorgeous creature. Why don't you come down here and chat with me?" She waved at him to land, appearing to be friendly.

He circled above her. "No, thank you. I'm happy here. Please state your terms. Why do you hold Neveah captive?" Alister, not wasting any time, got straight to the point. He was slightly distracted by the witch's physical appearance. Although the fire shifters had given him a detailed description of her, he wasn't quite prepared to see the face of Iris staring back at him.

"I want my magic back. My sister stole it and passed it on to one of her offspring. One of your witches. The one that looks like me." Alister could hear the fury in her salty tone. "I'm Elinor Butler."

Alister was taken aback by the woman's words as she admitted the family connection. The evil woman below him was the beloved aunt, known to be full of power-hungry energy.

"Your Iris's aunt? All you want is your magic back...nothing more? If you get that power returned, we all go our separate ways and no one gets hurt?" Alister asked, already knowing the woman wanted far more than just her magic, but he would leave it to her to start the war.

"Well...perhaps not just my magic. I also want your realm, all the others in the universe, and, of course, the grand battle where all your creatures die!" The woman voiced her list like it was no big deal. *How could she be so calm and cheerful?* She was obviously insane and he was not going to allow his people to go up against her if he could stop it.

Alister shot a fireball down at the witch. He anticipated she would move, run, flee; yet, she stood still, smiling, allowing it to hit her and the flame to die out. His eyes widened in surprise when she was left completely unharmed. In an instant, she brought the fireball back to its roaring intensity and shot it at him while she laughed, wickedly. Alister barely dodged his own flame; if it had made contact, it would have brought him down.

The witch had replied, challenging him to a battle between the two realms. Still smiling, she retreated into the castle and closed the doors quietly behind her. Alister couldn't help but be concerned for his people, especially the witches who would personally go up against her.

All the way back to camp, he thought about all the things that could go wrong.

* * *

Elinor walked away with the evil grin still plastered across her face until she shut the doors to the castle. Alister's strength had ruffled her feathers. She almost couldn't take his entire fireball and send it back up to hit him. The burning she felt inside from the fireball had only faded with the abilities she'd picked up from the fire shifters; by stealing their power, she was able to heal herself from any injury caused by flames.

The short meeting with Alister was enough for her to sense how primal, damaged, and dangerously unpredictable he would be. The beast was like nothing she had ever seen before. None the less, Elinor would be prepared. She had already tagged the beasts under her control. If they wanted their freedom, they would do anything she demanded. All she needed was to set up a meeting with seven of her most trusted and loyal followers.

"Your Highness," a woman bowed down at her feet. "Was that the King of Drakous?"

"Yes, it was, Charlotte. Not for long, though." Elinor smiled at her right-hand intern who she had been teaching for the past month. She had become most loyal and just as crazy as her own self, and Elinor planned to make her princess of all the realms if she survived this war.

"Shall I call for the others?"

"Yes, please do." Elinor replied with a smile. "How many shifting creatures are under my control?"

"Five hundred, ma'am, and seven of us loyal to you."

This news disappointed Elinor. "Go! Leave me be and get the others," she demanded.

While Charlotte slithered off to retrieve the rest of her followers, Elinor couldn't help but worry how little the number was—the number of those that'd chosen to be her servants compared to those who she'd forced. Thinking of prisoners reminded her of Adonis, still settled down in her dungeons. She wanted to pay him a visit to inform him of these new arrivals.

Walking down the steps to the jail cell, Elinor could hear Adonis's sweet voice speaking to the pathetic mouse that was with him; the rodent who he'd chosen to stay with instead of sharing her chambers and having the freedom to roam the castle...on a tight leash. Every time she thought of the other witch receiving his attention, her jealousy meter rose, but she wanted the man happy until the day she would take Neveah's life. One more day is all she would have to wait. Then, she will have defeated Alister and his army, be ready to take down the rest of his annoying realm, and have her husband with her to enjoy a happy ever after.

As she came around the corner and stared through the bars, she watched the gorgeous man doing sit-ups. The mouse sleeping peacefully on the cot sickened her, but the shirtless man was far too distracting to care much about the rodent woman. However, Elinor *did* care that he hadn't acknowledged her presence yet. She hit the bars loudly, waking up Neveah and halting Adonis's workout.

"Don't stop on my account," Elinor smiled. "Just wanted to make sure you knew your wife to be arrived."

Adonis sighed and raised himself off the floor. Grabbing his shirt folded neatly on the other end of his cot, he pulled it over his head to cover himself up.

"Awe. I was enjoying that sight."

"At least one of us is enjoying what we see. Is there something you need? Or you just down here to gloat?" Adonis spoke with disgust.

"No, my dear. I came down to inform you that Drakous Realm's finest are here to rescue your beloved," Elinor said, turning to stare at the mouse. "I plan to kill them all. So don't worry, our plans will not be stopped. We might have more guests for the wedding, though."

"How do you plan to take down multiple witches and an entire army that wants to rescue a mother, sister, and daughter? The love Neveah's family has for her is stronger than anything you could ever understand. It will make the witches more powerful than you. You know nothing about the power of that bond." Adonis lowered his voice to a whisper as he walked closer to her, "You can't win."

Elinor's smile turned to a frown while the anger built up inside her. Adonis simply laughed at the effect his statement had on her emotions. Raising her right hand to curse him or the mouse further, Elinor suddenly stopped, lowered her hand and sent him her signature wicked smile instead. "We will see about that. I have an unbeatable plan. Once those witches figure out what's going on, it will be too late, and I will destroy them."

Adonis quit laughing but kept his gaze directed at her. "I guess we will just have to see about that," he said. "Keep in mind, history has already shown what happens to those who do not take things seriously because they believe themselves to be the best already. Those are the ones who end up paying the most."

The amount of faith Adonis had in Elinor made her smile disappear again. Pouting, she stomped her foot and turned around to storm up the steps, slamming the door behind her and rushing to her throne room to wait for her loyal servants to arrive.

That stupid man has no idea what I am capable of! She tried not to allow his comments to bother her. No matter, she had enough confidence to conquer any adversary..all by herself.

"Your Highness. You sent for us?" Her loyal group gathered in her throne room; the frightened look in their eyes showed they were incredibly leery of her temper.

"Yes." She popped her head up and smiled at the seven who'd come to hear her plan.

Getting up from the royal chair, she walked to the line of people. Slowly pacing back and forth in front of them, she watched for any cowardly behavior in their posture. When she didn't see any sign of breakage, weakness or revolt, she spoke: "You are my most loyal subjects. I chose you to lead the army into a vengeful, bloody mess. I expect no mercy and everything to go as planned. If all else fails and any of you come back to my kingdom with an explanation of defeat, I will kill every one of you. This fight is to the death, with no retreat or treaty of peace. Do you understand?" Elinor watched them carefully for any fear hidden in their eyes.

"Yes, Our Queen. We understand," they replied in unison.

"Good. Now leave me." She waved her hand, dismissing them. "Except for you, Charlotte. We have more to discuss."

The group bowed their heads and walked backwards before turning and leaving her to settle the extra business with her female subject.

When the doors had closed, she circled Charlotte before walking up the steps to her throne. "You know what you need to do?" Elinor asked.

"Yes, ma'am. Happy to be of service to you," Charlotte replied with a bow.

"I couldn't be prouder. May you live a long and happy life. Off to bed with you. We have a war to win early in the morning," Elinor laughed, with Charlotte joining in her fun.

* * *

Waking up to the loud 'boom' coming from the direction of the haven, Adonis knew that war had been announced and his fighting troops were ready. He was happy that Neveah's family found his hiding spot, hoping they excepted his people to march into victory.

"Did you hear that, Neveah? That was the sound of our rescue party," Adonis picked up Neveah's mouse body carefully in his hands and laid on his back, setting her on his chest with a piece of gourmet cheddar cheese. "What do you want to do first when we are free?"

Adonis continued to speak to Neveah even though she never replied, because she couldn't speak or understand what he was saying. At least, he assumed she couldn't understand him. The squeaks she voiced, he thought, were just signs of hunger.

"If that evil magissa actually made this cheese on her own,

at least I will be eating like a king if the worst-case scenario happens," Adonis nervously laughed, as his body shuddered in disgust just thinking what his life would be like if he were married to that woman. "I would much rather marry you, Neveah."

"What is going on here? I told you *not* to feed that thing my cheese and not to have her resting on you like so! I warned you I would take her if I ever saw her so close to you," Elinor screamed, making Adonis jump up and off the cot. He tried to think up something fast to save Neveah.

"Your Highness," he addressed her calmly. "She's a mouse. It's not like we were kissing. She can't even communicate with me. You have nothing to worry about," Adonis reassured her, hoping to cool her temper.

"Prove it." Elinor eyed him suspiciously. "A kiss for good luck is a good start."

She grabbed the bars to his cell and stuck her face between them, her lips puckered, expecting Adonis to comply with her request. It was not going to happen. Just the thought of her lips anywhere near him brought a disgusted groan from his mouth.

Elinor retreated back a step wearing a displeased expression on her face. "You're going to regret that," she said, before sending a bolt of power from her right index finger and zapping Neveah. "Enjoy what time you two have left."

"Neveah!" Adonis yelled, running to pick her up.

"By the way," Elinor said, turning back, "If I die. You will die, too. My blood magic is what keeps you alive. So think about that the next time you hope I lose this war." She smiled, waving goodbye.

* * *

Elinor woke up refreshed from a good night's sleep. *Now*, she was pissed off.

Exiting the castle, Elinor found her army waiting right outside for her instructions. She looked at the people, the ones who had no desire to fight but were under her captivity, and those who were chomping at the bit to please her. She spoke, "Remember, we fight to the death. Leave no survivors, and as promised, you will earn your freedom—never having to see me again. Now attack and show no mercy!" Elinor started the war.

While the foinix creatures ran into battle, Elinor abandoned them so she could get prepared for the drakon and his witches. She was giddy inside at how genius her plan was. It was already in motion from the moment she'd started the attack.

Walking to the nearest part of the forest that offered good cover and bushes to conceal herself in, Elinor spotted the drakon in the sky and heard human footsteps running close by. Ducking down quickly, knowing Alister possessed exceptional hearing and sight, she was surprised he hadn't already seen her.

The two women were close to Elinor's hiding spot, so she projected an image of herself directly in front of them to have some early fun with her new toys. Her nieces halted in their tracks.

Angela was about to attack the image before Iris grabbed her elbow and stopped her. "It's not the witch. Don't move. She's watching us." Iris shook her head and put her finger up to tell Angela to stay quiet.

"Well, well, well.. aren't you a beauty for all to see?" The image toyed with Iris. "Powerful, too."

"Come out and fight us. Unless you're too afraid we will destroy you," Angela spoke.

"Don't you speak to me! Your voice is like nails on a chalkboard, so much like my sisters it makes me want to vomit," Elinor yelled back at Angela. "You're not looking well either. How about you save us all this trouble and let me put you out of your misery here and now?"

"That's big talk for a coward who hides in the shadows," Angela insulted.

"I am no coward!" Elinor screamed, ready to attack. She took her eyes off Alister who had spotted her from the sky and sent his fireball straight at her. With only seconds to react, she barely dodged the flame, landing flat on her back on the ground. Now they all knew exactly where she was; playtime was over.

Another fireball from a different direction went soaring up into the air, hitting Alister from behind and bringing him down to crash onto the ground.

"No!" Angela screamed. Calling her magic to the surface, she attempted to attack Elinor.

"I won't hurt my mother!" The magic refused to fight.

"Fine, you can die with the rest of us," Angela spoke out loud before forcing the magic back into its prison world.

"So...*you* are the one who has my precious baby. Well then, I will save you for last and kill my beautiful niece first," Elinor spoke, snapping her fingers to disintegrate Iris who was standing in front of Angela. But the magic had no effect at all.

"That's not possible!" she screamed, snapping her fingers repeatedly, only stopping when a figure appeared from behind her back. Carrying a chain in its hands, it blocked Elinor's magic from working.

"Hi there." Iris smiled, waving her hand at Elinor once she turned around.

Iris had pulled the same projection trick Elinor had. Sneering at Iris, she knew she'd been beaten by her own attempts to fool the two witches when they'd arrived. She hissed at Iris like a venomous snake. Although her magic may be contained, her shifting abilities were not; Elinor knew they were just taking a moment to come to the surface.

Footsteps came up from behind her. Turning, she stared at Angela who stood with a pendant necklace hanging from her fingers.

"What are you going to do with that?" Elinor hissed again, showing Angela she wasn't afraid.

Angela shoved the pendant in Elinor's mouth and stepped back to kick her in the chin. The sudden hit made Elinor bite down on the stone and crack it. The ink would now leak into her throat and kill the evil witch instantly.

Coughing and choking from the poison, Elinor was stripped of her magic, revealing a surprise transition. All the magic Elinor had provided her to hide her identity was taken away, making the witches in front of her gasp in horror that they'd just killed the wrong person and wasted the deadly ink. Charlotte was dying; Elinor had used her intern as a diversion. Now that Angela had used her secret weapon against the wrong woman, the witches knew the real Elinor could come out of hiding and destroy them, taking her magic back and winning the war in the process.

* * *

"Neveah.. are you okay? What has she done to you?" Adonis wept for the still unmoving, unblinking Neveah.

She heard him, but didn't try to reply. Even though Neveah had attempted to communicate with him for a month, to tell him she could understand everything he was saying, she'd learned that he was the only one who seemed to not understand her mouse squeaks. Neveah loved listening to every word he spoke, though. She'd laughed actually, knowing one day she would be able to tell him that she knew all his deepest, darkest secrets.

Knowing it would be another failed attempt to talk, she still tried to vocalize: "I'm fine. Nothing like a little static electricity," she laughed.

However, this time when Neveah spoke, she could hear her own voice loud and clear, free of squeaks. But why would the witch give her the power to speak to Adonis if she was so jealous of them bonding? Must be a sick joke.. allowing them to get close so she could torture them later.

"I can understand you!" Adonis spoke excitedly, lifting Neveah in the palm of his hand and twirling in a circle. "I thought I would never hear that sweet voice again. She must have messed up."

"I'm sure she didn't." Neveah explained why she thought Elinor had returned her voice; just to bring them down again. She believed that it was just a sick way of letting them know she had the control and power and they remained helpless.

"Shows what she knows. I'm going to enjoy hearing your voice and have you actually understand me when I talk, so I don't feel like I'm talking to myself," Adonis chuckled.

"That reminds me. Do you think she was serious when she said you will die, too, if she does?" Neveah smiled, though she was worried about Adonis's life.

"You could understand me this whole time?" Adonis gasped in shock, making Neveah laugh hysterically at his now wild, slightly guilty eyes.

CHAPTER 26

The morning of the battle everyone in camp was still sleeping, except for Leah. She wanted to enter her mother's tent before she woke so she could swap out her mother's pendant for a fake one she had forged. It would look like her mother's and emit similarly ill side effects to match the one holding the devil's ink poison.

Exiting her own tent, Leah saw Alister in the sky keeping watch for any spies the witch might send to the haven. But she wasn't concerned about him seeing her as she walked two tents down to her mother's.

When she entered the space, Angela was sleeping peacefully in her bed. Leah could sense powerful amethyst crystal energy in the air, knowing the source must be under her mother's pillow to help bring sweet dreams to her slumber. There was a box that contained the pendant necklace; it had been placed just to the left of the tent entrance, as far away from Angela as possible so it wouldn't harm her. Leah opened the box and switched the evil jewelry with the fake one, quickly sticking the other in her pocket.

Although the necklace would have similar side effects when Angela put it on, it wouldn't have the ability to actually kill her. It would also wear off before it did any actual damage to her mother's long-term health. In addition, Iris would cure Angela's illness with the same kind of magic Leah would use to protect herself while carrying the poison.

After Leah was done, she walked over to her happily dreaming mother and kissed her forehead. "I will protect you, Mother," she whispered, and walked away quickly to heal her own symptoms already cropping up from the ink.

Leah ran to her tent before she coughed up her lungs. Once safely inside, she walked to her own magic box and set the gem carefully inside, closing it and rushing to her bed to grab an obsidian crystal from under her pillow and absorb all its protective properties that would stop any physical harm the ink could do to her body. After her health was completely restored, she sighed with relief.

Sylvia's high-pitched voice, along with Simon's, coming from the tent next door brought memories flooding back into her mind. She needed their help on a task she couldn't explain until the exact moment it was supposed to happen. As she walked closer, she could hear the couple reminiscing over adventures they'd shared, promising each other that they would survive this war so they could have many more journeys across all the realms in the universe.

"Knock, knock. It's Leah. Can I come in?" Leah interrupted with no more time to waste.

"Of course, Leah," Sylvia spoke sweetly before Leah entered their tent. "Are you alright?"

"Yes, I'm fine. I need your help, though. Not now, but

when I yell for you. I'm sorry I don't make sense right now, but when the time comes, I need you to stay close and follow me," Leah spoke, visibly frustrated with herself.

"Take it easy, Leah. Don't stress. That's not a problem. We know what you can see. Arianna and Arik were close by when they were talking about you being an eye witch and that you get visions of the future but are unable to speak about the details. We will follow you without explanation," Simon assured her, speaking in a tone of absolute trust.

"Thank you." Leah smiled with gratitude.

"Love you." Sylvia walked to Leah and bent down to hug her tightly. Even though the two weren't ever close, she was glad that her cousin was there for her no matter what.

Just when Sylvia released Leah from her show of affection a loud 'boom' exploded above them and they all ran outside to see Alister's signal; it was time to march on to the castle.

Leah watched as Angela and Iris ran from their tents; the fake necklace was already dangling from her mother's neck. They didn't suspect a thing.

"Everyone gather in a group!" Alister yelled, hovering above Leah and the others, calling everyone outside into the center of the haven.

Once Alister had his army's full attention, he continued, "I know many of you are afraid, but I assure you I will be leading you from above and will keep you safe from the witch. Angela and Iris won't let her reach you on the ground, either. Just remember what you're up against with the other fire shifters, and never let your guard down. Offer them peace first and attack *only* when necessary. Some of you are fighting for your freedom, like they are. Others are on a rescue mission with me. Whatever the reason, we are all one, no matter where we come from. Drakous or Foinix Realm, we need to come together and live free. Now let us get the true king back on the throne!" Alister encouraged all the people just the way Leah had hoped, offering a merciful solution first before choosing bloodshed.

Cheers from all the people filled the air before Alister started the march. As promised, he flew ahead of his troops, leading Angela and Iris around the witch's army that was now coming straight toward the haven.

Warning the others, Alister sent a stream of fire into the air, notifying the rest that the fire shifters were closing in. Leah was waiting for the sign to set her plans in motion as she rushed to the front of the army, yelling for Sylvia and Simon.

"It's time! Follow me to the front!" Leah instructed.

Arriving at the front of the line, Leah could see a lionix coming in hot. "Simon, how many do you think you can drench?" Leah asked.

"All of them, of course. I run oceans, after all, not streams." Simon began by lifting his hands and concentrating. Creating a huge wave of water that mirrored a tsunami, he covered the witch's troops, stunning them long enough for Leah to prepare Sylvia.

"Sing a song and release them from the witch's clutches and I will work on the collars," Leah yelled, standing at a distance from Sylvia.

Opening her lips, Sylvia sent out the loudest song for all of the foinix creatures to hear, giving them a clear mind. Joining her, Leah used blood magic to remove the control collars wrapped around each beast's neck. The witch who'd put the spell on the contraptions was, after all, her great aunt. They were bonded: Elinor's blood had trapped them; therefore, Leah's could release.

Every metal bond connected to each creature instantly unclasped and fell to the ground. Once all of them noticed they were no longer at risk of losing their lives, they transitioned into their human forms, took to their knees, and surrendered.

Walking up to the boy who was the lionix Leah had first seen, she felt ill. He couldn't have been much older than herself. Bending down, Leah grabbed the boy's hand and brought him back to his feet. "You're free now." She smiled. "No need to bow."

"Thank you. Oh...thank you so much." He hugged her, making her burst with pride. When he drew back, he went in search of his mother. The army fighting on Alister's side copied Leah's actions and helped the others to their feet. Reuniting with lost family, making new friends—everyone was accepting of each other and thankful for their freedom.

No one saw a threat coming...

While they rejoiced in their happiness, Leah suddenly began to spot odd looks upon various faces. While there were so many who quite obviously wanted their lives back and didn't want to be a part of the witch's plan, some were as evil and dark as their queen. Leah could sense that there were some more than happy to serve her and carry out the plan even if they were now outnumbered and had no chance of winning.

Three men stood closely to Zack, looking suspicious. While Zack was busy laughing with other children his own age, Leah watched the men's every step. She heard Zack brag about his abilities and how he hadn't even been given the chance to use them because they'd surrendered so quickly. The trio of men triangled Zack and hissed. Long snake tongues protruded from between their lips as each swiftly turned into a large cobra with a diamond-shaped head that was formed with fire. Zack must have heard them before they transitioned because, not even a second later, he was one of them, hissing back.

No one moved. They were frozen in surprise because of Zack's powers and his beautiful, blue-colored flames. As quickly as Zack transitioned, he hypnotized the others, forcing them back into their human forms and bringing them to their knees. There, on the ground, the once frightening trio passed out immediately into a deep sleep.

Everyone cheered and clapped, but the excitement wasn't long lived. Since the snakes had failed in their attempt to bring about death, two other fire-covered monsters' bit as many humans as they could, making their way down the line to Nick and Jenisis.

"No!" Atticus yelled, galloping towards Jenisis and Nick at full speed. Trampling one of the fire monkeys, the other jumped onto the bucking stallion and wrapped his arms around Atticus's neck, biting into it before jumping away.

Sylvia and Simon combined their magic to get the monkey to stop, but no one expected Sylvia to issue a cruel song: "Boil from the inside out and melt until you are nothing but a pile of lava," Sylvia's voice was both angry and sad. The monkey, however, was now nothing more but a pile of molten lava and ash.

"Sylvia!" Simon yelled. "Why did you do that? You could have just put him to sleep." When she didn't answer or turn around, Simon walked in front of her. Her eyes were covered in darkness and leaked of blood. She blinked a couple of times before shutting them for good and falling to the ground.

* * *

It was crucial for Leah to leave and go after the evil witch now. She was feeling dizzy before flashes of a vision entered her mind.. stronger than they had ever been before. She closed her eyes to see what the future brought.

Her mother and Iris were facing Elinor; the evil witch was laughing, her eyes full of flames, before she struck Iris with fire that came from her open mouth and obliterated her. The sounds of her mother screaming filled Leah's ears before she watched the dark magic her mother carried get sucked out of her.. along with her last breath. Elinor turned around and was looking right at Leah. Raising her hands in the air, and then.. nothing.

Leah came out of her vision and fell to her knees crying. Getting up quickly, she ran as fast as her magic would take her to get to Angela and Iris. All she could think was she did something wrong. She'd waited too long before she left to rescue her mother and aunt. Thrashing through the brush and hopping on the sides of tree trunks, she finally made it close enough to hear her mother's voice.

Ducking down and moving slowly, Leah waited to see her aunt or mom come into view. Leah tip-toed around the back of a bush to watch what was happening. She spotted Iris sneaking behind the bush the evil witch was in and, seconds later, a flash of light came through the bush.

She felt like something was off. None of this had been in Leah's vision, so it didn't feel right at all. Leah observed the left and the right sides of her to see if anything unusual was lurking in the trees or bushes nearby.

A hand waved to the far left of Leah; rising from the prickly vines, it caught Leah's attention and pointed. There stood the witch that was going to kill her mother and aunt. Leah moved in a large circle so she would end up being right behind the evil one, stopping only when she saw another Elinor with her back to her, battling her family. Leah was so confused why her mother and aunt were fighting someone else if the witch was here.

Who was the person waving at Leah telling her where to go, and why hadn't she seen them in her vision? Her sight witch powers were still something to get used to, but it never left gaps or dark spots in her visions before.

Leah crawled closer to the witch. Soon she would have the evil woman close enough for her to release the ink and end everything. But the poison of the devil's squid ink had other plans; it was making Leah suddenly feel weak. This was the worst time; she needed a wealth of power to remove the ink from the pendant and put it into the witch without her noticing. As the cough formed in Leah's throat, she knew it was now or never.

Dancing her fingers above the pendant, Leah guided the

ink out of the gem in a string of black tar, through the air, and around Elinor's head so it could invade her eyes, nose, and mouth. She watched carefully as every last drop of the poison entered into the evil witch.

Elinor immediately clasped her hands around her throat, coughing and choking uncontrollably. Leah believed that without any protection crystals the witch couldn't survive.

Her mother and aunt ran in Leah's direction, hearing the sounds Elinor was making. When they saw the witch and Leah, it dawned on Leah that they were in the same spot where the witch had killed Iris and then Angela in her vision.

"No! You can't kill my family!" Leah screamed from behind Elinor making her turn around and show Leah the fiery eyes she'd seen earlier. A wicked smile spread across Elinor's face while Leah bolted toward her mother and aunt.

The trio of witches locked hands and chanted: "Katatrepste tin kakia magissa kai min epistrepsete pote." They repeated the line over and over again. The entire time they were chanting, the witch just laughed at them.

Angela looked down into Leah's eyes full of fear that they were going to die. Angela mouthed, "I love you," like she was saying goodbye, before returning her gaze to the evil woman who was in pain now, bringing hope to the family.

The painful look soon turned to one of pure anger. Elinor took a step forward with her left foot, exposing her chest to the right where Leah had seen the mysterious hand wave. An arrow coming from that direction now drifted through the air. It was as if her sight turned to slow motion as Leah watched the arrow's copper tip go straight through Elinor's heart.

The trio stopped chanting to see what the arrow would do to the witch. It didn't take long. The flame of life left Elinor's eyes and her body cracked like porcelain.

"Get down now!" Angela yelled, diving over the top of Leah, shielding her from harm as the pieces of Elinor's shattered body fell all around them. The witch was dead.

But *who* had been their savior?

* * *

Zack ran to Atticus, mimicking the same monkey that'd bit him; the only difference was the color of Zack's flames, once again being blue instead of red. Hoping that didn't make a difference to his abilities, Zack bent down and put his mouth over Atticus's wound, sucking the poison out of his injury. As if he was drinking the worst hot sauce in the world, it burned as it ran down his throat. Good thing he personally didn't mind a spicy flavoring, but soon the taste turned from spice to rust. With that, Zack knew he was just drinking blood and the poison was out of his dear friend's system.

"Thank you, son," Atticus spoke; weak but alive.

"He's okay!" Zack jumped up with cheer, watching his grandfather and Nick help him to his feet.

Remembering that the monkey had injured many others, Zack went in search of the ones it had bit. Although he saved two more, he wasn't successful with the rest. The poison had turned them to ash. All he knew was the last three were creatures from Drakous and he would have to figure out who in order to inform their families.

"Simon! Is my sister, okay?" Zack ran to Simon who was carrying Sylvia in his arms, heading back to the haven.

"She's sleeping," Simon spoke with a sour look on his face.

"Power crash. Had that before. She'll wake up in a couple days. Have you seen Leah?" Zack asked, looking around.

"No. I was busy tending to Sylvia. Sorry," he replied, continuing toward the haven.

"Leah!" Zack yelled for her.

"She ran that way. Time to fly, kid." Nick pointed towards the castle and transitioned into his eagle, waiting for Zack to copy.

Flapping his human arms and jumping, Zack turned into

the mighty eagle immediately in midair. "Let's go find her."

* * *

In the dungeon sat Adonis and Neveah, talking, unaware of anything that was happening outside the castle walls. Adonis spoke of the adventures he would take Neveah on—he gave a detailed description of the beautiful ocean and his favorite spot on the riverbed nearby. Fantasizing about the life they would share together.

"You're a fool," Neveah laughed at his big dream, even though she knew he wasn't kidding.

"You know all there is to know about me. It's your turn, missy. What do we have to lose? Will you tell me about you and your family now?" Adonis smiled, bringing Neveah to his chest and laying down as before.

"Stop picking me up like that. It's so weird," Neveah fussed.

"That explains why you bit me last time," Adonis chuckled, lifting his arm and putting it over his eyes, relaxing. "I'm ready to listen now."

"Are you sure? You look like you're ready to nap now."

"Come on. I want to hear."

Neveah sighed. "Fine. I'll tell you. What do you want to know?"

"I don't know. What do you want to do with your life? What's your family like? Do you want more children in the future?" Adonis asked, keeping his eyes covered.

"I opened a jewelry store back in Drakous; a business I transferred from Earth. Always been really great at making beautiful things for people. I would like to continue doing that and settle down, surrounded by my family and people who love me," Neveah spoke in a dreamy tone."

"That's great. They must love you if they came here to risk their lives in order to rescue you. What *is* your family like?"

Adonis asked her again.

"Well, my mom's human. She's not magic at all, but she can sure control any situation and others just..listen to her. My father is in Alaska, back on Earth, but we haven't talked in many years—even before we ended up in Drakous Realm, he wasn't in our lives much. My brother was a lost cause before we left Earth, and he fell in love with Iris, another witch. That whole situation gets complicated." Neveah talked while Adonis pretended to snore. "What the Hell!" Neveah scurried to his arm and bit into his flesh.

"Ow! I was joking," Adonis laughed "You have sharp teeth for such a little thing." He continued to rub his sore skin.

"You're not funny," Neveah said, even though she was laughing.

"Okay, Okay. Tell me why Iris and your brother are so complicated."

"You're lucky you were listening; you saved the rest of your flesh. Well...our sister was adopted. We just found out that little fact after thirty years, and it turned out that Iris was her older sister. Like her real sister and her real mother's name was Elizabeth Butler—" Neveah didn't get to finish the story, as Adonis jumped up, knocking Neveah off of him.

"Your sister's mother was Elizabeth Butler? Like...Elinor Butler? The evil magissa that locked us in here is her aunt?" Adonis yelled, feeling like he was going to murder someone.

Neveah landed on the floor and started coughing, "Adonis..something's wrong. I don't feel so good. I think my body is c-c-changing again."

Adonis set his anger aside and picked up Neveah. She was getting heavier... He watched her mouse body grow and change into the beautiful woman he deeply cared for, but now he knew who she was and the connection she had to the witch who'd killed his entire family.

When the transition was complete, Neveah laid in his arms. He stared into her glorious eyes with sadness.

"I'm free, Adonis! It's me," she spoke excitedly, feeling and seeing her own body, sighing in relief. "How do you feel? You don't feel like you're going to die, do you?"

"Not because of the witch's threat, no. I'm sure she's dead." He placed her on the cot and stared down at her. "I'm sorry, Neveah...for what I'm about to do. I'm going to kill your sister and everyone from that evil magissa's bloodline, and you can't stop me," Adonis issued his threat with complete sincerity. Turning, he rushed to the cell doors to see if they would open now that their owner was gone. When he pushed and the doors unlocked, Adonis jumped on the other side, slamming the door shut and melting the lock.

Neveah, still stunned, ran to the bars. "You *can't* kill them. Think about it, Adonis. You're only alive because of their blood line. And there are children...my nieces and nephew. Please!" Neveah clung to the bars, begging him to think about it.

Adonis lowered his head, feeling so dumb to think he had found his true love. Closing his eyes, he tried to find some kind of acceptance and forgiveness inside him; after all, he could just run away and never have to see her or be around her family ever again. Finally, the strongest emotion won out. His revenge may be strong, but he could never hurt Neveah by killing her family...he cared for her far too much.

"I won't touch them," he said in barely a whisper. "But I won't be around them either. When the evil witch rises inside one of your family members or comes out in an offspring, you will understand. Goodbye, Neveah." Adonis didn't release her from the bars; he just ran up the stairs and slammed the door. As he ran towards the doors leading outside, he turned into his lionix form and ran away, planning never to return.

CHAPTER 27

Everyone in Foinix Realm joined all who came from Drakous to celebrate the defeat of the evil witch. Although Neveah was ecstatic to be reunited with her family and friends, after being found and released from the cell, she didn't feel much like partying.

The crowd of people around her only made her anxious, most of them consuming alcohol and approaching her with stupid questions—asking if she was okay or asking what it was like to be targeted by such a powerful witch and survive. All she wanted to do was steal their drinks and tell them to go away. Instead, she donned her fake smile, nodded and waved like she was in a beauty pageant.

What could Neveah say that wouldn't make them pity her? And others feeling sorry for her was not what she wanted at all. At that moment, all she wanted was to grab a bottle and hide in a closet until she finished every last drop; only then would she be drunk enough to deal with everyone. But that wouldn't be a good idea either, because then she would want to fight someone, like anyone that came up to her and asked one more ridiculous question.

Neveah finally made it over to Angela who was listening in on Alister's conversation with the King of Foinix. Even to Neveah the conversation was intriguing. And, thankfully, it wasn't about her.

"My brother, how are you? It's been a long time," the Foinix king addressed Alister and attempted to hug him, but his wing was still damaged from the fall he took from the sky.

"What makes you brothers? Are you a drakon, too?" Angela asked, full of curiosity.

"Heavens, no. I was a Foinix," he laughed. "I'm King Thaddeus. Alister, here, married my sister, Alison. They were connected at the hip all through our childhood and—." When Thaddeus moved his gaze, Alister's look stopped him in his tracks.

Eyes as wide as golf balls, Angela downed her drink before excusing herself to refill it. Neveah realized she wasn't going to be up for a walk at the moment. Alister followed her to the table to engage in a new conversation. Neveah took that as a sign to go outside for fresh air and take a walk by herself.

* * *

"I'm sorry if that was awkward. I saw the look on your face," Alister said, joining Angela at the table full of wines, spirits, and snacks.

"Just shocked that you never mentioned your wife was a foinix, or that Basil calls you uncle because he is your *actual* nephew. Why didn't you just tell me? How did you end up in Drakous if you grew up here? I have so many questions,"

Angela sighed, while the heat from her wine-induced buzz reached her cheeks.

"Angela, I would love to tell you everything someday, but if you don't slow down on the drinking, you might do something silly..like the last time." Alister smiled, obviously reminiscing over the kiss she'd given him during her last intoxication.

Angela laughed into her drinking cup. "Although you are handsome in your drakon form, the glorious beast that you are now has nothing to worry about. I assure you; I won't be tempted to kiss you this time," Angela teased.

"I wasn't concerned about you kissing *me*. I just want you to be careful around other men. You might end up doing something you regret," Alister stated.

"You asshole. Here, take it," she said, shoving the drink in his hand. "I don't just go around kissing *anyone*, you know. I kissed you because I'm crazy in love with you!"

Angela didn't realize she'd voiced her emotions until she watched the biggest smile appear across Alister's large dragon face. "I meant..because I *was* crazy in love. Not that I am now...whatever, I'm going to find Iris."

Now Angela was smacking herself on the forehead. She couldn't *believe* she just said that. Telling Alister she was in love with him was going to make everything even more complicated, especially since she didn't know if they could ever be together with him stuck in his creature form. The heat in her face was from embarrassment this time, not liquor, as she thought of that one silly thing Alister spoke of that she *might* do if she drank too much.

She felt like an idiot. When she watched Alister fall from the sky after the fireball had connected, she'd been so afraid he was gone forever and she'd never have a chance to tell him everything. Yet now that Alister was fine, healing quickly from his injury, Angela chose to turn coward and run to her big sister's side.

* * *

The smell of the river was fresh and the sound was calming, as Neveah walked along the riverbed in search of agates. With luck, she found more than she could carry. Laughing excitedly in the silence, she made piles of the beautiful red, translucent crystals.

Neveah was the one who'd gotten Angela and the rest of her family hooked on rock hounding long ago. When they would all go together on a hunt, they would have friendly competitions on who could find the rarest or biggest agate the river or stream held. All fun and games to earn bragging rights. She would definitely be the winner this time and couldn't wait to rub it in her sister and Arik's face.

While Neveah was bending down to pick up yet another fantastic crystal, she heard a voice call out to her from inside the river. A familiar hypnotizing feeling lured her to the edge of the water. When she took a step farther, the water parted, making an aisle for her to walk down that led straight to a stone door.

Halfway down the aisle, Neveah turned to her left to look at the wave the water had created. Smiling, she reached out with her right hand to touch it but it retreated from her hand, like it was shying away. Silently laughing, Neveah dropped her hand and turned back to the door, continuing her walk towards it.

Arriving at the unique stone, Neveah remembered the writing and the handprint etched into the rock. She had been in the same position before and already knew how to open the door. Pressing her hand against the stone inside the print made it slowly open before her eyes.

"Hello!" Neveah yelled. When it opened enough to show her what lay inside, Neveah couldn't believe what she was seeing.

"Come in, my dear. I promise I won't bite," a beautiful, curvy, dark haired, tan skinned woman spoke. She was sitting in a chair at a table made completely of fire agate crystal.

Neveah walked inside feeling no fear this time as the memories flooded back into her mind about her ancestors and what she needed to do.

The woman smiled at Neveah while she took more steps, waiting for the door to slam behind her. The door shut, but it wasn't a frightening slam like before; it was a creaking, slow close. Neveah couldn't quite figure out which was worse.

The room was utterly spectacular. The shimmering, translucent fire agate covered the walls, floor, and ceiling, perfectly matching the table, chair, and other decorations placed around the room.

The red and brown hues offset the colors of gold, orange, and green making everything look like it was on fire. Even the heat in the room made you think you would burn if you dared to reach out and touch anything.

"This is quite different than the amethyst room in Drakous Realm," Neveah noted out loud.

"Yes, well..that would be my sisters' dramatic display. I am more of a sit down and have a drink kind of woman. I'm Lovena Talesman, the Agate Enchantress," the woman said, pointing to the chair across from hers. "Would you like to take a seat and have a drink with me?"

"Thank you," Neveah replied with a nod. Walking over to the open seat, she felt toasty warm. "I'm Neveah Michelson, but you probably already knew that."

"I did," Lovena said, staring at Neveah with a smile.

Looking down to avoid the woman's gaze, Neveah noticed she didn't have a glass to drink out of. Without asking, Lovena snapped her fingers and an agate glass immediately appeared in front of Neveah. But when she looked inside, it was empty.

"The glass has nothing in it," Neveah stated the obvious.

"Well, that part is entirely up to you. You can make

anything appear in it. What would you like to drink?" she asked, taking another sip from her own vessel.

"Okay." Closing her eyes, Neveah concentrated on a liquid she had been craving for weeks now. When she opened them, her glass was emanating the delicious smell of red wine. Picking it up, she emptied the contents in record time.

"You look like you needed that," the woman laughed. "Feel better?"

"Much," Neveah replied, looking at her glass that was once again full. "That's amazing! You have no idea what I have been through. My life has been Hell. I try to be the perfect mother, daughter, and wife...but it's never enough," Neveah spoke, then took another gulp.

"I understand what you must be going through. I had similar issues growing up. Just look at where I ended up. I messed up so badly, I couldn't free myself of all the negativity I had for the people and their problems in the outside world; I had no desire to aid, save, or help anyone. Being stuck here for thousands of years, however, will teach you a thing or two," Lovena snorted. "You don't want to end up like me, Neveah."

"Maybe not. Although, we *could* keep each other company and get drunk all day, every day without a care in the world," Neveah laughed, consuming more of her never-ending glass of wine before Lovena grabbed her wrist.

"You have a very important task ahead of you. You need to keep yourself grounded, Neveah, or you will never escape what worries you the most. I can feel your energy and it is out of control. If you don't let go of that energy, you will be consumed by all the negativity in your life and never have the ability to escape."

"I have been through this before with your amethyst sister. Why is it that these crazy rooms, completely made up of beautiful crystals, can be so damn demanding? What if I *like* the craziness in my life and just want to live it?" Neveah shouted, rising from her chair.

"*Is* that what you want? You can have the crazy and deny your destiny, Neveah. But the price you must pay will be up to you. The realms in the universe won't live long enough for you to decide what you want. Lucky for you the fire agate room doesn't demand much; all you have to do here is leave your negative energy behind. In return, it will give you positive energy and a different perspective on life. You must be ready, though. If not, you will have a long time to think about it while being trapped in here with me. What seem like hours in this room are actual decades passing by out there. If the negative energy doesn't burn you up inside before you can escape, then the sadness you feel when you leave here and find out everyone you loved grew up and died, will. You decide, Neveah." Lovena certainly didn't sugarcoat anything for her.

"So negative and harsh," Neveah responded.

"I just told you that's how I got here in the first place."

Neveah nodded. "How can I save anyone when I can't even save myself?"

"You have to be calm. I urge you to let go of the negative energy. You are strong and powerful. Channel that energy into saving all the realms and everyone in them. You can do it and you will," Lovena added. She walked forward and took Neveah's hands in her own to help calm her and remove the intoxicated feeling left from the wine. "It's time to go. Do you remember what you need to do?"

"Yes."

* * *

At the castle, people were leaving the party to return to their homes and enjoy their newfound freedom. Sylvia was awake and looking for her mother. She had missed all the excitement and reuniting with her. It was time to return home, yet Neveah still hadn't returned to the castle to join everyone else so they could enter the portal back to Drakous. Back to the safety of their homeland.

"Leah, have you seen my mother?" Sylvia asked. concerned.

"No, but we should get my mom and Iris to go find her," Leah answered.

The two went in search of Angela and Iris, both worried for Neveah's safety. Even though the witch was no longer a threat, the traitor, Adonis, was still wandering out there in the darkness. They found Angela and Iris laughing with the King of Foinix. He was going on about how Iris was a carbon copy of the evil witch, yet was far prettier than her. They were explaining how she was their aunt and had no idea why she was so evil. Iris's mother had never told her about a sister and had lied about why she had fled to Earth, even though it was probably to keep them safe from Elinor's madness.

King Thaddeus didn't seem to mind that he was in the presence of two gorgeous women, even if one *did* look like the hag who'd taken his immortality.

"Mom, we can't find Neveah," Leah walked up to Angela. "It's been hours."

"I'm worried about her," Sylvia added, feeling like her mother was somehow in grave danger.

The women curtsied, excusing themselves from His Majesty, and joined Sylvia and Leah in their quest to find Neveah. She had to have gone out for fresh air.

Sylvia just wanted her mother back. Not having her in her life for months was too long and too hard. She wanted to hug her and tell her everything she'd learned about herself and, above all, she wanted to make sure her mother was mentally and emotionally okay and wasn't falling off the deep end. Sylvia knew how her mother handled traumatizing situations in the past and didn't want her to repeat it after all she had done to stay away from the temptations of alcohol.

The four of them walked around outside asking anyone they saw if they had seen Neveah. With every "no" they were losing hope. Thinking she was somehow kidnapped again and they were on their way to another rescue mission, Sylvia thought about her mother's favorite things to do.

"I bet she's by the river looking for agates. You know how much she loves to rock hound. She would do that for hours back on Earth and lose total track of time. I'm sure she's down at the riverbed," Sylvia informed them, feeling excited again.

It was a short climb down the large boulders surrounding the castle to reach the river rocks below. Instantly, Sylvia spotted a glistening object on the ground. It was an agate; a clue that assured her Neveah must be there somewhere.

"Come on! I know she's out here if there are more of these," Sylvia turned around and yelled out to the others.

Reaching Sylvia, the ladies stared at the agate in her hand.

"Sylvia, look," Leah said, pointing behind her.

"What?" Sylvia turned around. It was her mother; she was standing on the riverbed facing the water. Sylvia ran towards her, breathing a sigh of relief that she was safe. "Mom!"

* * *

Neveah felt like she was in a trance as she walked back down the aisle to the riverbed. She turned around once she was clear of the water, and stared at the now replaced river that blocked the sight of the stone door below. She knew what she needed to do, but could not guarantee that anyone was going to be happy about it. The family crystals were not in her possession, they were back at the castle with Iris.

Coming out of her trance-like state, Neveah looked at the ground again searching for more crystals.

"Don't forget, Neveah. Stay focused," the river spoke to her.

"I will. I promise," Neveah replied.

"Mom!" her daughter screamed. Neveah turned around to see her beloved daughter running directly at her; Iris, Angela, and Leah trailed behind.

Bracing herself for impact, her adult daughter ran into her arms. Neveah embraced her tightly while she sobbed.

"Mom...I thought I lost you...and then I killed a monkey because it killed Atticus. I saw blood covering my eyes and I was so scared, Mom. I was so scared. Then I woke up and everything was over, and you were safe, and Zack saved Atticus," Sylvia spoke so fast and cried so hard that Neveah barely understood all her words.

"Honey, you're fine. We're alive and we're together. I love you. Calm down." Neveah thought about the irony. When she was a teenager like her daughter, everything was the end of the world. Now here she was an adult, and it could be the end of the world if she didn't save it.

Time was ticking by and Neveah knew she needed the crystals. Iris and Angela walked up to her and Sylvia wearing smiles, waiting for a moment to talk.

"Are you ready to go home?" Angela asked Neveah.

"I am. Do you have the crystals, Iris?" Neveah asked, holding out her right hand and trying not to appear suspicious.

"Don't you think we should get back to the castle before we open the portal?" Iris asked.

"I'm not trying to open the portal here. I just want to see the crystals," Neveah said. "They are mine, right?"

"Yes. Give Neveah her crystals, Iris," Angela instructed.

Iris looked at Angela, back to Neveah, then stuck her hand in her pocket. "Why do you want them now?"

"What's going on with you, Iris? Why are you stalling? Those are Neveah's crystals. She can have them whenever she asks."

"I feel like something is going on. Like you need them for something and aren't telling us. It's the energy in the air. I can't explain it," Iris said, pulling two stones out of her left pocket and handing them to Neveah.

"That's because something *is* going on," Leah interrupted. "Care to share with the rest of the group, Aunty?"

"The other two crystals!" Neveah demanded, holding out her left hand.

Iris reached into her right pocket for the other two stones and set those in Neveah's free hand. "What are you going to do? We can help."

"It's better if you don't. Just go back to the castle. Take my daughter and Leah with you," Neveah said, pushing the girls towards Angela and Iris.

"I know you're upset, but don't do anything rash. Don't destroy this beautiful land because you're hurt, sister. We all love you and we can conquer any threat together," Angela spoke, assuming the worst-case scenario.

"I'm not going to destroy Foinix, Angela," Neveah laughed. "I'm actually combining the realms." With that, Neveah turned around and sent the crystals floating into the air.

* * *

Stepping back to watch, they had no idea what Neveah meant when she stated she was combining the realms. As the crystals floated in the air above, the ground shook and the wind picked up all around them. Angela watched the scene with fascination, trying to huddle Leah and Sylvia between Iris and her own body for protection.

Neveah's chanting filled their ears: "Katarrípste tous toíchous anámesa stous drákous kai to vasíleio tou Foínika. Kánte tous eta. Kánte ta olóklira." She began to glow and hover above the ground.

It was amazing and beautiful. Neveah looked like a bright angel floating on top of the water. Soon, however, the scene turned strangely askew. Something was wrong. Neveah turned her head to look at her sister and mouthed the word, "help." Tears of blood began streaming from her eyes and ears.

"She's dying! We need to help her! Lock hands!" Angela screamed, linking the chain of her family to help Neveah. Together they were stronger and more powerful than any force. Whatever Neveah was attempting to do, they would accomplish it together or die trying.

Grabbing hold of Neveah's leg, Angela pulled hard until she was back on solid ground. "What do I do? How can we help?" Angela cried, looking at her sister's vacant face.

"Chant. Like me. All of you. Repeat after me: 'Katarrípste tous toíchous anámesa stous drákous kai to vasíleio tou Foínika. Kánte tous éna. Kánte ta olóklira,'" Neveah replied, taking Angela's hand in her own. All five of them repeated the chant three times before they were thrown backwards by a strong gust of wind, leaving them flat on their backs on the riverbed.

As Angela opened her eyes, she had no idea what was in store for her and her family. The words she chanted brought the Drakous and Foinix Realm together, making them one. It was going to be one hell of an adventure for all of the people, and she was thrilled to find out what awaited them just around the riverbend.

ACKNOWLEDGMENTS

It's no surprise that the title of my series refers to "Family," seeing as that my wealth of thanks goes to the ones I love. To begin, I would like to express my sincere appreciation to my family for backing me up and giving me the inspiration to create such relatable characters in my books. We have had so many hardships throughout time, and I adore you for wanting me to create new, exciting, and adventurous realms to "play" in.

Thank you to our local owners of Gordon's Select Market in McCleary, Washington. Lori and Jack Peterson, if it weren't for you Lori, encouraging me to contact local news releasing companies, I wouldn't have been featured in "The Daily World" newspaper with my first book. Jack, thank you for giving me the opportunity to have book signings outside your store. I was just starting to promote my first book. You both opened your arms out to me, giving me support and acceptance, when I was so nervous my work was going to be rejected.

A special thanks goes to my three incredible proofreaders and dearest friends. Talitha Cooper, who is always my first choice to review my writing. Like a sister we have been connected from day one of meeting each other. Lots of love and appreciation to you. Chelsea Williams, you came into my writing life in the most unexpected way. We had always known each other but never connected outside of family friends. Her passion was equal to my own when it came to my first book "Family Crystals." Her over enthusiastic need to read my second book "The Agate Enchantress" is what brought us together. Marci Zabel, we met recently while I was delivering over ten books to your doorstep. I just had to know you after that moment. Finding out that we were both mothers and shared the experience of having a child with autism, blew my mind. We connected through our children and their different abilities, creating a bond that I hope never goes away. To three amazing and wonderful people. I appreciate all your help with the last process before I published my second book.

Amy Lignor. I know we were both having a tough time in our own personal lives while working on this adventure and wished for the new year to come and make all our worries go away. I can honestly say that I love you like family. You're not only my editor and friend. You are my biggest motivator, number one fan, and inspire me to be a better writer every day. I hope that you are by myside not only for my series but all of my many books to come. "Thank you" is an understatement of how grateful I am to have you in my life.

Lastly, my deepest gratitude goes out to my readers. I couldn't have continued my series without all your support and reviews. The confidence you give me to continue my writing is greatly appreciated and keeps me going, even when life is tough and throwing boulders in my path. I keep writing for all of us. Thank you.

ABOUT THE AUTHOR

Born in one of the most stunning landscapes America has to offer – Juneau, Alaska – Amber Vonda was then raised in the small, quiet town of McCleary, Washington, with her two older brothers and one sister. Tragically losing her oldest brother at a very young age, Amber and family faced the hardship together. Moving forward in life, Amber was blessed with three amazing children who are the core of her world. When one of her beloveds was diagnosed with non-verbal autism, Amber's wealth of strength, courage, and huge heart took on the challenge, becoming a motivated stay-at-home mom. When she's not entertaining and finding fun things for her kids to do, she reads a good book or gets her hands dirty in the vegetable and flower gardens around her home. It was not a leap for Amber to enter into the literary realm, being that her own mind is constantly set on the "creative" channel. Inspired by her oldest daughter on a daily basis, a young girl who wished to write a book and loved brainstorming ideas with her mother, she asked Amber if she wished to write one, too. With that being said, Amber opened her laptop, released the ideas that were brewing, and typed until she had her first book written. "Family Crystals" to her second book "The Agate Enchantress" fantasy's that offer a tribe of unforgettable characters in action-packed realms that draw readers in from the first page to the last. These two books are just the start of a thrilling new series that will delight one and all for many books to come.